RÍO TINTO

AMERICAN LEGENDS COLLECTION

RÍO TINTO

A WESTERN STORY

MICHAEL ZIMMER

Copyright © 2013 by Michael Zimmer
Published in 2017 by Blackstone Publishing

Printed in the United States of America

ISBN 978-1-4708-6162-9

1 3 5 7 9 10 8 6 4 2

CIP data for this book is available
from the Library of Congress

Blackstone Publishing
31 Mistletoe Rd.
Ashland, OR 97520

www.BlackstonePublishing.com

For
Jon Tuska and Vicki Piekarski
Thanks for the opportunity

FOREWORD

A Word about the
American Legends Collections

During the Great Depression of the 1930s, nearly one quarter of the American work force was unemployed. Facing the possibility of economic and government collapse, President Franklin Roosevelt initiated the New Deal program, a desperate bid to get the country back on its feet.

The largest of these programs was the Works Progress Administration (WPA), which focused primarily on manual labor with the construction of bridges, highways, schools, and parks across the country. But the WPA also included a provision for the nation's unemployed artists, called the Federal Arts Project, and within its umbrella, the Federal Writers' Project (FWP). At its peak, the FWP put to work approximately six thousand five hundred men and women.

During the FWP's earliest years, the focus was on a series of state guidebooks, but in the late 1930s, the project created what has been called a "hidden legacy" of America's past—more than ten thousand life stories gleaned from men and women across the nation.

Although these life histories, a part of the Folklore Project within the FWP, were meant eventually to be published in a series of anthologies, that goal was effectively halted by the United States' entry into World War II. Most of these histories are currently located within the Library of Congress in Washington, DC.

As the Federal Writers' Project was an arm of the larger Arts Project, so was the Folklore Project a subsidiary of the FWP. An even lesser known branch of the Folklore Project was the American Legends Collection (ALC), created in 1936 and officially closed in early 1942—another casualty of the war effort.

While the Folklore Project's goal was to capture everyday life in America, the ALC's purpose was the acquisition of as many "incidental" histories from our nation's past as possible. Unfortunately the bulk of the American Legends Collection was lost due to manpower shortages caused by the war.

The only remaining interviews known to exist from the ALC are those located within the A. C. Thorpe papers at the Bryerton Library in Indiana. These are carbons only, as the original transcripts were turned in to the offices of the FWP in November 1941.

Andrew Charles Thorpe was unique among those scribes put into employment by the FWP–ALC in that he recorded his interviews with an Edison Dictaphone. These discs, a precursor to the LP records of a later generation, were found sealed in a vault shortly after Thorpe's death in 2006. Of the eighty-some interviews discovered therein, most were conducted between the years 1936 and 1939. They offer an unparalleled view of both a time (1864 to 1916) and place (Florida to Nevada, Montana to Texas) within the United States' singular history.

The editor of this volume is grateful to the current executor of the A. C. Thorpe Estate for his assistance in reviewing these papers, and to the descendants of Mr. Thorpe for their cooperation in allowing these transcripts to be brought into public view.

An explanation should be made at this point that, although

minor additions to the text were made to enhance its readability, no facts were altered. Any mistakes or misrepresentations resulting from these changes are solely the responsibility of the editor.

Leon Michaels
July 17, 2011

WIL CHAMA INTERVIEW

Alamosa, Colorado • March 18, 1938

❦

Begin Transcript

SESSION ONE

Is your machine running? Should I start?

All right. Well, when we talked about this last night, you said you wanted to hear everything I knew about the Tinto War. Since I was right in the thick of most of it, that's going to be quite a bit, so I hope you've got enough of those recording disks in your satchel there.

I probably also ought to warn you not to expect too much in the way of unparalleled feats of daring or fast-draw shootouts like they publish in the weekly pulps, because it wasn't like that. Oh, it was exciting enough, especially to those of us who survived the damned thing, and it was about as gritty as you'd want. As gritty as sand kicked in your eyes at times. It was pretty bloody, too, but I'll swear that when I look back on it, I'm not sure there were any real heroes to come out of that affair. Unless you lived through it, which I guess was accomplishment enough for most of us.

I came into the fray late, not even aware that it had been brewing for some time. So I guess for me, the Tinto War didn't start until that day in early March when I came back from what turned out to be my last weekly run to the Flats.

You know this was down in Texas, right, and that I was working for a man named Randall Kellums, who owned the Red Devil Salt Works? I was one of three drivers, mule skinners we were called back then, who hauled salt from the Tinto Flats to Kellums' processing plant on the Texas side of the Río Grande.

Although a lot of people will tell you that it was Randy Kellums who put Río Tinto on the map, that boast tends to ignore the fact that the original village, the one down by the river that we called Old Town, had been around for a good many decades before the first Anglo ever showed up in the Tinto valley.

On the other hand, if what those folks are talking about is Kellums' impact on both the town and the Flats, then they've got a valid claim. Up until Kellums got there sometime late in 1877, Río Tinto wasn't much more than a few dozen mud huts, perched on the banks of the Río Grande like a bunch of brown-shelled turtles sunning themselves on the low bench above the river.

The village of Río Tinto had just two reasons for existence. The first was the ferry that spanned the Río Grande there, a rickety craft only slightly safer than trying to cross over in a rusty bucket. The second was its proximity to the Tinto Salt Flats.

It was the Flats that brought Kellums to the valley, and which eventually led to what folks called the Tinto War. So I guess when you think about it, you could also make the argument that it was Randy Kellums who just about took Río Tinto off the map. Sure as hell, for better or worse, he changed that town forever.

Anyway, for me it all started that day in early March of 1880, coming in from the Flats with a load of unprocessed salt. In those days coming into Río Tinto from the east was like stepping out of a furnace, only to discover that the floor beneath you had been ripped away, dropping you into the cool basement. It was thirty-five miles—two days by wagon—of sun-blasted boredom from the Flats to the top of the bluffs overlooking the town, followed by fifteen minutes of belly-flipping exhilaration.

When I first started driving for Kellums, my heart would kind of scramble up in my throat whenever I got near enough to the top of the bluff to see all that empty space stretching out in front of me. The road just kind of all of a sudden ended, or so it seemed until you tipped forward over the cliff. Then it was a three-hundred-foot drop to the bottom, which you'd reach safely, grinning from ear to ear, if you'd done it right, or crumpled and broken and dead as a December weed if you didn't.

You might think I'm exaggerating the dangers. If so, I'd gladly point out the scattered bones and broken timber at the bottom of the bluff, all that remained of the two outfits that had gone over the edge the preceding year, killing both mule skinners and their teams. The skeletons of those mules were still visible from the top of the bluff, as white as freshly washed linens after being bleached in the salt and sun for a few months.

You might have thought we'd have learned a valuable lesson from those two tragedies, barely a year old when I started hauling for the Devil, but you'd be wrong. We were all young and brash in those days, and you know how youth responds to danger. Caution was just a word to us, death something that happened to someone else. I was as guilty of that as the next guy, because after the first few times negotiating the Cut—it was officially called Kellums' Cut, but we just naturally shortened it to the Cut—I became as cocky as the rest of them.

That day I'm telling you about, I had my mules moving along at a dandy pace. The trace chains were jingling a fine tune and the wheels were spitting up rooster tails of powdery caliche that the wind shredded and scattered behind us. Even above the creaks and groans of the running gear I could hear the grease bucket, hanging from the rear hitch, bouncing and clattering in its own wild dance of abandon. Just from those sounds alone, I knew I was going too fast. I should have slowed down, but I didn't. I jammed my heels against the footboard just as the lead mules dropped out of sight, and, even knowing it was going to happen, I could feel my muscles draw tight, my back stiffen up like a steel bar had been rammed down the hollow of my spine. As the middle team of my six-mule hitch seemed to cross over that threshold into oblivion, I let go of a lusty whoop that could have been heard in Mexico—granted, not that much of an accomplishment, being so close to the Río Grande, but it added to the excitement.

It wasn't until my wheelers dipped over the edge that I got my first real look at what lay beyond. There wasn't much to ponder. The Mexican state of Coahuila came into view across the river like a ratty old blanket dropped carelessly over the land, wrinkled with low hills and shallow dips, pilled with clumps of chaparral, a splotchy green in color, what with the coming of spring and all.

On the near side of the river there was just the tops of the giant cottonwoods, already leafed out and shielding most of the buildings from view. The rest was just sky, deep blue and nearly cloudless, as I recall.

The road hooked sharply to the right as soon as it curved over the lip of the bluff, following a track that had been gouged out of the side of the cliff by picks, shovels, and dynamite barely two years earlier. It was so narrow in places that I doubt a man could have stood to either side of the road when one of Kellums' wagons was passing without being crushed against the cliff on one side or tossed out into space on the other. The outer wheel trace was several inches lower than the one closest to the cliff, so that as you were going downhill the wagon would tip outward at the top.

It was that combination of the quick turn and the slanted surface of the road that cost Kellums his two outfits the year before. It was also why we were under strict orders to slow down before we started that last leg of the journey. But like I already told you, we never did. As the wheel mules made the turn, the big wagon lurched outward, then swayed back with a sensation like my stomach was being left to dangle over the emptiness of the cliff's face. I whooped again, louder than before, then fell back in my seat, laughing like crazy.

Lord, that was fun!

As the wagon righted itself, I got back to business, hauling in on the lines while working the brake lever with my foot to keep the rig from picking up too much speed. Kellums didn't use the big freighters and the long hitches that other companies did, primarily because of the Cut. Both of the wagons that had gone over the edge the preceding year had been high-sided Schuttlers, carrying close to three tons of salt apiece when they took the plunge. After losing his second rig that way, Kellums brought in smaller wagons, then reduced the size of the teams from twelve-mule jerk line outfits to simple six-mule hitches, the skinner riding a wooden seat high above the front wheels.

My own outfit was a John Deere wagon pulled by six big bay jacks. In that harsh climate and largely waterless terrain, it could carry a little over a ton of freight without trouble. The wagon had come to Texas with a coat of bright green paint, its wheels and running gear a cheerful yellow, but the sun soon dimmed the paint's luster to a dull, puke-like hue. Its regular cargo of loose salt hadn't helped the color much, either.

As soon as I reached the bottom of the bluff, I eased off the brake and let the jacks have their heads. The nice thing about mules is that, once they understand the routine, they'll pretty much do what's expected of them on their own. That's not to say their reputation for stubbornness isn't warranted, but I've found that there's a knack to getting along with jackasses—I'm talking about the four-legged variety here. It's just a matter of creating a sense of partnership with them. Treat a mule with respect and a certain amount of equality and you've got a partner for life. Treat them badly or with a heavy hand and you'll make yourself an enemy with a longer memory than you'd think possible.

Once the road curved away from the base of the cliff, it was a straight shot down a series of benches to the Red Devil plant. We made our way along the wide, dusty street in a shuffling jog, me sitting up there, high and proud, and probably a couple of pounds heavier for all the dust I was carrying in my clothes. After five days on top, battling the elements of a largely treeless, wind-ravaged desert, the shady thoroughfare we called Bluff Street felt pleasantly cool against my flesh, and the breeze off the river soon began to dry my sweaty shirt.

I couldn't help a wistful glance at Bob Thompson's Lucky Day Saloon as we rumbled past. The Lucky Day was the largest of the two drinking establishments in Río Tinto, and served a quality beer that Bob imported upriver from Brownsville. He had a poolroom in back where a lot of the boys hung out in the evening, myself included when I was in town. Or at least I did until everything went to hell.

Over the years a lot of writers and historians have tried to portray the Tinto War as a racial conflict between an invading Anglo population and the Tejano citizens whose ancestors had settled the town decades before. There might even be a kernel of truth in that, but I'll say right now that, despite my Mexican name and the dusky tint of my skin, I never sensed any animosity from the Lucky Day's patrons before the war busted everything open like a festering wound. I won't deny that a distinctive German accent and a largely Anglo view of the world, both by-products of growing up in my grandpapa's house, might have had something to do with my acceptance into the saloon's fraternity, but I can't say for sure that it did, either. Of course, once the war got started, all that changed.

Leaving the business district with its inviting shade behind, we rolled back into the sunlight. As we started down the hill toward the Devil, I spotted a keelboat approaching from the south.

Let me just say this now, then I'll not bring it up again. If at any time during these recordings you hear me refer to the Devil as providing something or doing something, I'll be talking about

Kellums' Red Devil Salt Works and its management, and not the demon of the same name.

And in case you're wondering, yeah, we were all aware of the—what do you call it? The double entendre? As you might've guessed by now, none of us thought too highly of Kellums. Most of us considered him to be a first-class jackass—my sincerest apologies to any mule that might take offense at the comparison.

At any rate, there was a keelboat coming in, and, not surprisingly, a lot of kids and even a few adults were making their way toward the wharf that Kellums had ordered built below the plant a few years before. I couldn't help grinning myself, wondering what new delights were being brought to town. Río Tinto was too isolated to warrant a spot on any stagecoach line, and the terrain in that part of Texas, especially along the river, was too rough for wagon traffic to be practical. Keelboats had become the town's primary connection with the outside world, bringing in not just fresh supplies that couldn't be produced locally, but also visitors and news from the outside.

The keelboat's outbound cargo would be a lot less diverse, consisting almost entirely of sixty-pound wooden crates stamped with the Devil's dancing red demon toting an oversize salt shaker above his head. Salt had been Río Tinto's lifeblood since the beginning. If not for the Flats, I doubt if anyone would have ever settled in the valley.

Wheeling my outfit into the wagon yard, I noticed that two of the three bays at the loading dock were empty. So instead of stopping at the corrals like I usually did, I went ahead and backed my rig into the number three bay. After setting my brake, I monkeyed down to loosen the coupling pin. I figured I'd ground-drive my mules to the corrals and pull the harness there, but I'd barely freed the wagon's tongue when a couple of stable boys showed up. I gave them a cursory glance, but, when they didn't say anything, I went back to work. Then Jim Houck came out of his office looking like a constipated bear, and I remember thinking, *somebody's ass is gonna get chewed out good.*

Houck was a longtime salter and Kellums' right-hand man when it came to processing the mineral. He'd been working around salt since he was a kid, harvesting brine out of the Georgia lowlands. He was in his forties then, a pretty hard-nosed son of a bitch according to the men and women who worked for him in the plant. Being a teamster, my supervisor was Chad Bellamy, who managed both the stables and the wharf for Kellums, and who was also the town's part-time lawman, when a lawman was needed. Although I seldom had any association with Houck, I didn't much care for him, based mostly on the stories I'd heard from others.

"Boss wants to see you, Chama," Houck said in his usual clipped tone.

If you've ever been called into the boss' office, you'll be familiar with the gut-punched feeling I got.

"What's he want?" I asked.

"Mister Kellums doesn't confide in me," Houck replied, looking put out that I'd waste his time with such a question. He nodded toward the two stable boys. "José and Sandro'll take care of your mules for you. I was told to send you up to the main office as soon as you got in."

Well, what are you going to do? Climbing up to the box, I fetched my revolver from where I always kept it when I was on the road, coiled like a snake next to my boots. It was an 1875 Remington with a seven-inch barrel that I'd done some work on with files and a honing stone to smooth out the action. It was as accurate as any gun I've ever owned, but I seldom wore it while skinning mules. The leather belt was heavy and hot, and the buckle had a tendency to bite into my belly whenever I spent too much time leaning forward with my elbows propped on my knees, which was my usual position while driving. Both Frank Gunton and Pedro Rodriguez, who were the Devil's other two drivers, were always telling me to wear it, and

I suppose I should have. That border country is a scary, dangerous place. It was then, and it still is today.

After strapping the belt around my waist, I loosened the buckles holding my rifle scabbard to the side of the box. Booted inside was a '73 Winchester, its butt slanted forward where I could grab it in a hurry if I needed it. My bedroll was bundled up in what we called the chuck box, bolted to the side of the wagon, along with a skillet and some eating utensils and what food I had leftover from breakfast that morning. The grub and cooking gear belonged to the Devil, so I just took my rifle and blankets and left the rest for José and Sandro to worry about.

The Red Devil plant sat like a squat, slumbering lizard on the first bench above the Río Grande's flood plain, a long, narrow adobe building with the loading dock on the Texas side of the building, the water mill that powered it all on the riverside. The stables and the barracks for the single men sat above the plant, and about thirty yards above that was the main office from which Kellums ruled his empire.

I was sweating again by the time I reached the veranda shading the front office. The cottonwoods might have done a good job keeping Río Tinto's business district cool, but the Red Devil and its buildings were fully exposed to the westering sun.

A burlap-wrapped olla hanging from one of the veranda's exposed rafters dripped moisture, and after slowly spinning the fired-clay jug on its leather straps to check for anything that might bite or sting, I tipped the mouth toward me for a long swig. The water was warm and gritty, but still tasty; a hot sun and dry wind can help a man overlook a lot of minor annoyances—like sand in his water.

Down below, the keelboat *Rachel* had already been tied up. Her crew had shipped their long sweeps and were even then lowering a gangplank toward the wharf. Standing on the *Rachel*'s deck, though keeping back out of the way, were a couple of Anglos wearing wide-brimmed hats and light, knee-length coats over pale linen shirts. Among the swarthy river men, they stood out like a pair of curried coach ponies in a herd of mustangs. My gaze lingered briefly on the two, then I shook off my curiosity and went inside.

I've got to admit the Red Devil's front office felt pleasantly cool after being out in the sun all day. I paused to let my eyes adjust to the dimness, then elbowed the door shut behind me. The Devil's chief clerk was Tim McKay, a smallish man not much older than my own twenty-four years, clean-shaven and rapidly balding, his flesh pale from long hours spent indoors, riding herd over invoices and order sheets. He commanded a desk next to a central hallway that led to Kellums' private office in back—a modern-day knight mounted on a wooden swivel chair, his lance a fountain pen of rich walnut.

Glancing up from a stack of paperwork, McKay made a quick grunting sound I couldn't translate, then stood and disappeared down the hall. I leaned my rifle against the wall, then dropped my bedroll beside it. Thirty seconds later, with a wag of his finger, I was following McKay down that same dark passageway. The door at the far end had been left open, and after ushering me inside, McKay quietly retreated. He hadn't uttered a single word the whole time.

This was my first visit to Kellums' private office. When he'd hired me last summer, the interview had taken place in Chad Bellamy's cramped office at the stables. Later on, I'd signed the necessary paperwork at McKay's desk, under the clerk's scowling supervision. Kellums hadn't been around that day, and I found out later that he made it a point never to associate with his employees or other underlings. I guess that's why he had line bosses and foremen, an almost military-like hierarchy to separate him from the masses.

The office McKay had escorted me to was a lot bigger than the one out front. It had better light, too, thanks to a trio of large windows set in the west wall, overlooking the plant, the stables, and the wharf.

Kellums was sitting behind a huge desk at the opposite end of the room, looking kind of small and dumpy in the distance. A row of wooden file cabinets along the inside wall, a large floor safe on steel rollers, and a horsehair sofa occupied most of the free space between me and him. A plain, walnut hutch next to the door held a silver tray filled with tumblers and shot glasses and several bottles of various brands of whiskey, none of which a salt-encrusted forty-dollars-a-month and found mule skinner like myself was ever likely to be offered a sip of.

Oh, and one more thing. There was a map of West Texas hanging on the wall behind Kellums' desk. Although I glanced at it as I walked in, I didn't attach any special significance to a pair of shaded rectangles close to Río Tinto that had been outlined in red.

Randy Kellums was a short, stocky man well into his fifties by then, with rubicund cheeks and close-cropped brown hair graying rapidly at the temples. I suspect that by this stage of his life, the furrowed brows and downturned mouth were more or less permanently etched into his face. I'd been working at the Devil for a little over six months by then, and if he'd ever smiled in all that time—I mean a real smile, fabricated from gladness—I'd never seen it.

Smirks and sneers were another matter.

I've sometimes wondered if Kellums' pudgy stature and bulldog visage had anything to do with the abrasiveness of his personality. If it did, then my presence in the room wasn't going to calm any waters. I pretty much towered over the older man. Standing just a shade under six feet, I was broad through the shoulders but slim in the waist and hips. I've heard that called a horseman's figure, although I've never been more than average in the saddle. My hair was straight and dark and thick, and I cultivated a fuller mustache then than the sporty little Clark Gable look I wear today.

I was dark-skinned, of course. My papa was Porfirio Chama, of the San Luis Valley in southern Colorado, not far from where Alamosa is today. My mama's name was Ana, the only daughter of Gabriela Gomez and Karl Wilhelm Holtz, a German immigrant who came to America in 1849 to look for gold. I was barely walking when Papa was killed in an avalanche trying to cross La Veta Pass on snowshoes in the middle of winter. His death forced my mama to move back in with her parents, who by that time owned a small hardware store in Pueblo. We moved to Denver shortly after that, and it was there I grew up. I was named Wilhelm, after my grandpapa, and it was from him that I received my Anglo views of the world, dosed liberally with Deutscheland values on discipline and finance.

If Grandpapa Karl didn't have the first dollar he ever made, I'll bet he could tell you where he spent it, what he spent it on, and what that item should have cost in an honest market. It wasn't until he gave up his pick-and-shovel work in the goldfields to open his own store that he learned to appreciate the term "markup."

Like Tim McKay, Randy Kellums had his nose buried in a stack of paperwork, one hairy-knuckled fist gripping a pencil like he was subconsciously trying to strangle it. I know he heard me come in, because, as soon as McKay shut the door, he raised his other hand to absently wave me forward, even though he didn't look up or otherwise acknowledge my presence.

Halting in front of his desk, I hooked my thumbs behind the buckle of my gun belt, then just stood there waiting. For a while, at any rate. As the minutes ticked past, I could feel my temper starting to bubble, crowding out my anxiety. I'd been on the road for five long days by then, the last two of them coming face on into a hot, unremitting wind. I was tired and still fairly parched, and after several minutes my gaze began to stray. That's when I spotted a sweating tin pitcher of water sitting on a small table next to Kellums' desk. A couple of tall tin cups were sitting beside it. With my hackles on the rise, I walked over to help myself.

Well, that got Kellums' attention quick enough. Leaning back in his chair, he regarded me through slitted lids as I downed a full cup, then poured a second and drank that, too. Afterward I returned the cup to where I'd found it, then sauntered back to stand in front of the old man's desk.

"Satisfied?" Kellums asked.

"Not all the way, but I'm getting there," I said.

See, at the time I thought he was talking about my thirst. It didn't occur to me that he'd been aware of my impatience all along, and that his question had been in reference to my little act of rebellion, not my comfort—the jackass.

Tossing his pencil onto the desk, Kellums said, "I'm pulling you off the road, Chama. I want you close by for a while."

Well, that was blunt, and not anything at all like what I'd expected. Feeling kind of panicky, I said, "I don't think I can work in your plant, Mister Kellums. No offense."

I didn't want to tick him off, but I knew even then that I'd quit before I started sifting salt or boxing it into crates. I'd seen the looks on the faces of the men and women who came out of that building at the end of a twelve-hour day.

A crooked smile flitted across Kellums' face. "I don't have any intention of putting you in my plant, Chama. I've got all the help there that I need, and I can hire more any time I want it. What I want you to do is deliver a message for me. After that, we'll see what develops."

A message? Now that was more to my liking. "Where do you want it delivered?" I asked, envisioning a long, pleasant ride to some place greener and cooler.

"Old Town."

"Old Town?" My head kind of rocked back in surprise. "Why me? You could've had Sandro or José deliver a message yesterday."

"They're boys, Chama. Their ... let's say their presence ... wouldn't have the same impact as yours."

I didn't know how to respond to that. Fortunately I didn't have to.

"How much experience did you have handling mules when you came here?" Kellums asked bluntly.

"None. I told you that when you hired me."

"That's right, you did. Yet I took you on anyway. Do you know why?" He raised a hand to stop me before I could hazard a guess. "There's no need to rack your brain, because you haven't a clue. So

I'll enlighten you. I hired you because of your skill with a revolver, and because of your involvement in the Gunnison affair last year."

Well, he might as well have yanked the whole damned floor out from under me. I'd come to Texas hoping to escape the taint of what had happened up there in Colorado, only to discover that Kellums had known about it all along.

"I'm not a fool," the older man went on. "That's a tough haul to the Flats and back. I wouldn't have put an inexperienced driver on that route without good cause." Yanking open the belly drawer to his desk, he pulled out a simple business envelope, which he tossed atop his ledger. "Right there is the reason I hired you. It took longer to put it all together than I anticipated, but it's done now, and that's all that matters."

"How'd you find out about Gunnison?" I asked, ignoring the envelope.

"It's my job to know what's going on in the world, and to understand how it affects me and my business interests here in Río Tinto."

My shoulders were sloping toward the floor, the wind taken neatly out of my sails. "What happened up there in Gunnison and Hogup, that's not something I'm proud of," I said quietly.

Kellums' laugh came out like the harsh bark of a choking dog. "I expect not. You're lucky the whole bunch of you weren't hung for murder."

I didn't have a reply to that, my own thoughts more or less running along that same line. After an awkward silence, I glanced at the envelope. "What's that?"

"That's what's going to make me rich. It could prove profitable to you, too, if you're game."

I guess he was expecting me to jump on whatever opportunity he tossed my way, because he got a real funny look on his face when I started shaking my head no before he even finished speaking.

"I've had my fill of killing, if that's what you're talking about," I told him.

Kellums' face grew thundery at my response. "I hope I didn't make a mistake hiring you, Chama. You mark my words, I'm going to move forward with this, whether I have your help or not. And as far as any killing that might occur, that's going to be up to Amos Montoya, not me."

"Ah, Montoya," I murmured, the pieces starting to tumble into place. My gaze returned to the envelope with fresh curiosity.

"It's from my attorney in Austin," Kellums said brusquely, still acting ticked that I hadn't jumped at his offer. "His assurance that my purchases are legal, and that all documents will be filed with the state of Texas within …" His words trailed off in a satisfied chuckle. "Hell, they've already been filed." His eyes narrowed on me as if to better gauge my response. "I bought that land out there, Chama. All of it. It's mine." Hooking a thumb over his shoulder, he added, "Go have a look. I've already penciled it in."

But I didn't have to look. I'd seen it when I came in and noticed the map on the wall behind Kellums' desk. I'd assumed then that the outlined sections, each one representing six hundred and forty acres of desert terrain, were to locate the Flats in relation to Río Tinto. Now I knew better.

"You bought the Flats?"

"Land and mineral rights, which means every damned red-veined flake out there belongs to me. Water, too."

I said just a while ago that I'd never seen Randy Kellums smile, but I believe he came close to it at that moment. Pushing around in his swivel chair, he eyed those highlighted sections on the map with all the pride of a new papa handing out cigars to strangers on the street. As for me, I was just beginning to grasp the significance of the transaction, the repercussions that were about to come down hard on the town of Río Tinto.

"Montoya's not going to stand for that," I said. "His people have been harvesting salt from the Tinto Flats for decades."

"Since about 1820, from what I've been able to gather," Kellums agreed, swiveling back to face me. "And they can still harvest salt for their own use ... with my permission, of course. They just can't sell it commercially anymore. That stops immediately." He took a deep breath, and his expression relaxed. "I sent Amos Montoya a letter several days ago, detailing my ownership of the Flats and my intentions toward anyone caught harvesting salt there without my consent. I have it on good authority that a letter from my attorney containing the same information was delivered to Montoya's store the same day. He's been warned, Chama, but just to be sure he understands, I want you to talk to him."

"Me? Amos Montoya doesn't even know me."

"Don't be naïve, Chama. Montoya probably knew who you were before I did. His connection to both the community and the outside world is something I envy."

I was staring at the map as Kellums spoke, studying the precisely outlined sections of land. Then I noticed a smaller area, also traced in pencil, and a grudging respect for his foresight began to take shape within me. Kellums hadn't just purchased the salt beds, he'd also bought the land surrounding Antelope Springs, that sole source of dependable water between the Flats and the town, vital to anyone traveling between the two locations.

"You've got it all tied down solid as a rock, don't you?" I said quietly.

Kellums' head moved in a barely perceptible nod. "I've had this planned for a long time. Even before I came to Río Tinto. It just took a while to put it all together."

"And me?"

He shrugged. "You were just a piece of luck. Another gunman to back my play." His eyes narrowed. "Not the only one, mind you, if you're thinking your presence here will garner you any special leverage."

What I felt was kind of like a sinking sensation, as if something dark and thick was swirling in on top of me. I'd felt that way once before, back in Gunnison, standing alone and half frozen in the top hall of the Atlantic Hotel, a double-barreled shotgun hanging in my hands like an iron post. The image was so vivid I nearly shivered from the cold.

"My message to Amos Montoya, through you, will be verbal," Kellums said, bringing me back to Texas and the lone bead of perspiration trickling down my cheek. "Are you ready?"

"If I say no?"

"It wouldn't change anything, other than the thirty minutes or so it'll take me to hire a new mule skinner, then find someone else to deliver the message."

"What if Montoya tells me, tells you, to go to hell?" I asked.

Kellums' eyes took on a fiery tint. "If he does, you tell him there won't be any need to go looking for it. You tell him I'll bring hell straight to Río Tinto, and dump it in his lap."

Excerpts from

Letters to My Sister

Being an Account of My Travels through Western Texas and Northern Coahuila, in the Company of My Husband, Dr. James Edward Furlough

by Mrs. Mildred S. Furlough

A Self-Published Diary • Dallas, Texas, 1880

• CHAPTER NINE •

A KEELBOAT RIDE ON THE RÍO GRANDE
SALT PLANT IN THE MIDDLE OF NOWHERE
THE PROCESSING OF A VITAL CONDIMENT
OBSERVATIONS OF A MEXICAN COMMUNITY

Sister, one cannot begin to describe the hardships encountered upon our journey to the little village of Río Tinto, on the Texas side of what the Mexicans call the "Río Bravo." After James concluded his business with banker McMurphy in Laredo, we booked passage aboard the keelboat *Yolanda*, bound for the quaint riverside community of the above mentioned, nearly a week's labors northward.

The *Yolanda*, I have been assured, is typical of the barges that ply this river ... single-masted and double-banked, with sixteen

"sweeps," that is to say, "oars," when the current is gentle enough …
[at] other times the boat is propelled forward by wooden poles
thrust into the riverbed like so many Roman lancers slaying a giant,
mud-encrusted beast … the *Yolanda* has a crew of twenty-two,
including its captain and first mate.

* * * * *

At Río Tinto I was introduced to a most charming acquaintance
from James' past, a Mr. Randall Kellums, with whom husband
served in the Quartermaster's Dept. during the late War of
Northern Aggression. Mr. Kellums operates a salt processing
plant here on the banks of the Río Grande River, and you will be
surprised to learn that this condiment is shipped throughout the
Southwest, and indeed to our own corner grocer, under the Red
Devil label.

That is correct, dear sister. I have discovered the source of that
pink flavoring we have both come to depend upon so dearly for the
meals the cook prepares for our families.

Did you know that the word *tinto* means tinted red? Or that
Río Tinto is also the name of the stream that meanders down off the
plateau above town? I have been told that white linens laundered in
these waters can begin to take on a pinkish hue after a time, which
might account for the coloring of so many of the shirts I see among
the laborers here.

* * * * *

While James and Mr. Kellums conducted whatever business
venture two such men of commerce might deem worthy of their
attention, I was afforded a tour of the Red Devil Salt Works
under the able guidance of Mr. Jim Houck, the plant's stalwart,
yet utterly captivating, foreman. You will be surprised to learn

that in this seemingly waterless wasteland, our salt is actually processed [and] packaged via the power of that same precious liquid, in the form of a waterwheel.

* * * * *

[After] the salt—which is very white at harvest, but laced with large, deep red "veins" that twist and swirl throughout the individual boulders—is removed from the wagons, it is carted through the plant by Mexican laborers who deposit the chunks of salt, some of them rather quite large, into a metal bin at the "upstream" terminus of the building. From there it is metered into a wooden trough with twelve-inch sides, where it is propelled forward by means of belt-driven iron slats, powered by the slow-turning blades of the mill wheel. This trough has been rendered as smooth as polished glass by the hundreds of tons of salt that passes over it annually.

The condiment is "pushed" to a series of heavy-mesh wire screens, where those grains, or "flakes," as they are referred to by Mr. Houck and others within the industry, that are fine enough to pass through these ever-tightening iron webs are deemed suitable for the table, and immediately moved forward by cart for shaping.

The chunks continue their journey along the belt through what Mr. Houck described as a "stamping mill," that is to say, a trio of hammer-like devices, each weighing close to five hundred pounds, and powered, like the belt itself, by the idyllic turning of the plant's waterwheel. As soon as these larger pieces are crushed to a properly-sized granule, they are moved forward to the "steam room."

* * * * *

There they [the salt flakes] are poured into funnel-shaped molds, which are then placed onto a leather conveyor belt—a different means of transport from the aforementioned device described, although ingeniously powered by the same mill via a series of gears and what Mr. Houck described as "clutches," a mechanical term I was unfamiliar with before our tour of the plant.

These metal cones then pass through a "steamer," or boiler room, which is encased in metal sheeting to prevent the mud bricks of the larger building from gradually melting under the effects of extreme moisture. Inside this large metal box, where at least two men constantly toil, enormous amounts of water are splashed onto highly heated stones, which creates a steam not unlike the summer humidity we experienced in New Orleans as young girls.

The steam causes the salt to adhere to itself in the shape of the aforementioned cone, which we both recognize so fondly.

* * * * *

After molding, the salt is then taken to the packaging area, where the division of labor is shifted by the sexes. That is to say, women actually do the final wrapping, which I deem as further proof of an assessment I made mention of upon our arrival in Brownsville, that the fairer sex is of a more hardy nature the farther one ventures into the wilderness.

Mr. Houck explained to me that the paper wrapper for our salt is imported from Mexico, and contains a high percentage of corn husks. The dancing, crimson imp with its oversized salt shaker, along with the slogan, RED DEVIL SALT, FROM THE LAND OF THE AZTECS, is stamped upon the paper at the plant.

After the cones are snugly wrapped and tied, they are placed, twenty-four at a time, into straw-padded crates—twelve cones "upwardly" pointed, the other twelve aimed toward the imp's own fire-saturated "lair," if I may speak so boldly of that place which all God-fearing men dread.

These crates, which are produced "in-factory," are then moved to the far end of the building, where they are warehoused until they can be shipped south by water craft. In fact, Mr. Houck informs me that the future cargo of the keelboat *Yolanda*, upon which husband and myself first journeyed to this isolated outpost of the frontier, shall, on its homeward journey, be composed almost in its entirety of the aforementioned product.

* * * * *

There appears to be an undercurrent of ungratefulness within the native population for the prosperity Mr. Kellums has brought to this region by his harvesting of the salt. Although my dear James has done his best to shield me from this uncomfortable ambience, one cannot but help to notice the sullen regard which Mr. Kellums receives from a goodly portion of the village.

I have been assured that Mr. Kellums' safety will soon be fortified by gentlemen skilled in the art of warfare. One can only pray that these knights of the revolver arrive in a timely fashion. I know that James has promised his every effort in assisting to locate men suitable for the endeavor, as it will safeguard not only an old and trusted friend, but an enterprise James seems most excited about, as it regards his aforementioned association with the arrival of the railroad to Laredo. (Editor's note: Corpus Christi, San Diego, and Río Grande Narrow Gauge Railroads reached Laredo, Texas, in September, 1881.)

WIL CHAMA INTERVIEW

❧

SESSION TWO

Kellums' message was short and blunt, although less threatening than I'd feared. Basically he wanted me to repeat to Amos Montoya the same information he'd just passed along to me, and which Montoya had already been advised of through at least two letters so far. Namely that Randall Kellums was now the sole and legal proprietor of the Flats, and that no one could harvest salt there without his permission. I was to also emphasize that any salt taken from the Flats with his permission should be for personal use only, and couldn't be resold.

I won't say the thought of being reduced to the role of a message boy didn't rankle me, but it didn't irritate me as much as I might have expected. I guess at that point I was still fairly intrigued by Kellums' ambitions, and especially how old man Montoya would react to Kellums' proclamation.

Tim McKay didn't even look up as I walked past his desk to where I'd left my rifle and bedroll, but he took plenty of notice when the front door was shoved roughly inward, as if the person doing the shoving wanted the room to know he'd arrived. McKay's head jerked up in alarm, his lower jaw dropping about an inch.

Standing to one side with my booted rifle in one hand, my bedroll tucked under my other arm, I paused to watch the two men I'd noticed earlier on the keelboat march boldly into the office. Although they paused speculatively when they saw me, they must have decided fairly quickly that I wasn't anything to worry about, and walked on over to McKay's desk without so much as a nod in my direction.

Although roughly dressed, they weren't bums. Each of them wore Colt revolvers, and one had a wicked-looking bowie angled forward over his left hip for easy reach. They were tall and whipcord lean, their deeply tanned faces honed by wind and sun. From a distance they could have been mistaken for brothers, but up close you could tell they weren't. One had dark hair and a scruffy beard, while the other was clean-shaven, with fine blond hair spilling over his collar in a way that reminded me of Wild Bill Hickok, whom I'd met a number of years before and admired for his soft-spoken ways. Neither of these gents seemed especially soft-spoken, and I would not have expected kindness from either of them, although I'd received generous portions from Hickok.

Studying the pair, I felt something uncomfortable stir in my breast. I've met their kind many times over the years, and the encounters always bring a faint chill to my heart. Like when you hear the whir of a rattlesnake behind the outhouse. You know it isn't an immediate threat, but it still puckers your bum.

The dark-haired man spoke first. "We're looking for Randall Kellums. The barge man said this was his office."

McKay's head bobbed like a blossom in the wind. "It is, indeed. Would you two gentlemen be Pope and Landors?"

"I'm Pope," the dark-haired man confirmed.

McKay glanced at the blond guy, but I guess he didn't figure additional clarification was necessary. It must have been an icy look Landors gave the clerk, because McKay seemed to turn a shade paler after peering into the blond man's eyes. Nearly stuttering, McKay said, "M-Mister Kellums has been waiting for you." He pushed awkwardly to his feet. "I'll let him know you're here."

When McKay had disappeared down the hall, Landors turned to me. "You got business here, or is staring at a man's back what they pay you for?"

"I wouldn't be here if I didn't have a reason for it," I said, making sure my own voice came out at least as firm as his.

Pope glanced my way. Both men, I noticed, had the eyes of predators, and it dawned on me then that the war with Montoya, which Kellums had claimed he wanted to avoid, had already begun. Had probably been set into motion weeks, if not months, before.

Tightening my grip on the Winchester's scabbard, I headed for the door. Low chuckles from Pope and Landors followed me outside, but I didn't feel intimidated by them so much as I felt ill about what I knew was about to rip through Río Tinto like a twister. Even though both Kellums and his Austin attorney had sent letters of clarification to Montoya, I figured that was as much for history's sake as it was a legitimate effort to avoid violence—proof that he'd done everything possible to preserve his rights as a businessman and property owner before resorting to force.

Oh, it was a crock, all right, a rich man's manipulation of justice. But it would probably go a long way if things got out of hand and the law had to be called in.

After leaving the Devil's office, I went to the barracks to drop off my gear. The barracks was a single large room with a dozen rope-sprung bunks lining the walls at one end and a small, seldom-used kitchen at the other, most of us preferring either the New Harmony Café or Rico De Azevedo's nameless joint down in Old Town when we got hungry.

As a rule the first thing I did when I got back from a run was to clean my guns. Salt plays havoc not just with the finish, but also with the internal mechanism. I was too worked up to tackle the chore that evening, though, so, leaving my gear piled on my bunk, I trudged up the hill to New Town. I needed a shave and a bath and a fresh change of clothes, but tonight I wanted a drink first. Maybe a couple of them, to dull the memory of my conversation with Kellums.

Like everything else in Río Tinto, the Lucky Day was constructed from adobe. It was two stories tall, with rooms upstairs for the working girls and a poolroom in back, which I've already mentioned. A hand-painted sign above the arched entryway to the poolroom proclaimed, IT'S YOUR LUCKY DAY, which I suppose is where the name came from.

The saloon was cool and dimly lit, and I could hear the clack and slow roll of the ivory balls from the poolroom when I walked in. Although relatively early—evening shade down below, but a smear of sunlight still spread across the upper reaches of the pale bluff east of town—there were already half a dozen customers scattered around the main room. My gaze lingered on a couple of men sharing a corner table. They both looked up as I entered, before turning back to their drinks and conversation. Normally I wouldn't have paid them much mind. Hell, even Río Tinto, as isolated as it was, caught its fair share of drifters. But something about those two attracted my attention.

I motioned for a beer as I walked to the bar. Bob Thompson had it drawn and waiting by the time I got there. I spun a nickel across the counter into his waiting hand.

"How was your run, Wil?" Bob asked.

"No trouble," I replied absently. For a mule skinner, comments about the road were as common as remarks on the weather to other folks, and I generally treated them as such. Catching the image of the two strangers in the wavy mirror of the backbar, their reflections half hidden behind a forest of whiskey bottle necks, I asked, "When did those two jaybirds show up?"

"Five or six days ago, I reckon," Bob replied.

"Who are they?"

Fixing me with an unblinking stare, he said, "Your coworkers."

I swore softly. "I didn't know it had gone this far."

"It's caught most of us by surprise," he allowed, leaning forward. "Those two came in right after you left last week, but there's been a few more show up since then. Mean-eyed sons of bitches, too."

"Was two more just got off the *Rachel*," I told him. "Kellums knew there'd be trouble."

"Sure, he knew. Randy makes a big show of sayin' he doesn't want trouble, but there's a mean streak in that ol' boy, and I've seen it more than once. You ask me, he's lookin' forward to kickin' them Tejanos off the Flats."

"You know about him buying the Flats?"

"I heard about it earlier this week, right after he got word from his attorney, although Randy Kellums ain't never been particularly quiet about his ambitions for that salt." Bob shook his head. "I doubt if Amos Montoya counted on him hirin' a fancy, cutthroat lawyer to do his dirty work for him, though. Or bringin' in a bunch of hired guns to back it up." Fixing me with a level stare, he added, "This is just between you and me, all right? I might not care much for Kellums, but I gotta live here, too."

"Sure, I'll keep a halter on it. Besides, I don't have a dog in this fight." I took a long sip of beer. It wasn't cold, but it was wet, and it lacked the grit I'd swallowed from the olla outside the Devil's office.

When I lowered my mug, Bob said, "You sure you ain't got a dog in this fight, Wil?"

"Me? Naw, I'm just a mule skinner." I paused, then shrugged as I recalled how I'd been pulled off of that job. "Kellums wants me to talk to Montoya, though. I don't know why."

"You're a Mex, ain't you?"

I met Bob's steady gaze. That was a subject that had never come up before, and I wasn't sure how to take it.

"I mean, with a name like Chama, you ain't Irish," he added.

"My grandfather was German."

"My grandfather was a horse thief who got hisself hung by a

Kentucky lynch mob. That ain't got nothin' to do with my tendin' bar in a Texas border town."

I didn't have a reply for that, either, and after a moment, Bob said, "I ain't sayin' it is, and I ain't sayin' it ain't, but it has occurred to me that, if I was Randy Kellums, right about now I'd be worried that this ruckus he's got brewin' with Montoya might grow into somethin' bigger."

"Like what?"

"Like a war between the Tejanos and the Texicans?"

I laughed softly, although there wasn't any humor in the sound. "If he thinks I can keep a lid on that kind of trouble just because I speak the language, he's crazy."

"It's not just the language, Wil. It's that that kind of trouble can attract too much attention from the outside world. You get a couple of killings over a product as well-known in Texas as Red Devil Salt, and it won't be long before reporters start showin' up. Then the politicians'll want to get involved, and the next thing you know, ol' Randy ain't got the upper hand no more. But if he can say ... 'See here, folks, this ain't anythin' atwixt Mexicans and Anglos, this is just some hotheads tryin' to take the law into their own hands,' ... well, that'd cool things off real quick. Then all he's got to deal with is Amos Montoya and his bunch. But Kellums is gonna have to convince folks that there are plenty of Tejanos on his side of the fence for that to work. I reckon that's where you come in. You and a few others."

"Son of a bitch," I murmured, swaying back from the bar. "I won't do it. I've gotten myself into that kind of trouble before. I won't let it happen again."

"I ain't wantin' to get caught up in the crossfire, either, but somebody ought to go talk to Montoya, see if they can't make that bullheaded old greaser see the light."

I hesitated, and I recall thinking, *that's twice, now.* Meaning twice in less than five minutes that Bob had brought up the issue of race. Stepping away from the bar, I said, "Thanks for the beer."

"Hey, ain't you gonna finish it?"

I shook my head and walked away.

"Watch your back, Wil!" Bob called after me. "The way things stand now, you could get a knife shoved in it from either side."

I threw a short wave over my shoulder but didn't look back. Outside, I paused on the boardwalk to roll a cigarette. It was getting on toward dusk, the sky kind of ash-colored with the sun gone, and the breeze had died to a whisper. I glanced at the cliffs above town. It wouldn't be long before the bats came peeling out of their dens among the higher crags, swirling across the twilight like a thousand tiny twisters.

Leaning against one of the cottonwood posts supporting the veranda, I smoked slowly, letting the tobacco take the edge off of my anger. My gaze roamed the length of the street. From here I could just make out the wharf and the crowd gathered around it. Neil Teague, who ran the hardware store, and Jay Landry, who owned the Tinto Mercantile, both had wagons parked near the end of the narrow dock, waiting as the *Rachel*'s crew off-loaded the merchandise they'd ordered from Brownsville. Other spectators stood watching the men work, talking and laughing, enjoying this brief respite from the monotony of their lives. Through the crowd I spotted Carlita Varga's red serape as she hawked tamales to the onlookers.

Before Kellums started the Red Devil plant and began shipping salt in quantity, keelboats were rare in Río Tinto. No more than four or five a year, nosing into the muddy bank to unload their nonde-script cargo of supplies, usually the merchandise other retailers downriver had refused. After Kellums showed up, those numbers increased steadily, until you could count on at least one keelboat every other week or so. Yet the townspeople never seemed to tire of their arrival. They'd walk down to the wharf in a lightened mood to hear the news the river men brought with them, to talk to people whose lives extended beyond these high bluffs and the vast desert.

In the other direction along Bluff Street, the town ended

abruptly about one hundred yards shy of the foot of the cliffs—with
one notable exception. That was Randy Kellums' sprawling adobe
hacienda, sitting atop a high knob just under the precipice.

The locals called that knob Rattlesnake Hill, because of the
large number of whirly-tails that could be found sunning themselves among the rocks and scree that had tumbled down off the
cliff's face over the ages. Old-timers to the area claimed there was a
den somewhere up there where the reptiles could ride out whatever
weather winter brought to this part of the Southwest. From what
I'd heard, these same old-timers had tried to warn Kellums not to
build his home there, but he naturally hadn't listened to what the
locals thought. From my experience, men like Kellums seldom did.

I don't remember if I've mentioned this yet, but Río Tinto had
two streets. In addition to Bluff, which ran in a straight line from
the bottom of the Cut to the wharf below the Red Devil plant,
there was a second street connecting the Anglo settlement with Old
Town. Little more than a rutted scar through the cottonwoods, this
thoroughfare started just off the Cut, then wound down from the
upper bench to join a narrow cart track that was the original Tinto
Cañon route to the top of the plateau. The one the Tejanos had used
for decades to reach the salt beds. Its route through the old part of
town was a winding course that befitted the wanderings of yoked
oxen going from door to door in colonial times. To me, it was a
reminder that civilization is a lot older than history.

Tossing my cigarette butt into the dust, I stepped off the
boardwalk to make my way toward that smaller, nameless artery
that would take me to Old Town. A man named Eber Cruz and
his wife Elsa ran the town's laundry down there, along with a
small bathhouse where Río Tinto's single men—those who didn't
prefer the waters of the Río Grande to save a little cash—could get
a hot bath and a fresh shave. They could get their hair cut there,
too, if their vanity allowed it. Eber Cruz had taught himself the
trade, but he'd been a poor instructor.

Eber's wife was standing outside smoking her own corn-husk cigarillo when I strode up. She smiled a welcome and waved me inside. I followed her to the door, where I met an equally beaming Eber.

"Señor Chama!" Eber exclaimed with the same feigned surprise I'd come to expect every time I returned from the Flats. "You are ready?"

I should probably mention here that Eber Cruz spoke only Spanish. Or more precisely, Mexican, true Spanish being a little formal for that part of the country. I probably also ought to add that a lot of the conversations that took place over the next several days, ones I'm going to be relating to you here, were in that same Tex-Mex lingo. Even so, I'm going to repeat most of what was said in English. Or rather, American, true English being a little formal for what we spoke back then.

"I'm ready," I told Eber—only I said it in Mexican, remember? Then I followed him through the kitchen to the fenced-in backyard where Elsa was already stoking a fire.

"The road was dusty this time?" Eber asked, leading the way to a chest-high adobe stall containing a galvanized tub, a wooden bench, and a coarse towel under a bar of yellow lye soap.

Tossing my hat onto the far end of the bench, I said, "That road's just about always dusty. I've only made the run twice when it wasn't, and both times made me appreciate it dry."

Eber laughed good-naturedly. "Better dust than mud, no?"

I agreed as I hung my gun belt on a peg. The rest of my clothes, I tossed over the top of the wall where Elsa could find them. Eber came in with a bucket of water that had been warming by the fire. Keeping his eyes decorously averted, he added it to the gray, sudsy liquid already lapping at the sides of the tub. I didn't protest. The idea of using someone else's bath water didn't really become repugnant until indoor plumbing came along in the twentieth century.

Stepping into the tub, I slowly sank down as far as my chin, then settled back to watch the twilight deepen. The first of the Tinto bats were already darting among the treetops, and it wasn't long before the main colony made its appearance, like globs of mud splattered against the gray canvas of the sky. The fluttering of their wings always reminded me of something dark and evil creeping through the forest, yet, in all the months I lived in Río Tinto, no one was ever bitten by a bat. Still, I was glad when the colony finally moved on in its sinewy, twisting journey into Mexico.

By the time Elsa showed up with fresh duds, I was ready to get out. This was my second set of clothing, scrubbed clean and neatly ironed, which I'd left with her the last time I was here. Eber came along with my boots and hat, both freshly brushed, the boots lightly polished.

It wasn't fastidiousness that brought me to Eber and Elsa's every week after my return from the Flats, but a desire to get as much life out of my clothes as possible. Salt was as hard on fabric and leather as it was on gun metal, and I'd learned early on that it was worth the money to have the Cruzes take care of my weekly laundering.

Full darkness had crept over the valley by the time I finished dressing. I studied myself as best I could in a mirror that had once belonged to the back of a dresser, a squatty, hog-fat taper illuminating my worn canvas jeans, a yellow-and-brown checked flannel shirt, and the black bandanna at my throat. My hat was flat-brimmed—more or less—with a low round crown and a horsehair band, my boots square-toed and low-heeled.

I forked over one dollar and fifty cents for my laundry and the bath. If I'd had more time, I might have splurged on a shave for an additional ten cents, but my business with Montoya was beginning to weigh on me. I figured I'd put it off for about as long as I could.

I liked Old Town, especially after dark. The low hum of family conversations coming from the adobe homes, the soft glow of lamp and candlelight, and the spicy aroma of Mexican cooking was warm and comforting.

Only a handful of businesses dotted the cart track that wound through town. Cruz's laundry was one. Rico De Azevedo ran a little hole-in-the-wall restaurant where he served a fare that could pretty much drill a hole in a man's stomach if he wasn't used to it. There was an old woman who made candles, an even older blacksmith with a permanently curved spine from a lifetime of shoeing horses and oxen, and, of course, Carlita Varga's little hut where she made tamales to sell to the single men who worked at the Devil. With the exception of Cruz's laundry, which drew a lot of its customers from New Town, they were all closed about as much as they were open.

The largest business in Old Town was Amos Montoya's store and cantina, both operated from the same squatty building. Behind that was the old man's private residence, a sprawling complex of rooms and hallways surrounding a private courtyard, and including living quarters for his extended family. Amos didn't have any children of his own, but there were nieces and nephews in all shapes and sizes.

Entering the mercantile, I was immediately struck by the smell, a combination of leather and oil and recently carded wool. Someone on a mandolin was playing border tunes in the cantina, separated from the store by a pair of batwing doors like you'd see on some of the fancier saloons of the day. There was a lamp mounted to a bracket on the wall beside a short counter, but the rest of the store was dark save for what light spilled in from the cantina, puddling on the floor like spilled cream. I nodded to a young man standing behind the counter, his neatly combed hair and thin mustache creating a dapper appearance on what might otherwise have been a plain face.

"I am looking for Amos Montoya," I said.

"What is your business with my uncle?" The kid's dark eyes were filled with suspicion, for which I couldn't blame him.

"I've got a message for Don Montoya."

"You are a Red Devil man, are you not? One of Kellums' muleteers?"

"Yes, I work for Kellums. He asked me to talk to your uncle. Is he here?"

The young man's gaze darted swiftly toward the rear of the

store, then just as quickly moved away. Turning toward the deepest shadows, I said, "Amos Montoya?"

There was a stirring in the darkness like parting waters, then a figure in a simple black suit stepped forward, toting a double-barreled shotgun. He was a large man, although not fat. His hair was gray, combed straight back from his forehead, his brows thick and black, wiggling like poked woolly worms every time his expression changed. Halting at the edge of the light, he said, "I am Amos Montoya." There was no apology, either for his subterfuge or the cocked shotgun in his hands. "What is this message you bring me?" he asked gently.

"It's from Randy Kellums," I replied, instinctively allowing the inside of my arm to casually brush the polished butt of my revolver, like I was reassuring myself that it was still there.

Amos glanced briefly at his nephew, then lowered the hammers on his shotgun. Setting the weapon aside, he motioned for me to follow him toward the rear of the store. I let go of a heavy breath when I saw that he was leaving the scatter-gun behind, although I didn't fool myself into thinking he was unarmed. I hadn't come here as an enemy, but it stood to reason that Amos and his clan would see me that way.

The dull thud of Amos' boots were my only guide as he led me down a lightless aisle toward the back wall. The faint squeal of iron against iron revealed a sliver of light that quickly grew as a thick plank door was pushed open to reveal a cluttered office not much bigger than an average-size horse stall. A slender taper set in a sconce drilled into the wall guttered briefly in the draft, then steadied.

Stepping out of my way, Montoya tipped his head toward the door. I entered, then halted as the room's contents came into view. Although the place was dark and cramped compared with Kellums' spacious office, it was much more fascinating. A simple, battered desk pushed into one corner represented the older man's business interests, but it was the rest of the room that caused my lips to part in awe.

Against the far wall was a large, glass-enclosed bookcase filled with time-yellowed artifacts. There were skulls and tusks from beasts

I failed to recognize, and demon masks that nearly chilled my spine just to look at them. More recent treasures included pieces of polished turquoise, a Comanche war shield with a bow and quiver of arrows, a ruby-spotted crucifix, and moccasins covered with an elaborate design of beadwork. On the top shelf was a seventeenth century escopeta— one of the earliest flint guns to come into that part of the country—its cock frozen open with rust, its wood dried almost to the point of disintegration.

On another wall hung a large buffalo robe with figures painted on the flesh side depicting a battle between Indians and men in metal suits and boat-shaped helmets, carrying lances and crossbows. Sitting on a table in front of the robe, and adding provenance to the illustrated encounter, was a badly tarnished Conquistador's helmet of the same skiff-shaped profile as those on the robe. Half a dozen iron arrowheads, their edges serrated by time and rust, were formed in a crescent around the front of the helmet.

My gaze roamed eagerly among these relics of an earlier time, when Texas was just an Indian word for "friend," and salt was harvested in leather sacks, dug up with stone tools. I didn't realize I'd come to a dead stop until I felt Montoya's hand on my shoulder.

"You like my collection?" he asked, sounding pleased even before I replied.

"It's impressive," I admitted, making no effort to hide the admiration in my voice. "Did all of this come from around here?"

"Most of it from within twenty miles of Río Tinto," he confirmed. "My grandfather discovered the older relics, the Spanish armor and the prehistoric tusks. Fortunately he had the foresight to save it. Much has been destroyed over the years by those who failed to recognize the significance of what they found."

"There are people who would pay a lot of money for some of this stuff," I said.

"They aren't for sale," Montoya replied curtly, then slid past me into his office. "Please." He motioned toward a comfortable-looking leather chair, sitting next to an open door that led deeper into what I assumed was his home.

Sinking into the cool leather, I removed my hat, then ran my fingers through my hair. Walking to the door at my side, Amos called: "Inez, we have a guest! Would you be so kind as to bring us something to drink?"

I heard a woman's answer from somewhere far off. Smiling, Amos returned to a simple, cane-bottomed chair in front of his desk. Sitting and crossing one knee over the other in the stiff yet dignified manner of a man posing for a photograph, he gave me a weary smile. "So, Señor Chama, you have come at last. I have been expecting you."

"Expecting me?"

He nodded. "For some time now."

"That's funny. I just found out about it myself a couple of hours ago."

Montoya tipped his head graciously. "Perhaps it was merely a lucky guess on my part." He paused when a young woman not much older than myself entered the room, bearing a tray with a tin pitcher and two tall, glazed tumblers. She set the tray on the desk, then quietly retreated, never once glancing in my direction. It made me wonder if she knew who I was, and if, like Amos' nephew out front, she considered me an enemy of the family, a hireling of El Diablo.

"Lemon juice, with sugar to blunt its sourness," Amos said, filling one of the cups. "Or I have other drinks, if you would prefer something stronger."

"Lemonade will do just fine," I replied, realizing only after his uncertain double take that I'd given the drink its American name.

He handed me the tumbler, then poured another for himself. I took a careful sip, then a series of greedy swallows that soon drained the cup.

"I believe you told my nephew you had a message from my good friend, Randall Kellums?"

"I didn't know he was your friend," I replied, setting the empty tumbler on top of a pipe stand next to my chair.

Amos shrugged, and I thought I detected a trace of bitterness in his voice. "He is not, of course, and I apologize for my weak attempt at humor. Tell me, what message does the owner of El Diablo Rojo send? That the salt of the Tinto Flats, which has been ours for so many generations, is now his because some lawyer in Austin has proclaimed it so with papers and fancy words and official seals? Or is it that he will have arrested and imprisoned any man who does not step out of the great Señor Kellums' path, as a proper peon should before a gentleman of such wealth?"

Well, if I'd had any doubts about the old man's feelings before, I didn't after that. You might have thought he'd half swallowed a piece of rotten meat that he was trying to hack back up before it slid on down. But Montoya's feelings toward Kellums, or Kellums' toward Montoya, for that matter, were subjects I didn't intend to get snagged on. So, as succinctly as possible, I relayed the message Kellums had given me, pretty much summing up everything Montoya had already surmised. When I was finished, Amos sat quietly for a few minutes, staring into space, and I wondered what he was really seeing in his mind's eye. The Flats? Or maybe Kellums with a noose around his neck? After a while he turned his gaze on me.

"Tell me, Señor Chama, what is your position on this matter?"

"You ought to call me Wil," I said. "And I don't have a position."

"Yet you work for Kellums, no?"

"I drive a team of mules for him, that's all."

Montoya's gaze dropped to the revolver on my hip. "Do you think your reputation as a gunman would allow such an effortless escape?"

"I wasn't aware that I had a reputation, at least not as a gunman."

"Ah, Señor Chama ..."

"Wil."

He smiled, seemingly pleased by my insistence that he use my

Christian name. "Very well then, Wil, I will tell you what I know of your reputation. I was an observer at last Christmas' rifle frolic, and I stayed afterward to watch the pistol competition. After your display of marksmanship that day, I am afraid all of Río Tinto is aware of your skill with the revolver."

Well, I guess that was something I couldn't blame on anyone but myself, and nothing to be ashamed of, either. Last Christmas, some of the town's leading businessmen had arranged a holiday shooting match, and I ain't bragging when I say I used to be a pretty fair shot with both a rifle and a handgun. In a total of five one-hundred-yard rifle matches, ten rounds each, I averaged an aggregate score of forty-six within a six-inch bull's-eye. That's forty-six rounds in the bull out of fifty shots fired, and pretty fair shooting for a lever gun. I didn't win, mind you. In fact I came in fourth, but that's out of sixty-plus shooters—three of whom were armed with single-shot tack-drivers—so I was well pleased.

Once the official matches were over and the prizes had been handed out, some of the boys decided to hold an impromptu pistol match. It was just a hat match, meaning the participants all ponied up a dollar, which we tossed into Frank Gunton's Stetson. There were no places such as first, second, and third, as in the rifle frolic. In the revolver matches, the winner took it all. Each match was six shots at a two-inch charcoal mark at twenty-five yards.

Now, back in those days, before my eyes got old and the front sights turned fuzzy, I was a more than fair rifle shot. But I was a whole lot better with a revolver. I'd practiced a lot up in Denver, but I also had a gun to back it up. Although I'd bought the Remington used, I'd done a lot of work on it under the tutelage of Matthew Dunn. You may not have heard of Matt Dunn, but if you were a shooter in Denver in the 1860s and 1870s, I guarantee you'd know who I was talking about.

Anyway, we shot four matches that day, and I took home nearly eighty dollars. Some of the boys were kind of tiffed at first, but they all settled down after I bought a couple of rounds for the house at the Lucky Day.

So, yeah, I guess I did have a bit of a reputation in Río Tinto as a pistolero, but I was also wondering if Montoya knew about my earlier brush with notoriety in Gunnison County, which included the mining camp of Hogup, and if he'd say anything about it. After a pause, I ventured, "How did you know I'd be coming here, Señor Montoya?"

"We are an old community," Amos replied. "We look out for one another. We would not have survived the Indian attacks and bandit raids if we didn't."

"Was it someone at the plant?" I knew most of Kellums' laborers were Tejanos from Old Town, and suspected that more than a few probably had ties to the old grandee.

Montoya shrugged. "Does it matter? They look out for me, I look out for them. It is the way it should be, no? Unfortunately your friend Kellums has never wanted to be a part of this community, of this family."

Thinking back to Kellums' smugness, the contempt I'd seen in his eyes every time he looked at the people who worked for him, brought back some of the anger I'd felt when I left his office that afternoon. "Randy Kellums isn't my friend," I replied coolly. "He's my boss, that's all.

"So when the fighting begins, will you side with him?"

"I think everyone is hoping it won't come to that."

"I think," Amos replied gravely, "that most of us realize this war with Kellums has already begun." He reached into a stack of papers under a heavy, blue-green stone on his desk and brought out a sheet of paper with the Red Devil's logo at the top. "The war was joined when I received this, informing me I am now a trespasser at the Flats, and a thief if I continue to do what my family has done since my father's father brought back his first kettle of salt. In truth, my friend, I believe the war actually started when Randy Kellums first learned of the Tinto Flats, and the salt that has yet to be harvested from them. His greed would allow no other option."

I couldn't argue with him about that.

"Will you fight, Wil?" Amos persisted.

I won't lie, there was a lengthy pause before I answered. After all, I worked for the Devil, and back then most men felt a certain loyalty toward their jobs. Riding for the brand is something I've heard it called in recent years, and I reckon that pretty well sums it up. But I was also thinking about what had happened up there in Gunnison County, running all that over in my mind and not liking the way it tugged at my conscience. Not just the final outcome, but how our actions affected the people involved, miners and citizens alike. Seeing their faces in my memory, I abruptly shook my head.

"No, I won't fight for Kellums," I said. Feeling a need to move, I started to rise. As I did, the side of my foot struck one of the pipe stand's thin legs with enough force to topple my lemonade tumbler. I grabbed it unconsciously before it could fall, a lightning-quick move that Montoya didn't miss. "I won't fight for you, either," I added, my face turning suddenly warm.

A faint smile wormed its way across the older man's face. "You were not asked to, my friend."

"All right, fair enough." I set the tumbler on a corner of his desk. "I appreciate your hospitality, Señor Montoya, but I won't take you away from your business any longer. Thank you for the lemonade, and thank ... Inez, wasn't it? Thank her for me, too."

I was heading for the door; Amos stopped me before I could open it.

"Tell me something, Wil."

I hesitated, my hand gripping the cool iron latch. Turning cautiously, I said, "What's that?"

"Will you fight for us?"

I think I might have actually reared back a bit in surprise at the old man's question. I'd just told him I wouldn't, and now here he was asking me if I would. The first word that came to my mind was an emphatic, *No!* But instead of speaking up, refusing to have any part in the coming battle, the best I could manage was a half-hearted shake of my head. Then I yanked the door open and stumbled back into the darkened store. I felt like a thief, fleeing into the night.

WIL CHAMA INTERVIEW

∼

SESSION THREE

Ready?

Well, if you remember, I'd just left Amos Montoya's office when your recording disk ran out of space. I was telling him about Kellums' ultimatum to quit harvesting salt, and then Amos asked me if I'd fight for his side, but I told him no.

Once I got outside, I paused and tipped my head back to stare at the heavens. That's an old habit of mine, going out after dark to look at the sky. On a clear night the stars remind me of spilled sugar, and the moon is an old friend I can always count on, no matter where I am or what kind of trouble I've gotten myself into. I recall it being comforting that night in Río Tinto, too, although I couldn't find any easy answers in the constellations.

The air was cool, like it generally is after dark in that desert country. I pulled my hat off to dry the sweat on my forehead. The mandolin from the Bravo Cantina was still playing slow songs next door, now and again interrupted by gentle bursts of laughter. Although I considered going in for a drink, I'd stopped there a few times just after I came to Río Tinto, and never felt as comfortable in the cantina as I did at the Lucky Day. I guess among the local Tejanos, I was as much an outsider as Bob Thompson or Randy Kellums. I'd been OK with that before, but it stirred up some odd feelings that night, along with an unfamiliar longing for—well, I wasn't sure what it was stirring up, so I just put my hat back on my head and made my way through the trees to New Town.

Although most of the stores along Bluff Street were already closed, the Lucky Day was still brightly lit. Someone inside was plucking out a rowdy tune on a banjo, accompanied by shouting and catcalls from the customers, mingled with the girlish squeals of the doves. I wondered briefly if Hattie Fender was working that night, then pushed the thought from my mind. I had other business to attend to.

Knowing the Red Devil's office had long since closed, I turned my steps toward Rattlesnake Hill, and Kellums' sprawling adobe mansion. My pace slowed after leaving New Town, then slowed even more when I turned off the road toward his house. I kept to the middle of the lane that led to the hacienda, my senses keenly alert. I'm not especially afraid of snakes, but I ain't partial to poison, no matter how it's administered.

In his continuing battle with Río Tinto's reptile population, Kellums had added a five-foot-high adobe fence around his property, its two-foot-wide crown adorned with close-growth prickly pear, broken shards of glass, and razor-sharp pieces of serrated iron, trimmed from old hay cutters. This was a familiar practice in the Southwest, a tried and true method of keeping out unwanted visitors. In the old days it was added to walls eight or ten feet tall to keep out raiding Indians or horse thieves, but it worked on snakes, too, if the top was sealed off tight enough.

The gate to Kellums' estate was constructed of thick mesquite planks, fit snugly into recesses in the adobe on both sides and against a wooden threshold at the bottom. It locked from the inside, although there was a small bell mounted next to the latch that guests could ring to announce their presence. I was just reaching for the cord when a voice from the yard ordered, "Leave it be."

I flinched. I hadn't expected the gate to be under guard. "Who's there?" I asked.

"Who the hell are you?" the voice countered as a stocky individual toting a sawed-off double-barrel stepped out from under the spiny branches of a paloverde. He wore a revolver on his hip and had a cartridge belt slanted across his chest. When he got closer, I saw that the belt was weighed down with 12-gauge shells for the shotgun.

"I'm Wil Chama. I need to talk to Mister Kellums."

"Well, ain't that a tough tit to pass," the man replied, coming to a halt on the opposite side of the gate.

"That's brassy talk for a house boy," I said. "Why don't you run along and fetch your master? Tell him I want to see him."

That's what I said, although I don't think the shotgun-toter heard much after the words house boy. He started cussing a blue streak, telling me what he was going to do to me and how many buckets it was going to take to haul away my remains—the usual trash you could hear most Saturday nights in your rougher saloons, although I'll confess he lacked the aroma of alcohol that made such threats easier to dismiss.

I waited until he finished, then said, "Well, before you start fetching buckets, why don't you tell Kellums I'm here? I expect he'll want to hear what I have to say."

Shotgun was reaching for the latch, I suppose to come outside and fulfill his promise, when the sharp bark of a command from the hacienda stopped him in his tracks. I glanced past him toward the house, where a tall gent in a black suit, wearing a brace of revolvers on his hips, had stepped into the light of a lantern hanging from the veranda.

"You Chama?" the leggy man asked.

"I am," I replied. "You'd best call off your mutt, before I kick him under the porch."

The leggy man chuckled. "You might want to watch yourself

around ol' Layton there. His bite is a whole lot worse than his bark. Matter of fact, his bite has been known to remove a few fingers."

"It's removed a few heads, too," Layton declared ominously.

"That may be, but the boss still wants to see him, Tom," the leggy guy said. "Let him pass."

Tom Layton yanked the heavy gate open, and I stepped through it. He tried to block my path, but I didn't let him. Our shoulders met, and it was his that swung back to allow my passage.

The leggy man grinned crookedly. "Looks like you've got some bark of your own, Chama. Let's hope you've still got it when you leave here tonight." He gave a jerk of his head toward the house, indicating that I should follow him. "I'm Charlie Anderson," he announced as we went inside, like that was supposed to mean something. "The boss is waiting."

This was my first visit to Kellums' house, and I was immediately struck by the chamber-like appearance of the front room. Lit only by a twin-wicked Tiffany lamp and a small blaze in the fireplace, its size was enhanced by barren walls and sparse furnishings. I saw only a sofa and arm chair, a small table holding the lamp, and a braided oval rug on the floor. The place reminded me of an abandoned house with a few oddball pieces of furniture left behind. There was no warmth, no sense of "home." This wasn't much different from the barracks down by the stables where the hired men slept.

An arched doorway to my right led to a dining room, with just a single setting at the head of a long table. I was guessing there was a kitchen beyond that, hidden behind a solid swinging door. The dining room was unlit, and in the shadows I almost missed the girl.

I'd heard about her, of course, down at the Lucky Day and around the Red Devil stables. Her name was Cierra Varga, and the regulars at the saloon often speculated lewdly on her duties at the Kellums' household—besides those of cooking and cleaning, for which she'd originally been hired. Yet for all the talk, I'd never seen her before, and she wasn't what I was expecting at all. I guess in my mind I'd built her into some kind of hardened whore, coarse in her manner, crass with her words. What I saw that evening was a short, full-figured woman with plump round cheeks and dark, penetrating eyes that followed my every move. I reckoned her age at sixteen, but found out later she was closer to twenty.

I came to a stop, my eyes locking on hers until Anderson broke the spell. With a prod to my shoulder and curt nod toward a door opposite the dining room, he said, "In there, sport, and let go of any notions you might have about that gal. She belongs to Mister Kellums."

I didn't bother to reply. The door Anderson had indicated stood open, and I walked in without announcing myself. Randy Kellums sat slumped at a desk similar to the one in his office, large and portentous, although not as cluttered. A cut-glass decanter sat to one side, reflecting light like pats of yellow butter clinging to the bottle's diamond-shaped ridges. An empty shot glass resided at his elbow, a trace of amber in a ring at its bottom. A short lamp with a dark green shade highlighted the wrinkles in his face, making him appear older than he actually was. Seeing Kellums in that light, my mind flashed back to the girl in the other room, and a lightning-quick sense of outrage stabbed through my guts. I swallowed it back, reminding myself that Cierra Varga was no business of mine.

Kellums was already in a foul mood when I walked in. "By God, it took you long enough."

"I'm here now."

"You should've been here two hours ago." He thumbed the stopper from the decanter and poured an ample amount of liquor into his glass. The powerful odor of bourbon filled the room. I glanced at Anderson, who was watching the slow swirl of spirits with undisguised hunger, yet he kept his silence as Kellums replaced the stopper and pushed the decanter out of his way.

Kellums took a healthy slug, then leaned back in his chair with his eyes half closed. You could almost trace the bourbon's progress through his system by the rising look of satisfaction that spread across his face. It lasted only a moment, but it told me more about the man than I'd learned in the last six months hauling salt for him. Then his eyes snapped open and he pegged me with a hard stare.

"Well, what did he say?"

"Montoya didn't seem interested in your message," I answered.

At my side, Anderson snorted contemptuously. "Suits me."

Kellums shifted his glare to the other man. "Don't get too full of yourself, Anderson. Montoya's a tough nut."

"He'll be like any other greaser I've ever run up against," Anderson replied. "Call his bluff, and he'll fold like a Chinese noodle."

I said, "You ain't from around here, are you?"

"Don't concern yourself with where I'm from, Chama. You're no different than Montoya, far as I'm concerned."

I wanted to say, "I'll take that as a compliment," but Kellums spoke first.

"You'd best mind what you say about Wil Chama, Anderson. He'll be riding with you after tonight."

You could tell this was fresh news to the gunman. Shifting his weight from one foot to the other, he said, "I don't ride with men I don't know, Mister Kellums. I told you that."

"You work for me now," Kellums returned bluntly. "You'll ride with who I tell you to ride with." He glanced at me with that crooked smirk I was becoming tired of. "Besides, Chama's got experience in matters of this nature. Go ahead, Wil, tell Charlie about Gunnison."

"Gunnison!" Anderson turned to me, his expression suddenly wary. "You were with that bunch?"

"I hired on to haul salt, Mister Kellums. That's all I want to do."

"You were hired because I knew that, sooner or later, I'd need your skills with a gun," Kellums replied.

"The way those boys botched that Gunnison job, I'd say we'd be better off if you kept Chama perched at the ass end of a team of mules," Anderson told Kellums. He tried to make it sound scornful, but I caught the trace of uncertainty in his words. There were an awful lot of conflicting stories circulating throughout the Southwest about what had happened up there in Gunnison County; I don't think Charlie Anderson was sure which ones he needed to believe, and which ones he wanted to dismiss.

My hackles were starting to rise at the way the two men were discussing me as they might a tool—where to use me, and how. Both of them were missing a central point. Taking a half step forward, I said, "I ain't riding with Charlie Anderson, Mister Kellums. I'll haul salt for you if you still want me to, or I can move on and look for work somewhere else."

Kellums didn't seem particularly cheered by my position. "I hired a gunman, Chama, not a goddamned mule skinner."

"I hired on as a mule skinner."

Kellums narrowed his eyes to half slits, like some men do when they think they can intimidate you into changing your mind. It didn't have much effect on me, though. I was Karl Holtz's grandson, and if I'd inherited anything from that old Dutchman, it was stubbornness. I met Kellums' stare evenly, determined to let him be the one who broke the strained silence.

"All right," Kellums said softly, after nearly a full minute. "If that's the way you feel about it, the hell with you. You're fired." He looked at Anderson. "Get him out of here."

Anderson started to reach for my arm, but lowered his hand when he saw my face. I've always been slow to rile, but, once the trigger's been pulled, it comes on strong.

Stalking from Kellums' office, I noticed the girl again, still watching from the shadows. Her eyes were large but unfathomable as they trailed me across the room. Behind me, the jingle of Anderson's spurs quickened as he hurried to catch up, but I didn't wait for him, and was through the door several steps ahead of him. Anderson stopped under the veranda.

"Chama's leaving, Layton!" he called into the darkness. "Help him find the gate."

There was a low rumble of laughter from the direction of the paloverde, then Tom Layton came into the lantern light, a grin spreading slowly across his face. "You wear out your welcome already, Mex?" he asked, reaching for my arm the same way Anderson had in Kellums' office.

I guess it was too dark for Layton to see the warning look I gave him. His fingers clamped tightly around my forearm, as if he thought he was going to hustle me toward the gate. But I wasn't in the mood to be hustled, and, when he tried to drag me forward, I dug in my heels and jerked my arm free.

"Hey, you little son of a ..."

I knew what he was going to say. You probably do, too. But I didn't let him finish it. A sharp jab to his gut cut him off in midsentence, and he grunted and took a step back, his face going pale and slack in the dim light. Then my anger got the better of me and I threw a fist into his mug that staggered him backward, into the thorny embrace of the paloverde.

I ain't proud of the way my temper flares up sometimes, but it can happen under the right circumstances, and it sure did that night. I went after Layton in a red fury, my fists hammering at his face and body. I'll say this for the guy, he kept his feet longer than most, although I suspect the clutching branches of the paloverde had a lot to do with that.

With Layton not mounting much a defense, I quickly began to slow down. There's not much satisfaction in pummeling someone who isn't fighting back. Then I heard the crunch of boots on the pebbly soil behind me and spun to see Anderson charging into the fray like an enraged bulldog, a long-barreled Colt revolver cocked over his head like a meat cleaver.

I swayed just in time to dodge the worst of that blow, although I still caught some of it on top of my shoulder. I cried out and nearly went down, then caught myself and straightened just as Anderson brought his revolver around in a backhanded swing that nearly took my head off. I went down hard, the stars above the cañon's rim jumping and darting like fleas. Through the popping lights I saw Anderson lunging forward to finish me off, and I struck out blindly with my heel. I fetched the son of a bitch a stout kick to the shin, neatly toppling him, then managed to clip him a good one with my fist as he tumbled past. I rolled onto my hands and knees, then shoved to my feet.

I'd figured Layton was down for good, but that ol' boy surprised me. Coming out of the darkness of the paloverde, he slammed into me from the side, and we both hit the ground. I twisted around before he could pin me, managing to elbow his nose solidly enough to draw a spurt of blood. He was still on top of me, though, flailing wildly, and, although I was managing to block most of his swings, I wasn't getting much of a stab at him. An even bigger concern was Anderson, hobbling toward me with murder in his eyes. I was in deep trouble, and knew it. Anderson was still carrying his Colt, but he'd reversed it so that the muzzle was pointed at my head. I figured he was waiting for a clear shot, which I was trying like hell not to give him. Then the night was shattered by a blast of light and sound, and all movement ceased. At the veranda, Randy Kellums was clutching a double-barreled shotgun. Its muzzles were pointed toward the stars, the left barrel dribbling powder smoke.

"Get your asses out of the dirt," Kellums grated, and we scrambled to comply. I don't think any of us were certain he wouldn't pull the trigger on that second barrel, cutting a swath of mangled flesh and bone through the three of us.

"I thought I told you to get off of my property," Kellums snarled at me.

"I got distracted," I said.

"That saucy tongue is going to earn you an early grave, Chama." He turned to Anderson. "I told you to escort him out of here. I didn't say anything about trying to turn his brains to mush."

"It was just a misunderstanding, Mister Kellums," Charlie Anderson replied.

"Yeah, and I'm beginning to wonder who made it. It looked to me like he was giving better than he got."

"Now, that ain't true," Layton protested. "He caught me off guard is all. Otherwise he'd be out on the street by now."

Kellums didn't even reply to that nonsense. Glaring at me, he said, "Chama, start walking."

That sounded like sage advice, and, grabbing my hat off the ground, I quickly headed for the gate. Behind me I could hear Kellums telling his men to get inside the house in a tone that reminded me of an irate mother, scolding her children for not coming in to bed—although I've yet to meet a mother who backed up her words with a scatter-gun.

On Bluff Street I stopped long enough to dust myself off—sliding my holster back around to my right hip, tucking in my shirt tail, lifting my hat to run my fingers through my hair to get it off my forehead. I think it was only then, staring back at Kellums' brightly lit hacienda, that it dawned on me that I was out of a job. I know I'd said earlier that I'd quit before I joined Anderson and his bunch, but I don't guess I really figured it would come to that. Now that it had, it hit me kind of hard.

I went to the barracks first to retrieve my stuff. Frank Gunton was sitting at the table in his long johns and socks, playing solitaire. His eyes grew wide when he saw me. "What the heck happened to you?" he blurted.

I'd thought that by tucking in my shirt and sweeping my hair back, I'd erased all signs of my scuffle with Kellums' gunmen, but a quick glance down my body showed me I hadn't come close. There was dust everywhere, and one of my sleeves was ripped at the elbow, the flesh underneath scraped red. I worked the arm experimentally, and I'll admit it was a little sore, although I hadn't noticed it until Frank's comment.

"I got into a tussle with someone," I replied vaguely.

"Who?"

"A couple of Kellums' new men." I walked down the room to my bunk, where I flipped open the lid to my wooden locker and began pulling out my gear and tossing it onto the mattress next to my rifle and bedroll.

"What are you doing?" Frank asked curiously.

"The old man fired me. Looks like it's just going to be you and Pedro hauling salt until he hires someone else."

"The hell you say." He stood and followed me down the aisle between the bunks. "Why'd he do that?"

"I guess he wasn't happy with the way I was working out. It ain't nothing I'm going to lose any sleep over, though. It was a good job, but I'll find another one."

"Not around here, you won't."

I stopped what I was doing for a few seconds, mulling over Frank's words and realizing he was right. My association with Río Tinto was about to come to an end.

"I guess first thing in the morning, I'll book passage on the *Rachel*," I finally said.

"Dang, Wil, I'm gonna to miss you," Frank said, and, from the tone of his voice, I knew he meant it. Awkwardly I shoved my paw toward him. Frank grasped it firmly. "Where will you go?"

"I don't know. Maybe Laredo or Matamoros. Or maybe I'll go all the way to Brownsville, then take a steamer from there. I haven't decided yet." I glanced at my gear. I'd already stowed away what I knew I wanted to carry in my saddlebags—my gunsmithing tools and the like. Now I began sorting through the rest of it, adding a few more pieces to my saddle pouches, then stowing the rest in a cheap carpetbag I'd brought with me from Colorado. I didn't own much in those days, so it didn't take long. After buckling the flaps tight, I slung the bags over my shoulder, tucked my bedroll under my arm, picked up my valise and rifle scabbard, and that was it. I was ready to go.

"You gonna write when you get where you're going?" Frank asked.

"I reckon not," I replied. Frank wasn't all that young, but he acted like it sometimes. Me, I wasn't all that old, but I was sure feeling fossilized that night. "Take care of yourself, Frank," I said, heading for the door. Then I paused and turned back. "When the shooting starts, don't forget to duck. This ain't your war."

He nodded gravely. "I'll do that," he promised. "Good luck to you, Wil."

I gave him a short wave, then walked outside with a unfamiliar lump in my throat. That lump grew a little larger when the door closed behind me. With my gear in hand and not knowing where else to go, I tramped back to New Town and the Lucky Day. It was a busy night for the saloon, but I got a place at the bar for me and my gear, and as soon as Bob saw me, he came right over. I noticed a chary look on his face that I'd never seen there before, but it disappeared when he saw my luggage.

"You goin' somewhere, Wil?"

"I'm looking for a room," I told him, having to raise my voice to be heard over the racket of the crowd. "Have you got one to spare?"

New Town had a saloon, a café, a grocery, two dry-goods stores, and a combination livery and blacksmith. It even had a small stone jail for when the need arose. But it didn't have a hotel, and it didn't have a boarding house.

"Sure, I've got a room I can rent you. How long?"

"I'm hoping just tonight."

"Sure, well, I guess a dollar ought to cover it."

That seemed high for what I knew I'd be getting, but I wasn't in a position to dicker. I slid a piece of silver across the bar, and he scooped it into his apron pocket.

"Top of the stairs, last door on the left," he said.

"Have you got anything to eat? The café's closed."

During the day, Bob ran a small lunch counter for his paying customers. It was just a table with nothing fancy on it—maybe some bread and cheese and pepper jelly, occasionally some cold roast. Enough to keep a man satisfied if he wasn't too hungry, and not go wandering off in search of a meal.

"There's food in the kitchen," Bob said, already moving off. "Help yourself to what you want. I'm too swamped to fetch it for you."

I made my way to the stairs, having to weave a crooked path through the crowd. Bob hadn't been lying about being busy. There must have been thirty-five or forty customers jamming the bar and tables, and I could hear more voices, along with the clatter of ivory, from the poolroom in back. I paused halfway up the stairs for a better view. I recognized just about everyone there, including a few Red Devil hands I would have expected to find back at the barracks with Frank, it being the middle of the week and all. Spotting Jake Murray and Roger Turner sitting at a table with the guy who ran the livery, I nodded a friendly howdy, but all three immediately looked away. I frowned at the snub, then shrugged it off. Jake and Roger both worked for the Devil, and had always been friendly in the past.

I saw Dora and Tina moving languidly through the crowded room like sharks searching for prey, but Beth and Hattie were nowhere to be seen. I wondered if they were upstairs with customers. Hattie's absence was a disappointment. She was my favorite among the Lucky Day whores, and I'd kind of hoped to see her that night, thinking it might be my last chance if the *Rachel* shoved off too early the next day.

I went upstairs, then down the dark hall to my room. Finding the knob, I gave it a twist and a shove, but the door only opened partway before banging into the foot of a narrow iron cot. I had to slide in sideways. The room wasn't much larger than a utility closet, maybe four feet wide by eight long. There was just enough space for the cot, a single chair, and a washstand with a pitcher and bowl on top. A towel hung from a peg driven into the adobe wall beside the stand. Although there was a lamp on a shelf next to the door, I didn't light it. Tossing my gear onto the cot, I backed out of the room and returned downstairs.

The kitchen was behind the bar, cramped and dirty and poorly lit. Pulling open the lid on a heavy oak chest Bob used to keep the mice and lizards out of his food, I rummaged around for something edible. Other than a mummified gecko at the very bottom of the tiny chamber, I didn't find anything unexpected, and I was hungry enough not to turn up my nose at what was there. Dropping some greasy roast pork, goat cheese, and red peppers on top of a couple of corn tortillas, I relatched the chest, then took my supper back to the main room and motioned for a beer.

Bob hadn't asked any questions earlier, but I guess he decided to get nosy this time. "Why ain't you stayin' at the barracks, Wil?" he asked, setting a frothy mug in front of me.

"I'm leaving town. Probably on the *Rachel* when she pulls out."

A thoughtful frown creased his brow. After a moment, he said, "Huh! We ... I mean, I kinda figured you'd stay and fight."

A chunk of cold pork seemed to jam up at the top of my throat. I had to swallow hard to get it down. "Why's that?" I asked, not at all sure I wanted to hear the answer.

"Well, hell, folks have been talkin', is all."

"Yeah? What are they talking about?"

His eyes flitted away, then came back. "About what happened up there in Colorado last year."

The muscles in my cheeks drew taut. "Who told you about that?"

"Kellums' clerk, that Tim McKay fella, stopped off here after work and told me about it. He was tellin' others, too, like he wanted folks to know. Or Kellums did."

I swore softly, my fingers tightening on the mug of beer. "I didn't know McKay was a customer here," I said, struggling to keep my anger in check.

"He ain't, as a rule, but I reckon ...." He shrugged uncomfortably. "I gotta admit I was wonderin' why Kellums was so set on you talkin' to Montoya," Bob went on after a pause. "I figured at first it was on account of you being Mex and all, but I guess not."

It irritated me that he kept bringing up my Mexican heritage. He'd done it that afternoon, too, if you recall. Anyway, he must have sensed my displeasure, because after a while he started to shuffle his feet nervously, like he was just now realizing that I might actually be a killer of men. I can't say I helped my situation any with my reaction. Never taking my eyes off of his, I said, "What's the matter, hoss? You're looking a little edgy all of a sudden."

"Hell, ain't nothin' the matter with me," Bob protested, but he was already moving away, and I swore again, wishing I'd kept my mouth shut.

Putting my back to the bar, I studied the crowded saloon with fresh perspective. My gaze fell on Jake and Roger and the liveryman. All three were studiously ignoring me, keeping their eyes glued to the table in front of them as if awaiting something magical to appear out of the whiskey-soaked wood. I shook my head in disgust. Before that night, if they'd seen me climbing the stairs to the upper floor, they would have hooted and hollered and shouted out ribald encouragement, figuring I was on my way to see Hattie. But not that night, and, with a sinking feeling in the pit of my stomach, I knew it would never be that way again. I was a marked man in Río Tinto, thanks to Randy Kellums.

Turning away, I wolfed my supper, then walked behind the bar to grab a full bottle of whiskey off the lower shelf. Normally Bob would have raised holy hell at that, but that night he just stood back and watched. I tossed a dollar on the bar to pay for the whiskey and the food, then headed upstairs. That time, I didn't stop to look at the crowd.

BATTLE OF THE HOGUP
PART I

by Eric Cranston

From
True Tales of the Old West magazine
May/June, 1956

Although made famous by the world's presses in the nineteenth century as the "Battle of the Hogup Mine," the events that transpired in the tiny village of Hogup, Colorado, during the winter of 1878–1879 have always been locally referred to as simply the Hogup Incident.

That this encounter, which resulted in the unfortunate loss of human life and personal property, probably wouldn't have occurred if not for an unusual set of circumstances put into play in the early part of 1876, has never been properly explored. Even today, the culpability of Donald Conlin in the murders of Lester H. Kerns and Columbus W. Wright is avidly disputed among scholars of the subject.

What is known is that in April of that historic year of our nation's centennial, Donald Conlin was introduced to Clifford A. Baker, the man Conlin later insisted acted alone in the hiring of Jesse Burgess, Wil Chama, Levi Pratt, George Tinslow, and Roy Washburn—the infamous "Gunnison Five"—to quell the riots that were threatening to topple the Hogup mining operation. Whether

Conlin's introduction to Baker was formal, or made at the end of a gun barrel, as Conlin himself implies, is still debated, although historic evidence seems to support at least the possibility of Conlin's claim.

Papers on file with the South Dakota Historical Association confirm that in 1876, Conlin was operating a claim near Harney's Peak in the Black Hills of Dakota Territory, and that in April of that year he abruptly relinquished title to his claim to one Lawrence V. Mueller of Deadwood. Cliff Baker was an employee of Mueller at the time, although the nature of his duties for Mueller's numerous enterprises has never been fully disclosed.

Cliff Baker's influence in the Deadwood matter is speculation, at best, and might not have raised more than an occasional eyebrow among dedicated historians if not for a letter signed by Conlin and published in the *Denver News* in 1888, alluding to Baker's involvement in his decision to return to his old stomping grounds along the western slopes of the Rocky Mountains.

Conlin's long and often frustrating history with Colorado's rugged landscape is well recorded in regional newspapers. In 1874, he and two partners, Edwin Turner of Rockport, Indiana, and Winston Hart of Tell City, Indiana, filed a claim on a northern tributary of the Gunnison River named Hogup Creek (Editor's note: Later renamed Conlin Creek), after an unusual hill formation nearby. There, the partners reportedly enjoyed moderate success in their panning efforts, until their labors were interrupted in the fall of that year by a war party of Ute Indians. Hart was murdered on the claim, his body mutilated by warriors who ransacked the camp and destroyed what equipment and supplies were not carried away. Although Conlin and Turner were able to escape the worst of the savagery, Turner was so seriously wounded in the encounter that he later had his left arm amputated at the shoulder, due to infection caused by a Ute arrowhead embedded in the joint.

Turner returned to Indiana the following spring, but Conlin remained in the West. His name turns up again with the purchase of an existing claim on a tributary of Fountain Creek, near present-day Manitou Springs.

Things seemed to have gone reasonably well for Conlin until the summer of 1875, when his ownership of the Manitou Springs site was challenged by a Denver conglomerate, alleging an 1874 purchase of some twenty established and unestablished claims along the same tributary, including Conlin's. One can only imagine Conlin's reaction to this unexpected setback, especially when, in a letter addressed to Turner, now back in Rockport, he alluded to "some unusual success" at his Manitou Springs location.

Although Conlin instigated a legal challenge against the larger corporation, his claim was eventually dismissed by a miner's court in Blackhawk. ("The Blackhawk Conspiracy," *True Tales of the Old West* magazine, January/February, 1952)

Since Conlin had filed his purchase with the Blackhawk District's claims office in good faith, he was awarded compensation for his losses, although his settlement was widely speculated to be less than twenty-five cents on the dollar. In the above-cited letter to the *Denver News*, Conlin states the award was closer to twelve cents.

After leaving the Manitou Springs area, Conlin next turns up in the aforementioned Black Hills of Dakota Territory, where his luck seems to have briefly changed for the better. He filed a claim on a piece of ground "near, and slightly northeast of, Harney's Peak," and immediately built a brush shelter and a new rocker box.

Conlin worked the Black Hills claim throughout the fall of 1875, and once again seems to have enjoyed some "unusual" success for his labors. Yet despite his presumed satisfaction with the site (letter to Turner; December 16, 1875; author's collection), in the spring of 1876, Conlin once again left a profitable claim under suspicious circumstances. Although he would later state that he was forced to sell by ruffians hired by mining magnate, George

Hearst, no proof of Hearst's involvement in the Conlin site has ever surfaced. Nor did Hearst himself appear in the Black Hills until well after Conlin abandoned the Dakota Territory. (Editor's note: Hearst did not arrive in the Black Hills until October of 1877, when he took over management of the Homestake Mine.)

While some historians argue that Conlin's presumably false statement against Hearst brings the entirety of his testimony into question, others present the thesis that, while Hearst himself may not have arrived in the Hills until the autumn of 1877, it would be presumptuous to assume he didn't have operatives working in the area well before that date.

In fact, some historians speculate that it is this seemingly improbable accusation against Hearst (what would Conlin have to gain from such an outlandish statement if it weren't true?) as much as the files with the South Dakota Historical Association that substantiate the transfer of ownership of Conlin's claim to Lawrence Mueller, that strengthens the argument for a hostile takeover of Conlin's Black Hills site. Records from Hearst's mining ventures in South America do list an L. V. Mueller as an associate of Mr. Hearst in Bolivia, although no further identification of that person, or his subsequent return to the United States, has been found.

Others, however, maintain that Conlin's allegations of coercion were merely attempts to solicit the sympathy of public opinion, and to focus the blame for the Hogup murders more firmly upon Baker's head. To claim otherwise, they suggest, begs the question: Why would Conlin send for Baker to run his Hogup operation if Baker had been party to the forced eviction of Conlin from the Hills?

These Black Hills allegations aside, it is well documented that by the summer of 1876, Conlin had once again returned to the western slopes of Colorado, where he renewed the claim he, Turner, and Hart had filed on Hogup Creek two years earlier. Also submitted at this time was a relinquishment of title document from Turner, still in Indiana.

With legal ownership of the Hogup now seemingly secured, Conlin surprisingly brought in operatives from a Black Hills mining corporation owned, in part, by Lawrence Mueller. Among the individuals to arrive in Gunnison was the Hogup Mine's new manager, Clifford A. Baker.

Cliff Baker's reputation in Western mining circles in the 1870s was less that of a skilled, hard-rock miner, and more that of a sharp and resourceful businessman. One contemporary of the times summed it up rather succinctly when he stated that Baker "got things done," and apparently in an efficient and timely, if not always ethical, manner.

For a man like Donald Conlin, already forced off of two claims by shady legal maneuvering and a third by Indian attack, Baker's reputation, as well as his willingness to take over the Hogup's day-to-day operations for a percentage of the profits, must have seemed heaven sent. And profits did seem assured, as Conlin's initial belief in the Hogup site in 1874 proved extremely well-founded. By early 1877, the mine was employing some two hundred men, working twelve-hour shifts for an around-the-clock operation that, at peak production, delivered nearly a ton of high-grade ore every seventy-two hours. Estimates at the time placed the gold content as high as seven percent, although others deemed those numbers inflated in an attempt to sell shares in the Hogup against the mine's eventual depletion.

By December of 1876, Donald Conlin had retired to Denver, a wealthy individual by all accounts, enjoying the "high life" on his share of the Hogup's dividends.

With Conlin out of the picture and Cliff Baker in charge, all seemed right in the town of Hogup, until a series of cave-ins in the fall of 1878 brought an end to the harmony within the mining community, and the arrival of a band of strike breakers called the Gunnison Five.

WIL CHAMA INTERVIEW

❧

SESSION FOUR

I woke up the next morning groggy and hungover, my tongue woolen with the taste of cigarettes and booze. I don't drink anymore, and I didn't drink a whole lot when I was younger, but I won't deny a certain amount of experience with the bottle. That night in the Lucky Day was one of my worst.

After rolling my blankets into a bundle and gathering my gear, I shoved what was left of the whiskey into my saddlebags and squeezed out the door. Downstairs was nearly deserted. Only Bob Thompson remained from the crowd the night before, sitting at a table near the front door with a cup of coffee steaming in the cool air. Bob looked up guardedly.

"Howdy, Wil."

"Bob."

A strained silence filled the next couple of minutes. Finally I said, "Take care of yourself," and headed for the door. Bob didn't try to stop me. He didn't offer me a seat or a cup of coffee or even a final good bye. I guess that was just as well, the way things turned out, but I still slammed my fist into one of the batwing doors on my way out, just so that he knew my feelings.

Río Tinto had two eating joints, but my favorite was the New Harmony Café, just a few doors down from the Lucky Day. It was run by an elderly African couple who'd told me they'd been house servants for a large plantation in Alabama before the war. With freedom granted, they'd come West. I don't know how they ended up in Río Tinto, but I was glad they did. Mama Belle might have perfected her culinary skills in the South, but it was out here that she'd melded them into a near perfect blending of Southern fried and Tex-Mex. A few of her concoctions were spicy enough to blister the roof of your mouth, but I liked her Southern stuff best.

The breakfast crowd had already cleared out by the time I got there, so I had my choice of tables. The old man, Jerome, came over as soon as I was seated.

"How are you this morning, Mister Chama?" he asked kindly. In all the months I'd known the couple, I'd never heard a cross word or seen a sour expression from either of them. Río Tinto might not have amounted to much in the eyes of an aristocrat, but I reckon it must have looked pretty fine to someone born and raised in slavery.

"I'm hungry, Jerome," I said.

"Might could be some fried eggs and bacon and flapjacks'll take care of that."

Both Jerome and Mama Belle had deep Southern accents that were occasionally difficult to grasp with my Western-trained ear. I mention that as I mentioned yesterday how most of my conversations in Old Town were in border Spanish. I'm not going to try to mimic the way folks talked, because that was as varied as the people who lived there, which was an assorted crowd in those days.

Anyway, Jerome's breakfast suggestions filled my mind with images my belly immediately rejected. Stifling a whiskey belch, I said, "Maybe just some bread and cheese this morning. And coffee. Lots of coffee."

Jerome smiled knowingly but didn't comment. He was back

in a few minutes with a large bone-china cup and a steaming pot, which he sat in front of me. Heading back to the kitchen, he said, "I'll go fetch that bread and cheese now."

Taking my time, I managed to get everything down, then keep it there afterward. I was even feeling a little better by the time I paid my bill and went outside. Wandering up the street, I ducked into the Tinto Mercantile to arrange passage on the *Rachel*. Jay Landry's gawky stare told me he'd heard about my involvement in the Gunnison affair. I guess by then, most people had.

Río Tinto didn't have a regular shipping center, but Landry had volunteered time and space for the job, just as he had the postal chores for a community that didn't rate its own post office. It was a pretty shrewd move on his part, offering a service that was bound to bring folks into his store, and maybe generate a little extra revenue in the process. After dumping my gear on the floor next to the door, I walked over to the counter. "Can I still buy a ticket for the *Rachel*?"

My request brought a relieved smile to the storekeeper's face. I don't know what he expected—probably that I was going to shoot up the place or try to rob him or something. In a kind of gush of words, he said, "Sure, Captain White was in here not thirty minutes ago and said he wants to shove off by noon, can you make that?"

I nodded and dug a wad of bills from my pocket while studying the printed schedule Landry placed on the counter in front of me. A ticket to Laredo was fifteen dollars; it was sixty-five dollars to Brownsville. I waffled over destinations for a minute, then decided to book passage all the way to the Gulf. I figured I could catch an ocean-bound steamer from there and go just about anywhere in the world that struck my fancy—maybe some place like Australia or Africa, where I could leave my reputation behind forever.

Now, sixty-five dollars pretty well emptied my pockets, but I had a couple of hundred bucks stashed away in the pouch I carried my gunsmithing tools in, plus my pay from the Devil for my last two runs to the Flats. Knowing I wouldn't have to worry about money for a while, I bought some extras to take with me—crackers and sardines, a new pair of socks, extra ammunition for both my rifle and revolver. Leaving my gear at Landry's, I walked down to the Devil's main office to collect my pay. Kellums must have already told McKay I was fired, because he had my money waiting for me.

Back in New Town, I made myself comfortable on a bench in front of Neil Teague's hardware store and rolled a cigarette. I was lounging there with my ankles crossed, soaking up the morning sunshine, when I spotted a group of horsemen riding up the street from the Red Devil stables. My muscles contracted immediately, as if someone had turned a crank at my feet, drawing everything from my scalp on down a little tighter.

Oh, I recognized them right off, you'd better believe that. Remember me mentioning Pope and Landors, the two gun hands who had gotten off the *Rachel* the day before? Well, that was Wade Pope and Pinky Landors, and I'd heard of both of them while working for Matt Dunn up in Denver. Especially Pope. A lot of hide hunters used to hang out around Dunn's place, and Pope's name would come up every once in a while. He'd been a hider himself back then, hunting out of Dodge City, and they said he was easy to rile and quick to shoot. Rumor was that not all the men he'd killed had been gunned down in a fair fight, either.

Sitting up cautiously, I watched the gunmen jog past on R. D. branded horses. Pope and Landors were out front, riding stirrup-to-stirrup. Tom Layton came next, slumped in the saddle, his face lumpy from last night's fracas, one eye swollen nearly shut. I was kind of proud of that, but tried not to let it show. Although Layton glared at me with his good eye, he didn't say anything. Bringing up the rear was one of the men I'd seen yesterday in the Lucky Day. I'd learn later on that his name was Ike Bannon. Ike was a small and ribby, and other than Jerome and Mama Belle, the only African I ever saw in Río Tinto.

Although none of the new men Kellums had hired looked especially tame, I'd have to say Ike Bannon had the meanest air about him. When the others turned their gaze my way, it was like they'd be happy to squash me like a bug if I got in their way. Ike just looked like he wanted to squash me, period. Like he'd be more than happy to go out of his way to do it. Maybe it was his shrimpy stature that gave him such a need to prove himself. Whatever the reason, he stared at me that day like he hated me to my core. Glared even worse than Layton, who had good cause to glare.

I won't deny a wave of relief when they jogged on past without stopping. Getting to my feet, I strode to the edge of the boardwalk to watch them out of town. They took the Cut, quickly growing smaller as they made their way toward the desert's rim. Hearing the soft thud of shoes, I turned to find Neil Teague standing behind me, looking at Kellums' hardcases.

"Where do you figure they're off to?" I asked, not really expecting an answer, but dang if ol' Teague didn't surprise me.

"Probably going after Montoya's men. He sent two of 'em out a couple of days ago for salt."

Now, that brought a quick chill to my gut, and, after a pause, I said as casually as I could, "I wonder if Amos Montoya knows about it yet."

Teague gave me a hard look, then turned and went back inside. I've got to say that, for the way everyone kept insisting how unexpected Kellums' actions were, it seemed the lines were being drawn between the two factions mighty quick.

It didn't seem fair to me that Kellums' men were getting a free pass out of town, so, since I still had a couple of hours before the *Rachel* shoved off, I decided to put my nose where I was pretty certain it didn't belong. Stepping off the boardwalk, I made my way down a footpath through the trees to Old Town.

A boy of ten or so was hunkered down on his calves in the shade of the veranda fronting the Bravo Cantina when I got there, a solemn-eyed kid wearing gray cotton trousers nearly worn through at the knees and a too-thin shirt he was growing out of. He was holding the lead rope to a burro loaded down with enough kindling to make it look like a blood-swollen tick. I gave the burro a wide berth, having learned to respect the range and speed of a jackass' heels as thoroughly as I did a mule's, and ducked through the low door to the cantina.

The Bravo was about as different from the Lucky Day as a couple of drinking establishments could be. The room was low-ceilinged but spread out, wide and dark and cool as a cavern. The bar ran along the right-hand side of the room, simple but not crude, carved out of a single cottonwood log. There were a few tables scattered around, but nothing for gamblers; no chuck-a-luck cage or faro table or roulette wheel. Not even a pool table or a dart board. In the wall opposite the bar was the entrance to Montoya's store, making it easy for a man who came in for supplies to stop off for a drink before heading home.

There was nobody behind the bar, but Amos Montoya was sitting at a table near the back wall with a bald Tejano in a dirty white apron. Both men eyed me warily as I approached.

"Welcome, Señor Chama," Montoya greeted tentatively. "Have you brought another message from El Diablo?"

"I don't work for Kellums anymore."

Montoya didn't look surprised, and I was guessing he'd already heard. Probably knew about my scuffle with Anderson and Layton, too. That man had a communications network set up that would make the military envious.

"Then a drink?" Montoya glanced at the bartender, who immediately stood.

"No, sir. I came to tell you about Kellums' men."

Montoya nodded graciously. "I am aware that Kellums has hired a number of hombres *malos*," he said. "They will be dealt with when the time is appropriate."

"Did you know a bunch of them just rode out, heading up the Cut?"

That got a quick response. "No," he replied, frowning and sitting up straighter. "That is news. When did they leave?"

"Maybe ten minutes ago."

Hearing a stir of movement behind me, I half turned, my hand sliding instinctively toward my Remington—something it wouldn't have done on its own even twenty-four hours before—but it was only the boy I'd seen outside. He moved almost shyly to one side of the front door, keeping his back to the wall. Only his eyes betrayed any emotion. Curiosity, I thought, or fear.

Glancing at the bartender, Montoya curtly tipped his head toward the door. As the man hurried out, Montoya rose and moved behind the bar. "Perhaps you would join me in a drink now, señor, if it is not too early?"

I hesitated only a moment. Although I wasn't eager to pour any more liquor down an already touchy gullet, some niggling sense of inquisitiveness urged me to accept. "Sure, a small one."

I walked over to the bar where he was already pouring mescal into a pair of red-tinted clay cups with thick, crooked rims—homemade and home-fired, like most of the stuff you'd find in Old Town. I took a prudent sip, then nodded approvingly. It wasn't bad for a local brew, although I could tell even before it hit bottom that it was going to be too soon after last night's binge to truly appreciate. I must have made some kind of face, because Montoya cocked an eyebrow in question.

"The taste is bad?"

"No, it tastes fine," I assured him. "It's just a little early in the day for me."

A rare smile breached the older man's lips. "Lately my days and nights have become as one. Breakfast at midnight, dinner at dawn." He took a healthy swallow, then set his cup aside with a suppressed shudder. "I will confess that I did not expect to see you again, Señor Chama. Word had come to me that you would depart on the *Rachel* this afternoon."

"It doesn't sound like much goes on around here that you don't know about," I remarked.

"Perhaps, but I am glad you brought me this news. Three days ago I sent two men to the Flats with carretas to bring back more salt." He nodded toward the silent youth, still seemingly pinned to the wall next to the front door. "Felix's father is one of them. I fear now for their safety."

I stared quietly at the kid. He met my scrutiny without flinching, the somberness of his expression, the deerlike wariness in his eyes, triggering a vague memory deep in my brain. I tried to bring it to the surface, but it refused to rise.

"You ought to be afraid for them," I told Montoya. "I had words with a couple of Kellums' men last night. They're a rough-barked lot." After a pause, I added, "Have you got anyone who can stand up to them?"

"A gunman, you mean?"

I nodded. I hadn't wanted my question to be perceived as an insult, and I was glad Montoya didn't take it that way.

"I have a man, yes."

"A man? Just one?"

"I am afraid I lack Señor Kellums' financial resources," Montoya admitted. "Guns, and especially men skilled in their use, cost much, and Río Tinto is a poor town. I could have a hundred goats in my pens by nightfall, but a hundred dollars would be much harder to come by." He took a sip of mescal, staring reflectively at the far wall. "Much harder," he added, then brought his gaze back to me. I was already shaking my head "no" when he said, "Perhaps you would change your mind?"

"I've already paid for my passage downriver," I answered. "I'm going to ..."

There was a loud thump behind me, and I whirled lightning

quick, my hand diving for the Remington for the second time in less than half an hour. I swore under my breath when my gaze fell on Felix. I guess he'd been heading for the door, but had somehow managed to bump into a chair along the way, accidentally shoving it hard against a table.

The kid froze with his hands on the back of the chair, his dark eyes staring into mine, and my mind flashed instantly to Colorado, the little mining camp of Hogup, north of Gunnison. A warm flush of embarrassment spread across my face, and I looked away. I wasn't very proud of that time in my life, although not for the reason Kellums had implied in his office the day before. The truth is, I'd been on the wrong side of that affair from the very beginning, and the memory of some of the things we'd done up there shamed me more than I wanted to admit. I'd made a promise to myself when it was over that I'd never get involved in anything like that again, and I didn't intend to break my vow now. Not for Randy Kellums or Amos Montoya.

The batwing doors separating the store from the cantina swung open and a large man dressed in black trousers and shirt, a leather vest and wide-brimmed sombrero, stepped into the room. His gaze raked hard over me and the kid, then moved on to Montoya.

"Carlos said you wished to speak with me," the man said in a low rumble, like the words were rattling up through his throat on iron rails.

"I did," Montoya acknowledged, then inclined his head toward me. "This is Wilhelm Chama, but we call him Wil."

I could tell by the big man's unaltered expression that he'd never heard of me, which I found refreshing after the preceding night.

"And this," Montoya continued, turning to me, "is Angelino Sandavol, although he prefers to be called Angel." Swinging back to face the burly Mexican, he added, "Our friend Chama is a Kellums man."

Sandavol's eyes came back to me hard as stone, although he

didn't put his feelings, as obvious as they were, into words.

"No, that is no longer true," Montoya corrected himself. "Señor Chama was a Kellums' man, but he no longer works for El Diablo. In fact, he is leaving Río Tinto this afternoon ... unless we can persuade him to stay and help us."

"And you feel we need a Kellums man?" Angel asked, his expression clearly indicating he didn't.

"I think we need this Kellums man," Montoya replied solemnly. "When I asked you to come to Río Tinto, Angel, I did not know the extent of Kellums' desire to crush me. I expected one man." He turned to me with a wry smile. "This man."

"This one?" Angel's eyes narrowed. "Ah, yes, the gunman from Colorado."

"So I had once thought," Montoya conceded. "But friend Chama has surprised me. He has quit El Diablo Rojo, rather than fight his own people."

Now, that wasn't true. Neither Montoya's heritage nor my own had anything to do with my decision not to become involved in the Tinto War. Besides, back then I considered myself as much German as Mexican.

"Did he truly quit, or does he only pretend to quit?" Angel asked.

"That is a good question," Montoya agreed, keeping his eyes on me. "It is one I have asked myself several times since he and I spoke last night. To be honest, I don't have an answer. Not yet."

"Well, let me give you one," I said, pushing away from the bar. "I quit the Devil last night, and when the *Rachel* shoves off this afternoon, I'll be on her." I started for the door, my stride long and purposeful.

"Are you sure that is really what you want to do?" Montoya called after me.

I kept walking.

"Perhaps there is still a way in which you could atone for the horrible wrong you did in Colorado."

That brought me up sharp, my fingers snapping into white-knuckled fists like a pair of steel traps hanging off my wrists. Turning slowly, I could see the concern on Montoya's face, the fear that he'd gone too far, pushed too hard. There were a lot of thoughts bucking around inside my skull at that moment, a lot of conflicting emotions, a lot of things I could have said. I'm glad now that I didn't, that I kept my response short and sweet, even if it did sound like it was squeezed out of a sausage grinder.

"I've got nothing that needs atoning for, either here or in Colorado."

"Perhaps I am wrong," Montoya said. "If that is the case, then I wish you a safe journey and a long and healthy life."

I nodded uncertainly, then started again for the door. I heard Angel crossing the room to the bar, the musical jingle of his large-roweled spurs sounding strangely out of place in the taut silence of the cantina. At the front door I paused to watch the Bravo's bartender hurrying down the path from New Town, his white apron flapping around his knees. I should have kept walking, but I didn't.

The bartender's name was Carlos Mendez. There was a sheen of perspiration across the top of his bald head, and his mouth was open in the manner of an out-of-shape man in a rush. He must have really been moving since leaving the cantina to find Angel Sandavol, then climb the bench to New Town and make it back here in the time he did. I noticed his chest was heaving mightily as he burst through the door and made a beeline to the bar.

"It is as Chama says," Carlos managed between raspy gasps. "Four hombres." He quickly named off the men I'd seen from the boardwalk in front of Teague's hardware store. "It is said they go to the Flats to cause trouble, but I do not know if that is true." Then he shrugged expansively. "But if not the Flats, then where?"

Montoya nodded grimly. "Then word has reached Kellums that Antonio and Cesar are digging salt, and he has sent his hombres malos, his bad men, to stop them. There can be no other explanation." He looked at me, asking a question with his eyes.

I wanted to say no. The word was right there on the tip of my tongue, like a watermelon seed just waiting to be spit out. But before I could utter a refusal, I felt my gaze being drawn to the kid, standing silently at my side. Felix's eyes, veiled by an unruly mop of coal-black hair, were large and luminous in his olive-skinned face. I could tell he was making an effort to keep his emotions in check, but he couldn't hide the rigid set of his shoulders, the scar-like tautness of his lips. I think I might have cursed, I'm not sure. I do know it took me a moment to drag the words out, and that I was still looking at the kid when I spoke.

"I'll go," I said raggedly. "Just this once, just ... just to help."

At the bar, Angel growled. "I do not need this one's help, *patrón*. It will be difficult enough, knowing there are four men before me who wish to see me dead. To have another at my back who I cannot trust would be more trouble than it is worth."

"If it bothers you so much, I'll ride out front and let you bring up the rear," I said pointedly, turning my back on the kid.

Montoya held up a hand. "Señor Chama will go. I have decided."

Angel's nostrils flared. "As you wish, patrón," he said. "But I cannot promise he will come back."

Montoya glanced my way. "Friend Chama ... Wil?"

I nodded brusquely, my pulse throbbing loudly in my temples. "I'll go, but I'll be damned if I'm going to waste time trying to prove anything to that big ape." I jutted my chin toward Angel. "And if he tries anything funny, it might be him that doesn't come back."

Montoya nodded. I guess he figured that was about as much as he was going to get from either of us. I looked around for the kid, but Felix was gone.

WIL CHAMA INTERVIEW

❧

SESSION FIVE

I think that recorder of yours runs uneven. Or maybe it's the way I'm remembering what happened down there in Río Tinto. It seems like sometimes it's hours between having to change disks, and at other times—I don't know. I guess it doesn't matter.

Anyway, getting back to what happened, after I agreed to go to the Flats with Angel Sandavol, Montoya instructed his bartender to have Flaco bring me a horse. Flaco was the nephew I'd met the night before, behind the counter in Montoya's store.

"Tell Flaco to bring Señor Chama my good bay horse, and have him use my range saddle," is what the old grandee said, and Carlos replied, "Sí, patrón," and vanished into the store.

A couple of minutes later I heard the back door—the same one me and Amos had used the night before—open, then shut. Grumbling too low for me to make out the words, Angel exited through the cantina's front door.

"You have a rifle and enough ammunition?" Montoya asked me.

"Yes, but it's still up at the Mercantile. I'll pick it up on the way out of town."

"That won't be necessary." He glanced at the front door. "Felix!" he shouted, and the kid ducked back inside just long enough to nod, like he could read the old man's mind, or more likely had been eavesdropping, then scooted out of there quick as a whip.

Coming out from behind the bar, Montoya sank tiredly into a chair. "I must confess I share some of Angel's distrust," he told me. "But instinct tells me more strongly that you are being truthful. Still, it is only fair that I warn you that, if I am wrong, if you are not as you portray yourself, I will not hesitate to exact justice. What we attempt here is too important for all of us. We cannot allow treachery to undermine our efforts. You understand this?"

I walked back to the bar. The cup of mescal the old man had poured me earlier was still there, and I drained it in one large swallow. This time I didn't grimace when the hard liquor hit my stomach. After a couple of minutes, Montoya nodded satisfaction.

"Good," he murmured. "It is good that we understand one another. Now we must speak of other matters. I am paying Angel Sandavol two hundred pesos per month, but his reputation justifies such an extravagant wage. For you …"

"I don't want your money," I cut in. "You can pay my expenses, what food I eat and a place to sleep, but that's all I'll need."

Montoya's eyes narrowed suspiciously. He might have thought he was bucking Randy Kellums for the people of Río Tinto, but he was a businessman to the core, and the idea of getting something for practically nothing made him uneasy.

"It's personal," I added after a pause.

"Ah," he said softly, bobbing his head as if he understood.

Hearing the clop of hoofs outside, I walked to the cantina's door. Flaco was leading a tall bay gelding toward the hitching rail, and I whistled appreciatively. I'm not a horseman, but that doesn't mean I can't recognize a quality animal when I see it. That bay was the best-looking horse I'd seen since coming to Río Tinto. It made me wonder where the old man had been stashing it. When I went outside for a closer look, Montoya joined me.

"You are satisfied?" he asked.

"It's a fine mount," I replied.

"One of the best in my stables."

As Montoya stroked the bay's long neck, I studied the rig cinched to the gelding's back. It was a pale amber color from its rawhide covering, the leather scraped so thin you could see the darker colors of the wood underneath. It had one of those big, platter-shaped saddle horns you normally associate with Mexico, and taps on the stirrups to protect your toes from the thorny stings of cactus. But the slats were bare, without even a piece of hide to soften the miles. I eyed that seat with considerable trepidation, already envisioning what my hind end was going to feel and look like by the time we reached the Flats.

We were still standing there when Felix returned with my rifle and the extra cartridges I'd purchased that morning from Landry. At Montoya's command, he moved around to the gelding's offside to fasten the scabbard to the saddle. Angel appeared from behind the store astride a big, black gelding that must have been cut late, judging from its heavy muscles and broad chest. The sharp curve of its neck was bowed against a tight rein as the horse cavorted sideways down the street, kicking up little clouds of dust in its eagerness to be off.

Angel's rig was a lot nicer than mine, with a leather seat, skirting, and full fenders. Silver conchas winked smugly in the sunlight, and there was a bedroll and saddlebags fastened behind the cantle, reminding me that I'd still have to swing past Landry's store to fetch my own blankets and bags before riding out for the Flats.

Angel pulled up a few rods away, his expression clearly showing that his opinion of me hadn't changed. Keeping my own feelings to myself, I went around the far side of the bay to help Felix secure my scabbard to the saddle. Montoya walked over to talk to Angel, trying to ease the scowl off the big man's face. I couldn't hear his reply, but I could tell by the agitated rumble of his voice that Montoya's efforts were largely wasted. Angel Sandavol didn't trust me any farther than he could throw me, although that might be a poor analogy, considering the man's size.

Carlos came out of the cantina carrying a cloth sack bulging with food that he handed to Angel. I stepped into the saddle, the bay spooking and jumping like it hadn't been ridden in a while.

Coming over, Montoya reached up to shake my hand. "Go with God, Wil, and good luck."

I nodded curtly, knowing we were going to need it. As we rode away, Angel remained true to his word by making it a point to bring up the rear. I kicked the bay into a canter, heading for the Cut, but Angel called me back before we reached the trees.

"That way," he said, nodding toward the ancient cart track that spilled from Tinto Cañon like a dog's lolling tongue on a hot afternoon.

I started to tell him about my bedroll, then thought, *the hell with it,* and reined toward the cañon. Being more familiar with Kellums' wagon road, I found the old route to be winding and slow, twisting between fallen boulders that had tumbled so close together over the eons that it's a wonder anyone had ever found a path through them. It didn't take long to figure out why Kellums had gone to the expense of dynamiting a road out of the side of the cliff, rather than trying to negotiate his wagons through this maze of rocks and cactus. We followed the cañon for several miles before it finally came out on top.

I guess you'd call that country between Tinto Cañon and the Flats gently rolling, but for a boy who'd grown up in the evening shade of the Rocky Mountains, it just mostly looked flat and uninspiring. As we moved out briskly across the cactus-studded plain, Angel maintained his position at my back.

Although it was hot and windy up top, we made good time. I pulled up when we reached the main road to point out the tracks Kellums' gunmen had left in the powdery caliche earlier that day, cleaved in places by the deeper cuts of a wagon heading in the opposite direction. I figured the wheel tracks had been made by Pedro Rodriguez, another of Kellums' mule skinners. Pedro would be heading home with a full load, while Frank Gunton was probably somewhere behind us yet, making his way to the Flats to pick up his next cargo.

I wondered briefly what Pedro would think when Frank told him about my being fired. Would he call me a fool for turning my back on such a good-paying job, or would he understand? Pedro had a wife and three small children in Old Town, and needed employment a lot more than I did, but I wanted to think he would approve of my decision. In time, of course, I'd find out how wrong I was, but on that day, my first riding for Amos Montoya, I still believed I was doing the right thing.

We'd lost a lot of time following Tinto Cañon's labyrinthine course. I tried to make up for it by keeping the bay clipping along at a short lope, but it was probably fifteen miles to Antelope Springs by that old route, and nearly noon before we came in sight of the pale green carpet of its chaparral, still several miles distant.

The Springs was a series of shallow pools running along a quarter-mile stretch of mostly dry riverbed, just above where Antelope Creek joined the Tinto River. I pulled up well out on the plain. Angel rode alongside, scowling into the distance.

"Are those the Springs?" he rumbled.

"Uh-huh. If we're lucky, that's where we'll catch up with Kellums' hombres malos."

"Where?" he asked, his eyes scanning the stubby motte.

"The road passes a stone hut near the head of the Springs. There's good grass there and plenty of wood for a fire. It's where I always camped during a run."

It was two days by wagon between Río Tinto and the Flats, five days total on the road. On two of those nights I'd camp at Antelope Springs, so I was fairly well-acquainted with the area.

Angel slid a long gun from his scabbard, a Whitney-Kennedy chambered in the same .44 caliber as my Winchester. I made that assumption based on the size of the bore, which was pointed more or less in my direction when he lowered the rifle across the pommel of his saddle. Although he did it casually, I knew what he meant.

"We will go forward slowly," Angel informed me. "You will ride in front and I will follow. If you are leading me into an ambush, I will shoot you first, and make certain that you are dead before I turn away. Is that understood, hombre?"

"If there's an ambush, it won't be my doing," I replied. "But just so you understand, I'll be shooting back at any whore's son who shoots at me, I don't care what direction the bullet comes from."

That was a reckless response, what with Angel's rifle already pointed in the general direction of my spine, but I was a lot more hot-headed in those days than I am now.

Motioning toward the distant trees, Angel said, "*Vámonos.*"

That's Mex for "git movin'."

I heeled the bay toward the lower end of the copse, figuring that if Kellums' men were still laid over at the upper spring, me and Angel would stand a better chance coming at them through the chaparral.

That last hundred yards was about as nerve-racking an ordeal as any I'd ever put myself through. Only that night in Gunnison was worse. My eyes were shifting constantly as we approached the chaparral, although in the bright sunshine it was hard to see anything under the spreading limbs of the scrub oak. I hauled my Winchester from its scabbard, and didn't look back to see what Angel thought about it, either. As soon as we penetrated the edge of the thicket, I drew up once more. Angel heeled his black horse close, and this time all of his attention was focused on the surrounding brush instead of me. I could tell he was feeling as edgy as a fresh-scraped wound.

"How far?" he queried.

"Another quarter of a mile to the upper spring."

I suppose necessity was beginning to chip away at Angel's

distrust, because the next thing he said was, "We will split up now. You will take the west side of the creek. I will follow the east side."

I nodded agreement and moved out. Despite the fifteen miles already behind us, the bay was pulling restively at its bit, no doubt sensing my own nervousness.

Maybe my going ahead and telling you this now will spoil the suspense, but Kellums' men weren't there. Surprised the hell out of me. Reaching the stone hut, I pulled up to look around, but there wasn't hide nor hair to be seen of them in any direction. I was still gawking when Angel kicked his mount across the stream and rode over.

"Where are they?" he demanded, as if I'd hidden them away before he got there.

Not bothering with a reply, I dismounted to cast about for sign. It didn't take long to find some—the shod hoof marks of horses over the larger prints of the Devil's mules, a cigarette butt ground out under a heel, a discarded matchstick. I picked up the remains of the cigarette, rolling it between my thumb and forefinger until it crumbled and fell apart. Sitting his horse a few yards away, Angel swore viciously.

"It was them?" he said, his words more statement than question.

"More than likely," I agreed. "Not many people use these springs unless they're on their way to or from the Flats. I don't see any other tracks here except for Pedro's, and he uses dried corn husks for his cigarettes. This is store-bought paper." I brushed a few loose flakes of tobacco off my fingers. "They stopped, but not for long."

Angel was staring east through the trees, toward the pale ribbon of the road. "How much farther?"

"Too far," I replied grimly. I knew he was anxious to push on, but we needed to pace ourselves. The fifteen or so miles we'd already covered from Río Tinto via the cañon trail hadn't taken too much out of our horses, but it was another twenty-five miles to the Flats, and that over a parched and waterless landscape. Our mounts would need the rest and water they got here.

Angel's jaw was working aggressively, like he was chewing on gristle. For a minute I thought he was going to order us to keep riding, but he finally leaned back in his saddle with a frustrated growl. "Thirty minutes," he said. "No more."

That was about half the time I would have preferred under normal circumstances, but just about right considering who we were chasing, and why. Angel dismounted and we pulled the saddles from our mounts, then removed their bits so they could more easily drink and graze. My bay immediately laid down in the dust to roll, and looked like he enjoyed it, too. I'm glad he did, because all I could do was stand there tense as a banjo string. I think I killed three or four cigarettes while we waited, a sure sign of anxiety, since I usually didn't smoke that many in a day.

We pushed on after half an hour, setting a faster gait than we should have in the growing heat. That country between Antelope Springs and the Flats was just more of the same—a gently rolling short grass desert, dotted with cactus and rabbitbrush. Overhead, the sky was clear but pallid, like a well-washed blue chambray shirt. The breeze died around midafternoon, and beads of sweat began to creep out from under my hat. The bay suffered even worse. A dirty lather had gathered along the cinch, and the hair on its neck and shoulders was wet and matted from perspiration.

It was approaching dusk by the time we reached the spot where the Tinto River veered sharply northward toward the Bow Mountains, rumpled up on the horizon like blankets kicked to the foot of the bed. Our route continued straight east, and I heeled the bay into a hard lope for this final leg of our journey. Angel was close beside me when we topped a low rise and saw the Flats rolled out before us.

Now, I'd seen that same sight at least once a week for six months, but it was Angel's first view of the beds, and he hauled back on his reins with a startled exclamation. The Tinto Flats are a series of saltbrush-ringed playas with no observable exit, which accounts for the heavy levels of saline. I've been told that toward the middle of the dry lake the salt crust is upward of four feet thick, and I'd guess the size of the shallow basin at between two hundred and fifty to three hundred acres. Its most distinctive feature, of course, is its rosy coloring, noticeable at any time, but especially vivid in the early morning hours when the dawn light is just beginning to brush its surface.

The road terminated at the Chute, which is what we called the place where Kellums' harvesters lived and toiled. Although we could see the buildings from where we'd stopped, I knew Montoya's men wouldn't have gone that far. The local Tejanos had a place near the southern end of the playa where they gleaned their salt. I'd never been there, but it wouldn't be hard to find.

"This way," I told Angel, reining off the road toward a twisting cart track that wound through the desert flora. The sun was down by then, twilight softening the harshest edges of the terrain as we approached a grove of cottonwoods where a small, freshwater spring, uncontaminated by the salt flats, provided grass for the Tejanos' oxen. Not seeing any sign of life among the trees, I yanked the Winchester from its scabbard and laid it across the bend of my left arm.

Angel spotted them first, hanging like bundles of chiles from a sagging cottonwood limb. I swore and levered a round into the Winchester's chamber. My gaze swept the deepening shadows under the trees, but nothing moved in the still air. Not even the dead.

We rode in stirrup-to-stirrup, our horses turning skittish at the scent of death. Other than Cesar and Antonio, there was no one else around. Kellums' men had done their job quickly and efficiently, then moved on. The oxen lay close to the carts, all four of them shot once in the head, and the carretas had been set afire, although the flames hadn't caught and the worst damage was a pair of scorched hubs on the nearest cart.

Although there wasn't any doubt that Cesar and Antonio were dead, we cut them down as quick as we could, then pried the nooses from around their necks and started gently slapping their faces and rubbing their arms, as if that might bright them back. It probably looked fairly macabre, but I didn't know what else to do, and I don't think Angel did, either. As darkness settled in we gradually ceased our frantic efforts to raise the dead. I remember sitting back in the tall grass and taking my hat off. With the sun down, the breeze began to stir again, drying my sweat. I rolled and lit a cigarette while Angel walked over to the salters' camp. He came back a few minutes later with a pick and shovel that he threw at my feet.

"You dig their graves," he commanded hoarsely.

It was the wrong approach to take with me feeling the way I did, and I came up fast, wrapping my fingers around the Remington's time-scarred grips. "Back off, big man," I snarled.

Angel's eyes were blazing as he squared around to face me, one massive fist hovering over his holstered revolver. "You will dig, or I will bury three men here tonight," he threatened.

"You try it, and I'll leave that ugly mug of yours above ground to feed the buzzards," I fired back.

We stared hard, but in the end I think we both realized it wasn't each other we were mad at. After a couple of minutes I slowly peeled my fingers off the Remington, and Angel relaxed his forward-hunched pose and straightened. Following a strained pause, he said, "I think I saw another shovel in one of the carretas. I will get it, and we will both dig."

I nodded, satisfied with the compromise, and strode off to find a likely spot. There was another grave near the edge of the trees, an older one with a wooden cross pounded into the dirt at its head. We buried Antonio and Cesar next to that, then went to fetch our horses. I had a pretty good idea where Kellums' gunmen had gone, and Angel and me—well, we had a score to settle with that bunch.

Excerpts from
The Colorful World of Salt

∞

by Harold Teaberger

Ocean Front Publishing • 1936

[An even] partial list of the earth's more exotically shaded salts reveal a rainbow of colors—from Peruvian pink and Hawaiian red to Indian black and Argentine yellow.

* * * * *

These colors are usually subtle and almost always naturally occurring, the result of nonsaline minerals so intricately compounded within the seasoning that its extraction becomes fiscally prohibitive, if not physically impossible.

* * * * *

This tinting, especially in salt harvested from ancient lake or sea beds, is seldom more than the decomposed remains of various algae or other plant matter, or microscopic animal life.

* * * * *

Many of these salt pans have been harvested by indigenous peoples for thousands of years, and can be expected to produce this vital condiment for many more thousands of years, but … smaller beds scattered throughout the world, and including numerous locations within the United States … suffered a much shorter life span.

* * * * *

The Tinto Flats of West Texas are an excellent example of these limited-resource beds, and perhaps explains the desperation of the native population to limit its harvest in the latter part of the nineteenth century.

* * * * *

[It was] West Texas' low rainfall and high evaporation rate that created the underground brine … the reddish-pink color came from a pigment called carotene, secreted from algae, thus giving the Tinto Flats salt its uniquely veined shading.

* * * * *

The Tinto Flats produced a light, delicate flake that melted rapidly when applied to warm foods, making it ideal as a finishing or table salt.

WIL CHAMA INTERVIEW

❧

SESSION SIX

I'm glad you told me yesterday how most of the people you interview begin to remember more and more about the incidents you're interviewing them about as they go along. That's sure been the case with me. Last night, lying in bed, I started thinking about all the stuff that happened out there at the Flats when we found those two guys, and I began to get the shivers. Like I was reliving the whole thing all over again. I finally had to get up about midnight and fix myself a cup of cocoa before I could go to sleep.

Anyway, after we buried Antonio and Cesar, me and Angel saddled our horses and rode for the Chute. We still weren't talking much to one another, so I can't say what he was feeling, but I know I was about ready to tear the world apart with my bare hands.

I didn't mention this last night, but unless Kellums' thugs had taken some better weapons with them, Antonio and Cesar had been pretty poorly armed. The only guns I saw in their camp were a double-barreled shotgun and a single-shot rifle, both muzzle-loaders.

I'm telling you this now because, as we rode out of the trees, I noticed Angel was carrying the shotgun across his saddle bows. I wish

I'd thought to grab it first. A shotgun is a handy weapon to have in a close-quarters fight, and possesses a mighty fine intimidation factor as well, although I didn't know how much good that was going to be against men like Wade Pope and Pinky Landors, or that mean-eyed little runt, Ike Bannon. I suspected it would work real fine against Tom Layton, though. Of the ones I'd met so far, Layton seemed like the biggest bully in the lot, a personality trait I've never had much respect for. Although there was no trail linking the cottonwoods where Antonio and Cesar had been murdered to the Chute, where Kellums' harvesters lived, the vegetation that close to the salt beds was sparse enough that we found our way without trouble.

As a description, the word "chute" is misleading. The structure was really nothing more than an earthen ramp that led to a wooden platform just slightly higher than the sideboards on Kellums' tallest wagon. The light sleds his crew used to haul the salt in from the playa were dragged to the top of the ramp by a team of mules wearing sturdy leather moccasins to protect their feet from the corrosive qualities of the salt—hang around a place like that with even a tiny cut on your finger, and you'll soon learn what I'm talking about.

With the flat-bottomed sleds on top and one of Kellums' freighters down below, laborers would shovel the salt onto a wooden slide that funneled it into the wagon. Kind of like a chute, although not that elaborate. We just called it the Chute because we had to call it something.

In addition to the ramp and platform, there was an adobe barracks similar to the one in Río Tinto, with half a dozen bunks at one end, a kitchen in the middle, and a small, sparsely furnished office at the other end. The place was managed by a middle-aged man named Hank Waite, who I'd always gotten along well with. Waite was slim but paunchy, with thick, gray hair and pale, sad eyes. He didn't do much physical labor anymore, but everyone agreed he was a good manager, and most of his crew liked him. Waite normally kept five or six men working under him at the Flats, with one man always taking a week off to blow his pay in Río Tinto.

There was a corral with a lean-to shed behind the barracks where the mule skinners kept their teams, penned in with the stock Waite's men used to work the salt flats and usually a few saddle horses. Hay and water were hauled in monthly, the water brought in by tanker hitched to the rear of a salt wagon. It was a heavy SOB when full. I knew because I'd hauled it behind my wagon more than once.

That night with Angel, the first thing I did was ride around back to check the corral. There were four unfamiliar horses inside, their hair spiky with dried sweat, heads drooped in exhaustion. The other horses—Waite's saddle stock—were all missing, although I had a good idea where they'd gone. Riding back to the front of the barracks, I gave a shout, and Hank Waite came outside carrying a lantern above his head.

"Wil?" he said uncertainly.

"Yeah, it's me."

"Who's that with you?" He was peering into the shadows, where Angel had pulled up about twenty yards out to observe the inter-action between me and Hank with a distrustful eye.

"I'm looking for the four men who rode in here on those horses you've got out back," I said, ignoring Hank's question.

The foreman's lantern sagged a little. "What's going on?"

"Yeah," chimed a voice from the barracks as the rest of Hank's crew shoved outside. The person who'd spoken, a kid named Danny Fuller, pushed up beside Hank. "What the hell's goin' on, Chama? Them crazy-eyed sons a bitches that come here earlier said you wasn't haulin' salt for the old man no more."

Looking back on it now, I can see the irony of Dan Fuller calling anyone "crazy-eyed." There's a term you hear sometimes called "having a screw loose." That was Danny Fuller to the core, kind of dumb and a little loco, and not someone you'd want to turn your back on if he was mad or had been drinking. That night at the Chute, though, I was feeling frazzled, and in no mood to suffer a fool's babbling.

"They still around, Hank?" I asked.

"No, they ain't. They rode in here a couple of hours before sunset and told me they worked for Kellums, then said they needed fresh horses. I don't know if they really work for the Devil or not, but I wasn't going to argue with 'em."

"That little niggah looked mean as hell," Danny added thoughtfully, then his expression abruptly changed. "Mind you, I ain't sayin' I'm scart of the boy. Anybody says that, they'd better not do it to my face or I'll pluck their damned tail feathers."

"Pull back, Danny," Hank chided mildly. "Nobody said you were afraid."

"I'm just sayin they better not, is all."

"Then they've already pulled out?" I cut in before Danny could work himself into a frenzy.

"Switched saddles and rode on without a backward glance," Hank confirmed. "Didn't even take time to see to their stock. I had to have a couple of my boys take care of 'em, else they might've keeled over from exhaustion. Them ponies was rode hard, for a fact."

I nodded reflectively. "That sounds like them," I said, then started to rein away. "Much obliged, Hank."

"It's starting then, huh?" Hank asked morosely.

I knew what he was talking about, but I didn't answer. Guiding my horse over to where Angel waited, I related the information Hank had given me, then pointed out that Kellums' gunmen had a good three-hour head start on us, and mounted on fresh horses, to boot.

"We ain't likely to catch up," I added as we fell in side-by-side, following the road back toward Río Tinto. "Not unless they stop somewhere along the way."

Although I could tell it galled him to say so, Angel agreed. We'd already covered better than thirty-five hard, hot miles that day, and our horses were tuckered. Besides, we knew where Kellums' hombres malos were headed, and that they wouldn't be hard to locate when we got back to town.

We rode on for a few miles, then made a cold camp in an arroyo. I didn't have my bedroll with me, but lay down in the soft sand and pulled my saddle blanket over my shoulders. It was damp with sweat and stank of horse, but I've slept worse. Coming awake at dawn, chilled and sore, I pushed groggily to my feet.

We breakfasted on the grub Carlos had sent along—goat's meat and cold refritos wrapped in tortillas—then saddled our horses and moved out. Me and Angel still weren't talking much, but I was beginning to sense a lessening of the big man's distrust. Some hours later we spotted a cloud of dust on the horizon. It turned out to be Frank Gunton, making his weekly run to the Flats. Frank hauled back on the lines when we met.

"I thought you was leavin' on the *Rachel*," he blurted to me.

"I changed my mind."

He glanced at Angel, no doubt curious about what the two of us were up to. I don't know if he was aware of who Angel was at that point, but he kept a straight face if he did. I repeated the same query I'd made of Hank Waite the night before.

"Yeah, they came through the Springs about midnight." Frank shook his head as if recalling a bad dream. "I was already bedded down under my wagon when they rode in, but there was still some coals left from my supper fire. They asked if I had any food, so I gave 'em what I had." He chuckled dryly. "I heard a fella say one time that God created man, but that it was ol' Sam Colt made 'em all equal. That wasn't a theory I wanted to test last night."

I smiled in spite of my sour disposition. I liked Frank. Hell, I liked a lot of those boys who worked for Randy Kellums. If not for Kellums' greed, his desire to own it all, I could have gone on working for the Devil for a long time.

"You were smart to give them what they wanted," I said. "They killed a couple of Amos Montoya's men out at the Flats yesterday."

Frank's eyes widened, shifted briefly toward Angel, then came back to me. "You working for Montoya now, Wil?"

"I … no, I just volunteered to ride out and see if I could stop Kellums' men before somebody got hurt. Unfortunately we were too late."

"Damn." Frank shook his head sorrowfully. "I hate to hear it's gone that far. If it keeps up, I ain't sure I'm going to hang around long myself."

There was a stack of supplies for Waite's crew in the back of Frank's wagon, including a couple of crates stacked on top of a bed of straw. I knew what he was carrying, but asked anyway.

"Dynamite?"

"Yeah, two cases of the stuff. Hank sent word last week that he was running short." Hank's crew resorted to dynamite fairly regularly to break up the salt that was, in places, compacted to a granitelike hardness. I'd watched them do it a few times. They'd drill a series of holes in a rough quadrangle, then light the fuses and run like their britches were afire. The explosion would loosen the salt into manageable chunks that could be hoisted onto the sleds and hauled back to the Chute. What always amazed me was how, when a charge was set off, the salt bed would kind of ripple under my feet, even from a quarter of a mile away. If you've ever stepped on a snake curled up in tall grass, you know the feeling.

We said good bye to Frank, then rode on to the Springs, where we stopped to let our horses graze and rest for a couple of hours. We took our time returning, and didn't get back—following the cart track down through Tinto cañon—until dusk. The bats were just exiting their caves as we came into town, swirling above us like columns of black smoke. A cold shiver passed along my spine as I watched them. I don't think I breathed easy until the colony finally veered south, following the Río Grande out of sight.

Me and Angel were a pretty subdued pair as we climbed down in front of the Bravo Cantina. A couple of boys, no more than eleven or twelve, came out to take our horses. I unbuckled my scabbard first, then stepped back as the bay was led around the far side of the building, its head low after two long, hot days.

Although not eager to face Montoya, I figured I'd come this far, and that I might as well see it through to the end.

You could tell right off that news of the killings had already reached town. Spotting Amos in his usual place against the rear wall, me and Angel walked over. A couple of men I didn't recognize vacated their chairs so we could sit down. Angel didn't beat around the bush.

"I am sorry, patrón," he said solemnly. "We were too late to stop the injustice."

Montoya's head moved in a slow nod. His gaze slid toward me.

"Kellums' men just about killed their horses getting there," I said. "I didn't expect that."

"I was told that they returned on different mounts," Montoya acknowledged. "They were hung, Antonio and Cesar?"

"Yes," Angel confirmed.

"The bodies?"

"We buried them there."

That nod again, slow and sad. "Then all that can be done has been done."

Tentatively I said, "Have you talked to Chad Bellamy?"

Several of the Bravo's customers laughed derisively. Montoya merely shook his head. "Bellamy might wear a badge, but he is a Kellums man. He is not to be trusted."

"I used to be a Kellums man," I pointed out, then immediately wished that I hadn't. You could almost feel the animosity among the cantina's customers.

Montoya, though, remained unmoved. "Chad Bellamy is an Anglo, Wil. You are not. Besides, I have not yet decided if even you are to be trusted."

I guess I shouldn't have been surprised. Even after two days in the saddle, chasing the dust of Kellums' hombres malos, I was still an outsider, still a "Kellums man." Scraping my chair back, I pushed tiredly to my feet. "I reckon I'll move on," I said, unconsciously switching to American.

"Where?" Montoya queried. "The *Rachel* has already left for Matamoros."

"I'll get a room at the Lucky Day for tonight. I can decide later how I want to leave." Then, even though it was petty and more than a little childish, I added, "I ain't staying where I'm not welcome."

A whisker of a smile darted across the older man's face. "You will not find much welcome at the Lucky Day, mi amigo. Word that you have ridden for Amos Montoya and his salt thieves has already reached the ears of the Anglo community. The news was not kindly received."

That brought me up short. I hadn't considered that agreeing to help Angel Sandavol at the Flats might somehow affect my standing among New Town's businessmen.

"There is, if you are interested, an empty room behind the store," Montoya said. "You are welcome to it, if I have not too thoroughly mangled your feelings."

I shrugged, aggravated but exhausted. "I reckon my feelings can take it," I replied. "I'll need to fetch my gear from Landry's store, though."

"That won't be necessary, either. Señor Landry took it upon himself to throw your things into the street when he heard you had ridden out with Angel. I had Flaco bring everything here. In fact, it is already in your room."

My room? Montoya's words held an odd ring, like I'd been out in the desert for months rather than days, and that life back here had moved forward without me. There was movement at the door to the store, and I looked over to see Inez standing there with a lamp already lit against the growing darkness.

"My niece will show you the way," Montoya said kindly. "There is food as well, if you are hungry."

I nodded, then followed Inez into the store. Angel stayed behind. I figured he and Montoya still had quite a bit to discuss, not the least of which would be me.

You might recall me mentioning Inez Montoya the other night, the woman who brought the lemonade to Amos' office. I didn't dwell on her then because we were talking about other things, but I sure noticed her. I was noticing her that night as we left the cantina, too. She was of medium height and full-figured, with glossy black hair that fell nearly to her waist in shimmering waves. Her face was a near-perfect oval, her complexion soft and smooth, and the small mole at the corner of her mouth added uniqueness rather than distraction.

You might think me forward to describe her in such intimately physical terms, but I won't deny that I was as smitten by her beauty as any lonely, homeless drifter was likely to be. I didn't hold out much hope for a relationship, though. I hadn't been in that border country long, but I'd seen enough to know that its menfolk were as protective of their women as men were anywhere else.

We exited through a back door into a small courtyard, the type of quadrangle you'd often see on bigger ranchos. It had high walls against Indian attack, and rooms along each side that opened toward the center. Like the walls surrounding Kellums' compound, this one also had cactus planted on top to thwart intruders.

I followed Inez across the dusty yard to a heavy plank door. She pulled down on a leather thong to release a wrought iron latch inside, then pushed the door open and stepped aside for me to enter. It was a simple room, although quite a bit nicer than the oversize closet I'd paid Bob Thompson a dollar for at the Lucky Day. There was a bunk against one wall, a couple of chairs, a washstand and basin filled with fresh water, a sweating olla and a tin cup, and a sconce screwed into the wall, holding a pair of candles. The floor was dirt, but recently sprinkled and freshly swept, and the single window beside the door had been thrown open to allow the room to air out.

Inez came in just far enough to light the candles, then stepped back to the door. "Do you wish food?"

"I wouldn't turn it down."

"I will have some sent to you." As she started to turn away, I impulsively grabbed her arm. She stopped with a startled, half-frightened expression altering her face, and I immediately dropped my hand.

"I'm sorry," I muttered. "That was rude of me."

Her dark eyes searched mine. I thought for a minute she was going to speak, then she abruptly spun away, hurrying across the yard toward the store. I watched until she disappeared inside, then slammed my own door closed with an angry curse. I figured I had maybe five minutes before her uncle showed up with a scatter-gun to kick me out, which was what I deserved. Had I not been so tired and dejected, I might have gone ahead and gathered my gear so that Montoya wouldn't have to wait for me to pack, but ten minutes passed, and I began to wonder if maybe the gods hadn't decided to overlook my earlier transgression.

My bedroll had already been unfurled atop the bunk. After another five minutes, I went over and lay down. I might have dozed. I say that because I remember flinching badly when the door swung open and Inez stepped into the room carrying a wooden platter filled with rice and beans and a bowl of chili Colorado. There was freshly baked bread on the side, toasted and smeared with butter, and a little cup of grape jam. She'd also brought along a pot of coffee, the wire bail hanging over her bent arm like a stew kettle in a fireplace.

She set the tray and the coffee pot on the table, then moved out of the way. I expected her to leave, but she didn't. She didn't speak, either, but just stood there with her eyes cast toward the floor. Pushing uncertainly to my feet, I moved a chair around for her to sit.

"Would you like to join me?" I asked.

She hesitated only a second, then slid into the chair. I filled a heavy china mug with coffee and set it in front of her, then used the tin cup next to the olla for myself. I sank into the second chair, as wary as a mouse creeping under the nose of a dozing cat. In the glow of candlelight, Inez's eyes looked like polished obsidian, her manner shy and demure, as befitted a lady of breeding. She wore a dark skirt with a white blouse cut low enough to hint at the fullness of her breasts. The vision, as a whole, nearly took my breath away.

After an awkward silence, she said, "I was saddened to hear of Cesar and Antonio's deaths. They were good men, but I know that you and Señor Sandavol did all that was possible to prevent their murders."

Of all the subjects Inez Montoya could have brought up, that was probably the worst. She must have noticed my discomfort immediately.

"I am glad you agreed to help my uncle," she hastened to add. "He is a proud man and would never admit it, but I think he worries that the opposition is too strong."

"Do you work for your uncle?"

"Yes. Ever since the Apaches killed my mother and father."

I murmured an apology, for which she thanked me. "It was a long time ago," she added. "I was just a child."

"Did the Apaches attack Río Tinto?"

"No, it was outside the village. Father had gone to gather wood for the winter's fires, and mother went with him. They never came back." She took a tentative sip of coffee, then set the cup aside as if the taste disagreed with her. "Tío Amos says you come from Colorado, and that you are well-known in that place."

"I don't know how well-known I am. I was born in a little town in the San Luis Valley, but I was raised in Denver."

"I have heard of Denver. They say it is a very big city."

"Big enough, I suppose."

"What did you do there?"

"I worked for a man who outfitted the buffalo hunters."

"You were a hunter, too?"

"No. Mostly I helped out in the warehouse, although sometimes I'd work the counter."

"Like Flaco?"

"More or less. If there was time, I'd help the owner work on guns. He was a capable smith."

Her eyes brightened. "I watched last Christmas when you shot the revolver matches down by the river. You were very good."

I'll confess to a certain stirring of pride that she'd noticed, although I tried to keep my chest from puffing out too far. "I used to practice a lot," I admitted. "And my boss showed me a few tricks, like how to control your breathing, and how to keep your front sight from bobbing around too much."

"Is that why tío hired you? Because of your skills with the revolver?"

I remember thinking, *I hope not.*

Knowing how to control your breathing in a shooting match was one thing, but those little gems of knowledge Matt had imparted to me hadn't helped much in Gunnison or Hogup. Not when a bunch of people were shooting back. Still, I figured old Montoya's reasons for wanting me to side with him, instead of Kellums, had to be common knowledge by then, so I just nodded. "I guess he thought I'd be able to help stop Kellums' hired guns, but we didn't have much luck."

"It will be different next time."

Inez meant for her words to reassure me, but instead they caught me off guard. I'd told myself when I agreed to ride out to the Flats with Angel that it would be a one-time deal. I wasn't sure I wanted a second chance. Yet of all the images seared into my brain from the past couple of days, none burned hotter than the face of the kid, Felix Castillo, whose father I had failed to save.

Sensing my distress, Inez stood up. "I should go. Tío will start to worry."

I rose with her. "Thank you for the food, and ... I'm glad you stayed to talk. It was nice."

She smiled briefly, then hurried away. I followed as far as the door, and, for the second time that night, I watched her disappear into the main house.

I ate everything on that platter, and could have done some serious damage to another helping, but figured it would be impolite to go hunting for more. I set the dirty utensils on a bench outside, then smoked a final cigarette before stripping down and crawling into bed. I was asleep almost before my head hit the pillow, but was jolted awake some time later by a pounding at my door. Grabbing my revolver, I leveled it at the latch. "Who's there?"

"Open," a graveled voice commanded. "We need to talk."

I recognized that throaty rumble right off, like tumbling boulders deep inside a mine shaft, but I didn't lower the Remington. "What do you want?"

"I want you to open this door, before I kick it down," Angel replied. He banged on the frame again, rattling the danged thing near enough to shake it loose of its pegs.

After a pause, I said, "Hang on while I get dressed."

I heard a muttered curse from outside, tinged with humor. After throwing on my clothes, I flung the door open with the Remington still clutched in my hand.

Angel pushed inside without invitation, the shotgun he'd brought back with him from the Flats propped over one shoulder. "Put that pistol away, you fool," he told me. "If I'd wanted to harm you, I wouldn't have knocked before entering your room."

I lowered the hammer but didn't holster the gun. "What time is it?"

"It is after midnight. Listen, we have work to do, you and I."

"What kind of work?"

"To finish what we didn't finish in the desert. The killers of Antonio and Cesar are in the Lucky Day, bragging about what they did."

"Bragging!"

"Do not act so surprised. What did you expect from such men?"

"I expected them to keep their mouths shut, in case the law gets involved."

Angel snorted. "What law? Your good friend, Señor Chad, who

the Devil owns like a dog? Or maybe the rinches?"

So you know, Angel was referring to Kellums when he spoke of the Devil, and rinches was a less than flattering term used to describe the Texas Rangers.

I've never personally had any dealings with the Rangers, so all my knowledge of the organization is second-hand at best, but I've got to admit that, if even a third of what I've been told over the years is true, their brand of justice was not only heavy-handed, it was tilted significantly in favor of Anglo interests.

A lot of folks down in Texas claim that just about all the hatred between Mexicans and Texans, and the Rangers in particular, could be laid at the feet of Santa Anna and his treatment of the freedom fighters at San Jacinto and the Alamo. Being neither Tejano by birth, nor living down there even a year, I couldn't say if that was true or not, but I've yet to meet anyone from Texas who denied it.

All that aside, I was still stunned that Kellums' men were bragging about stringing up a couple of innocent laborers, men just trying to make a living. I said as much to Angel.

"They do not brag for bragging's sake," he told me. "It is their wish that everyone knows what happens to those who defy El Diablo's injunction against harvesting salt. The patrón suspects Kellums himself ordered these cowardly boasts, but I intend to change that. I intend for Kellums to know that the people of Río Tinto will not be intimidated by his toughs, anymore than they were intimidated by the Comanches and the Apaches." He paused. "We, Chama. You and me. We will make them see the error of their ways, eh?"

I nodded grimly. "Count me in," I said, shoving the Remington into its holster, then strapping the gun belt around my waist.

The night air seemed cooler than usual when I stepped outside, the sky clear. There were no lights anywhere in the courtyard. Angel led the way through a heavy wooden gate on the river side of the compound, then down to the stables where Montoya kept his livestock. The low, contented purring of hens in the chicken house accompanied us through the deeper shadows next to the buildings.

"This way," Angel said, gliding silently between a pair of weathered carretas.

I'd never been this way before, but, as soon as we left the protection of the stables' adobe walls, I spotted the faint trace of a path, climbing the bench behind the town's small stone jail. Although the destination seemed ominous, I didn't question Angel's route, and we were soon making our way through the towering cottonwoods. We paused on top, and I put my back to the cool stone wall of the solitary cell, my pulse racing.

Río Tinto's lockup didn't include an office. Barely ten feet square, it was little more than a low-ceilinged cubicle where Chad Bellamy could store the town's drunks until they sobered up enough to be sent home. In the six months that I'd lived there, until the murders of Antonio and Cesar, I'd never known of any crime more serious than public intoxication.

Across the street, the Lucky Day was still brightly lit, although the boardwalk out front was surprisingly empty. On a normal night, there would have been several customers loitering outside to cool off, chewing the fat while they worked on their beers or cigars. Tonight everyone was inside, and I began a slow boil, imagining them crowded around Kellums' gunfighters like a bunch of feasting vultures.

At my side, Angel cupped his hands over his mouth to mimic the clipped, jarring cry of a nighthawk. The call was answered immediately from beyond the saloon, and a couple of minutes later a slim figure in a battered porkpie hat slipped furtively out of darkness next to the New Harmony Café, then sprinted across the street toward us. It was Flaco, carrying a Spencer carbine in his right hand, its muzzle pointed toward the ground.

"Señor Sandavol?" the youth called softly.

"Sí, over here."

But Flaco had already spotted us. Eyeing me skeptically, he said to Angel, "I did not think you would bring this one."

"Chama has earned his right to be here," Angel replied.

I was struck by an unexpected sense of gratitude, and wondered if his distrust of me was finally starting to abate.

"Are they still there?" Angel asked.

"Yes, all four of them, and several others as well. But not Kellums."

"Kellums wouldn't be," I said. "A guy like that likes to keep a healthy distance between himself and the blood-spillers."

Angel flashed a grin in my direction. "You know this type, eh?"

"I once fought for his kind."

"As have I," Angel assured me. "It is the same in Mexico as it is in Norteamérica. The *ricos* always seek another to do their dirty work, while they stay home to drink good wine and fuck beautiful women."

In my mind I saw Cierra Varga standing at the entrance to Kellums' kitchen, and wondered if his pleasure was a part of her duties.

"Anderson is there," Flaco said, interrupting my thoughts. "He is their *jefe*, their boss man." He glanced at me. "You know him, no?"

"I met him the other night. What about the others?"

"There is Pope and Landors and the man you fought …"

"Tom Layton?"

"Sí, plus Bayless and Potter."

Angel turned a questioning eye upon me. "You know these men?"

"Not Bayless or Potter, but Pope, Landors, and Layton are three of the men we trailed to the Flats." I glanced at Flaco. "What about the negro? Is he there?"

Flaco shook his head. "Just the men I have already mentioned."

"Well, it's a start," I growled, stepping away from the jail's wall.

Angel grabbed my arm and hauled me back. "Where are you going?"

"To the Lucky Day. I owe those bastards something."

"We all owe them something, but not our lives. Those men in the saloon have been drinking. If you go in there now, they will kill you before you can order a beer."

"I'm not going in there to order a beer," I said, but Angel's words chilled my anger. He was right, of course. The men inside the Lucky Day had been drinking steadily for some time, and would be feeling their oats. I might have been welcomed among them in the past, but not anymore. Like it or not, I was a Montoya man now, and I sagged back against the stone wall, my rage subsiding.

"We can do nothing from here," Angel said. "Let's find a different location."

We crossed the street to the empty lot beside the New Harmony Café, then out the other side and into the brush behind the line of businesses that made up the bulk of New Town. We didn't stop until we were opposite the Lucky Day's back door.

There was a lantern hanging from a hook beside the saloon's rear exit; a second lantern dangled from the eave of a trio of slabwood privies about thirty yards behind the building. A path connected the two, but other than that it was all dry grass and patches of prickly pear—the bane of many a drunk over the few months that I'd lived there.

"Now what?" I asked Angel.

"Now we wait," he answered, squatting with his back to a slanting cottonwood, making himself comfortable.

After a pause, I hunkered down nearby. Flaco walked over to the tree where Angel was quietly studying the rear of the saloon, but he didn't sit down. I could sense his anxiety even in the dark, could see it in the way he kept wiping his palms against his pants to dry them.

Flaco reminded me of my first time waiting with a gun for a man, a target, to come to me. That had been up in Gunnison, of course, a frigidly cold night in January of 1879, with snow drifted up as high as the sills on the windows. I want to tell you about that. Some of it, anyway. Tomorrow, first thing.

BATTLE OF THE HOGUP
PART II

by Eric Cranston

From
True Tales of the Old West magazine
July/August, 1956

The men who became known as the Gunnison Five were an eclectic gathering of gunfighters of varying reputations. Among the worst of them were George Tinslow and Jesse Burgess, both reportedly former members of William Clarke Quantrill's Missouri bushwhackers, who had aided in the sacking of Lawrence, Kansas, in August of 1863.

A third member of the Five was Levi Pratt, who had made a name for himself in Nebraska as a guard for the Wells Fargo Express Company, and for his participation in cleaning out the Remer Gang at their Brushy Hollow hideout. ("The Brushy Hollow Scrap," *True Tales of the Old West* magazine, March/April, 1955)

Of the two final members of the Five, Roy Washburn and Wil Chama, even less is known. The Denver Directory for 1877 lists a "Washburn, Roy Edward," at 640 Arapahoe Street, but there is no clear connection between this man and the alleged killer of Oren Bruthens in 1878, or of his having any involvement with the Hogup strike in general.

Likewise, a Wilhelm Chama is mentioned in several Denver

newspapers of the era as an employee of the Matthew J. Dunn Outfitting firm, although, again, there is no ascertainable link between this Chama and the hired gun at the Hogup Mine. What is thoroughly documented, however, is that Dunn was a well-known supplier of firearms and other goods to the buffalo hunters who worked the plains of eastern Colorado and western Kansas. Dunn was also reportedly an excellent gunsmith, with his own shop and a small shooting gallery behind his store on East Colfax Avenue, offering, at the very least, a place of practice for Chama.

The incidents which led to the introduction of hired strike breakers to the mining community of Hogup were a series of three cave-ins, which occurred in as many months in the autumn and winter of 1878. Local newspapers reported a combined loss of thirty-six lives, and a sense of great despair among the survivors and their families. Although sizable contingents of both Mexican-American and Chinese laborers were employed at the Hogup Mine, it was the Irish who suffered the highest number of fatalities, as it was the Irish who organized the mine's first strike on November 9, demanding better equipment and enhanced safety measures for the underground laborers.

According to testimony collected by the courts in 1879, allegations of poor bracing and "soft" lumber had surfaced from the Hogup almost from the beginning. There seemed to be consensus among all three ethnic groups that not only were the headers constructed of green pine, but that the dimensions of the timbers were inadequate for the depth of the shafts, by that time reaching several hundred feet below ground in three main "branches."

Perhaps there shouldn't be any surprise that it was the Irish who would initially challenge the Hogup's management. For more than a decade, immigrant groups from Ireland, such as the Molly Maguires, had battled coal mine managers in Pennsylvania and other states for more safety and better wages. Although accusations were made that members of the Maguires instigated the Hogup's first strike, no evidence has ever surfaced to support that allegation. In light of the extensive legal battles plaguing the Maguires in the East prior to the Hogup incident, it seems doubtful that there was any connection. Yet secret Irish societies were rumored to, and probably did, exist in Hogup, as did similar consociations among the Chinese and Mexican-Americans.

The first strike against the Hogup ended without violence when mine foreman Harold T. Richter promised that action would be taken immediately to shore up the sagging infrastructure of the shafts. Unfortunately for all parties involved, no plans were apparently ever made to fulfill that promise. When the second cave-in occurred on December 4, resulting in the loss of eighteen lives—the worst of the mine's three structural failings—an immediate strike was called by the Irish contingent.

Although this time the miners seemed more organized, and more inflamed, the age-old barrier of race and culture would quickly rear its head. While a small element of the Mexican-American community did support the Irish in their December rebellion, the Chinese, under the leadership of Ling Longwei (loosely translated as Clever Dragon) refused to participate. Allegations—an admittedly well-used and often vicious tool in any strike—that the mine's operators intended to bring in more Asian laborers from Sierra Nevada mines only augmented the unrest sweeping through the Hogup community.

If the management of the Hogup Mine needed any intimation of outside involvement in the Irish resistance, it could hardly have done better than the arrival in Gunnison of two individuals with easily traceable lineage to the Molly Maguires—Lester H. Kerns and Columbus W. Wright.

While the true identities of Kerns and Wright have long been a matter of contention—fine old English names associated with what more than one source described as rich Irish brogues— their devotion to the radicalization of the strike has never been questioned. From their lodgings in Gunnison—Hogup was a company town, and therefore off limits to anyone the mine's management deemed minacious—Kerns and Wright conducted a series of meetings throughout December with the more anarchistic members of the Irish faction.

Either despite the influence of Kerns and Wright, or possibly because of it, the second Hogup strike was abruptly called off on December 21, and all operations at the mine were resumed at full capacity. Promises were once again made to the miners that the framework of the three main branches would be reinforced, and, this time, management actually seemed to have taken steps toward that end. A contract renewal with the Gunnison Timber and Framing Company stipulated a 33.3 percent increase in the number of timbers delivered to the Hogup every month, and the thickness of the shafts' main bracings was increased from four-by-six inches to six-by-six inches.

As production at the mine resumed, everyone seemed content until the third and final cave-in occurred on December 27, resulting in the loss of eight miners, all of them of Mexican descent. Rumors of inferior bracing and soft lumber once again circulated throughout the town, and within twenty-four hours a third strike was called, this time attracting the nearly unanimous support of the Mexican-American community under the leadership of Juan Ortiz Gomez.

Very little is known even today of Juan Gomez. What few scattered reports can be found describe him as a stocky, middle-aged man of retiring disposition—hardly the sort of firebrand one might imagine in a position of authority during such volatile times. It was Gomez's seemingly effortless ascension to leadership that has fueled speculation among historians regarding the influence of Kerns and Wright in the matter, as well as accusations that the third Hogup cave-in was a deliberate act of sabotage, manufactured to further an ever-growing call to unionize. ("The Hogup Conspiracy: A Further Examination of Incidents Leading to the Infamous 1878 Strike,"

Colorado's Weekly Journal of History, August 14, 1950)

On the evening of December 28, a mob of Irish and Mexican insurgents descended upon the mine headquarters, where Clifford Baker and Harold Richter were residing with a trio of out-of-work cowboys, identified in court records as Ernie Davis, Floyd Cochraine, and John Wanczyk, hired as security guards. Jeffrey Callahan, writing for the *Denver News*, reports that a crowd of nearly two hundred souls converged on the mine's headquarters at the foot of Hogup Mountain, nearly half of them women and children. Callahan's article states, in part: "A stand-off quickly ensued, with the beleaguered hierarchy gathered in a knot on the front stoop of the operations office, as a rowdy gathering of the unwashed and unbarbered swelled around them like flood waters breaching a levee. Messrs, Baker, and Richter calmly stood up to the horde, and quickly placated its bloodthirsty leanings."

Other reports were not so forgiving of the Hogup management's handling of the situation, and insist that Baker and Richter's Cowboy Guards fired indiscriminately above the heads of the crowd, coming so close to flesh and bone in a few instances that "hats and bonnets were tumbled from the protesters' heads." It is widely accepted that, despite this omission from the *Denver News*, several shots were fired into the sky, and at least one bullet, most likely from one of the strikers, smashed a windowpane in the mine office's front window directly behind Baker, Richter, and the Cowboy Guards. Nevertheless, there were no reported injuries to either side during the encounter, and the mob soon dispersed.

Unfortunately it was to be a short-lived truce, for by the morning of the twenty-ninth, five horsemen rode into the town of Hogup to take up residency at the mine's office. They were George Tinslow, Jesse Burgess, Levi Pratt, Wil Chama, and Roy Washburn—soon to become known as the Gunnison Five.

WIL CHAMA INTERVIEW

❧

SESSION SEVEN

I mentioned last night how Flaco's nervousness reminded me of my own that night in Gunnison. I was dwelling on that incident heavily while me and Angel and Flaco waited behind the Lucky Day for one of Kellums' hombres malos to make an appearance.

If you recall, my Grandpapa, old Karl Holtz, owned a store in Pueblo where me and Mama went to live after Papa died. We didn't stay in Pueblo long, though. I was just a toddler when Grandpapa moved us all to Denver, where he opened a little grocery on Olive Street. He bought a house just behind the store, and I guess he was doing all right for himself and his family, which still included me and Mama.

Grandpapa never made any bones about the fact that he expected me to take over the grocery business someday. "I vill give you dat start, by Gott," he'd tell me at least twice a week in that thick-as-molasses German accent of his. "But den you vill 'ave to grow der business youself. Is a gift I giff to you, young one, and a goot damned living you can make with it, too, for you vife and der little ones ven dey come along."

Problem was, I had about as much interest in grocering as I did in shoveling manure down at the Rocky Mountain Livery, which I'd been doing after school for twenty-five cents a week ever since I was eight years old. Maybe even less, because at least at the livery I was outside, around livestock most of the time, instead of cooped up in a store that reminded me of nothing so much as a cramped jail cell.

I think Grandpapa Karl consented to my working at the livery only because he thought I'd jump at the chance to come indoors when I finally graduated, but he was dead wrong about that. I had other plans, and by the time I was thirteen, I'd skipped so many days of school that the teacher finally came down to the store to ask Grandpapa if I was ill.

Ain't no doubt I was feeling pretty poorly by the time that old coot put his belt away, but that beating didn't change my mind about attending classes. If anything, it just hardened my resolve to halt my education where it was. Finally Grandpapa said, "Den, fine, by Gott, if you don't vant to make youself smarter, den you can vork in der store vit me."

But I didn't do that, either, and we had a pretty tense couple of months around the house that year. Grandpapa pulled me out of school like he'd promised, and I started wandering around town when I should have been at the grocery or making deliveries. More than once that old man threatened to sic the law on me if I didn't shape up. Then one day, on the opposite side of town, I wandered into Matt Dunn's store, and it was like I'd come home. Instead of shelves filled with tinned goods and boxes of dried fruits, I found aisles sprouting lead and gunpowder, primer caps and empty brass, all waiting to be put together in the big cartridges the hunters used to shoot buffalo. There were crates of skinning knives and casks of salt to cure the tongues and hams the hunters took, bottles filled with poison for the bugs that liked to destroy the green hides in summer, and heavy clothing to withstand all but the worst plains blizzard.

Oh, there was foodstuffs, but it was all men's grub, like slabs of salted pork and tins of sardines and fifty-pound sacks of pinto beans, plus coffee, salt, sugar, pepper, and bottled medicines for their bellies, for as a grizzled old-timer once told me, "They ain't nobody ever more constipated than a buff'ler hunter, son."

Matt confirmed it. "Buffalo hunters and cowboys. Just about all they eat is meat and beans. It's a wonder their bowels move at all."

Matt sold plenty of whiskey, too. I don't recall a single outfit that left for the buffalo ranges without at least a five-gallon keg of the stuff stashed away in the wagons for medicinal purposes.

I started hanging out at Dunn's every day, and, after a couple of weeks, Matt offered me a part-time warehouse job, sorting skins and inventorying merchandise. It was gut-busting labor—a green bull's hide can weigh close to one hundred pounds—and I soon reeked of uncured pelts and raw meat, but I loved it. Even when I'd get a dose of lice and Mama would make me take a bath in the carriage house in water so hot I'd come out looking like a boiled lobster, my flesh on fire from the strong lye soap and disinfectant she forced me to use. Rain or shine, winter or summer, she never let me into the house until she was sure my body was free of graybacks.

Matt took a liking to me right off. So did the hunters and trappers who came in to trade, and it wasn't long before I was moved into the store, where the skills Grandpapa had taught me from an early age about clerking and keeping books assured me of steady employment. It also exposed me to Matt's talents as a gunsmith.

Matt didn't do a lot of the fancy modifications that some of the smiths around town did, like Carlos Gove's under-levers or the Freund Brothers' improved extractors. Mostly he just slicked up the factory guns he sold, making them smoother and more reliable, or changed out the sights for something a little easier to read under a blazing summer sun or against the freezing albescence of a snow-covered plain.

I loved hanging out in Matt's little shop at the back of his store, and I made no effort to hide my fascination with firearms. Not just the shooting of them, which I enjoyed, but also the way all the parts fit together so precisely. A good gun is as much a work of art as a fine Swiss watch, in my opinion, and a hell of a lot more practical. You can tell time by the sun, but it takes a weapon to put meat on the table or save your life when someone is trying to take it away from you.

I started staying late after the store closed to help Matt in the shop, sweeping up and the like, but also doing some filing and polishing on the guns. Eventually he let me start taking them apart and putting them back together again, so I suppose it was inevitable that when a beat-up old Colt Navy percussion came into the shop that no one else wanted, I purchased the thing myself, then began refurbishing it after hours. The final result wasn't too shabby, thanks to Matt's tutelage, and I put a lot of lead downrange in the covered shooting gallery behind his shop—thirty yards into a stack of crossties pilfered from the Denver Pacific railroad yards.

I became a pretty good shot with that old gun, but it wasn't long before I started hankering for something better, like one of the new cartridge models flooding the Western markets. My first was a .46-caliber Remington that a Dodge City hide hunter brought in to trade for a new Colt Peacemaker. I bought the Remington from Matt after the trade was completed, then switched out the cylinder and relined the barrel to shoot .45s. I also slicked up the action until it handled about as smooth as melted butter on a hot griddle. I won't lie. I was damned proud of the finished product, and practiced with it religiously—a fifty-count box of ammunition every couple of days—until Matt talked me into doing my own reloads. I'd get better accuracy by tailoring my cartridges to my gun, he said, not to mention saving a chunk of money over factory ammunition.

He was right about improving my accuracy. Once I found a combination of bullet, powder, and primer that the Remington liked, I was able to tighten my groups down to a shade under four inches at thirty yards. There are shooters out there today who can do a whole lot better than that, but there weren't many back then.

There was one, though, and it might be bragging to mention it here, but I'm going to. There was a drifter came into the store one afternoon, a long-haired gent in a frock coat and a wide-brimmed hat. A few of us were having a friendly shooting match out back, with the money we were wagering tossed onto a loading bench built against the store wall, and this guy wandered outside to see what all the racket was about. We talked him into trying his hand, and he cleaned up in short order. His name was Hickok, and I reckon just about everybody knows who I'm talking about.

I shot against Bill just that one time, and lost a dollar for the privilege. I wish now that I'd purchased that coin back from him, even if it had cost me two dollars, just so I could have had it framed. There aren't many men who can say they were outgunned by the famous Wild Bill, even if it was just a shooting match at glass insulators.

Bill left for Cheyenne the next day, and not long after that he was gunned down in Deadwood, Dakota Territory, by a coward named Jack McCall, but I guess most folks know about that, too.

Anyway, word started getting around that I was a pretty fair shot, which I suspect is what brought Cliff Baker and Larry Mueller into Dunn's one early December afternoon in 1878. We were just getting ready to close up shop when the two wandered in. You could tell right off that they weren't hiders. Oh, they had the same rough-barked demeanor as any plains tough, but they lacked the leathery hue of an outdoorsman. Their skin was too soft, their hair too clean and short, and both of them sported mustaches that were neatly trimmed and recently curried. Their dress was that of a dude as well, wide ties and derby hats and polished shoes, although, in fairness, I've seen more than one buffalo hunter deck himself out in a fancy suit of clothes after a few months in coarse wool and buckskins.

The two men approached the counter where I was tallying the day's receipts, and for a moment I wondered if they were going to rob the place. They had that look. Instead, one of them, Mueller, asked if I knew of a young gunman who was supposed to work there. I said no, of course, and the dude frowned like I'd insulted him.

"A youngster by the name of William Chama," the other guy, Baker, said.

"Chama? That's me!" I exclaimed, hearing of my reputation as a pistoleer for the first time. "What do you want with me?"

"We have need of men who are proficient with firearms," Mueller said. "Your name was offered."

I shrugged. "I'm pretty good against bottles and such. I don't know about being a gunman, though."

"We were informed that you shot against James Butler Hickok some years ago, and that you lived to tell of the experience," Baker remarked.

I laughed at that. "Some of the boys must have been hoorawing you, mister. Bill Hickok was in here a couple of years ago, and we shot at targets out back, but it was all in fun."

Both men were scowling by then, exchanging perturbed glances. "This was a tall man with reddish hair and a large mustache who related this information," Baker said.

"That was probably Murray Green. He used to work here. Was a senior clerk for a while, but he got caught stealing coal oil and was fired." Then, in a juvenile attempt to protect Matt's honor, I added, "The boss would have loaned him the stuff, had he asked."

"It's a prank Mister Green shall dearly regret, if I see him again," Baker promised darkly.

"If you were talking to him at the Pinto Saloon, you'll probably see him again," I said. "He does most of his drinking there nowadays."

"Wil," a voice interrupted quietly from the back of the room. Matt came forward carrying a silver-plated Colt revolver and an oily rag, and although I didn't understand this at the time, I do now—the Colt was loaded. I could see the lead tips of the bullets through the front of the cylinder.

Baker and Mueller smoothly shifted around to face him, like they had steel bearings under their heels. "You're Dunn?" Mueller said, more statement than question.

"What do you boys want with young Wilhelm?" Matt asked, emphasizing my name, although by that time I'd become used to folks assuming my full Christian name was William.

"That would be a personal matter," Baker replied.

"Not in my store, it ain't," Matt said.

Mueller and Baker exchanged another annoyed glance, then Mueller slipped me a business card. "We are staying at the Denver House, if you'd care to discuss a part-time position with the Hogup Mining Company. The salary would be significant, if you're interested."

"He ain't," Matt said, but the two dudes were already heading for the door. When they were gone, Matt came over, holding out his hand for the card Mueller had given me. He studied it a moment, then tossed it on the counter in front of me like trash. "You would do well to add that card to the kindling bin," he said. "You won't find anything gainful working for that type."

"What type?"

"The kind that's little better than crooks and murderers themselves," Matt said. "They hire others to do their dirty work for them, but their hands are just as bloody."

"What kind of dirty work?"

Matt gave me an irritated look, like I was asking why the sky was blue or the grass was green. "Ask your grandfather," he said bluntly, then went back to his shop, ejecting the loaded rounds into a oil-darkened palm.

I know now that I should have listened to what he told me, but I didn't. I lay in bed that night pondering the consequences of earning a "significant salary" with a gun, wearing a holster full-time, instead of a clerk's apron. I didn't say anything to Grandpapa, and I didn't say anything to Matt the next day, but, that night after work,

I stopped by the Denver House on my way home.

It's funny the way a man never suspects he's stepping into a viper's den until it's too late to back out. I thought I was just going in to talk, but that ain't what happened at all ...

Anyway, that's what I was thinking that night behind Bob Thompson's saloon with Angel and Flaco. My thoughts were still mulling over the events that had led me to Gunnison County when Angel jerked to attention at my side. My head came up sharply, the memories of that long ago encounter with Mueller and Baker quickly fizzling out. Angel used his chin to point out a man just exiting the rear door of the Lucky Day, making his way carefully toward the row of privies. I say carefully because he was obviously drunk and was having a hard time staying on the path.

"Son of a bitch," I said, standing. "That's Pinky Landors."

Angel got up with me, while Landors continued his erratic course to the privies. You'd think after having struggled so hard to get there, he would have gone inside, but he didn't. Instead he stopped in front of the nearest outhouse, unbuttoned his fly, and began to urinate against the door. I don't know if he was trying to make a statement of some kind, or if he was just whiskey stupid. From where I was standing, he looked wobbly enough that it could have been plain confusion.

"*Vámonos*," Angel whispered, striding briskly across the rough ground.

Even as preoccupied as he was, Landors immediately spotted us. I was half afraid he'd make a move for his revolver before we got close, but I guess he didn't recognize us in the dark. It didn't hurt that we were angling toward the rear door of the saloon, too, instead of the privies. He kept his eyes on us, though, and by the time we reached the saloon, he was buttoned up and on his way back.

Both Angel and Flaco had kept their long guns by their sides and out of sight as we crossed the empty lot. At the door, Angel turned and stepped forward, swinging the muzzles of his shotgun up to belly-level. Pinky Landors cursed and started to reach for his gun, but Angel said, speaking better English than a lot of Anglos I knew, "If you do, amigo, I will blow your fucking head into the next cañon."

Landors froze with his gun half drawn, and, in the lingering silence of the next moment, I said out of the side of my mouth, "I thought you couldn't speak American."

"I don't know where you got that idea, but now is not a good time to discuss it."

Well, he was right about that, but it caught me by surprise, nonetheless; the guy'd spoken nothing but Mexican ever since I'd met him.

Keeping one big thumb curled over both hammers, Angel started forward.

Staring hard at me, Landors snarled, "You're gonna regret double-crossin' us, Chama. Kellums is gonna nail your ears to the side of his house."

"He'll have to come and get them first," I replied, tightening my fingers around the Remington's grips.

Turning his gaze on Angel, a crooked grin played across Landors' face. "I know you. You're that greaser who killed Milo Barnes last year in Sonora."

"Sí," Angel concurred. "Your friend, Barnes, chose the wrong side of a shotgun to stand up to." That was all he said, but the implication was clear. The gunman's gaze dropped to the twin muzzles pointed at his stomach, and his face, even under the weathered tan, flushed a faint shade of red. I knew then how he'd gotten the name Pinky.

"Pull your *pistola* and let it fall," Angel instructed.

Landors shook his head. "Nuh-uh. You're gonna try to kill me anyway, and I sure as hell ain't gonna make it any easier on you."

I sensed Angel stiffening at my side. "Do you wish to greet death that much sooner?" he asked.

"Go ahead and pull the triggers, you pepper-gut son of

a bitch!" Landors cried, flipping his revolver up so fast I could barely follow its arc.

Angel's shotgun roared at my elbow, and Landors was flung backward like so much discarded trash.

If I'd wanted to live up to my reputation, I probably should have had my own gun drawn by then—but that's the trouble with reputations. They ain't often built on fact. I was a good shot, all right, but I wasn't a hardcase. The name I'd made for myself in Colorado had been constructed mostly out of chance and misunderstanding. I guess what I'm trying to say is that everything that happened behind the Lucky Day Saloon that night happened so quick it pretty much left me standing there with my mouth agape, instead of handling myself with the cool professionalism of a gunfighter. I ain't ashamed to fess up to that, either. I never wanted the reputation I'd been given after that Gunnison affair.

Flaco was caught just as flat-footed as me, but Angel'd been down this road before, and was already in motion. Grabbing Flaco by the arm, he gave the youngster a hard tug. "Wake up," he snapped, pulling the youth away from the still-twitching corpse.

I hung back a moment longer, staring numbly at Landors' twisted form. It wasn't even twenty seconds before that Pinky Landors had been a real threat to everyone in Old Town, me included. Now he wasn't going to bother anyone again, and I was having a little trouble getting my mind wrapped around that fact.

"Chama!" Angel called sharply, drawing me out of my own brief stupor. He and Flaco were already halfway to the chaparral. Shaking my head as if to clear it of floating cobwebs, I hurried after them. They were well into the brush behind cottonwoods when I caught up, Angel reloading his shotgun with calm efficiency.

"You killed him," Flaco gasped, like he was having trouble catching his wind. I felt the same way, as if the shotgun's blast had sucked most of the oxygen out of the air.

"It was him or me," Angel explained. "I chose him."

Flaco nodded excitedly. I don't think he was protesting Angel's action so much as he was stunned by its swiftness. Belatedly I drew my revolver and waited. It wasn't long before the saloon's back door creaked open and a man peered out. After a moment's hesitation, he reached for the lantern hanging outside the door and turned the wick down until the flame was snuffed. I don't know what he hoped to accomplish, since the light hanging from the privy's eave was still burning brightly.

"Should I shoot?" Flaco whispered, half raising his carbine.

"No," I said quickly. "We don't know who that is."

"Whoever it is, he was there, listening and laughing at how Antonio and Cesar kicked and gurgled while they died."

I glanced at Flaco's youthful face, the dark thunder in his eyes, and knew he was on the verge of ignoring my command.

Fortunately Angel sided with me. "We cannot know that, young one. Not with certainty. It is better that we allow a guilty man to live than risk injury to one who is innocent." He was speaking Mex again, which I sourly commented on. Giving me a patient look, he said, "Do you not understand the language of your parents?"

My cheeks grew warm, but I let the matter drop. It was a fact, though, that my grandpapa had frowned on Spanish being spoken in his house, and that my command of the Mexican tongue was as shaky as Angel's American.

"We should go," the big man said abruptly, returning his ramrod to the thimbles beneath the shotgun's web. "We have exacted some measure of justice for the murders of Antonio and Cesar, and we have given Kellums and his hombres malos something to think about. Maybe next time they won't be so quick to boast of their accomplishments."

Maybe, but I doubted it.

We eased though the chaparral, circling wide around the short stretch of businesses that lined Bluff Street. We'd made it as far as the feed store when we heard shooting from the direction of Old Town.

"That comes from Tío Amos' stables," Flaco blurted after a pause.

"Are you sure?" Angel asked.

"Yes, see!" He was pointing toward the cottonwoods lining the south side of the street, the dark bulk of Montoya's stables barely visible through the thick trunks. I cursed at the quick burst of flames rising near the hen house.

We raced into the empty lot between Teague's Hardware and the feed store. We were about halfway across Bluff Street when I saw a couple of men run out of the trees behind the jail and make a beeline for the Lucky Day. I skidded to a halt. "Hold up, you two!" I shouted.

One of the men spun fast, a lance of flame erupting from his side. The bullet made a faint whumping sound as it passed between me and Angel, a distance of no more than two feet separating us. Then all three of us fired as one, and the guy who'd taken the first shot fell as if his feet had been jerked out from under him. The other man kept going, and, although Angel emptied the shotgun's second barrel at him, he didn't stop. It looked for a moment like he was going to run inside the saloon, but he changed course just before reaching the boardwalk and sprinted into the alley between the grocery and Teague's.

Powder smoke was still swirling its slow waltz over the street in front of us when a volley of gunfire opened up from behind the saloon. I ducked instinctively, then bolted for the cottonwoods. Angel and Flaco were tight on my heels when I plunged over the bank toward Old Town. We found Amos waiting for us under the veranda with a Sharps carbine held tightly in both hands.

"Where have you three been?" he demanded as we came panting up to the cantina. The question caught me off guard. I'd assumed, when Angel knocked at my door, that he'd been sent there by Montoya.

"There was some unfinished business that needed our attention," Angel replied. He was staring toward the stables, although there was no longer anything to see in that direction.

"Someone tried to set fire to the haystacks," Montoya explained gruffly, "although I suspect their real target was the salt carts. Some hay had been forked under them, then doused with coal oil before the fire was struck. It was my good fortune that I had sent Carlos down there after nightfall with some men to keep watch. They were able to scare Kellums' arsonists away, then extinguish the flames before they could cause serious damage."

"Did you see who it was?" I asked.

The older man shook his head. "No, but I have not yet spoken with Carlos. Perhaps he or one of his men were able to identify someone, although the men I saw wore sacks over their heads."

"Sacks?" Flaco repeated.

"Flour sacks," I supplied. Tinslow had wanted us to wear them in Colorado, but we'd refused. I'm glad we did. The use of masks or hoods is a coward's act; I thought so then, and still do today.

Montoya was studying us closely, and I realized he must have heard our shooting from New Town. After a couple of minutes, he asked, "Was anyone hurt?"

"Sí, I am afraid so," Angel replied soberly. "The man called Landors was killed, and another was shot. I do not yet know if that one lives, but I doubt it."

"And who gave you these orders?"

"I did not request orders," Angel replied evenly. "The man called Landors helped hang Antonio and Cesar. It was my job to protect them and, when I failed that, to seek justice for their murders."

"Do not forget that it is I who pays your salary," Montoya said stiffly. "Or that I also command."

"I am paid a salary to do a job, patrón," Angel replied respectfully. "If you do not wish for me to do that for which I am paid, then perhaps I should return to Mexico."

The two men stared silently at one another for a long minute, then Montoya glanced at Flaco. "Return to your room. I will speak with you later."

When the younger man was gone, Montoya turned to me.

"And you, Chama? What is your excuse?"

Now, I had one, remember? I'd thought Angel was acting under Montoya's orders, and I could have stood my ground, but I'd be damned if I was going to turn my back on Angel Sandavol after what we'd been through. Not to mention I wasn't too keen on the old man's tone of voice. I wasn't one of his nephews, and I sure as hell wasn't some flunky drawing Montoya wages, a fact I was just about to remind him of when Angel cut in.

"I asked Señor Chama for his assistance, patrón. It was my fault."

"It wasn't anyone's fault," I said stiffly. "It was a good idea, and needed to be done. Besides, if not for the three of us and the ruckus we made up there, we might all be throwing water on your haystacks right now, instead of standing out here arguing with one another."

Montoya glared at me like I was some kind of bug, but then that granitelike expression of his abruptly relaxed, and he said, "You are right, of course. Come, let us go inside where we won't be a temptation for any of El Diablo's riflemen."

We went into the Bravo and Montoya closed the door firmly behind us, double-checking to make sure it was latched before crossing the room in the dark to light a lamp. As the cantina sprang into view, I walked behind the bar and grabbed a bottle of beer floating in a wooden tub of water. It wasn't cold, but it was cool, which was about as much as you could hope for in that border country.

You might have noticed I said bottle, which would have been unusual for a village as isolated as Río Tinto if it had been something like Coors or Budweiser, but this was just some homemade stuff put up in an assortment of discarded whiskey bottles, Mason jars, and whatever else they had that could be sealed with rubber or wax. I asked Angel and Amos if they wanted anything, but both men declined. Taking my jar over to the table where they were already seated, I lowered myself into an empty chair, then stretched my legs out to one side. My feet hurt and my socks were damp with perspiration. I would have given a silver dollar to kick my boots off for a few minutes, but I was afraid that I wouldn't be able to get them back on again.

We didn't speak much, just sat there waiting and listening. It was another hour before Carlos finally slipped in through the courtyard door, a couple of men trailing uncertainly behind him. They stopped out of the light, as if reluctant to be identified, while Carlos came over, carrying his hat in one hand, a Springfield rifle in the other.

"All is quiet, patrón," Carlos reported.

"Good," Amos said softly. "Take your men back to the stables. I doubt if Kellums will make a second attempt tonight, but we can no longer be certain of anything."

Carlos nodded, and he and his men quickly disappeared.

Montoya glanced across the table at me and Angel. "Now we wait some more, eh?"

"For what?" I asked, still wet behind the ears in such matters.

"For El Diablo to make the next move," Angel said.

I didn't reply to that, and the deep silence returned. I nursed my beer and smoked an occasional cigarette, and after a while I moved to another table where I could fold my arms on top and rest my head in the warm cove they created. I dozed but never really slept, and after a while I got up and moved outside. The air was chilly but invigorating, and the early-morning chatter of birds brought my attention to the pearl coloring of the sky above the cliffs. I glanced around to see if I could spot any late-returning bats, but the heavens were clear. I shuddered anyway, and tossed my cigarette butt into the dirt. Although exhausted, I have to admit I felt better. I could hear voices coming from the village, and it wasn't long before I caught the odor of mesquite smoke, along with the pleasant scent of baking bread. Soon afterward a stubby woman with graying hair came out of the cantina to announce that breakfast would soon be ready.

Standing at her side, one hand clamped affectionately atop her shoulder, Montoya said, "We will be there soon," but he sounded distracted, and following his gaze up the narrow road to New Town, I spied a solitary rider making his way toward us on a dun mule. Almost under his breath, Montoya added, "I expected Kellums."

Well, he was wrong. It was Chad Bellamy, and he was wearing his badge.

The woman eyed the approaching rider briefly, then turned away without hurry. My eyes quickly swept the trees separating the two Río Tintos, but didn't find anything threatening. Chad kept his mule, one of Pedro's string, to a steady walk, and drew up not twenty feet from the cantina's front door. Keeping both hands folded in plain sight atop his saddle horn, he nodded a cautious greeting to Montoya, then turned to me and Angel. I thought I detected a faint trace of bitterness in his eyes, but I couldn't be sure.

"What brings you to our humble village?" Montoya queried.

"It ain't your village, Amos, and it ain't Randy Kellums', either. It's one town, although I'll grant you it's gonna blow apart real quick if we can't get a lid on this thing."

I thought Montoya's smile seemed condescending. "And your suggestions, señor?"

Chad sighed loudly. "Was two men killed outside the Lucky Day last night. Folks seem to think you might have had a hand in that."

"Two, you say? I wonder if their killers might be the same men who tried to burn my salt carts?"

"No, it ain't likely," Chad said bluntly, then turned to me and Angel. "Where were you two last night?"

Before either of us could reply, Montoya said, "They retired early last night, Sheriff. I am afraid both men were very tired after returning from the Flats, where two close friends of ours were likewise murdered. You have heard of the hangings of Antonio and Cesar?"

"Yeah, I heard about it, but I don't have jurisdiction over the Flats. You'll need to contact a United States marshal if you want someone to look into that for you. Or a Ranger," he added with a taut smile, indicating that he was well aware of how folks along the Río Grande felt about the rinches.

Frowning at the lawman's remarks, I said, "Is that funny to you, Chad?"

"Not as funny as finding you down here working for Montoya," he replied. "Frank said you'd left on the *Rachel*, so I didn't believe Jim Houck when he claimed you'd turncoated on us."

"Are you talking about the Devil, or the law?" I asked.

Chad's face got a little flushed at that. "You might be interested to know that one of the men killed last night was Pedro Rodriguez. You and him and Frank were pretty good friends, weren't you?"

Well, that brought me up short. I stood there in near disbelief, trying to assimilate the idea that Pedro must have been the man we'd shot crossing the street last night. One of the men who had attempted to set fire to Montoya's hay supply and salt carts.

"Tell me, Sheriff," Montoya said, "was there an odor of coal oil on Rodriguez's hands? Something to indicate whether he might have been one of the men who attempted to burn us out?"

"I didn't sniff the man, Amos. I just had his body hauled down here to Old Town so that his wife and family could bury him."

Chad was watching me as he spoke to Montoya, and I suspect he could tell by my expression that I knew who'd killed Pedro Rodriguez, and why. There wasn't much he could do about it, though. Not unless he could dig up a witness.

My anger getting the better of me, I took a menacing step forward. "Why don't you tell Kellums to drop this damned war before someone decides to toss a torch inside his plant?"

Montoya's hand shot out to grab my arm. "Easy, my friend," he murmured. "Do not make threats you can be accused of later."

I don't know if Chad heard the older man's words, but his reply was basically the same. "Be careful what you say, Chama. Someone decides to set fire to something belonging to Mister Kellums, I'm going to remember your words."

I gritted my teeth in frustration, but did the smart thing and kept my mouth shut. Chad pulled his mule's head up. "I'll be back, Amos. If you know anything about who killed Pedro or Pinky Landors, you'd best spill it. If I have to find out who did it on my own, it's going to go a lot harder on everyone involved."

Chad reined away, and we watched quietly as he rode up the bench trail to New Town. When he was gone from sight, Amos spat disgustedly into the dust.

"What next, patrón?" Angel asked.

"After breakfast, I want you and Wil to return to the Flats with some men. I want to bring in the bodies of Antonio and Cesar, as well as the salt carts that are still out there. And while there is protection for my diggers, I want to send out the rest of my carts, too." He glanced at me and Angel. "I want both of you to go, and to take Flaco with you. Carlos is a good man and can manage things here, but I want Flaco out of Río Tinto until tempers have cooled."

"That could be a while," I pointed out.

"Perhaps, but it will take several days, maybe a week, for the carts to get out there and back. Hopefully that will be enough time."

I exchanged a guarded look with Angel. I could tell he was thinking the same thing I was, that, if we returned to the Flats to harvest more salt, Randy Kellums was going to be more or less obligated to send someone out to stop us. But maybe that's what Montoya had in mind, to keep the war away from Río Tinto, clear of his home and business, and the homes of his family and friends.

But if that was the case, why send Flaco along? Why risk his nephew's life when he had me and Angel to stick our necks out for him?

I think that was the first time I ever questioned Amos Montoya's motives, but it wouldn't be the last.

WIL CHAMA INTERVIEW

❧

SESSION EIGHT

We ate breakfast at a long table in the courtyard. I don't recall what we had, but I do remember that Inez wasn't there, and that I was disappointed.

There were a lot of other people on hand, though, way more than I would have expected. It kind of reminded me of the monthly pancake breakfasts we used to have at St. Alonzo's Church in Denver when I was young, although there wasn't any laughter or light-hearted banter among the adults, and none of the children was running around shouting and getting underfoot at every turn.

A lot of the men were carrying Springfield rifles like the one Carlos had been toting the night before. These were Civil War surplus weapons that had been converted to shoot the old .50-70 government cartridge. I'd done my fair share of modifying those old battlefield work horses when I was with Dunn. They weren't as accurate as a lot of the newer guns, but they were tough and reliable, and made up for with punch what they lacked in precision. I'd find out later on that Amos had bought twenty of these relics and several hundred rounds of ammunition last fall, at his own expense. Apparently he'd discerned Kellums' aspirations long before any of the rest of us had.

After breakfast, Carlos brought me a dun mare already saddled. I led her over to my room to fetch my bedroll and saddlebags. Montoya's salters were already waiting when me and Angel rode around the front of the cantina. There were only two carts, plus the two we'd left at the Flats. You'd have thought for all the fuss Kellums had been making of the matter, that Montoya owned fifty of the damned things.

The carretas were each pulled by a single, yoked team of oxen, with an extra team hitched behind for the carts still out at the Flats. There was also a light spring wagon parked nearby with a pair of horses standing in harness. If anyone had any questions regarding its purpose, the two empty coffins tied down in back would have answered their queries quick enough.

We started off without fanfare, once again following the old cart track through Tinto Cañon, rather than the route Kellums had blasted into the face of the bluff. One thing I never found out was why the Montoya faction refused to use the Cut. I always assumed it was because Kellums had had the thing built for his own use, and they didn't want anything to do with the man or the improvements he made to the community. I'm just guessing, mind you. Like I said, I never asked, and no one ever volunteered an explanation.

It was slow going because of the oxen, and well after noon by the time our little caravan came out on top, the harsh desert flowing eastward like a hot brown sea. We paused to let the animals rest, then pushed on at a snail's crawl. It wasn't long before Angel loped over.

"The men in the wagon are becoming impatient, and I will confess that I am also growing weary of the oxen's slow progress. Flaco and I have decided to push on with the wagon. It is to be hoped that our grim chore will be completed by the time you and the *boyeros* arrive at the Flats."

"I appreciate your concern for my welfare," I replied wryly.

"Not to mention promoting me to captain of the carts. Have you told the drivers yet?"

Angel shook his head, a rare smile twitching at the corners of his mouth. "No, I will let you inform them of your new position, but I am sure they will be thrilled."

"Uh-huh. Maybe you ought to put spurs to that pony of yours, before I decide it might be more fair for us to flip a coin to see who gets to ride ahead and who gets to stay back here listening to those steers break wind every other step," I replied in American.

This time, Angel laughed outright, the first time I'd ever heard him do that. It was a high, kind of girlish sound, and so out of character from his usual solemn manner that I think my jaw might have dropped a little in surprise.

"¡Vaya!" he called, suddenly kicking his horse into a lope, as if wanting to flee the embarrassment of being discovered in such a light-hearted mood.

Free of the plodding gait of the oxen, it wasn't long before the spring wagon and horsemen were lost to sight over the distant rim of the horizon. I stayed close to the carretas as the miles reeled past like a river of cold molasses. It was well into the gloaming before we reached Antelope Springs. I rode in first, my rifle handy across my saddle, but the place was deserted. Angel and his men had passed through hours before, then pushed on for the Flats.

After waving in the boyeros, we made our camp near the upper spring, then dug out the food the women had sent along—chili con carne and stone-ground tortillas, along with a small cask of wine from Río Tinto's own vineyards. It was good eating, and I slept soundly that night for the first time in quite a while.

We got an early start the next day, stopped twice to rest the oxen, then about midnight finally rolled into the cottonwoods where Antonio and Cesar had been hung. Angel and the others must have expected us, because they were still up, with fresh coffee brewing and a good supper sitting warm by the fire. Me and my boyeros dug in hungrily, while the others saw to the oxen and Flaco took care of my dun mare. Squatting across the fire from me, Angel nursed a cup of coffee until I finished my first helping. As I was dishing up more beans, he said, "I think it best if we start back tomorrow."

I glanced at the spring wagon. The caskets were still there, the lids nailed down tight.

"We packed them in salt to slow their decay, but they should be returned to Río Tinto as soon as possible," Angel added.

I nodded agreement. Although the spring wagon was parked quite a ways away, I could smell the faint odor of death emanating from the twin coffins. "Without the oxen to slow you down, you ought to be in Río Tinto by tomorrow evening."

"I think so," Angel concurred. "I will leave Flaco with you, and return as soon as the dead are placed in the arms of their families. With a fresh horse, I can be back here in two days. The carretas will be loaded by then, and we can all return to Río Tinto together. It will be safer that way."

I studied the big man thoughtfully. "Something troubling you, amigo?"

"Sí. There is an itch between my shoulder blades that a stick cannot satisfy. I have felt this sensation before. It has always preceded trouble."

"Kellums' men?"

"I would think so. We will soon have four carts loaded with Tinto salt. El Diablo has made his position clear. He believes the salt is his, and he will do whatever is necessary to see that no one else profits from it."

"We'll keep our eyes open," I assured him.

Angel nodded, then rolled his shoulders as if the itch had worsened. "Perhaps, but one more set of eyes might see what others miss. I will return in two days. Wait for me before you pull out."

Angel left before dawn the next morning, taking one man with him to drive the spring wagon and leaving me with Flaco and three others to fill the empty carts. After breakfast I sent Flaco out with the others, and, while they grubbed salt, I rode up to the low ridge west of the Flats where I'd have a better view of the surrounding country.

I could see the Chute from there, with the barracks behind it. I could even see some of Hank Waite's crew far out on the Flats, shouldering salt into their flat-bottomed sleds. I watched absently as they filled a dray, then hauled the clumsy vehicle off the flat plain behind a team of rawhide-shod mules.

While part of the crew guided the sled to the top of the ramp, a couple of men hurried out to where the salters had been digging. I watched with growing interest as they set about their task. It took nearly an hour to drill a trio of wrist-size shafts into the hard bed, then drop a few sticks of dynamite down each shaft. After lighting their fuses, the two men ran like hell. I had to grin, watching their frantic scrambling. A few minutes later, the muffled boom of the explosions rolled across the flat plain. The dun threw her head up at the sound, snorting like a deer, although she didn't try to bolt. Down on the Flats, the salt that had been flung skyward in salmon-colored geysers was now falling back to earth. Within seconds a fine pink haze had settled over the newly blasted crater, lingering there for some time before it began to dissipate.

I glanced over my shoulder at the mare, but her attention had been drawn elsewhere, and I surged to my feet with my rifle across my chest. A single horseman was approaching through the sprawling cactus beds. Hauling up a few rods away, Hank Waite nodded a cautious greeting. "How are you, Wil?"

"I'm good, Hank. What brings you this far from the Chute?"

A quick shrug lifted the slim man's shoulders, then lowered them back to their familiar, work-worn slope. "Saw someone sitting up here and figured I'd better check it out."

"Thought it might be some of Montoya's men?"

"Isn't it?" he asked in an oddly stoic tone.

Now it was my turn to shrug. It was funny, but I still didn't consider myself one of Amos Montoya's crew. I could see where Hank might, though, and probably the rest of them, too. Nodding toward the cottonwoods, I said, "We came to get the bodies of the two men Kellums' gunmen murdered."

"Looks like they're doing more than that," Hank observed.

"The Tejanos figure that salt is as much theirs as it is Kellums'. Maybe more so, considering how long their ancestors have been harvesting it. I guess I kind of see it their way."

"It's an argument I hope to circle wide of," Hank avowed. "I wish the rest of my crew felt the same, but they don't. Not all of 'em."

"Who doesn't? The kid?"

Hank nodded glumly. "Danny Fuller went back to town with Frank Gunton. Says he's gonna offer his services to Kellums." Hank sighed, then glanced at the sky as if wishing he could just stop talking and let it all blow away on a good stiff breeze. "Danny says he wants to kill some Mexicans, and I reckon he's dumb enough to try to do it. I'm sorry to have to tell you this, Wil. It ain't a position I share or condone, but I ain't brave enough to quit my job over it. I'm fifty-eight years old, and that's too long in the tooth to start over. Not if I don't have to."

"I don't fault you," I said.

"There's something else you should know. Danny's real fond of dynamite, and he's good with it. He kept pushing us to teach him how to use it, so we finally did. Hell, anyone who's done much blasting eventually reaches a point where he'd just as soon not have to deal with the stuff. It gets on a smart man's nerves after a while. Trouble is, Danny's too young to be afraid of blowing himself up. He doesn't respect it, and he'll take chances with it that an older man won't. Maybe you ought to tell Montoya about that. I'd hate to think what would happen if Danny got it in his mind to toss a couple of sticks of dynamite into the Bravo. It could kill a lot of innocent folks."

A chill whispered down my spine, an image flashing through

my mind of the carnage just two sticks of dynamite could cause inside a low-ceilinged room like the cantina.

"He's a crazy little son of a bitch, Wil," Hank said quietly. "Watch out for him." He pulled his mount's head out of a patch of grass. "I reckon I'd better get back."

"Thanks for the warning, Hank."

He waved a hand vaguely in my direction. "*De nada*," he replied, reining away.

Watching him ride off, I wondered if I should have offered him a similar caution. Maybe if I'd spoken up out there at the Flats that day, fewer men would have died. I doubt it, but still …

BATTLE OF THE HOGUP
PART III

by Eric Cranston

From
True Tales of the Old West magazine
September/October, 1956

With the arrival in Hogup of the Gunnison Five, an already volatile atmosphere would quickly turn explosive.

Although the gunmen initially moved into the back rooms of the mine's main office, it wasn't long before they began impinging upon the community at large. Jeffrey Callahan, of the *Denver News*, reports that the actions of the Five were arrogant at best, and often deliberately provocative.

Hogup, Colorado, was a company town in every respect. Although in official state records it has never existed, for the estimated four hundred to four hundred and fifty souls who lived under the evening shadow of Hogup Mountain, the community of tiny, drafty shacks and corporate-owned businesses squeezed into the narrow cleft of Conlin Cañon was as much home as the finest mansion in Denver. Not surprisingly, the camp's inhabitants resented the arrival of Baker and Mueller's hired thugs, and chafed at the seemingly deliberate rude treatment they received from the Five. According to court records gathered after the battle, the five men seemed intent upon "creating trouble in every instance."

Callahan goes so far as to suggest that, from the very beginning, the motive behind the aggressive behavior of the Five was murder. He states, albeit without verification, that their targets were the leaders of the Irish contingent, as well as Juan Gomez of the Mexican-American community and Ling Longwei, for the Chinese.

Despite resentment from the three major factions within Hogup—the Irish, Mexican, and Chinese—reaction to the Five seemed timid. Whether the strikers were withholding their anger at the request of others, or were intimidated by the arrival of the gunfighters cannot be determined with the limited information currently available, although later actions in both Gunnison and at a roadhouse owned by a man named Elmer Beeson, located between Gunnison and Hogup, might suggest the former.

Although by all accounts the most prominent of the three largest factions within the Hogup community during the earliest days of the conflict, the Irish suffered noticeably from a lack of leadership. At least four individuals seemed to have held the chief's position for brief periods throughout November and December of 1878, but with the arrival of Lester Kerns and Columbus Wright, that mishmash of captaincy was quickly corrected, and, by the latter part of December, the Irish had accepted Oren Bruthens as their official spokesman.

Oren Bruthens came to America in April of 1866. By May of that same year, he was working on the Union Pacific Railroad as a gandy dancer, during that company's frenetic push across the continent. Bruthens arrived in Denver in the summer of 1868, after breaking a leg in a track-laying accident west of Laramie, in Wyoming Territory.

In an interview with the Arapahoe County Register in 1902, Bruthens' son Rodney states that his father accepted employment in the mines above Denver before his leg had fully mended, resulting in a permanent limp and seasonal pain. The younger Bruthens goes on to state that this injury, although serious in nature, "in no way diluted the man's devotion to his employers," and that his loyalty remained as true in the mountains as it had on the plains working for the Union Pacific.

UP records offer a contradictory view of Oren Bruthens' time with the railroad, listing numerous infractions by, and disciplinary measures against, Bruthens and an associate identified as Darren O'Brien, whose name also turns up in connection with the Hogup strike. In a deposition made public by the prosecuting attorney's office on April 2, 1879, Clifford Baker names O'Brien as Bruthens' lieutenant, and a key figure in the final conflict of January 12, for which the incident has become famous.

Just exactly who killed Oren Bruthens in the early evening hours of January 3, along the road between Gunnison and Hogup, has never been clearly established, although sources close to the struggle have suggested the murderer was Roy Washburn. They cite as proof the fact that Bruthens was ambushed from scrub growth along Conlin Creek, just south of Beeson's Roadhouse, where Washburn had been observed earlier that day "lingering suspiciously," and that the weapon of choice was a shotgun, the same style of firearm Washburn was known to brandish regularly upon his rounds through the Hogup community in the days prior to the murder.

Although George Tinslow, Jesse Burgess, and Levi Pratt all testified to Washburn's presence in the mine office that day, Edith Fains, the woman who oversaw the domestic responsibilities for the group, and who was on site on the day Bruthens was killed, stated she never saw Washburn after the noon meal. Also conspicuously absent in court records is Wil Chama's testimony, although Fains states she noticed Chama in the office numerous times that afternoon and evening.

If Bruthens' murder was meant to cow the citizens of Hogup, its efforts have to be deemed a failure. As word of Bruthens' assassination spread throughout the Irish community the next morning, a mob of angry laborers began to gather at the Hogup's main office, "cursing and throwing rocks." While Baker and Mueller were not at the mine that day, having previously returned to Gunnison, foreman Harold Richter stated for the record that, in his opinion, there was never any danger from the protesters, and that the group had dispersed by midmorning.

Although a two-day peace settled over the Hogup facility following Bruthens' murder, it was clearly the calm before the storm. By the end of the second day, minor incidents of vandalism began to occur at the mine, and Baker, now back in Hogup, reinstated his Cowboy Guards to secure the structure. Operations were shut down completely on the morning of January 6, and the company stores in Hogup were closed later that afternoon by order of Lawrence Mueller.

With supplies, especially of kerosene and food, cut off, the atmosphere in the camp rapidly began to deteriorate. The rumors of a private army riding into town to torch the buildings and drive its citizens into the maw of a Rocky Mountain winter spread throughout the camp in the following days, and few bothered to question its validity. As one survivor of the conflict later lamented, "It seemed like the worse the news got, the more willing we were to believe it."

By January 10, conditions had become so severe that individuals within the community began to call for an end to the strike, and a withdrawal of demands for better bracing and worker safety. Whether these pockets of crumbling resistance would have spread cannot be known, as it was that very afternoon that several wagonloads of supplies arrived at a point just off of mine property, courtesy of Kerns and Wright.

With the miners' insurgency seemingly thwarted, Baker and Mueller set out for Gunnison in an enclosed and curtained carriage. Edith Fains would later testify that the passengers inside the coach also included Levi Pratt and Wil Chama. At some point after that, George Tinslow and Jesse Burgess were reportedly seen riding out on horseback, following a "roundabout path and in a skulking manner," according to one witness.

Meanwhile, with adequate supplies of food and coal oil once again on hand, resentment against the Hogup's management reportedly flared to new heights. As dusk settled over the town, strikers began to converge on the mine office, where only Roy Washburn and Baker's Cowboy Guards were left to defend the structure. Mine foreman Harold Richter later stated that the Irish contingent was led by Bruthens' lieutenant, Darren O'Brien. Although the Irish remained the most vocal force in the Hogup conflict, Richter acknowledged that both the Chinese and Mexican-American communities were "well represented" by this time.

Threats of violence that included death and maiming, the destruction of valuable mine equipment, and "blowing the [mine's] entrance" by means of explosives, were voiced by the increasingly agitated mob. *Denver News* reporter Jeffrey Callahan, perhaps the most prolific writer covering the Hogup strike, also recalled demands for the surrender of Roy Washburn for the murder of Oren Bruthens.

Despite the growing peril for the tiny group at the Hogup's office, Richter remained firm in his defiance of the laborers' demands, and the protest slowly fizzled. By 3:00 a.m. on the eleventh, Callahan writes that the number of demonstrators had dwindled to less than twenty, all of them of Irish descent.

As an interesting aside, after Harold Richter's statement that O'Brien was not only present at the January 10 protest, but that he was also its instigator, no mention of his further involvement in the strike has surfaced. With Bruthens' death, leadership within the Irish contingent had apparently once more been fractured. The strikers' situation would be further derailed on the night of the tenth by additional murders, this time leaving little doubt as to the culpability of the Gunnison Five.

WIL CHAMA INTERVIEW

❧

SESSION NINE

Man, I hate the sound that dictating machine makes when it runs out of space. It claws at my nerves like fingernails across a chalkboard. But I guess it can't be helped if you insist on recording everything, and, to tell you the truth, I kind of appreciate that you do. It makes me believe that what I've got to say is going to be heard in my own words, instead of twisted around by some historian who wants to interpret my meaning. I hate when people do that. Like they know better than I do what I was thinking or feeling, or why I did the things I did.

Anyway, getting back to what I was talking about, Angel showed up as promised two days later, just after sundown. While Flaco took care of his horse, Angel and I made ourselves comfortable by the fire. We'd kept a kettle of beans and meat warming at the edge of the flames in anticipation of his return, and there was a little coffee leftover, too, although turning gritty as the pot was drained. I gave Angel a few minutes to take the edge off his hunger, then asked about the news from Río Tinto.

He shrugged without looking up. "There is not much," he replied around a mouthful of goat and refritos. "Kellums' gunmen have all but taken over the Lucky Day, while your sheriff amigo continues to ask questions about the deaths of Landors and Rodriguez."

"No more fighting? No more fires?"

"None, although there is not much laughter, either." He looked up, squinting at me across the slow dance of firelight. "A very solemn place, your Río Tinto."

"It isn't my place," I replied.

Angel smiled briefly, then resumed eating. When he finished, he leaned back on one elbow with a contented belch. "Are the carts loaded?"

"They filled the last one this afternoon."

"Then everything is ready for our return?"

"I was planning to roll out at first light, whether you were here or not."

He nodded wearily. "I fear it will be a dangerous journey. Kellums' hombres malos have been making threats, and it is said that even El Diablo himself has promised that our carts will not reach Río Tinto."

The boyeros, who had been sitting quietly to one side listening in on our conversation, stirred nervously. One of them blurted, "Will the patrón send more men?"

Angel shook his head. "Señor Montoya has hired myself and our good friend, Wil Chama, to see that you are returned safely to your homes. Flaco is also here. That will be enough."

After an exchange of worried glances, the drivers stood as one and moved away from the fire. I could hear them over by the carts, huddled close and talking among themselves. Flaco, who had been sitting with them, sidled closer to the flame. "We are outnumbered, Señor Sandavol, and Wil was told by Kellums' jefe at the Chute that the crazy-eyed gringo called Danny Fuller has gone into Río Tinto to join the fight."

Angel looked at me. "This is true?"

"It's what Hank Waite said," I confirmed.

Angel nodded thoughtfully. "It is rumored that others from the Devil have volunteered their services, as well," he murmured. "Plus three additional gunmen have arrived on the keelboat *Joker*."

I perked up at that. "Who?"

"A man called Elwood Hardisty and two others whose names were not yet known when I left." He smiled bleakly. "El Diablo has been busy, no?"

"His name is Kellums," Flaco responded tautly. "You do us all a disservice by referring to him as Satan."

Angel laughed good-naturedly. "You mean I do your nerves a disservice, eh, Flaco?"

The young man jerked his head toward the boyeros. "Do they look like they are benefiting from your words?"

"No, they do not," Angel conceded with a heavy sigh. "Perhaps you are right. I do not respect this man, Kellums, so maybe that is why I call him El Diablo. To show my disdain for him and all that he represents."

Pushing clumsily to his feet, Flaco began rubbing his palms along his trouser legs, as he had that night behind the Lucky Day. I recognized the symptoms, the keyed-up anticipation of knowing a fight was imminent, and that people were going to die soon. I'd felt the same way in Colorado, waiting for Lester Kerns and Columbus Wright to come back from the Hogup that night at—well, I guess that doesn't matter. Not anymore.

We were all up early the next morning, in such a rush to get away from there that we skipped a breakfast fire and just chowed down on cold beans and cabrito. There was barely enough light to see the trail when our little caravan creaked out from under the trees. A stiff breeze was blowing out of the northwest, and the air was cooler than it had been in recent days. The sky was clouded over, the smell of rain a welcome change from the land's normal acridity.

Angel took the lead, riding out about fifty yards in advance of the lead cart. I brought up the rear with my Winchester resting across my saddle in front of me, my hat pulled low against the blowing sand. Flaco rode alongside one of the boyeros, a young man about his own age.

The massive wooden wheels of the carretas sent up a piercing squeal for want of grease, and the deep, solid-walled beds swayed ponderously under their heavy loads. We stopped at noon to rest the stock, and I pulled my jacket on against the rising tempest. Because of the cooler temperatures, we decided not to stop for our usual midafternoon break, and that, coupled with our unusually early start, allowed us to reach Antelope Springs shortly after sundown.

I swung down next to the upper pool to water my horse, exhausted not just from the long day in the saddle, but from the buffeting I'd taken from the wind. Angel was already there, looking cold and miserable in a brightly colored poncho.

I've already mentioned the stone hut at the upper spring. It was small and dusty and barely tall enough for an average-size man to stand upright in, although it was also wind-tight and sturdy. I'd only used it a few times in all the months I hauled for the Devil, preferring instead to throw my blankets down next to my evening fire if it wasn't threatening rain. But I'd made up my mind that afternoon that I was going to bunk inside that night, out of the wind. I guess Angel and Flaco had the same notion, for they quickly accepted my suggestion to share the spartan quarters. Not surprisingly, the boyeros declined.

"They are uncomfortable around you," Flaco informed me and Angel later that night, inside the hut with the door propped shut, the latch having long since disappeared. Not that his statement was much of a revelation. I'd noticed the cart drivers' reticence from the time we left Río Tinto. Maybe that's why I haven't been able to recall their names; they were there with us, but, then again, they weren't.

I asked Angel if we needed to keep watch, but he said no.

"We are too well-fortified here," he replied. "If Kellums' men attack, it will be between here and Tinto Cañon, or more likely in the cañon itself."

His reasoning made sense, and, after another skimpy meal of cold meat and beans, we crawled inside our bedrolls. The boyeros stayed outside, curled up under their carts with their blankets tugged over their heads, and I remember Angel cracking a joke about how, if they weren't careful, they'd end up blown all the way back to the Flats by morning. I chuckled politely, and then immediately fell asleep.

Angel was up first the next morning, awakening me by smacking his upturned boots on the heels with a closed fist to dislodge any creepy-crawlies that might have slithered inside during the night. I'd never worried much about scorpions and centipedes in Denver, but they were a caution I'd taken to heart after coming to Texas and having Elmer Griffith, who worked at the Devil's stables, show me the nub of his left trigger finger that he'd lost—in a damned painful ordeal, to hear him tell it—to a centipede's sting.

I was just skinning into my socks when Angel pulled the door open and stepped outside. I watched sleepily as he walked away from the hut, then paused to stretch languidly, his arms extended wide above his head, fists clenched. He was still in that pose when a volley of gunfire opened up from the surrounding chaparral. I saw at least half a dozen lead slugs plow into his body as I lunged for my rifle. He dropped to one knee, then pitched forward on his face before I'd chambered my first round.

Flaco, closer to the door, grabbed his Spencer on the way out. I doubt if he even heard my warning shout to get back inside. Staying low, he ran to Angel's side. By the time he got there, I was at the door, firing as rapidly as I could work the Winchester's lever. I sent one shot toward a clump of mesquite where at least two of the ambushers were holed up, then several more into the brush along a shallow arroyo. A cloud of powder smoke blossomed from a low ridge about one hundred yards away, the bullet slamming into the stone wall at my side before spinning off with a shrill whine. I snapped a round at the tiny gray bloom, then began pumping more bullets into the mesquite. Flaco dropped the Spencer, slipped both arms under Angel's shoulders, then heaved upward and back, yanking the big man's torso off the ground. He backed toward the hut in a series of staggering strides, bullets kicking up dust on every side. Meanwhile I shot my Winchester dry, then threw it behind me and drew my Remington. By the time I'd emptied the revolver, Flaco had Angel nearly to the door.

I don't know, maybe I should have gone outside to help. Maybe things would have turned out differently if I had, although I've told myself a thousand times over that I did the right thing by ducking back into the hut to retrieve Angel's Whitney-Kennedy. I was gone no more than a couple of seconds, but by the time I got back, Flaco was down, clutching his side with bloody fingers, Angel sprawled across his lower limbs like a two-hundred-pound sack of coal.

Angel was dead, that much was clear even in all of the mayhem. I suspect he was already dead when Flaco ran outside to help him. But Flaco was still alive, and I darted through the door in a crouch, keeping up a swift, methodical fire until I reached the boy's side. Shifting the Whitney-Kennedy to my left hand, I grabbed the younger man's collar in my right and hauled backward.

"No," he groaned, clawing weakly for Angel's outstretched arms. "We cannot leave him here."

Crazy kid. Bullets kicking dirt and dust all over us, whining past our ears like hornets sprung from a fallen hive, and he was still trying to save a dead man. Tightening my grip on his shirt, I dragged him into the hut, both of us tumbling over the threshold in a tangle of flailing limbs and bloodied clothing. I kicked the door closed with my stockinged foot, pushed Flaco out of my way, then grabbed a saddle and threw it against the door to brace it shut.

"Angel," Flaco wheezed, reaching toward the door like a sinner pleading for salvation.

Not feeling particularly religious at the time, I shouted for him to shut up. "Angel's dead," I added none too kindly. "Leave him be and start shooting."

Well, he didn't, and I could see with a second glance that he probably couldn't have even if he'd wanted to. He fell back with a groan, his chest heaving, blood turning the fabric of his shirt a gummy crimson. There wasn't anything I could do about it. Not with the rattle of gunfire from every side, the splatter of lead against rock and the thump of bullets hammering.

With Angel's Whitney-Kennedy in hand, I moved to a small window—there was one in each wall, although no shutters to close them off—and cautiously peered outside. As soon as I did, a rifle sang out from the motte. The bullet smacked the wooden sill at my shoulder, a hail of splinters arrowing into my jaw and shoulder. A second rifle barked from the opposite side of the hut, the bullet coming inside with an odd whistling sound to strike the wall above my head in an explosion of fragmented lead and shattered stone chips.

I dropped instinctively to the dirt floor and wrapped both arms over my neck.

"Wil!" Flaco gasped.

I raised my head. The stark terror in that kid's eyes is something I'm going to carry with me to my grave. He was dying, and I think we both knew it. I'm convinced he did. For the first time since the shooting started, I realized a fear of my own, a dread that I would perish there alongside Flaco and Angel, shot to pieces in a tiny stone hut in the middle of West Texas, the goddamned middle of nowhere!

Grabbing my rifle, I crawled over to my saddlebags and dug out a box of .44s. I began reloading as fast as I could fumble the cartridges from pasteboard to port. Outside the firing tapered off, then ceased altogether.

"Wil," Flaco said, more softly this time.

I kept shoving cartridges into the Winchester, and, when that was full, I pulled the Whitney-Kennedy over and reloaded it, too, grateful that both weapons fired the same cartridge. I listened as best I could for the sound of approaching footfalls, anything that might warn me of a rush on the windows, but, after all of the shooting I'd done, my hearing was as muffled as if I had wads of cotton packed into each ear. After a time I began to make out a faint sucking sound that caused the hair across the back of my neck to stand up. Even concentrating, it took me a moment to place the low, wet sighs. They were coming from the wound in the side of Flaco's chest, playing a gentle death's tune with the escaping air from a punctured lung. Feeling a tremendous guilt, I scooted over to the youth's side.

"Hey, amigo," I whispered gently. "Are you still with me?" He was alive but no longer conscious, and my lips drew thin in frustration. "Damn it, kid," I grated.

I guess, judging from them Hollywood movies I've watched in recent years, I should have added something more heartfelt or dramatic, like, "Don't you die on me," or "You hang in there, son." But I hadn't been, what's the word—conditioned? By the cinema, I mean. Hell, back then, none of us had. So all I said was, "Damn it, kid," like it was his fault he'd gotten himself shot and was about to die.

Flaco Montoya has been dead for nearly sixty years now, but I still feel bad that I hadn't gone to him when he called for me that first time.

With the shooting stopped, I took time to pull on my boots and shirt, then rose cautiously to my feet. Keeping my back to the wall where I wouldn't be easily spotted from outside, I quickly took stock of my situation. I had plenty of guns and ammunition, but no water or food. I had a dying man at my feet and a dead one just outside the door, and Lord knew how many men waiting in the surrounding chaparral, eager to make sure I didn't escape.

In addition to those larger issues, I had numerous splinters impaling my shoulder like miniature spears, and at least two of them in my jaw that I could see by bending my gaze down past my cheek. I plucked out what I could find with my fingers, but there wasn't much I could do about the smaller wounds on my chest and shoulders and the left side of my face—slivers of stone gouged from the rock walls by bullets, tiny pieces of lead burrowed under my flesh.

With my head tipped back against the cool stone, I felt a wave of panic rush upward from the pit of my stomach. I believe it was pretty close to overwhelming me when I heard a voice, wrapped inside my grandpapa's thick German accent, growling for me to "Valk it oof, boy. Is from your heart too far to kill you."

"You bitches," I recall muttering, but the old coot's advice salvaged my composure. Leaning both rifles against the wall, I drew my Remington and began punching out the empties. In doing so, I must have tipped forward a bit, because immediately a pair of shots came slamming through two of the windows, ricocheting off the walls in jagged, thumb-size shards.

I don't know if you've ever seen a spent bullet after it's been bounced around a rock house a few times, but it's a scary thing to imagine what one of those misshapen chunks of lead could do if it struck your body. It's bad enough just getting shot, but the thought of getting hit with something as twisted and saw-toothed as a ricochet can just about turn your knees to noodles. I've also heard that ricochets are more apt to cause infection later on—you know, assuming you survive the initial impact.

After a while, Kellums' men began a sporadic rifle fire that, although never again reaching the intensity of those first several minutes, did a fine job of keeping me unnerved. I'd duck and curse every time a bullet came through a window, although I also managed to keep up a fairly steady return fire, picking my targets judiciously and being careful not to show myself at the window. What I'd do was hang back in the shadows where I couldn't be as easily spotted, slam three or four rounds into an area where I thought one of the ambushers might be hiding, then hit the floor as a fresh volley came screaming through the windows.

It went on like that for a couple of hours before I began to detect a change in the pattern of gunfire. The shooting seemed to be growing thinner, as if some of the ambushers were holding back. That worried me, as I could well imagine one or two of them keeping me pinned down while the rest crept stealthily forward. Slipping over to the door, I peered through a crack between a couple of planks, but the little clearing in front of the hut, though hazy with gun smoke, was empty save for Angel's body lying to one side of the entrance. Cautiously making the rounds of the windows, I didn't see anything I considered cause for alarm. After a while I became convinced that there was only one or two men left out there, with most of the shots coming from the chaparral fronting the door.

In case you're wondering, Flaco had passed on by then. I'm not sure when he died, just that at some point I became aware that his chest was no longer rising and falling erratically, and that the fishlike suction of his breathing had ceased.

You might think I'd have been bothered by Flaco's death, or by having his corpse lying close by, but the truth is, with all the shooting going on, I'd barely noticed. That changed quickly once the firing from outside tapered off. Almost instantly I began to feel the slow rise of panic in my breast that had nearly overwhelmed me earlier. I kept checking the windows, as if expecting charging hordes of gunmen at any second, but there was nothing to see, which only increased my anxiety. I was at the window closest to the arroyo when the whole damned building blew to hell and gone.

I was flung against the opposite wall. I seemed to hang there a moment, elevated midway up the wall, before plummeting to the dirt floor. I hit the ground hard, nearly choking on dust so thick I swear I could have carved my name in it. My head throbbed and my ears rang and tears streaked my cheeks, while a sulphuric stink filled what was left of the shattered structure. I shook my head dizzily, then pushed weakly to my hands and knees. I recognized the smell, and knew immediately that some low-down son of a bitch had tossed a stick of dynamite against the outside wall of the hut. And just about the time I figured that out, the entire east side of the shack was blown inward from a second blast, which seemed to suck all the oxygen out of the building.

I must have lost consciousness for a few seconds, because when I became aware of my surroundings, the air was already starting to clear out, the sky above such a brilliant blue it hurt my eyes to look at it.

Stifling what I thought at first was a silent groan, I rose to my knees, then sank back on my calves while the world danced and bobbed around me. The east wall was completely destroyed, burying Flaco's body beneath its rubble, and the ceiling on that side of the ridge pole had collapsed in a tangle of broken limbs and sod. My Winchester and Angel's Whitney-Kennedy, along with my saddlebags containing the extra ammunition, had also disappeared under the debris. I still had my revolver, though, and I drew it as I lurched clumsily to my feet.

The panic was gone, retreating from a growing rage that swelled into suffocating proportions. Through what remained of the west wall I could see two men approaching with awestruck expressions on their faces. They were looking at what remained of the hut, rather than in it, and had failed to notice me rising phoenix-like from the smoke and dust.

I recognized both men instantly, and, with a harsh cry, I stepped out through the west wall, my finger already tightening on the Remington's trigger. The guy nearest me was Danny Fuller, and I shot him first, without aim or hesitation. Danny was carrying two sticks of dynamite in his left hand, the fuses entwined but unlit, and he had an old percussion revolver in his right hand, its muzzle pointed toward the ground. His mouth flew open when he saw me, and his eyes grew wide, but that was as far as he got. My bullet took him square in the forehead and he crumpled on the spot, the reddish-brown sticks of dynamite bouncing once, then rolling away.

The second man was Joshua Tibbets, one of the mechanics who

helped keep the Red Devil plant in operation. He was carrying a rifle, which he tried to bring to bear as soon as he saw me, but I snapped off my second shot before he could get the hammer back. My bullet caught him in the stomach, and he coughed out a grunt as he dropped the rifle and wrapped both arms over his belly as if to smother the pain.

Not knowing if there was anyone else around, I spun a circle with the Remington thrust before me. My legs were shaky and my vision was less than eagle-sharp, but I didn't see anyone, and by the time I came back around to Tibbets, he'd already fallen to his knees and was bent forward with his forehead nearly touching the ground. Keeping the Remington's muzzle trained on the top of his head, I walked over to kick the rifle out of reach, then jerk a handgun from his belt that I tossed after his long gun. Stepping back, I said, "Who else is here?"

He didn't answer. Hell, the shape he was in, he may not have heard me. Cursing, I leaned forward to knock the hat from his head, then jerked his face up by his long, dark hair. "Can you hear me, Tibbets?" I yelled. "Who else is here?"

His expression curdled in pain. "No one."

"Like hell," I growled, giving his head a shake.

"Jesus, Wil, they ain't here."

"Where are they?"

His lips moved slowly, and his eyes were starting to glaze over. "Not here."

"Where?"

"They went on."

"Where?" I shouted, tightening my grip on his hair.

"The Flats."

Now we were making progress. "Who? How many?"

Like the croak of nails drawn slowly from hard wood, I heard the names tumble from the wounded man's lips. "Tom ... Layton. John Potter, El- ... Elwood Hardisty."

"Why are they going to the Flats?"

I was thinking of the Chute, you see, and not considering the cottonwoods where Montoya's men usually camped when they went after salt. There was an old jacal there that they used in bad weather, in addition to a good-size spring that had been dammed to create a pool where they could water the stock.

"Gonna tear ... tear it down ...," Tibbets whispered. Then he stopped talking, and a peculiar look came over his face. His gaze seemed to turn inward, as if no longer aware of me standing above him, holding him up by his hair. An expression of puzzlement briefly narrowed the mechanic's eyes—and then he died.

Of all the men I've seen killed in my life, all that I've killed myself—and that's a whole lot more than I want to contemplate—I think Joshua Tibbets' death is the one that haunts me most. More so than even Flaco and Angel. Because I was there, staring into his eyes when the life went out of them like a snuffed candle, knowing even as I watched that I was the one who'd put it out.

I was so taken aback that I instinctively let go of his hair. He rocked forward, still on his knees, then kind of serenely tipped over like he was going to take a nap. I moved back two or three paces, staring at the corpse. That's all it was, too. Just an empty husk, once used but now discarded.

Swallowing hard, I raised my eyes to the fringe of chaparral, noticing for the first time the vague outlines of Fuller's and Tibbets' mounts, deep within a feathery screen of mesquite. Staring numbly at their horses brought to mind my own dun mare, but she was nowhere to be seen, nor was Angel's black, or Flaco's grulla. Most of the oxen were gone, too. Only three remained, stretched out flat on their sides—a couple of brindled steers and a cow with a depleted udder, a rust-colored halo of drying blood pooled above her head.

Other than the ashes of last night's fire and the discarded blankets from their bedrolls, there was no sign of the boyeros.

That was a big relief for me, as I'd been half afraid I'd find all four of them lying murdered among the dead oxen. Keeping my revolver to hand, I walked out a ways to see if I could find the horses, but they must have hightailed it out of there with the cart drivers when the shooting started.

I should admit now that I didn't blame the boyeros for running. Had I the option, I might have done the same thing.

Abandoning my search for our own stock, I went to fetch the horses I'd seen hitched inside the chaparral. One of them turned out to be a dainty little sorrel filly, a two-year-old that, in my opinion, was too small yet to be carrying a rider. The second was a long-legged gray gelding, rigged out with a standard American stock saddle. After stripping the tack from the filly's back and giving her a smack on the rump to convince her she was free to go, I loosened the gray's reins and led him over to the crumbled stone hut. Instead of taking off on her own, the bay followed, and I decided that, if that's what she wanted to do, I'd let her.

I didn't bother Flaco, buried under the rubble of the collapsed hut, but I did drag Angel inside, finding a place for him among the scattered stones. The door had been blown off its hinges in the first blast, and I hauled it inside and laid it over Angel like a coffin lid, then weighed it down with rocks to discourage scavengers. I left Fuller and Tibbets lying where they'd fallen, and never regretted it.

Passing Flaco's Spencer on my way to the gray, I picked it up and brought it along. There was a scabbard on the saddle's offside, slanted backward above the gelding's hip, and I shoved the carbine inside. I was about to pull myself into the seat when I remembered the two sticks of dynamite Fuller had been carrying. I went back to get them, then creaked into the saddle, my muscles protesting all the way to the top. Still feeling a little woozy from the morning's events, I eased the horse away from the Springs at a walk, the bay following as docilely as a pet fawn.

I took my time on the ride back, not really caring if I made it in before dark or not. As the miles crept past, I began to feel better. My hearing began to clear up and my thinking became less befuddled. My anger remained high, though, and would spike sharply every time I thought of Angel or Flaco.

Although it was still windy, yesterday's clouds had moved on and the air felt warmer. I hadn't been able to find my hat after the explosions, and I could feel the sun against the pale flesh of my forehead, like a hot rag over fevered skin. From time to time I would ride over swaths of damp soil where it had rained overnight—some little more than pocked dust in the road, others a crusted, hardening mud, breaking into shards beneath the gray's hoofs. It was probably noon when I spotted a group of horsemen spurring toward me from the south. I pulled up, my hand dropping instinctively to the Remington's grips, but I didn't draw it. When I recognized Amos Montoya riding near the front of the pack, I slid my hand forward to rest it lightly atop my thigh.

Montoya brought his men to walk while still some distance away. He was riding a tall chestnut with four white socks and a diamond-shaped snip above its muzzle. As he came closer, I saw a look of fear come over his face, and I swore softly. I guess I'd forgotten that Flaco was his nephew.

"Mi amigo," Montoya greeted, pulling his horse to a stop barely a dozen feet away. He scanned the desert to the east, then turned back reluctantly. "Was it El Diablo's men?"

"They ambushed us this morning at Antelope Springs," I reported sadly. "Flaco was killed trying to help Angel."

The look on the older man's face was like watching a pair of invisible screws being tightened into his leathery cheeks. His knuckles grew pale around his reins and his lips trembled briefly. I don't know how far it would have gone, because about that time a broad-shouldered man with a giant mustache kicked his horse forward. I would find out later his name was Gilberto Varga, a brother to Cierra Varga, the young woman who kept Randy Kellums' house. The Vargas were cousins to Flaco on his mother's side.

"And where were you, Chama, that you are still alive when the others are dead?" Gilberto challenged.

I glanced at him, then away. I had no intention of being drawn into a mire of senseless accusations.

"From the looks of him, I'd say Wil was right there in the thick of it," a man stated loudly from the rear of the crowd. The horsemen parted to reveal Frank Gunton astride a sorrel mule, a sheepish grin coming over his face at my astonished reaction. "Howdy, Wil," he said with a quick, low wave of his hand. At his side was another gringo I knew and liked, Dave Madison, who operated the steam room at the Red Devil plant.

"Wil," Dave offered by way of greeting.

"Dave, Frank," I replied. "What are you two doing here?"

"The Devil's been shut down," Frank explained. "Folks are starting to choose sides, and me 'n' Dave decided we didn't want to ride for the old man no more. Not with the kind of men he's been hiring lately."

Growing impatient, Montoya abruptly cut in. "What happened to Flaco?"

My unexpected happiness at finding Frank and Dave among Montoya's men plunged toward my boot heels. In quick, cutting strokes, I outlined the morning's attack, making an effort to emphasize Flaco's bravery in attempting to rescue Angel, as if that might somehow soften the family's grief.

"You killed two of them?" Montoya asked when I'd finished.

"Danny Fuller and Joshua Tibbets," I confirmed, and toward the rear of the group, I saw Frank and Dave exchange regretful glances. I'd never met anyone who cared much for Fuller, but a lot of us liked Tibbets.

Studying my knee-torn trousers and shredded shirt, measled with the stains of dried blood across my shoulders, Montoya said,

"And your own injuries?"

I shrugged. "I'm still kicking."

"I think maybe you are lucky to still be kicking, amigo," the older man stated, and, although I was inclined to agree, I kept my mouth shut.

"Go back to Río Tinto and have your wounds attended to," he instructed. "We will go on, and bring this foolishness of Kellums to an end." His lips drew taut. "El Diablo has much to atone for after today."

The heavy-roweled Mexican spurs on the heels of the old man's boots snapped backward, and the tall chestnut snorted its surprise and took off like a gust of wind. Most of the others flew after him. Only Frank and Dave hung back.

"Dang, Wil, you gonna be OK?" Frank asked, frowning in concern. "You look tattered, for a fact."

"I'll be fine," I said. "You boys go on, but be careful. That's a mean bunch you're hunting."

Frank grinned good-naturedly; his was a hard mood to keep down. "We'll see you when we get back," he promised, then spurred after the others, Dave Madison riding close by his side.

For a minute I watched them go, thinking about everything that had happened so far, and what was yet to occur. Then, glancing at the little bay filly still shadowing the gray, I said, "Let's go, *chica*. I've got some unfinished business of my own in Río Tinto."

BATTLE OF THE HOGUP
PART IV

by Eric Cranston

From
True Tales of the Old West magazine
November/December, 1956

The subsidization by Lester Kerns and Columbus Wright of supplies delivered to the entrenched citizens of Hogup in the late afternoon of January 10, 1879, has been well documented and needs no further discussion here. Even though neither man was present as the crates of food and supplies were passed out, their involvement in the relief efforts was already common knowledge among the hungry strikers. Perhaps it was equally well known to Clifford Baker and Lawrence Mueller.

Jeffrey Callahan, that indefatigable chronicler of the Hogup conflict, was in Gunnison on the evening of the tenth, telegraphing an update on the strike to his editors at the *Denver News*, when the vehicle carrying Baker and Mueller arrived in town. He "observed its course down Gunnison's snowy main avenue through the frost-etched windowpanes of the telegraph office," and would comment later that he thought it odd when the coach turned down an alley between the Atlantic Hotel and a cooper's shop. He claimed to think it odder still when the coach reappeared only minutes later to continue its journey to the Muncie Boarding House, where Messrs,

Baker, and Mueller maintained separate accommodations on the third floor. Callahan reported that their time of arrival in Gunnison was shortly after 7:00 p.m., well after dark at that time of year.

According to depositions collected in the weeks succeeding the strike, Baker and Mueller ordered a hearty supper at the Coal Creek Café, next door to the Muncie, then returned to the lobby of the boarding house where they enjoyed an evening of lively conversation and "enchanting music," the latter provided by the proprietor's twelve-year-old daughter, Alice Stevenson, on the piano. In a telephone interview conducted with the now eighty-seven-year-old former Miss Stevenson, currently a resident of Santa Monica, California, she made it a point to inform this chronicler that Lawrence Mueller seemed especially intrigued by her ministrations of the ivories that night, and encouraged her to continue on well past her usual bedtime, until the recital was "disrupted by that awful unpleasantness at the Atlantic."

The unpleasantness in question was the eruption of gunfire from two blocks away, involving, according to witnesses, at least two shotgun blasts and "three to four" reports from a revolver. Upon investigating the source of the shooting, the Atlantic's night clerk discovered the bodies of Kerns and Wright lying in the upstairs hallway of the hotel's second floor. An autopsy performed that same evening by Gunnison physician E. J. Hunsaker determined that the cause of death to both men were multiple .31-caliber pellet wounds from what appeared to be buckshot from a 10- or 12-gauge shotgun. The physician's report also noted that both men had been delivered a coup de grace to the head by a bullet of at least .44/100 caliber.

The murders of Kerns and Wright, and, indeed, it was never considered anything less than homicide by the citizens of Hogup, were investigated by then Acting Sheriff Benjamin Meeks.

It is interesting that Meeks was never a permanent resident of Gunnison, nor was he considered a qualified lawman by the Colorado Sheriff's Association—points made repeatedly by the prosecuting attorney's office in Denver during its examination of the evidence presented in the twin assassinations.

In actuality, Meeks was a part-time deputy from Ouray, hired temporarily when Acting Sheriff Maxwell Chapman was called to Denver to answer a challenge to an earlier arrest. The timing of Chapman's summons to the capital was another point of contention made by the prosecuting attorney, especially in light of the charge against the prisoner in question—failure to pay a restaurant bill totaling thirty-five cents. As deemed by a January 29 *Denver News* editorial, Chapman's presence in the Mile-High City that second week of January 1879, was, at best, an "exercise in excessiveness."

Not surprising to representatives of Kerns and Wright, Meeks' investigation concluded that the two men were murdered by persons unknown who "more than likely took off as soon as they could." Meeks listed the probable motive for the killings as a botched robbery attempt.

On the same night as the murders of Kerns and Wright, attempts were also made on the lives of Juan Gomez and Ling Longwei. Gomez received superficial wounds from a shotgun blast to his left wrist and hand; Longwei escaped injury altogether, thanks to a system of bodyguards and lookouts established outside his residence by other members of the Chinese community.

At dawn the next day, January 11, a search was made for Darren O'Brien, the quasi-leader of the Irish element, but he could not be located, nor was he seen in the area afterward. His name turns up again only in depositions gathered by the prosecutor's office. Whether O'Brien was another victim of the violence surrounding the Hogup strike, as many historians believe, or received word of the impending ambuscade before the attacks could be executed and fled the region has never been determined.

News of the deaths of Kerns and Wright did not reach Hogup until nearly noon on the eleventh. Accusations against Chama and Pratt spread quickly through the camp, thanks in no small part to Edith Fains' declaration that she had observed the two men entering the coach with Baker and Mueller the preceding evening. By midafternoon, a crowd had once again gathered in front of the Hogup's main office, but the atmosphere seemed different this time, according to numerous witnesses. Callahan, of the *Denver News*, reported an "eerie calm" taking possession of the throng, and that there were no angry calls for justice, nor any further demands for mine safety.

Violence, Callahan stated, seemed imminent, and the Hogup's representatives—mine manager Harold Richter, striker breakers George Tinslow, Jesse Burgess, Levi Pratt, Roy Washburn, and Wil Chama, and Cowboy Guards Ernie Davis, Floyd Cochraine, and John Wanczyk—judiciously retreated to the sturdy log structure of the office, rather than stand outside to treat with the strikers as they had done in the past. The first shots were fired late in the afternoon, coming from the increasingly volatile crowd of miners. Richter ordered a return volley, but with instructions to "aim high," perhaps in an attempt to repeat their actions of December 28, when shots fired over the heads of the crowd by Davis, Cochraine, and Wanczyk were successful in dispersing the demonstrators.

Their efforts seem to have had the opposite effect this time, as the strikers not only quickly returned fire, but also scattered and took cover.

Sporadic gunfire continued until dusk, when a cold darkness settled over the camp. Callahan writes that the sky was overcast and "heavy with snow that threatened to fall at any moment," and that the temperature had dropped well below the freezing point.

For the strikers, small fires soon sprang up out of range of the guns trained on them from the cabin, offering warmth and sustenance, but for the nine men and one woman—Edith Fains—trapped inside the cabin, no such luxuries were available for fear of sniper fire from the mountainside above the mine office.

Although the bulk of the fight had tapered off at nightfall,

Callahan states that occasional bursts of gunfire would erupt, and that the strikers kept up a constant barrage of taunts and insults to the individuals inside the cabin. Shortly before dawn, the situation worsened when noises of destruction began to emerge from the mouth of the Hogup's main shaft. Recalling earlier threats to blow the entrance with dynamite, Richter ordered the men known as the Gunnison Five—Tinslow, Burgess, Pratt, Washburn, and Chama— to relocate to a small equipment shed closer to the mine's entrance, where they could maintain better protection of the shaft.

Taking along several saddlebags filled with ammunition for their rifles, shotguns, and revolvers, the five men made a daring break for the shed, eighty yards west of the main office and less than thirty yards from the mine entrance. Although the Five were quickly spotted, and numerous shots were exchanged, they managed to attain the illusionary safety of the shed without injury.

One must wonder at the gunfighters' reaction when they discovered the vulnerability of their new location. Unlike the main office, constructed of sturdy, well-chinked logs, the Hogup's equipment shed was made of slab wood, those outside pieces of logs whose inner timber had been cut into bracing and planks. Weak at best, and of indeterminate thicknesses—thin at the sides, seldom more than an inch or two at its center—the walls would offer scant protection from the striking miners' guns.

Recognizing their predicament, Tinslow immediately ordered four of the five gunmen to start digging trenches close to the shed's walls, while a fifth man kept watch against an armed rush. Their situation was helped somewhat by a large selection of shovels and picks stored in racks against the rear wall, but the ground inside the shed had been frozen for nearly two months by then, and progress was slow. By sunup, the Five had gained less than a foot on the hard earth.

The actual conflict that became famous as the Battle of the Hogup began with the rising of the sun on January 12. Tinslow, crouched near a gap between two slab planks, spotted several men at the mine's entrance. Claiming to observe actions that mimicked the preparation of dynamite, Tinslow opened fire, wounding one of the men and driving the others inside. Within seconds of Tinslow's first round, the striking miners who were scattered along the mountainside retaliated. Inside the shed, the gunfighters took cover in their shallow pits as bullets from the miners' weapons pierced the thin pine plank walls. According to Callahan, within thirty minutes of opening fire, the shed looked like "a chunk of Swiss cheese," as the men inside "cowered trembling beneath a blanket of shredded bark and sap-filled splinters."

Other accounts of the battle were more respectful of the Five's sharp-shooting skills, and none other than Edith Fains herself, an acknowledged sympathizer of the strikers' plight, stated that the gunfighters put up a "lively" resistance. Fains witnessed the battle in its entirety from one of the main office's rear windows, something of a front-row seat when compared to the miner's shack nearly two hundred yards away from which Callahan was forced to view the battle.

Verifiable facts related to the actual conflict on the twelfth are in short supply, although wildly differing eyewitness statements abound. Estimates of the number of strikers actually engaged in the exchange of gunfire vary from fifteen to one hundred and fifty; Callahan says fifty to sixty, mostly Irish and Mexican, as the Chinese were poorly armed.

Although Harold Richter contends that his Cowboy Guards only returned fire when fired upon, other witnesses claim that the men still inside the cabin kept up a steady .45-caliber support for their comrades trapped inside the equipment shed. Fains concurs that Davis, Cochraine, and Wanczyk were willing participants in the fight, and shot until their gun barrels were as "hot as flat irons." (Editor's note: Fains is referring to the common laundry iron here, the older style which required heating on a stove top before use.)

Fains also states that throughout the day, she never saw Richter with a gun. Witnesses to the Hogup's earlier demonstrations agree that the mine manager never actually took a physical part in any armed conflict, although he did issue the orders for his guards to open fire.

Inside the rapidly disintegrating shed, the Gunnison Five kept up a formidable front. It probably helped that the strikers contained themselves to an area close to the base of the mountain, where there was better cover among the stumps and boulders. Juan Gomez stated that many of the strikers barely returned fire out of respect for the gunfighters' aim, although that position conflicts with other reports, as well as a photograph of the equipment shed taken on January 16 by *Denver News* photographer Augustus Kresse, which shows a "well-ventilated" structure.

Estimates of the number of rounds fired vary even more widely than the number of participants. Callahan insists no less than two thousand cartridges were expended over the course of the day; Fains says "several hundred." Richter calculates between five hundred and one thousand. An examination of the Kresse photograph reveals approximately eight hundred seemingly fresh bullet holes in the planks on the east wall, which received the brunt of the strikers' fire. Other sides of the shed were also heavily perforated, although bullets passing completely through the building cannot be discounted.

The five gunfighters made at least two attempts to escape the shed during the day-long battle. The first occurred at approximately 8:00 a.m., when Tinslow threw open the front door and made a gesture that seemed to represent a command for his men to follow him toward the stronger walls of the main office. A hail of bullets from miners perched along the mountainside quickly drove him back inside. Around noon a second attempt was made when one of the Five kicked out two of the planks in the rear wall, apparently believing that the ground behind the building wasn't adequately guarded, but several shots from the miners trapped inside the Hogup's main shaft seems to have dashed that hope.

The Battle of the Hogup lasted until dusk of the twelfth, when a posse of eighteen citizens dispatched from Gunnison by Acting

Sheriff Benjamin Meeks arrived at the mining camp to arrest the strikers. Although warrants had been issued for Darren O'Brien, Juan Gomez, and Ling Longwei, Sheriff Meeks wisely changed his mind upon viewing the scene and declared that he had come instead to arrest all members of Hogup's management, including its "agents and guards." Said prisoners were to be immediately escorted back to the Gunnison jail.

Although there was some protest from the strikers, Meeks managed to place his prisoners in a wagon and escort them out of Hogup without incident. As darkness settled over Conlin Cañon on that bitterly cold January night, the citizens of Hogup quietly returned to their homes.

Richter, his Cowboy Guards, and the Gunnison Five were taken to the town of Gunnison, where, after a flurry of telegraphs between Meeks and Sheriff Maxwell Chapman, still in Denver, Meeks was ordered to forward all nine prisoners to Denver, where they would be charged with inciting a riot. Meeks chose a southern route to avoid the snow-clogged mountain passes along the Continental Divide, and didn't arrive in the Denver with his prisoners until the twentieth.

On the twenty-second, the Gunnison Five and the Cowboy Guards were incarcerated in the Denver City jail, while Richter was released, without having once stepped foot behind bars, on a five hundred dollar bail posted by Lawrence Mueller. Within twenty-four hours, the remaining prisoners were also freed on a collective bail of eight hundred and fifty dollars, or slightly more than one hundred dollars per individual. On January 30 all charges against Harold Richter were dropped. Charges against Ernie Davis, Floyd Cochraine, and John Wanczyk were dropped on February 4.

The courts were not as lenient with the Gunnison Five, however, and an investigation was ordered by a deputy prosecuting attorney for the state of Colorado. Depositions, many already cited above, were gathered until early May, when the attorney general's office issued an announcement that, due to conflicting testimony from the numerous factions involved, as well as the questionable legal tactics of the strikers themselves, no charges against the Five would be pursued.

In light of the actions taken by the five gunfighters upon their release, it has been suggested that a verbal stipulation of the dropped charges might have been the immediate vacating of the state by all parties involved. Whether true or not, it is known that within three days' time, the Gunnison Five had disbanded, and appeared to have left the area entirely. George Tinslow's name has turned up in Wyoming annals in the 1880s as a suspected cattle rustler; he was reported hanged in 1888 by persons unknown. Levi Pratt was killed attempting to rob a mine payroll office outside of Price, Utah, in 1884. Wil Chama reportedly went to Texas, and is claimed to have been involved in the Tinto Salt War in that state in 1880. The whereabouts of Jesse Burgess and Roy Washburn after leaving Colorado have never been documented.

Despite their sacrifices, the plight of the miners at the Hogup Mine improved only slightly after the murders of Lester Kerns and Columbus Wright. Shaft bracings were strengthened, and better lighting was added along all three branches. Although a citizens' committee was formed to assess the stability of the shafts, reports afterward indicate their suggestions were largely ignored, except for the introduction of canaries, the delicate birds whose sensitivity to toxic gasses deep underground could warn the miners of danger before human life was lost.

Even with these limited measures, however, there were no further cave-ins at the Hogup operation, and the mine was closed permanently in 1908. Annual deaths after the 1878–1879 strike were in keeping with the average for that era, one to three men per quarter. No records were kept of the injured.

Total casualties for the Hogup strike were five dead. In addition to Kerns, Wright, and Bruthens, Isidoro Cortina of the Mexican-American contingent, and Irishman James O'Roarke were killed during the siege on the equipment shed. One woman, name unknown, and twenty-one unidentified males were wounded, including Juan Gomez, who was shot in the hand on the night of the tenth. One man, Darren O'Brien, vanished.

There is little doubt that a large number of questions remain unanswered in regard to the Battle of the Hogup Mine and the events which led up to it. Even a partial listing of the gaps in the complete story would require more space than this magazine can justify. Suffice it to say that as research continues through the efforts of *True Tales of the Old West* magazine and its reporters, any new evidence will be presented within these pages as speedily as possible.

THE END

WIL CHAMA INTERVIEW

❧

SESSION TEN

Time seems to be really flying by now. I can't believe it's already dark again. It feels like we just started recording a few hours ago. But, yeah, to answer your question, I remember where I was when we broke for supper. I was on my way back to Río Tinto from Antelope Springs, having left the bodies of Angel Sandavol and Flaco Montoya under the ruins of that stone hut Danny Fuller and Joshua Tibbets dynamited down on top of us.

It was late afternoon by the time I got back, hurting more than I wanted to admit and dragging-my-tail-feathers-in-the-dirt tired. But I didn't go straight to Montoya's, like you might have expected. I guess I was more mad than I was worn out, and I rode down Bluff Street with a feeling in my gut like a ten-pound chunk of ice. I kept the gray to a walk, my eyes moving back and forth in anticipation of an ambush, although I'd realize later on that I had no reason to fear one at that point.

A group of men were standing on the boardwalk in front of the Lucky Day, and as I drew closer, I recognized Charlie Anderson, Wade Pope, and a third man I'd had pointed out to me named Clyde Bayless.

Bayless was tall and slim and even more blond than Pinky Landors.

A fourth man standing with them was as much a surprise to me as Frank and Dave had been riding out to the Flats with Montoya. Bud Atkins had a Mexican wife down in Old Town. He was an ex-Confederate who had come to Texas trailing Jo Shelby and what remained of the general's old Iron Brigade after the Civil War. Bud had apparently given up pursuit of the general at the Río Grande when his horse stepped in a badger hole and broke its leg. Folks said Bud was the first Anglo to settle permanently in the Tinto Valley, and that he had ties to the Tejano community that went deeper than just his marital status. I'll confess that seeing him there with Kellums' gunmen was more than a bit disconcerting.

Anderson and his crew had already spotted me, and I could tell from quite a ways out that they'd also recognized the gray. That I was riding in on a mount one of their own had ridden out on was bound to trouble them, I figured, although they held their positions on the boardwalk, and allowed me to come to them.

I reined up about fifty yards away, across the street from the Lucky Day but up a ways—about even with the alley that ran between Ty McGiven's grocery and Neil Teague's hardware store.

In case I haven't described this before, Jay Landry's Tinto Mercantile sat between McGiven's grocery and the Lucky Day. So, west going east, it was the Lucky Day, Landry's, then McGiven's grocery, and finally Teague's hardware.

There were other businesses along the street, of course, like the New Harmony Café and the feed store, but I don't want to muddy the waters anymore than I have to. I'll just mention these four, and you'll understand why in a minute.

As soon as I dismounted, I reached across the saddle to yank Flaco's Spencer from the scabbard, all the while keeping my eyes on those men across the street. I let the reins drop, and the gray wandered off a few paces to pull at some grass growing at the edge of the cottonwoods. The little bay filly that had come back with us from the Springs followed it to the trees.

I started across the street at a walk, not toward the saloon, but toward McGiven's grocery, carrying the carbine in my right hand. With its stubby barrel, the Spencer carbine is light enough to be handled like a pistol, at least for the first shot. I'd have preferred my Winchester, not only because it held twice as many cartridges as the Spencer, but because it didn't require that extra step that a Spencer did, namely having to cock the hammer separately after levering a round into the chamber. On the other hand, the Spencer's big .52-caliber slug was going to pack quite a bit more wallop than my Winchester's .44-40 round, and that was going to come in handy real soon.

I was about halfway across the street when the men in front of the Lucky Day began to break apart, moving toward the edge of the boardwalk with their hands edging toward their holsters. I was sorry to see Bud Atkins stay with them. I'd hoped he wouldn't be a part of this.

Clyde Bayless was the first to leave the shade of the veranda, brushing the tails of his dusty black jacket back to expose the pearl grips of a silver-plated Colt. Bayless wore his light blond hair long, in the style of the late Wild Bill Hickok, and I still remember how it fluttered in the breeze off the river, gleaming like spun silk in the slanting rays of the afternoon sun. No one spoke. I reckon we all knew what was going to happen next.

As Bayless moved deeper into the street, I continued my path toward the boardwalk in front of McGiven's. It turns out they had a plan, although I was too green at the time to realize it. Anyway, with the bulk of my attention focused on Bayless, I was a split-second slow in responding when Charlie Anderson went for his gun.

It shouldn't come as a surprise to anyone that a split second can make all the difference in the world in a gunfight, but luck was on my side that day, and Anderson's shot missed me clean. Bayless' didn't, though. While I snapped the Spencer up to fire at Anderson,

Bayless' bullet hit me in the stomach and sent me sprawling. But my luck was still holding, see? You will. By getting knocked on my ass, those shots fired almost simultaneously from Pope and Atkins missed completely. Meanwhile I lurched to my feet and made a run for McGiven's boardwalk, throwing myself to the street and rolling under the skimpy shelter of the front steps even as more bullets peppered the ground around me.

No, I wasn't gut-shot. I wouldn't be sitting here talking into a Dictaphone machine if I had been. What happened was that Bayless' bullet caught the buckle of my gun belt, mangling it badly before gouging a deep furrow along the well-oiled leather just under the billet. There was some blood, but no worse than what I'd brought back with me from the Springs, what with all the little rock chips I was still carrying under my hide.

Out in the street, Bayless was advancing on my shelter, firing methodically as he closed the distance between us. He must have figured I was wounded worse than I was, but that was his tough luck, not mine. Levering a fresh round into the Spencer's chamber, I brought the piece to my shoulder, eared back the hammer, and fired. My bullet caught the gunman square in the chest, and his legs kicked out from under him as if spring-loaded, dropping him on his butt in the pale, ankle-deep dust. A gout of blood burst from his mouth, spraying the front of his white linen shirt. Then he flopped back with a surprised look on his face, and didn't so much as twitch after that. I'm guessing he was dead before his shoulders hit the ground. Like I said, a Spencer packs a pretty hefty punch.

With Bayless down, I wiggled farther back under the boardwalk. I could feel the warm spread of blood soaking into my shirt, but didn't dare check it out for fear of what I'd find. Making my way to the far end of the boardwalk, I timidly poked my head above the level of the porch. The street was empty, and with a sweet, grateful curse, I jumped to my feet and ducked into the alley.

I paused there with my back pressed against the grocery's

side wall, breathing more heavily than my exertions should have accounted for. I guess it's safe to say I was scared. Only a fool wouldn't have been. After a while I peered around the corner, but Anderson and his men were gone. Figuring they must have taken shelter in the saloon, the first thought that occurred to me was that at least one of them would probably sneak around back to flank me. Making sure I had a round chambered, I hurried down the alley to the grocery's rear corner.

Now, I might not have been the most experienced gunfighter on the street that day, but I wasn't an idiot, either. That's why I got down low before easing an eyeball around the corner. It was a good thing I did, too, because Atkins and Pope were both back there. Pope was circling wide, already into the chaparral where me and Angel and Flaco had waited the night Angel killed Pinky Landors. Atkins was staying close to the buildings, and had already climbed partway up the back stairs to the second story of Landry's store, where the merchant had his home.

Pope saw me first and fired. His bullet passed just inches above my head in a shrill, angry whine. Stepping away from the building, I swung the Spencer toward him and pulled the trigger. I'm pretty sure I missed, but my shot must have come close, because Pope yelped and dived for cover behind a live oak.

Atkins pulled the trigger barely an eye blink after me, his bullet whomping into the side of the building like a sledgehammer on a wedge. Not thinking—which I don't recommend in a gunfight, by the way—I moved into the open, levered a live round into the Spencer's chamber, then lifted and fired in one fluid motion. My slug hit the bottom of one of the wooden steps close to Atkins' knees and he howled loudly, whether in pain or surprise I couldn't say, but when he continued climbing, it was a lot faster than before. Twisting partway around, I sent another bullet sailing toward the live oak where Pope was crouched, then leaped back into the alley.

Don't ask me why I turned when I did, because I couldn't tell you. All I know is that, after jumping backward into the alley, I spun around real fast to discover a short, stocky man with a heavy black beard standing at the other end of the alley, a cocked revolver leveled at my spine. I'd find out later his name was Oliver Swanson, out of Louisiana.

In turning, I'd moved slightly away from McGiven's store, so that the gunman's bullet passed between me and the grocery, right where I'd been standing just a fraction of a second before. I chambered and fired a round as quick as I could, but a Spencer ain't built for speed, and Swanson managed to fan off a second shot while my finger was still drawing slack off the trigger. This time, luck finally let me down. Swanson's bullet burned high across my left side, and I cried out and fell heavily to one knee. I fired, but the little shit was already darting back around the front of the building. Pushing to my feet to give chase, a wave of light-headedness sent me stumbling into the side of the building, gasping as a white-hot flash of pain lanced my ribs.

I saw the Spencer lying in the dirt in the middle of the alley, although I didn't recall dropping it. Figuring any effort that would require me to bend over might be a mistake, I left the carbine where it was and drew my revolver. That ol' Remington felt mighty good in my hand, like an old friend I knew I could count on.

I was leaning against the grocery with my legs braced in front of me to keep me from tipping over, but I knew I couldn't stay that way for long. I figured I was already wearing out whatever luck I might have had left for one day.

What you've got to understand is that, up until that point, everything had been done just about as close to nonstop as you can imagine. So far I'd managed to keep my opponents off balance, guessing as to what my next move would be, but I was afraid that if I gave 'em even a few minutes to regroup, they'd figure out a way to trap me in that alley, and I couldn't let them do that. Not if I wanted to live, and believe me, as reckless as I'd been with my life that day, I still wanted to live. So with the Remington in my right hand and my left arm pressed firmly against the wound in my side, I sucked in a deep breath, then stepped around the rear corner of the grocery.

What happened next seemed to happen in slow motion. Oh, I was moving, all right, and probably pretty fast, considering that Pope and Atkins were firing right back just as quick as their thumbs and trigger fingers could work their revolvers, but it felt like everything had slowed down.

Atkins had gained the top of the stairs and was down on one knee where he wouldn't make an easy target, but he was also lacking even the limited experience I had in these situations, and he was watching Wade Pope, who had left the trees and was sprinting toward the alley's rear entrance.

I shot Pope first, my bullet striking him high and spinning him partway around. Moving to my right, I snapped a shot at Atkins just as he stood up to take aim at me. Although I was a shade quicker, my bullet went high and caught him in the jaw. Atkins' eyes kind of popped out in surprise as a good-size chunk of bone and tissue was torn from the side of his face. He fell backward, then tumbled loosely down the stairs.

Bud Atkins didn't stop rolling until he reached the bottom, and he didn't get up afterward. Pope was also down and not moving, so I didn't waste a second shot on either of them. I ran back through the alley, the wound in my side bringing tears to my eyes and making my nose run snot. I hesitated only long enough to swipe a sleeve across my nostrils and catch a deep breath, then stepped around the corner with the Remington leveled at my waist.

There were two men standing on the boardwalk in front of McGiven's grocery. One of them was Ty McGiven. The other was Jay Landry. Landry threw his hands up when he spotted the Remington, and McGiven squawked and jumped back, slamming into the front of his store hard enough the rattle the glass in the window.

"Don't shoot, Chama," Landry squawked. "We ain't armed."

Ignoring those two, I stepped out into the street. The bearded guy, Swanson, he was lying face down in the dirt just off the boardwalk, one arm flung above his head as if he'd died trying to hail a carriage. A puddle of blood was solidifying the dust at his side. Glancing at McGiven, I said, "What happened to him?"

The grocer looked puzzled. "Didn't you shoot him?"

After thinking about it for a moment, I allowed that maybe I had.

"Well, he came staggering out here from the alley and collapsed. We assumed it was you who shot him."

"Is he dead?"

Landry guffawed. "I'd say he sure looks like it."

I felt like smacking him upside his head for such a smart aleck response. "Where's Anderson?" I asked.

"I assume he's still in the saloon," McGiven replied.

"How many men does he have with him?"

McGiven shook his head. "I don't know. Three, four."

Landry suddenly lowered his hands. "Now see here, Chama, I want this madness stopped. We can't have people like you shooting up the town over something as trifling as who owns a piece of property."

"This ain't none of your business, Landry," I replied. "Shut up and get out of here, before you get hurt."

The two businessmen exchanged peeved glances, but departed without further bluster. Not knowing what else to do, I returned to the alley, then made my way to its far end. I wouldn't have been surprised to find Anderson or some of his gunnies putting a sneak on my location, but the big, cactus-studded rear lot was empty save for the bodies of the two men I'd left there.

Leaning weakly against the grocery's wall, I punched the empties from my revolver and replaced them with live rounds. Then I edged around the back of the building. The Lucky Day's rear door stood wide open, but, from the sun-washed outdoors, the saloon's interior looked as dark as the belly of a mine shaft. For the first time since riding into town that afternoon, I felt a twinge of uncertainty. Hugging the grocery's back wall where I wouldn't be as easily spotted, I contemplated my next move. Did I wait out Anderson and whoever else he might have with him inside the Lucky Day? Or did I go in after them?

Another consideration—and it was a big one—was that Anderson wasn't bleeding. I was. Not to mention there was no way I could cover both the front and rear of the saloon by myself. No, I was either going to have to go in after them, or give it up and make a run for it. In the mood I was in, it didn't take long to make a decision.

Atkins was still lying at the foot of the stairs behind Landry's Mercantile, and hadn't moved as far as I could tell. Spotting his revolver in the dirt under the steps, I eased forward to grab it. It was a simple Colt conversion, chambered for the old .44 Henry round, which meant I wouldn't be able to reload from my own dwindling stock of ammunition, but a quick check showed four live rounds still in the cylinder, so I tucked it into my belt.

Like a stalking cat, I continued on through the weeds toward the Lucky Day. My pulse started hammering as I imagined Charlie Anderson crouched inside the dark saloon, taking aim at me as I crept closer. Drawing Atkins' Colt with my left hand, I rocked the hammer back to full cock.

Have you ever wondered what goes through a man's mind just before he rushes forward toward his probable end? Well, it's probably not as much as you might think, which is likely why he's able to accomplish the foolishness that others might call bravery. For me, at least, that's the way it was right before I made my charge on the saloon's rear door. I went in fast, firing left-handed with Atkins' Colt in the hope of startling anyone watching the door to duck for cover. I also went in at an angle, so that I wasn't silhouetted against the outside light any longer than necessary.

Going in blind like I did, I had no idea where I'd land, and, sure enough, it was into a stack of whiskey crates. I grunted loudly as my already bruised body slammed into the wooden containers, setting them to swaying precariously above me. Spotting a slim, dark figure sprinting toward the door to the main room, I snapped off the last round from the Colt. My bullet struck a twenty-gallon keg standing upright next to the door with a sharp crack of splintered wood, followed by the splash of spilling beer. Flinging the empty Colt aside, I lunged to my feet, then quickly threw myself back down as a volley of gunfire raked the storage room.

The fusillade was loud but brief, and, having already abandoned common sense for the day, I took its termination as the opening I'd been waiting for. Jumping to my feet, I made a dash for the entrance to the main room. I was expecting to be instantly fired upon. Instead I made it to the door without incident. Pausing for the space of a heartbeat—not very long, the way my pulse was racing—I shouted out some senseless promise to kill every mother's son in the place if I saw so much as the hint of a gun barrel, then dived through the opening.

Anderson wasn't there. I remember sitting on my butt on the floor with the Remington sweeping the room left to right, blinking stupidly at the half a dozen or so individuals who hadn't fled the saloon. Bob Thompson was standing behind the bar, looking as worried as you might expect the owner of the place to be, what with my threat of chaos still echoing across the room, the fumes of spilled beer and whiskey rolling through the door behind me like a toxic fog. Hattie Fender and Beth Knight were huddled in a corner with several customers, all of them looking like they were about to soil themselves. But Anderson was gone, and, across the room, the batwing doors to the street were still swinging.

Cursing, I surged to my feet, heading for the door in a lurching run. I was almost there when I skidded to a stop in the spit-slick sawdust and swung around with the Remington raised shoulder-high. Behind the bar, Bob's eyes shot wide, and he dropped the sawed-off shotgun he'd been swinging toward my back.

"You son of a bitch," I grated, leveling my sights on a bead of sweat clinging to the bartender's nose.

"Jesus, Wil," Bob croaked. "Don't shoot! Please, God, don't pull that trigger."

"Wil ..." Hattie said tentatively, half standing. "He didn't mean nothing."

"Where's Anderson?"

"He took off out the front door," she said.

"Who else is in here?"

"No one. Least ways, none of Kellums' toughs."

When Bob started to lower his hands, I let the Remington's muzzle twitch a warning. "You keep 'em high," I snarled, and he reached for the ceiling, fingertips stretching. "Kick that shotgun to the far end of the bar," I ordered. After he did that, I said, "If you ain't standing in that exact same spot when I come back, I'm going to blow your goddamned head off. Savvy?"

If I'd been smart, I would have gone ahead and shot him then. I was risking my life turning my back on him, especially after he'd made his intentions so clear with that scatter-gun. The thing is, me and Bob had a history, and our friendship hadn't been all that bad until that last week. Maybe that's why I unconsciously gave him the benefit of the doubt, although I hope I never do anything that dumb again.

I spotted Charlie Anderson as soon as I exited the saloon. The gray horse I'd ridden in on had lingered in the tall grass across the street, and Anderson was just throwing a leg over the saddle when I stepped to the edge of the boardwalk. He spotted me right off, and I believe he was swearing as he jerked his revolver up and fired. His lips were moving, at any rate.

Anderson's bullet slapped the dobe wall about a foot to my right, spraying my cheek with dried mud. He fired a second time, then dug his spurs into the gray's ribs. I didn't flinch or seek cover. Instead I braced my shoulder against one of the veranda posts and cradled the Remington in both hands. The gray was making good time, the dip over the bench toward the Río Grande coming up fast, but I didn't hurry my shot. I knew I'd get only one. Sighting carefully, I squeezed the trigger, then stepped clear of the billowing powder smoke.

The gray continued on toward the river, but its stirrups were flopping, the saddle empty. On the ground in front of the jail, Charlie Anderson was still tumbling limply across the hard ground, stopping only when he came up hard against the stone wall beside the front door.

There was movement behind me and I spun with the Remington cocked. Bob Thompson was standing behind the batwing doors, but he had the fingers of both hands plainly visible, clamped to the scalloped wood like they'd been glued there. Hattie and Beth stood on either side of him, all three of them looking at me like I was some kind of monster dredged up from the bottom of the Río Grande. I didn't care. Right at that moment, I just didn't give a damn about anything or anyone.

Turning away from the trio of heads perched like owls atop the doors, I walked across the street to where Anderson was lying on his back, his arms spread wide. A big cherry-red stain covered the front of his shirt where my bullet had exited the body. He was dead, and I didn't have to get too close to see that. I remember standing there, just staring at the body for some time before I slowly holstered my revolver and walked off through the trees toward Old Town.

After what I'd been through that long day, the Bravo Cantina seemed cool and dark and quiet, a haven of tranquility, even if that tranquility was largely illusory. Carlos Mendez was standing on the sober side of the bar when I walked in, talking to a guy in a leather vest, with a broad-brimmed sombrero and fancily carved holster worn high on his waist. I gave them both barely a glance as I walked around behind the bar to where the shotgun Angel had brought back from the Flats leaned against the wall. It was freshly cleaned, loaded, and capped, and I nodded in grim satisfaction to visualize him scrubbing the piece thoroughly before riding out that last time. Old man Montoya had been right about me and Angel. I'd really gotten to like that rumbling bear of a man; it saddens me still that I never got to know him better.

With the shotgun in my right hand and my left arm still pressed firmly against my throbbing ribs, I went back outside. The day was nearing its end, the sun already nudging down against the earth as if seeking its bed. I glanced at the sky but it was still too early for the bats to leave their dens. The spots I saw swirling up there were my own, and I sank into a chair sitting beside the door before my knees gave out and dumped me on the ground.

After a while Carlos came to the door, pausing there to study me thoughtfully. "There was shooting?" he observed after a moment.

"I heard it."

"It was not you?"

"It was me."

He seemed to consider that for a spell. "Señor Montoya instructed me to stay close to the cantina and store, otherwise I would have come to your aid."

I didn't know him well enough then to know whether or not he was telling the truth, but I was glad that he hadn't. Especially now that I'd come through it all alive, if not entirely in one piece, as Carlos quietly pointed out.

"You are hurt bad?"

"Just some scratches."

"That is a lot of blood for scratches, my friend."

I didn't reply. There was some kind of commotion going on in New Town. I couldn't tell what it was, but figured I'd be finding out soon enough.

Carlos must have noticed it, too, because he disappeared into the cantina without waiting for my opinion on the blood that was soaking through my shirt. A few seconds later I heard him and the guy in the black vest talking in low tones from somewhere back in the cantina.

It was only then that I started to feel some minor curiosity about the stranger in the leather vest, especially the way he carried his gun. I was annoyed with myself for not asking Carlos who he was or what he was doing here. It was just another example of how poorly qualified I was for that job. When I look back on those days now, I believe I made a fair showing for myself, but I was awfully lucky, too. More so than a normal man has a right to expect.

The crowd up on Bluff Street was becoming more agitated by the minute, their voices swelling in anger. I pushed to my feet, caught my balance when I started to list to one side, then moved to the edge of the veranda to await whatever came my way. I was still dripping a little blood from where that damned Louisiana swamp rat, Oliver Swanson, had shot me, although I didn't think it was bad. I figured if it was, I'd already be stretched out unconscious on the ground.

Still, I was lucid enough to recognize how wobbly I was becoming, and that the sweat pouring down my face in salty rivulets wasn't entirely caused by the day's heat. It scared me to think what would happen if I passed out too soon, so I tried to keep my thoughts focused on the activity up on Bluff Street. Sure enough it wasn't but a few minutes later that a congregation of New Town's finest began making its way toward the cantina. Most of the crowd—McGivens, Teague, and Landry among them—was on foot, following closely behind Randy Kellums' fancy carriage, but I couldn't stop a knot of rage from tightening my jaw when I spotted Chad Bellamy riding in that shiny black rig beside Kellums.

Kellums' driver halted the carriage about thirty yards away, the crowd of pedestrians lapping up on either side like a wave, although I noticed folks were careful not to step too far forward. Most of them were yammering for justice, calling for an end to the "senseless violence" and the restoration of "law and order." When I heard my name shouted out as an instigator, I took a quick step forward and swung the shotgun up as if to empty both barrels into the crowd.

Talk about a sudden silence. You couldn't have whacked a cork into a bottle of noise and shut a crowd up any faster. After a couple of tense moments, Chad Bellamy cautiously raised one hand, then climbed down from the carriage's rear seat. I admired his spunk, if not his wisdom. He edged forward a few hesitant steps, his left hand raised palm out, although keeping his right close to his Colt.

"Easy, Wil," Chad called. "I just come down to talk."

"I noticed you brought along plenty of help."

"It's a free country. Ain't no law says they can't come down here if they want to, but no one means you any harm, I'll promise you that."

I laughed at the absurdity of his words. "You take a good look at what's left of my best shirt, then tell me your people don't mean me any harm?"

"Now, Wil, you know you brought this on yourself. My goal is to stop it before anyone else gets hurt."

I'd been teetering on the razor's edge of mad ever since seeing Angel Sandavol chopped down in his tracks that morning; at Chad's words, I went off like a cheap firecracker. I don't recall everything I said in reply to the part-time lawman's nonsense, but I do remember threatening to yank the head off of every son of a bitch there and spit in the hole.

I told them a few other things they didn't want to hear, too, like how it wasn't anyone's fault but their own that things had blown up in their faces the way it had, and that it had been Kellums who'd imported all the hired guns into Río Tinto, then gotten the ball rolling by sending those selfsame hombres malos out to the Flats to hang Cesar and Antonio and leave a bunch of kids fatherless. I also told them what had happened out at Antelope Springs that morning, and that two good men—meaning Angel and Flaco, not Fuller and Tibbets—had been murdered there because of Kellums' greed.

When I finally stopped to catch my breath, I was standing about ten feet in front of where I'd been when I started, and the small brass bead of my shotgun was fixed on a spot right between

Randy Kellums' eyes. Kellums' face looked as pale as a bucket of milk, and Chad had backed away until his heels were pressed up against one of the carriage's front wheels. The driver was making a real effort to keep his team under control, what with all the yelling going on and the tension in the air.

I had the shotgun pressed deep into my shoulder, and noticed that I'd cocked both hammers at some point after starting my tirade. Feeling kind of embarrassed—not by what I'd said, mind you, but because I'd lost control of my anger while doing it—I took a step back and allowed the shotgun's muzzles to drop a few inches.

"Get out of here," I said huskily, speaking to Chad. "And take that sorry piece of trash with you." I nodded toward Kellums.

Chad swallowed visibly, but I guess he realized the worst of the danger was past. "I've got to take you in, Wil," he said almost apologetically, and, again, I admired his grit for standing his ground like that, even if his voice did quaver a little.

"No," was my simple response.

"I've got to. I've got a warrant for your arrest."

"There ain't no judge in Río Tinto, Chad," I reminded him.

"I know, but Mister Kellums swore it out, and I'm duty bound to honor it."

I chuckled softly, shaking my head. "And if I swore out a warrant against Kellums?"

"You'd have to have proof to back it up."

"Git, Chad," I said wearily. "Before I do something I'll regret for the rest of my life. And throw that damned badge away while you're at it. It doesn't mean anything out here."

Chad flushed red, but he did a better job of hanging onto his temper than I had. "All right. I've still got to arrest you, Wil, but I don't have to do it today. I'll come back tomorrow, when folks ain't so riled up."

"It won't be any different tomorrow," I told him.

He nodded, licked nervously at his lips, then glanced behind him. I still sometimes wonder what went through his mind when he saw how far back New Town's businessmen and other outraged citizens had retreated from him, Kellums, and my shotgun. "All you men just go on home!" he shouted. "I'll take care of this tomorrow."

Oh, they grumbled to let the world know what they thought about it, and that it was a good thing they were feeling generous, else they would have taken that shotgun away from me themselves, and shoved it some place the sun doesn't normally shine, but I figured that if Chad came back tomorrow at all, he'd come alone.

In the carriage, Kellums, arrogant to the end, was firing up a thick Cuban cigar, jammed into the corner of his mouth like a chunk of firewood. Smirking through the curling smoke, he said, "I won't forget this, Chama, even if the others do."

"They won't forget," I promised darkly. "I won't let them forget."

Kellums guffawed, then spoke curtly to the driver, who swung his team in a tight circle and set off up the road at swift trot, forcing Chad to jump aboard on the move.

With the mob gone, I turned toward the Bravo, and I don't mind telling you I was taken aback to see Carlos and the guy in the leather vest standing to either side of the cantina's door. Carlos was holding a sawed-off shotgun across his chest like he'd done it before. The stranger was just standing there, although I noticed his hand hanging solidly beside his holstered revolver. He looked like he'd done that before, too.

Lowering his scatter-gun, Carlos came out to meet me. "Damn, hombre, you are one tough son of a whore, no?"

I nodded, grateful for the compliment, humbled by the support I'd earlier doubted. Then my leg gave out and I dropped to one knee.

Carlos helped me back to my feet. "You should come inside, amigo," he said kindly. "Hector and I will keep watch after this."

I glanced at the guy in the vest. Hector was probably in his early forties, more stocky than fat, with deep-set brooding eyes and the shaggy, unkempt appearance of a man who had come a long way to be there.

"Hector Flores," he said by way of greeting. "And you are Wilhelm Chama, no?"

I think I might have nodded. I know I was heading for the cantina, but the danged thing was shimmying around in front of me like a game of keep-away. Carlos was saying something, but his words sounded garbled and far away. Then the cantina kind of slid off to one side, replaced by a darkness I couldn't stop myself from tumbling into headfirst.

WIL CHAMA FOLLOW-UP INTERVIEW

❧

THE HOGUP INCIDENT

Thanks for coming. I was afraid you wouldn't, that you'd feel this was a waste of time after being here so long last month.

I know we talked about the Hogup strike the last time you were here, but I tried not to dwell on it too much because you'd said you wanted to hear about the Tinto War, and my part in that. The thing is, the more I've thought about it, the more I've realized just how interwoven those two incidents are. Not historically, but for me personally. What happened in Hogup influenced just about every decision I made down there in Río Tinto, and it all started with that kid, Felix Castillo.

I want to tell you about him, but I need to tell you about Colorado first, about what happened up there in Hogup that changed me so much. Not that I realized it then, of course. I was well into my thirties before I began to put it all together, to make sense of the decisions I later made in Río Tinto.

I've already told you about Cliff Baker and Lawrence Mueller approaching me that day in Matt Dunn's store, then asking me to come talk to them at the Denver House if I was interested in their proposition. Well, I was, so I did. I went in there like a lamb to slaughter, and never even saw the knife that cut my throat. So to speak.

Back in its heyday, the Denver House was a pretty fancy place. It was one of the first in town to have an elevator, and the first to offer in-room telephones that connected to the main desk. It kept a small army of bellhops in a room off the lobby, too, all of them decked out in those funny little pillbox hats with the straps under their chins, red suits with red bow ties, and black shoes polished to such a luster you could have shaved in the reflection.

The echo of my hobnail boots followed me across the polished granite floor of the lobby. I presented the card Cliff Baker had given me to the desk clerk, who rang up one of the kids in their monkey suits to go find out what Baker wanted done with me. This was before they got those in-room telephones, you see? Anyway, I think it impressed the clerk and bellboys alike when Mueller and Baker both came downstairs with the chubby bellhop, big grins plastered across their faces. After warmly shaking my hand, they ushered me into the hotel bar and bought a round of expensive Scotch that made the cheap whiskey I'd previously consumed taste like kerosene.

Baker did most of the talking, and it soon became apparent that neither man actually owned the Hogup, or even had a significant interest in the place other than for the money it made them. As Baker put it: "We are hired to increase the production of gold from the Hogup, and to that end we will not be discouraged."

He talked fancy like that sometimes, but you could hear the hard rock in his voice whenever some plan of his fell apart, which would happen more and more frequently over the following weeks. In time I'd come to realize that Cliff Baker was an uneducated clod who'd managed to smooth off enough of his rough edges to pass as something slightly more respectable.

Lawrence Mueller, on the other hand, was both educated and well-read. He just seemed to lack several key moral ingredients. Baker's tactics were crude because, deep down, he was a crude and frightened man who gained some small measure of reassurance in bullying others. But Mueller, well, I think that son of a bitch actually enjoyed cruelty. Like he got some kind of thrill from inflicting fear and pain on others. Unfortunately I lacked Matt's insight at the time, and wouldn't come to appreciate his contempt for men like Baker and Mueller until I was already chin-deep in the quagmire that became the Hogup strike.

The crux of Baker's sales pitch was that he and Mueller were working for a man named Donald Conlin, a local resident and freshly minted millionaire, of which there were quite a few back in those days. I'm talking about men who'd been dirt poor almost their entire lives, only to stumble—sometimes literally—onto a vein of ore rich enough to blind Midas. Guys like that would think nothing of spending a thousand dollars for a private audience with some well-known traveling orchestra, only to show up at what should have been a top-hat-and-tails affair in broken-down, sockless shoes and the same grungy overalls they'd worn wading the streams and creeks as half-starved bums.

For me, what Baker and Mueller's offer amounted to more than anything was adventure—a chance to get out of Denver and spread my wings a little. The promise of a significant salary and a chance to become a man of influence didn't hurt, either. I'd have respect, is the way Mueller worded it, and that sounded pretty darned good to me.

When I told Matt what I'd done, he just walked away, but his disappointment in my decision was keenly evident in the downward slope of his shoulders. I didn't even try to explain my decision to my family, although I left Mama a note telling her I'd gotten another job, and that I'd be gone for a few weeks. I suspect she knew the truth as soon as Grandpapa returned from Dunn's store, where he'd surely gone to find out what had become of his grandson.

The Denver and Río Grande railroad hadn't yet penetrated the mountains west of Pueblo in 1878, and the higher passes were all closed by snow, so we went north to Cheyenne instead, and caught the UP to Ogden, Utah. When I say we, I mean me and Cliff Baker, Levi Pratt, who I knew slightly from Dunn's, and Roy Washburn, who had a house over on Arapahoe. Mueller had already departed, but we caught up with him in Salt Lake City, where he was waiting for us with George Tinslow and Jesse Burgess, both men being old acquaintances of Baker and Mueller from their Deadwood days.

We rode the stage from Salt Lake City to Gunnison, a hazardous journey considering the lateness of the season and the depth of snow in the mountains. Comfort was about what you'd expect with seven men crammed inside a tiny icebox that rocked so violently on its leather thorough braces that it's a wonder the whole bunch of us didn't get sick, instead of just Washburn, who puked more or less the entire way.

We were a tight-lipped and snappish bunch by the time we arrived in Gunnison just after Christmas. Baker and Mueller put us up in the Atlantic Hotel for a night, then moved us to a roadhouse some miles north of town run by a man named Elmer Beeson. The grub was poor, the rooms cold and cramped, and the bedding was liberally infested with bedbugs that I like to never got rid of, but Beeson also had a bar where Mueller ran a tab, and a wife who was what I'd politely call "accommodating." A few days later, we all moved on to Hogup.

Hogup was a company town, meaning all the homes and businesses were owned by the same conglomerate that ran the mine—Donald Conlin himself being so far removed from the scene by then that I doubt if he even knew what was going on.

A company town is a pretty handy operation for the people who own it, but just about every one I ever had any association with reeked of corruption. Even the most basic and easily obtainable items, like toothbrushes or baking soda, were overpriced, and outside options were few at best, and more often nonexistent. Under such circumstances it didn't take long before the miners owed more than they'd ever be able to pay off, finding themselves locked in debt to the company store as securely as if with chains and bars. Before I went to Hogup, I'd thought slavery in the United States and its territories had been abolished, but I soon learned that it had just taken on a different form.

The Hogup's main office was a snugly built log cabin with a bunkhouse in the back for us and separate rooms for the mine's manager, a man named Harry Richter, and a bull-like woman who cooked and kept the place clean. I don't recall her name.

One of the first things Baker wanted us to do was make our presence known among the townspeople. At least that's what I thought he said. I guess Pratt and Burgess and them heard it differently, because, from the very beginning, they all went out of their way to intimidate the local citizens. They'd shove folks around for no reason, or make them step off the boardwalk when they passed, or cut in front of them in stores. They made sure they had their own tables in all the saloons, too—the Irish, Mexicans, and Chinese all having their own establishments, like you'd naturally expect—and woe be to the man or woman who didn't respect that.

I'll tell you, it was damned disgusting the way we treated those folks, and it didn't take long before I realized just how big of a mistake I'd made in joining the Baker outfit. Oh, I did what I was told, I won't lie about that. At the time, being as young and inexperienced as I was, I didn't figure I had much choice. But I never liked it. Not the way the others did.

But the worst thing I did—I'm going to tell you about that now. It's why I asked you to come back, and it's what made me stay there in Río Tinto after having already booked passage out of town on the keelboat, *Rachel*.

After a couple of days in Hogup, George Tinslow got it into his head to walk into one of those shacks the company had put up for its laborers. The first time he did this was in the Mexican part of town, where, I found out later, there had been a good-looking Spanish woman living with her father and siblings. I don't think

Tinslow did anything inappropriate, other than enter the house uninvited, but I guess it scared the hell out of the people inside.

That night in the Irish saloon where the five of us normally met, Tinslow told us about it, and everyone but me had a good laugh. After that they started walking unannounced into houses all up and down the gulch, and it didn't take long before they were helping themselves to whatever they wanted. Not the women, I'm relieved to say—although they might have gotten a little grabby with some of the prettier ones—but small things, like food off the table or maybe knocking some pretty something off its shelf with a shoulder, then acting like it was an accident. Basically they were just ratcheting up the level of intimidation that Mueller and Baker had been encouraging all along.

I did it once, and only once. Me and Levi Pratt were making our way down the street early one morning when the smell of baking bread caught our attention. It was coming from one of the two-room shacks the company furnished for men with families. Giving me a snaggletoothed grin, Pratt tipped his head toward the door.

"Let's go," he said, but I was already shaking my head no.

"Naw, I ain't hungry," was my reply, but Pratt wouldn't be deterred. He pushed roughly through the door, and, after a moment's indecision, I followed.

The whole front room couldn't have been more than ten-foot square, crammed tight with a small cook stove, a table with benches, and a floor-to-ceiling cabinet made out of old dynamite crates stacked one atop the other.

There was a woman standing at the stove when I walked in, tall and gaunt as a cadaver, with dull blue eyes and a chunk of fresh-baked bread in her hand that wouldn't have adequately fed one of the four children gathered around her table, let alone the whole brood. Her clothes were ragged and threadbare, her hair like gray wire. I thought she was old at first, but a second look convinced me she was just tired—bone-weary exhausted and about to run out her string.

The kids were frozen around the table, the oldest a boy of twelve or so, the others all girls, ranging in age from about six on up to ten. They were as dirty and as poorly dressed as their mama, but it was the boy's attire that caught me off guard.

"What do you want?" the woman demanded in a rough Irish brogue I'm not even going to try to mimic. She looked frightened, but I don't believe it was me or Pratt she was scared of.

Levi said, "We smelled your cookin', honey, and decided to invite ourselves in for the feast."

"Ain't no feast here," she returned smartly, "nor enough food for outsiders."

Pratt laughed. "We ain't outsiders, darlin'. We're company men, here to protect your interests against them damned union-izers. Surely you wouldn't turn a man away hungry when he's here to help."

"It doesn't look like they've got enough, Levi," I interjected, staring at the table. There was a skillet in its center, but I counted only five greasy fried eggs inside. That's not much for a hungry family, even with a half-burned loaf of bread for sopping.

Pratt's voice took on a dangerous edge. "Then next time she'll know to make more, won't she?"

I looked at the boy. "What are you doing?"

It was a stupid question, I guess. He stared back silently, dressed in the dirt-encrusted clothing of a deep-shaft miner, the broken leather bill of a cheap eight-piece cap pushed back on a mop of unruly copper-colored hair, his cheap sack coat worn nearly through at the elbows. He didn't reply, but the woman did.

"He's eating his supper."

"He works the night shift?"

"Aye, he does, and never misses a day, he don't. The company's got no right comin' down here, causin' us all such a fret."

"Then you'd best tell Bruthens and O'Brien and that bunch to quit talkin' to them union men," Pratt growled.

"Where's your papa?" I asked the boy.

"His father's dead," the woman stated harshly. "Killed in the cave-ins, he were."

Pratt sneered. "Then that's just one less dumb mick we gotta deal with, ain't it?"

Me, I just kept staring. The look in that boy's eyes was like nothing I'd ever seen before. Part of me wants to say they were as vacant as the busted-out windows of an abandoned house, but that would be misleading, because there was something still in there. Something clinging stubbornly to life, down there past the hurt and the loss and the mind-numbing responsibilities no twelve-year-old boy should ever have to face. I really don't think it was hope I detected in those cold depths. I guess, truth be told, I don't know what it was, although I do recall that it put a chill all the way up my spine.

Then Pratt grabbed the loaf of bread out of the woman's hand and we left. But that kid's expression, the look in his eyes as we walked out, that never did leave me. Just like Felix's eyes. All that helplessness, the haunting fear and overwhelming opposition that's life's lot for far too many people. Children especially.

Back then I was younger and tougher, and I was able to handle my emotions better. Today when I think of those kids, of that boy in Hogup and Felix Castillo in Río Tinto—well, sometimes at night, in bed, I weep. My wife holds me when I do, because she knows what's eating at my soul, and sometimes she cries, too.

Nothing else that happened in Hogup ever mattered after that. Even today people want to know who killed Kerns and Wright, or who murdered Oren Bruthens along Conlin Creek, or what it was like lying on my belly inside that equipment shed while the striking miners shredded the place around our ears with their guns, but none of that ever mattered. Not to me.

There were five men killed and a lot more hurt, and I'm old enough now to accept the fact that there wasn't anything I could have done at the time to change what happened. But I changed, and I swore, when I got out of that mess, that I'd never let myself be drawn back into anything like it. That's why I was so determined to leave Río Tinto after Kellums fired me. Thank God I didn't. Thank God I stayed, because I realize now that leaving would have been no different than what I did in Hogup, when I followed Levi Pratt out of that shack with the woman's loaf of bread under his arm, turning our backs on those starving kids.

Turning my back on them.

I guess I finally realized it wasn't avoiding a fight I needed to do if I wanted to feel right about myself. It was choosing the right side. And that's why I wanted you to come back, what I wanted to try to explain. And now that it's done, I don't think I even came close. It was just—that look in their eyes, you know?

WIL CHAMA INTERVIEW

❧

SESSION ELEVEN

My world moved as though through a dream, hazy and indistinct. There was light—sometimes from the sun, at other times smaller and more intimate, as if from a candle or lamp—and there was water to cool a parched throat or fevered brow. Periodically a liquid warmth would slide past my lips to swirl briefly in my stomach, then spread its heat toward my outer limbs. There was a woman, too, with quick, gentle hands and a round face that would hover above me like a bronzed moon.

These images came and went on a regular basis, along with a distant rumble of conversation that reminded me of far-off thunder. I didn't recognize my surroundings when I finally woke up, but I sensed that I'd been there a while.

My gaze wandered in curiosity, exploring the richly furnished room from a cushion of pillows tucked under my head and shoulders. I had a hard time crediting such luxury to an out-of-the-way place like Río Tinto, yet I knew I couldn't be anywhere else.

The room was large and pleasantly cool, with tall windows in two of its walls, the light playing through, muted by ivory sheers.

I was lying in a large four-poster bed, half submerged in a thick feather mattress. There was a walnut rocking chair sitting next to one of the windows, a bedside table containing a tumbler of what I hoped was water, a dresser, chest of drawers, full-length mirror on its own stand, and a tall armoire with a scalloped wooden crown—all made from the same richly polished oak as the bed. I might have imagined myself dead and gone to heaven if not for the rough adobe walls and earthen floor.

At first I couldn't recall what had brought me here, but when I tried to sit up, a detonation of pain clubbed me back to prone. After a moment spent catching my breath, I tipped my head forward to discover a swath of bandages drawn tight around my ribs, a faint pink stain showing through the fabric on the left side. I ran my fingers lightly over the bindings, but other than awakening a few deep, warning twinges, I didn't learn much.

I must have made some kind of noise when I tried to sit up, because it wasn't long before I heard a rustle of cloth through an open door. A few seconds later a short, stocky woman came into the room. The same woman who had come to fetch me and Angel to breakfast the morning we pulled out for the Flats. She regarded me silently for a moment, while I stared back like a nitwit, at a loss for words. Then she turned away, the brush of her long skirts over the hard-packed floor fading into the deeper recesses of the house.

I cautiously filled my lungs, stretching the torn flesh across my damaged ribs as far as I dared before exhaling. I'd thought the room cool only moments before, but now my brow was damp with perspiration, my palms clammy. A taunting ache lingered in my side. It wasn't long before I drifted back to sleep.

It couldn't have been more than a minute or two later when the sensation of being watched drew me from my slumber. As my eyelids fluttered open, I saw Amos Montoya standing quietly at the side of my bed. You might have expected him to smile when he saw me awake, but he didn't.

"Rosa informed me that you had returned to the land of the living," he said in a tone as somber as his expression. "I thought she must have been mistaken."

"No, I'm here," I said, the words croaking out in spits and spurts.

Montoya's eyes went to the nightstand, and the woman called Rosa hurried forward. Lifting the clay tumbler from the bedside table, she slipped a callused hand behind my head to steady me while I drank. I drained the vessel greedily, and when I was done, I lay back against the pillows, sated but without energy. Observing my weakness, Montoya said, "You lost a lot of blood, but the injury is not as serious as it might feel. The bullet passed between two of your ribs, but neither were broken, and the wound is clean and does not look infected."

"It'd take a few days for an infection to set in," I reminded him.

He nodded stoically. "Yes, it would."

I let that sink in for a bit. Well, that and the fact that the last time I'd seen Montoya, he'd been on his way to the Flats, hot for revenge.

As if anticipating my next question, he said, "You have been here for forty-eight hours, unconscious for much of that time. Besides the wound in your side, there is a cut across your stomach where a bullet struck the buckle of your gun belt. Fortunately the buckle deflected the bullet's path. There is a bruise, but it was the buckle that cut into your stomach, not the bullet. That wound also appears to be healing well, as one would expect from someone as young and strong as yourself."

I glanced down my body at the tiny punctures peppering my chest and shoulders like a healing case of smallpox.

"The rock chips you collected at Antelope Springs," Montoya needlessly reminded me. "Rosa counted forty-seven such wounds from the waist up. Apparently your trousers were sturdy enough to withstand the assault, for she did not find any below the waist. She was able to remove nearly forty pieces of stone or lead. Others may still be buried there. If so, they should eventually work themselves out. Or perhaps they already have. She couldn't tell."

I touched one of the more inflamed wounds, high on my right bicep. My finger came away faintly greasy, the smell reminding me of the salve I used on my mules when they got a cut. Meeting Montoya's eyes, I said, "What about Angel and Flaco?"

"We brought their bodies home for a proper burial. The two men you killed, Fuller and Tibbets, had already started to feed the vultures. I saw no reason to interrupt their feast."

"And the boyeros?"

"They are safe. By hiding in the scrub along Antelope Creek, they were able to escape the wrath of Kellums' hombres malos. They followed the Antelope to the Río Tinto, then followed the Tinto home, unharmed but frightened." A faint scowl tinged the older man's features. "I should have furnished them with better weapons before sending them out," he said as if speaking to himself. "Muzzle-loading rifles are no match for Winchesters. Perhaps if they had been better armed, Flaco and Angel would still be alive."

"Or else your boyeros would also be dead."

"Perhaps, but I think they would have preferred to fight as men, rather than cower like rabbits under the shadow of an eagle."

I could empathize with that. I've come to the conclusion over the years that there are times when a man needs to run, but there are also times when he needs to stand up and fight. To run when he should fight can cripple a man's spirit.

Rosa returned after a few minutes with a fresh tumbler in one hand, a stack of folded clothes pressed between her bosom and the other arm. After setting the tumbler on the night stand within easy reach, she placed the clothes on top of the dresser, then exited the room with an air of brisk efficiency. At the time I wasn't yet certain Amos and Rosa were man and wife, but I suspected it.

"Your own clothes were ruined," Montoya informed me—again, needlessly, since I'd been in them at the time of their destruction. "I have furnished you these from my store." He left the room then, pulling the door closed behind him.

I laid there a moment, gathering my strength, then pushed the quilt off and carefully slid out of bed and onto my feet. Although stiff and sore, I wasn't as gimpy as I'd feared, and after that initial burst of pain the first time I tried to sit up, I wasn't hurting too badly, either. Not bad enough that I couldn't get around.

The clothing Rosa had left for me was pure Mexican. The shirt was blue cotton with mother-of-pearl buttons from the throat to about halfway down my chest, the pants a lightweight leather, tanned to a soft honey-brown color. The trousers had side seams that opened from hip to ankle, but could be closed with a vertical row of small silver buttons. Angel had worn a pair much like these, although made from black wool instead of buckskin, and had considered himself quite the dashing figure when he unbuttoned the legs from the knees on down to expose his *calzoncillos*, the old-fashioned bleached cotton drawers he wore underneath.

A lot of folks today don't realize that back in the nineteenth century, our clothing was a lot different than it is today. Belt loops and zippers and shirts that button all the way down the front were rare when I was a boy. I remember the fit Grandpapa Karl threw the first time I came home wearing a pair of center-fly pants, rather than the old-fashioned drop-front style that buttoned at the sides. He'd considered my attire scandalous, although that's about all you see nowadays.

Of my own duds, only my boots had survived the assault at Antelope Springs. They were scuffed and worn down at the heels, but that was just from hard use. I pulled them on last, then stood in front of the full-length mirror. I can still recall the shock I'd felt, the effect those new clothes had on my identity.

Hell, I knew I was Mexican. Always had. I was the progeny of Porfirio and Ana Chama, of the San Luis Valley in Colorado, and I was proud of my parents. But I don't think I was aware until that day of the impact my Grandpapa Karl had had on my upbringing, or the manner in which his domineering personality had diminished my own sense of heritage. Even with the influence of a Mexican mother and grandmother, my accent then, as now, was as much German as it was Mexican, thanks to Grandpapa's insistence that Mexican never be spoken in either home or store. But that day in Montoya's bedroom, I was seeing myself in a way I never had before, part of something bigger than just a scrawny junior member of a bull-headed old Dutchman's household.

Unaccountably shaken by the image, I turned away from the mirror and left the room. I found myself at the deep end of an unfamiliar hallway, windowless and poorly illuminated. I felt like an intruder as I walked its length, coming eventually to an arched doorway on my left. Hushed conversations from within drew my attention, and I paused at the entrance.

There must have been eight or ten women inside a cramped parlor. Most of them were sitting primly on horsehair settees or wooden folding chairs; others stood around the room holding tiny cups with saucers, or thin white handkerchiefs wrapped over their knuckles to dab gently at their eyes. I didn't see Rosa, but Inez Montoya was there, sitting stiffly erect on a straight-backed chair in one corner, seemingly alone despite the press of femininity around her. I almost spoke until I noticed the rigid set of her jaw, the iron-hard rejection in her smoky eyes. Like the others, she was dressed in black, her face partially concealed behind a lacy veil of the same ebony hue. Grief hung in the still air like tobacco smoke above a poker table. I stared into Inez's unwelcoming gaze as if struck mute, until a voice from farther down the hall broke the spell and I moved on, oddly grateful for the intervention.

Rosa stood before an open door at the far end of the narrow passageway, waiting to usher me inside. I recognized the room as soon as I entered. It was Montoya's office, just off the back of his store, and I knew then where I was, and where I'd been. Recalling the last time I'd visited here, delivering Kellums' ultimatum, brought up a strange sense of disconnection.

Amos was already there, already seated at his desk. He motioned toward the same plushly upholstered chair where I'd sat last time, and I made myself as comfortable as my protesting ribs would allow. A tired smile creased the older man's visage.

"You look properly presentable," he remarked. "Like a true son of *la raza*."

There was more truth to Montoya's words than I cared to acknowledge, which might be why I resented them so much.

"I don't know about that," I replied, speaking American, which I knew he understood, with a deliberate emphasis on Grandpapa's Bavarian inflection.

"Well, on the outside," he conceded, apparently not wishing to antagonize me. Shifting around to face me full on, he said, "Tell me what you know of our current situation."

"Not much," I admitted. "I remember Chad Bellamy coming down here with Randy Kellums and a bunch of New Town businessmen to try to arrest me."

"And you threatened to remove their heads and spit in the cavities?" Montoya laughed softly. "Carlos told me of your response. He insists the faces of the gringos turned even whiter than usual."

"I was pretty mad."

"Are you still mad?"

It seemed an unusual question, but I didn't have to ponder it long to come up with an answer. "Yes, I am."

The old man nodded as if pleased. "Much has been accomplished during your recuperation, but there is still much to be done."

"How much?"

After a reflective pause, Montoya began to speak, and I don't guess there's any need to repeat everything he said. At least not word for word. He mostly just brought me up to date on what had happened after we parted company out there in the desert.

Montoya took his men on to the Springs like I'd figured he would, and after pulling Flaco and Angel from the rubble, they'd packed both men onto a couple of horses—they'd combed the chaparral downstream from the hut and located the mounts me and Angel and Flaco had been riding—and sent the bodies back to Río Tinto with a two-man escort. Keeping the rest of his small army with him, Montoya continued on to the Flats.

"Our hearts were black with rage," he told me, and I reckon they were, based on what he went on to describe.

They'd been too slow to save the jacal and the spring with its pool of fresh water, although Montoya insisted the damage had been minimal. A couple of posts supporting the pond's stone dam had been pulled down, allowing the water to drain out, and the jacal set ablaze—but nothing that couldn't be repaired.

After leaving the cottonwoods, Montoya took his men to the Chute, where Hank Waite and his crew were still harvesting salt as if there was no such thing as a war erupting between the Kellums and Montoya factions.

To Waite's credit—and probably what saved his life and the lives of his men, Montoya and his Tejanos being as angry as they were—Hank hadn't made any attempt to deny that several of Kellums' hombres malos had been there earlier that day.

"Kellums' assassins stopped only long enough to eat, then they returned to Río Tinto," Montoya informed me. "But Waite identified them. Tom Layton, Ike Bannon, Emillio Robles, and Elwood Hardisty. Only Johnny Potter remained in Río Tinto as El Diablo's personal bodyguard. I learned just this morning that Layton has been made el jefe, the leader of those men who are left of Kellums' crew now that Anderson is dead."

"Who's Emillio Robles?"

"El Diablo's latest killer. A very bad man, that one."

Although Kellums' hombres malos had been less than half a day's ride ahead of them, Montoya hadn't taken his army to the

Flats in their pursuit. He'd gone there to start evening the score with Randy Kellums. He gave Hank and his men five minutes to gather their personal belongings, guns excluded, and get out. Then he called out to Gilberto Varga. I told you about him, remember? Stout guy with the loud mouth who'd been riding with Montoya the day I met them on my way back to Río Tinto. Gilberto had always been one of those guys you sort of notice on the fringe of things, but never really pay much attention to. I guess he'd started moving to the forefront when Montoya gathered his army, taking over in the field as Carlos did in town.

Anyway, Montoya told Gilberto to bring that place down like the walls at Jericho, and he did. In a grand style, too. Waite still had nearly a case of dynamite out there that they used to blast salt, and Gilberto sank half a dozen sticks along the base of the Chute, then lit the fuses. I guess he blew that thing just about level to the ground, then did it again with the barracks. By the time it was all over, the only thing left standing was Waite and his crew, all of them bug-eyed and scared, but still alive. Which, despite my fluctuating feelings toward Montoya, I had to acknowledge was probably more than Kellums would have allowed, had the shoe been on the other foot.

"We left Waite and his men at the Flats," Montoya continued. "The walk home was long and difficult, but they arrived intact yesterday." A grimace twisted the old man's lips. "That dog, Kellums, did not even send a wagon to bring in his men."

What Montoya said next caught me completely off guard, and might have accounted for why Kellums neglected to send a wagon after Waite and his crew.

"When we returned to Río Tinto, I was determined to finish this war between my people and Kellums," he said. "No matter what the cost."

What they did was go straight to the Red Devil office down by the salt plant, where everything was business as usual until Montoya fired a shot into the air to bring Kellums to the door.

Montoya ordered him to surrender, but Kellums refused. He slammed the door shut, then ran to a window and opened up with a revolver, while Montoya's men scattered into the trees and brush south of the office. Before things got too far along, Tom Layton and his boys, who had apparently been at the Lucky Day for a little debauchery after they got back, heard the gunfire and came hoofing it down to Kellums' rescue.

In that hard, monotonous voice of his, Montoya admitted it might have been one of his own men who first opened fire on the window, but only as a warning for Kellums to do as he was told. Unfortunately, when Layton and his boys got down there, any hope of forcing Kellums to surrender was lost. By the time the shooting stopped, one of Montoya's men had taken a bullet to the calf of his leg and another had broken his wrist diving for cover. In the confusion, Kellums and his men managed to escape out a back window.

"They retreated to El Diablo's hacienda on Rattlesnake Hill," Montoya said, "and have been holed up there ever since. If we had dynamite, I would throw a stick into the house myself, but, sadly, Gilberto wanted to make a point at the Flats. He used up all of the explosives he could find to bring down the Chute and the stone barracks."

"What about Kellums?" I asked. "Has he got all his men in there with him?"

"Yes, his hombres malos, plus his clerk, Tim McKay, the plant foreman, Jim Houck, and a few others. I don't know what their situation is for water, but it is known that he has enough food to last for at least a week, maybe more."

"Where's Bellamy?"

Montoya's lips curled in distaste. "Your friend, Bellamy, fled on the same day Kellums and his men were forced to retreat to their fortification among the serpents. That Kellums should choose such a location as his home should come as a surprise to no one, as it is common knowledge that men tend to seek their own kind."

"Bellamy," I reminded the older man gently. "Where'd he go?"

Appearing mildly embarrassed by his distraction, Montoya said, "Your friend left on horseback. He went downriver."

I thought about that for a moment, picturing in my mind the lay of the land to the south, the locations of the towns and forts. "He went for help," I said finally. "It's the only thing that makes sense. He may or may not be in Kellums' pocket, but he isn't a coward. He didn't run."

Montoya nodded as if to confirm my assumption. "Señor Bellamy was heading for Fort Duncan when Hector Flores and Gilberto Varga caught up with him."

I was almost afraid to ask, but I had to know. "Is he dead?"

"Would it upset you if he was?"

"Yes. Bellamy's a good man."

"Yet he works for El Diablo."

"So did I, once."

Montoya seemed irked by my reply. With a dismissive shrug, he said, "Your friend wasn't killed. Hector and Gilberto caught up with him at Monte Bajo and brought him back alive, although in somewhat worse condition than when he left. He resides in one of the rooms off of the courtyard now. The door is chained and padlocked, and a guard watches outside his window. I've given orders that, if he tries to escape, or if an attempt is made to free him, he is to be shot immediately."

I leaned back in my chair, ignoring the sting of pulling flesh over my ribs. Despite the old man's effort to display confidence in his control of the situation, I could sense his uncertainty, and I was pretty sure I knew what caused it. Monte Bajo might not have been much of a town, but it was only seven or eight miles upstream from the military post of Fort Duncan. If Chad had talked to someone at Monte Bajo, or managed to get a message off to the commanding officer at Duncan before Hector and Gilberto caught him, it could play havoc with Montoya's plans. While I doubted the military would get involved in a civilian matter, it was entirely feasible the officer in charge would send word to the US marshal's office in Brownsville, or to one of the Ranger camps along the Río Grande.

To tell you the truth, I wouldn't have minded some outside intervention. I was recalling what happened in Hogup the preceding year, and the relief I'd felt when we'd been arrested by that Gunnison posse and shipped off to Denver. Even surrounded by a bunch of tin stars, I hadn't been overly confident we'd get out of that camp alive, but I do believe with every fiber of my being that if those lawmen hadn't showed up when they did, we'd have been rushed as soon as the sun went down, and wouldn't have lived to see it come back up the next day.

Perhaps sensing my empathy for the part-time lawman, Montoya said, "Are you aware that your friend made good on his promise to return the next day to arrest you?"

The old man's words brought a smile to my face. Say what you want about Chad Bellamy, the guy had sand. "What happened?" I asked.

Montoya's lips thinned again in displeasure. "Hector and Carlos saw to it that he did not achieve his goal."

"Then I guess I owe them my thanks."

The door opened before Montoya could reply, and Rosa entered with a tray of food. A girl of twelve or so followed with a jacket, sombrero, and gun belt piled in her arms like religious offerings. Rosa spoke softly to the girl and she set the clothing on top of Montoya's desk. Rosa placed the tray next to it.

"There is chili verde and tortillas, plus some hard-fried eggs," the older woman said, then lightly touched a small clay jar sitting next to the platter of food. "Here is goat's milk, but I can bring coffee if you wish."

Montoya looked at me, cocking a brow.

"I could stand some coffee," I said. "And a cigarette. I'd dang near kill for a smoke."

"I will bring tobacco and papers with the coffee," Rosa promised.

"*Gracias,*" I murmured as she left the room.

I was hungry enough that, as soon as she was gone, I scooted my chair closer to the desk and dug in. Montoya quietly smoked a cigar while I ate. His gaze was on the opposite wall, but I could tell his thoughts were much farther away.

I ain't as a rule a hoggish eater, but I made short work of that good food, and even had polished off the jar of milk by the time Rosa got back with my coffee and a fresh bag of Lone Jack tobacco and a little bible of smoking papers. She poured coffee for me and her husband while I rolled a cigarette, then quietly retreated. When the door was closed, Montoya looked at me as one might a son he is about to send off to war. His earlier annoyance was nowhere to be seen.

"There is one more thing I must ask of you, Wil, if you have the strength."

I felt a quick prickle of wariness. "What's that?" I asked.

"There is a message I need delivered to Kellums. Much like the one you brought here to me."

"You want me to tell Kellums to stay off the Flats?"

Smiling faintly, Montoya shook his head. "No, but I do wish you to deliver another ultimatum, that Señor Kellums should surrender immediately or suffer the consequences. I won't ask you to memorize the details. I've written them out for him, so that there can be no misunderstanding."

I thought about the older man's request for a minute, then said, "If you already have it written out, why haven't you already sent it?"

"I would prefer that you deliver the message personally."

"Why?" I asked, none too gently.

He never blinked. "Because you have no relatives in Río Tinto, and because I think Kellums would be less likely to hold you hostage than he would someone who has lived here all his life, whose family and friends are here."

"You could tie that message to a rock and throw it over the

wall," I suggested. "That way, no one has to take any risk."

I could tell I was starting to irritate him again, but I didn't care. Finally he admitted there was another reason. Two, actually.

"The first," he started, "is that having the same man sent to him that he sent to me will be to my … to the town's advantage. It will show Kellums that he does not control Río Tinto as he once thought he did. And two, because Kellums is already holding a hostage behind his walls. Fortunately he isn't aware of it yet."

I started to ask him who, then it dawned on me like a bucketful of bricks dropped on my head. "The girl!"

"Sí. Cierra Varga."

"So that's how you always knew what Kellums was up to. I figured you must've had a spy in the plant. It never occurred to me that it might be her."

"It has occurred to no one yet, but I fear that it could. She needs to get out of there, before it is too late."

"And you want me to help her?"

"I want you to convey the message that her services inside the hacienda are no longer needed. There is a sign that she and I have already agreed upon. When she sees it, she will know she is to give up her double life and return to her people."

Montoya's words triggered memories of past conversations and crude speculations that had circulated among the riffraff of the Lucky Day. I included myself in that crowd, and felt shame vying with anger. "Do you know what the people of this village think of Cierra Varga?"

"They think she is a whore, a Jezebel who has turned her back on her people for a rich man's pleasure. Her sacrifices were great, Wil, but the rewards will be greater."

"For who?" I damned near shouted.

Montoya reared back in surprise. "I did not force her to accept Kellums' offer."

"But you encouraged her, didn't you? You sold out a girl's reputation for your own gain."

The old man's face turned hard as stone. "I'll not have an outsider question my motives, Señor Chama. What was done was done for the good of the all."

"Varga," I muttered, frowning. "What is Gilberto to her? A brother?"

"Sí."

"And the old woman who sells tamales at the wharf when the keelboats come in?"

"Carlita Varga is the girl's mother."

"Where's her father?"

"Rubio Varga is dead," he stated flatly. "Like so many others. Flaco's parents, Inez's."

I blinked and looked away. "I didn't know about Flaco's parents."

"He seldom spoke of them. Nor does Inez. Both lost their parents to the Lipan Apaches, but years apart. Cierra's father was killed by Comanches, although I suppose the difference is minimal in the eyes of a child. Parents lost, orphans left behind. But they were young when their parents were killed, and life has always been harsh along the Río Grande. You think this war which Kellums has brought to us is a terrible thing, and it is, but you must also remember that our people have been dying in terrible ways for many generations. That is why Kellums will not win, why he cannot win. We have survived too long to be brought down by one man's greed."

"What about your greed?" I asked coldly.

"It is not my greed, Wil. It is my vision, for the village and its people."

I shook my head in rejection of Montoya's attempt to justify his actions. My thoughts reeled at the unfairness of his decision to sacrifice someone who had already suffered so much, for what, in the end, would turn out to be so little.

"You would rather see us all subjugated?" Montoya demanded. "Little more than slaves to a fat, self-serving gringo?"

"It wouldn't have come to that."

"Wouldn't it? If Kellums takes control of the Flats, we would all have to work for him, struggling at wages too low to sustain even the most frugal of families." There was fire burning deep in the old man's eyes now. "You saw as much in Colorado. You cannot deny that."

"What I saw in Colorado sickened me," I replied harshly, pushing to my feet and reaching for the door that led to the store.

"You would turn your back on this girl, Wil? Leave her to Kellums' jackals?"

"I'm not the one who put her there, god damn it. If you want her out, you'll have to do it yourself."

"I cannot," Montoya replied, his voice softening. "Not without putting a man inside, and you are the only one who can do that. The only one I can be certain Kellums would want to see, would allow inside his hacienda."

I stood there on the verge of yanking open the door and walking through it to—where? My hand had been reaching for the iron latch. It came back slowly, falling to my side. Montoya was right, at least about my chances of getting inside Kellums' stronghold. Lord knew the Red Devil's owner held a special hatred for me, for my perceived double-cross of his grandiose plans. Yeah, I thought grimly, I could probably get inside. The question burrowing into my brain was if I could I get out.

Montoya waited silently. Finally, like a growl emitted from deep in my throat, I gave him my answer.

"Yeah, I'll do it. But for the girl, not you."

Montoya smiled with relief. I don't think he gave a tinker's dam why I did it, just so long as it was done—the bastard!

WIL CHAMA INTERVIEW

❧

SESSION TWELVE

Montoya handed me the jacket first, lifting it off the stack of clothing the young girl had brought in when Rosa delivered my chili verde and eggs. I started to refuse it, but he insisted, so I took it, hefted it a few times, then wrinkled my brows in puzzlement.

The old man smiled broadly. "Look inside."

Pulling the lapel back, I spotted the curve of a revolver's grip peeking out from a slit in the cotton lining. I glanced at Montoya, then slid the gun from its hiding place.

"I had Rosa modify the jacket," Montoya informed me. "When the garment is on, not even a lump can be seen to spoil the wearer's profile, yet the pistol can be drawn as easily as if from a belt."

The revolver was a slim, silver-plated .38 Colt with black gutta-percha grips. It was a self-cocker, what they call a double-action today, which means that in a tight situation you didn't have to cock the hammer first to fire it. You could just pull hard on the trigger and it would cock and fire itself.

"Try it on," Montoya said, motioning toward the jacket. He seemed unusually proud of the design, as if he'd created it himself.

The jacket was a vaquero style, short-waisted and snug-fitting, in a shade of brown similar to the buckskin trousers I wore. With the jacket on, I returned the Colt to its form-fitting pocket under my left arm, then rolled my shoulders experimentally. I've got to admit, if not for the extra weight, I wouldn't have known it was there. Drawing it once more, I checked the cylinder. It was fully loaded, and I returned it to the jacket's lining.

The gun belt was unfamiliar, but the heavy Remington cradled inside was an old friend. I slid it free, glad to see that someone had cleaned it properly. I checked the Remington's loads as I had the Colt, but found only five cartridges in the cylinder, the hammer resting on an empty chamber. That's not always a bad practice, keeping your hammer down on an empty chamber, but things had bypassed normal in Río Tinto about the time the first of Kellums' hombres malos had arrived in town. I popped the gate and dropped a live round into the sixth chamber, then returned the Remington to its holster.

Montoya handed me the hat next, a broad-brimmed, tall-crowned sombrero, the color of a mourning dove. It was used but clean and still in good condition. Yet I couldn't bring myself to try it on. I think I feared the transformation might be too complete—or too permanent.

Montoya nodded in understanding as I placed the hat back on the desk. "Your own was destroyed," he explained. "We found it in the hut, but it had been cut nearly in half when the walls fell."

"What about my rifle?"

"We found that under the rubble as well. The wood on the right side of the stock was badly chewed by falling rocks, but the action functions properly and the barrel is straight. It is in your room, if you wish to have it."

"No, no point in making Kellums' men anymore nervous than they likely already are." I pulled the jacket's lapels closer. "I'm ready if you are."

"Almost." He reached into a desk drawer to withdraw a sealed envelope addressed to Randall Kellums, of Río Tinto, Texas. "For El Diablo," he said, smiling wryly.

I tucked the envelope inside a pocket. "I'll see that he gets it, or at least do my best."

"Then there remains but one final act of preparation," Montoya said, and, from the same drawer as the envelope, he pulled out a heavy iron cross with twin arms, called a Cross of Lorraine. It was about four inches tall and two across, with a few simple lines scored into the unpolished metal for decoration. A leather thong was strung through a flat loop on top.

"Is that what I'm supposed to give to Cierra?"

"There will be no need to give it to her. Just be sure that she sees it. She will know its meaning, and slip away at the first opportunity."

"She might not be there," I said. She had been the last time I'd gone to Kellums' hacienda, but what if she was in the kitchen or out back, or what if one of Kellums' men had pulled her into another room?

"It is important that she see this," Montoya said. "In all like-lihood, you will have but one opportunity. You must not fail, Wil."

I lifted the cross from Montoya's hand and slipped the thong around my neck. The metal lay solidly against my chest, heavier than it looked. If Cierra was there, I'd make sure she saw it, but I doubted if I'd have a lot of options if she wasn't.

We walked outside, and I paused when I saw the soft, late afternoon light bathing the tops of the cottonwoods. I'd assumed the time was shortly after dawn, when I normally rolled out of bed. It surprised me to realize it was nearer to dusk. Although the sun's rays were still blasting into the high, fragmented cliffs east of town, Río Tinto itself was already in shadow.

It felt good to be outside and moving. I could feel my strength returning as we hiked up through the trees to New Town. The first thing I noticed when we came out of the trees was the eerie silence engulfing the row of businesses along Bluff Street. Everything was shut down, even the saloon, and the street was deserted except for Montoya's men, patrolling the boardwalk with their Springfield .50s. A pair of salt carts had been rolled across the road at the eastern end of town, with a cluster of Tejanos crouched behind them. Beyond the carts was Kellums' hacienda, perched atop Rattlesnake Hill like a miniature castle.

"Looks like you've got a stand-off," I observed.

"More of a siege," Montoya replied. "It is only a matter of time now before Kellums must surrender to our demands."

Unless a United States marshal or a company of Rangers showed up, I mused.

Hugging the trees below the bench line, we quickly made our way to the carts. As we drew closer, I could see additional men stationed around the house, hidden from snipers inside the compound, yet able to cut off any attempted escape. The sight tightened my gut, reminding me of that long day trapped inside the equipment shed at Hogup with the rest of the Five—the hopeless desperation, the taut anger and hair-trigger tempers. The memory brought images of Cierra to my mind, holed up inside Kellums' hacienda and probably scared to death.

Hunched low, we made a run for the carts. I was surprised to find Gilberto Varga there, a single-shot carbine butted authoritatively to one thigh. He practically sneered when he saw me, but otherwise ignored my presence.

"*¿Que pasa*, amigo?" Montoya questioned the stoutly built Tejano.

"All is quiet, patrón," Gilberto replied. "We send a few shots their way from time to time to remind them that we are here, but they seldom fire in return."

Scowling, Montoya said, "Do not waste ammunition if it can be helped. Our supplies are limited until the next keelboat arrives."

"My apologies, patrón," he replied, the broad brim of his sombrero dipping slightly in acknowledgment of his master's displeasure.

While Gilberto groveled—all right, I'll admit that's a little harsh, but I didn't like the guy; I didn't like the way he'd spoken to me out in the desert or the way he was treating me there in the street in front of Kellums' hacienda, and I sure as hell didn't like it that he'd stood still for his sister being sent into Kellums' hacienda as a spy—I went over to one of the carretas for a closer look.

The compound, being at a higher elevation than Old Town, was still bathed in afternoon light, its cactus-topped walls pocked with fist-sized craters from Montoya's Springfields. From the gap between the cart's wheel and its bed, I could see the bobbing crowns of a couple of hats behind the wall close to the gate. I assumed they had a hole drilled through the mesquite planking where they could keep an eye on us without exposing themselves to our rifles.

"Señor Chama," Montoya called gently, bringing me around to where he was standing beside the rear of the next cart, a piece of white cloth tied to the tip of a Springfield's steel ramrod. "It is time, mi amigo."

I straightened slowly, sucking in a deep breath. "You reckon that little piece of linen is going to stop them from shooting me as soon as I poke my head around this carreta?" I asked.

"I hope so," he replied soberly. "Otherwise, all of my planning will have been for nothing, and we will have to resort to more violent means to end this war."

Well, you can't say the man didn't speak his mind. Accepting the ramrod, I checked both the Remington in its holster and the Colt inside my jacket's lining, then lifted the flag above my head and stepped into the street.

I'll tell you what, that was a damned long walk from the carts to the gate. The sound of my pulse fairly roared in my ears, and my scalp wiggled and jumped in a primitive dance born in the time of saber-toothed tigers. My gaze was locked tightly on the entrance to Kellums' compound, and I don't think an exploding cat could have broken that link. I halted about twenty yards out, hooked a thumb in my belt in what I hoped was a nonchalant manner, and called out to the men gathered behind the wall.

"It's Wil Chama! I've got a message for Randy Kellums!"

"I know who you are, you double-crossing son of a bitch," was flung back at me.

I grinned recklessly, recognizing Jim Houck's voice. "You're going to be out of a job real soon, Jimbo," I replied loudly. "You might want to take your hat in hand and ask Mister Montoya if he's got a place for you. Maybe he'll let you shovel horse shit out of his stables."

Yeah, can you believe that? Not two minutes earlier I'd been worried that, when the time came, I wouldn't even be able to squeak out a howdy, but there I was, trading taunts with the bad guys like I was the coolest customer ever to come down the pike. Don't ask me where all that swagger came from, because I couldn't tell you.

Houck responded in anger, like you'd expect from someone wound up as tight as he was. Let's just say his opinion of me and my heritage wasn't awfully high at the moment. I will say this, I don't hold the man's crudeness against him, having been known to make some pretty wild statements myself in similar situations. Like ripping off heads and spitting in holes.

It wasn't but a couple of minutes later that I spotted a new hat bobbing back and forth behind the gate, and soon after that the latch popped open and the gate was swung back to reveal the yard inside.

"Come on in, Chama," said another voice I instantly recognized. "Mister Kellums is anxious to see you."

A little shiver ran down my spine, but I tried to keep my expression stoic as I started forward. Tom Layton waited inside, wearing a wicked grin of anticipation.

"By God, I been waiting for this," he chortled as I stepped through the gate.

Elwood Hardisty kicked the gate shut, then moved up behind

me. My Remington was jerked from its holster, then the hem of my jacket was yanked up high enough to expose the waistband of my trousers, although fortunately, Elwood didn't notice the extra weight in the garment's lining. Satisfied that I wasn't carrying a hideout gun at the small of my back, he quickly patted the tops of my boots, then stepped back and tossed my Remington to Layton, who caught it deftly with one hand.

"That's all he's got," Elwood announced.

Layton was eyeing me closely, like he was measuring me for a new suit of clothes, or a coffin. Finally he said, "You sounded mighty full of yourself out there, Chama. Me 'n' the boss was listenin', and we agreed you needed to be whittled down some."

"And you think you're the man to do it?" I asked, but I've got to confess that the gunman's mean little eyes had already drained away most of my bravado.

His grin widening, Layton tipped his head toward the hacienda. "Let's go, boy. The boss wants to talk to you."

I walked up the path to the sprawling house with Layton on my heels, but stopped after entering the big front room. There were probably a dozen men sitting around on blankets, talking quietly among themselves or playing cards. Everyone shut up when I walked in, no doubt wondering what new twist I'd brought to the saga. Jutting his chin toward the office, Layton said, "You know the way."

I took a couple of steps in that direction, then stopped again when I sensed movement from the arched entry to the dining room. My heart beat a little louder when I saw Cierra Varga come out of the kitchen. She paused, staring, and I casually reached up to pull the lapels of my jacket back, throwing my chest forward like a strutting rooster. Her gaze dropped briefly to the front of my shirt, then skidded off to the side. Although no trace of emotion crossed her drawn features, I had to believe she'd noticed the heavy, double-barred cross hanging around my neck. Then

Layton gave me another hard shove, and I stumbled toward the office with my back to the girl.

Kellums was seated at his desk when I walked in, his ruddy cheeks sagging, jaw stubbled gray. A normally dapper man, he didn't look like he'd groomed himself or changed clothes in a couple of days.

John Potter was also there, sprawled lazily in a padded armchair. He was lanky and unkempt, although the look seemed more natural on him than it did Kellums. Potter wore a Smith & Wesson top-break revolver in a holster on his left hip, the butt tipped forward for a cross-belly draw.

It was Kellums who got the conversation rolling. "You greasy-faced little son of a bitching cock-eyed bastard," he spat, glowering at me with his heavy-lidded eyes. "I should have strung you up the last time you were here."

I cast about in my mind for some wisecrack reply but couldn't think of a thing. Remembering the envelope Montoya had given me, I plucked it from my pocket and tossed it onto the desk.

Kellums glanced at it suspiciously, then picked it up and ripped it open. Shaking out a single sheet of foolscap, he began to read, and I swear his cheeks were fairly glowing by the time he finished. Raising his eyes to me, he said, "You got anything to add to this, Chama?"

"Nope."

"You sure?"

"I'm just a messenger."

Kellums glanced at Potter, who had uncoiled himself from his seat with the lazy grace of a rattler. "What do you want done, boss?" the gunman asked softly.

"Kill it," Kellums growled, then leaned forward with his elbows propped on his desk to reread Montoya's carefully printed missive.

Layton grabbed my right arm, Potter my left. Without looking up, Kellums added almost distractedly, "Take him outside to do it. I don't want him stinking up the house."

Thus ended my final conversation with Randall Kellums, the

man who had entertained such high expectation of my abilities as a shootist, only to be disillusioned in the end by my refusal to join his army of toughs.

As Layton and Potter hauled me roughly from the room, my mind reeled from his cold-blooded command: Kill it! Not kill him, mind you. Not execute Chama, or take Wil out back and cut his damned throat. But just eliminate it, as if in his mind I'd ceased to be human.

No one said a word as I was half dragged through the front room to the kitchen. Not even the men I'd worked with at the Devil. I was mad about that for a long time afterward, although I eventually came to realize that most of them were probably too terrified to speak up, what with the mood Kellums had been in those days.

Layton kicked open the swinging door to the kitchen, and they manhandled me through sideways, my feet scrambling to keep up. Cierra was standing beside a massive stove set against the rear wall, stirring a five-gallon pot of what smelled like ham hocks and pinto beans. She barely looked up as I was hauled past, and I wondered if she'd noticed the Cross of Lorraine so prominently displayed on my chest. I didn't know whether to say something to draw her attention to it, or keep my mouth shut and not risk giving away her relationship to the Montoya faction.

Before I could come to a decision, Layton yanked the door open and started outside, growling at me to quit struggling. He was mostly just wasting words. Heck, I wasn't fighting him. The truth is, I was having trouble making my limbs function because I knew I was being taken outside to be shot. Then a voice as sweet as a bird's song stopped us.

"Señores."

We all three ground to a halt, turning as one as Cierra Varga came forward carrying that steaming pot of ham and beans. She was smiling prettily, her fingers protected by thick towels, and for a second I wondered if she was going to offer us a taste. I think I was as surprised as anyone when she threw the bubbling contents of that kettle straight into Potter's face. Potter fell back with a screech, clawing frantically at his face while me and Layton yelled loudly at the splatter striking our exposed flesh.

"You blanking whore!" Layton shouted, pushing me back into the kitchen even as he pawed for his revolver.

I threw myself against him before he could get it drawn, both of us careening into the hot oven. Layton screamed as his hand came down on top of a burner. He dropped my arm and was reaching for his own blistering palm when Cierra's heavy, cast-iron pot slammed down on top of his head.

Layton crumpled as if every bone in his body had turned to mush. Throwing the pot aside, Cierra ducked past me through the door. I stood there flummoxed by the unexpected turn of events, until she reached back inside and grabbed my wrist.

"This way," she cried, tugging on my arm.

There were a couple of men out back, reclining along the wall. They rose uncertainly when Cierra and I burst out of the kitchen. I recognized both of them from the Devil. One, Jerry Wallace, took a hesitant step forward. "Hey, where are you two going?"

Drawing the Colt from my jacket's lining, I pointed it at them and shouted, "Hit the ground, you sons of bitches!"

Well, they weren't heroes, neither of them, and I'd be hard put to say who planted his face in the dirt the quickest. Meanwhile, Cierra was racing toward a stout-legged table set close to the rear fence. A pair of galvanized laundry tubs and a cold fire pit identified the purpose of the arrangement, but I also noticed an additional objective in the table's location, one which I doubt Kellums or his gunmen had been aware of.

Cierra got there first. Leaping nimbly to the table top, she sprinted along its length to pick up momentum, then flew over the wall without disturbing a single thorn in the row of cactus planted along the top. She was a regular mountain goat in a skirt, and I wanted to cheer as she disappeared from sight, her long hair flowing off her shoulders like a cape.

Slower to get there, I instinctively hesitated before launching myself skyward. That half-a-second pause was nearly my undoing. Just as I was getting ready to take the plunge, I heard a shout from the house commanding me to stop. Whirling into a crouch, I snapped off a shot that struck close enough to the men crowding through the kitchen door that they all ducked back inside. I spun toward the fence and jumped, but I was awkward and low, and hooked my boot in a tangle of prickly pear as I went over the top.

The ground on the outside of the fence was bare of rocks and thorns, but harder than hammered hell. It wretched a strangled cry from my throat when I landed, jarring the wound in my left side so bad I came close to passing out. For a minute all I could do was lie there gasping, listening to these shrill little whistling sounds coming from my throat. But even hurting and with the wind knocked out of me, I knew I couldn't linger. I'd driven Kellums' gunmen inside with my first shot, and might have bought myself a minute or two, but no more than that.

Cierra had come to a halt among the rocks at the base of the cliff, maybe fifty feet away. Her eyes were large as she motioned wildly for me to get up. Grimly I pushed to my feet with all the dignity of a fat cow on pasture grass, then ran a staggered path toward the maze of boulders that had peeled off the towering cliff who knew how many eons before. I wasn't quite among them when a bullet struck a shoulder-high rock at my side, causing me to flinch and duck.

"Hurry!" Cierra urged.

I nodded foolishly. My breath was rasping in my throat and my ribs felt like they were on fire as we moved deeper into the rocks. It was several minutes before the pain began to subside enough for me to start taking notice of our surroundings. We were climbing rapidly, worming past boulders as big as carriages, over others no larger than a sack of oats, staying low and moving fast.

I was following Cierra without question, putting my faith in her knowledge of the terrain as we made our way up the fractured cliff face. In fact, I was glad she was leading. Not only did that allow me to keep an eye on our back trail, but there were dozens of routes to choose from, and I didn't know which ones led to the top. What I didn't know then, but soon found out, was that Cierra didn't know the way, either. It wasn't ten minutes later that we came to the top of the scree and were forced to halt. Above us soared another hundred feet or so of crumbling stone ledges and sheer drops, bathed in the golden light of the setting sun. If there was a path out of there, I didn't see it. I looked at Cierra, and I don't know what my expression was like, but she suddenly burst into tears.

"I didn't know," she cried.

A sensation like a bellyful of worms invaded the pit of my stomach. Down below, several men were moving stealthily among the rocks along the lower slope, cautiously making their way toward us.

At my side, Cierra was already drying her eyes with the back of her hand, getting her emotions under control. "There is a way … maybe."

I looked at her, desperate for any possibility. "Where?"

She pointed at the cliff face in front of us. At first I didn't see what she meant. Then I spotted it, a narrow fissure cutting vertically toward the top of the cliff, like a trough carved into the rock by a giant's fingernail. I counted several hand- and footholds spaced at irregular intervals along the shallow flute. Unfortunately I also noted numerous stretches of bare rock, some half a dozen feet or more in length.

"We can do it," Cierra said determinedly. "We have to do it."

Well, she was right about that. We had to do something, and we had to do it quick. Then, as if to reinforce what we already knew, a rifle bellowed from below, the bullet coming so close we both ducked, and Cierra let out a small, startled yelp.

Moving behind a stone monolith jutting obliquely from the cliff's face, we exchanged worried glances. "I'll go first," she volunteered.

"No, I'll do it." My eyes were already climbing the route above us, gauging the odds. My fear was that as soon as either of us rose above the level of the rock we were hiding behind, the men below would have clear shooting all the way to the top. Even if they missed the first few rounds, they'd soon find the range. And we weren't going to be making much time climbing that treacherous stretch of stone. Hell, our chances wouldn't have been all that great even if we didn't have a bunch of killers closing in behind us.

"There is no other choice," Cierra said.

With my jaw clenched in frustration, I thumbed the Colt's hammer all the way back; it might have been a self-cocker, but I knew I'd get better accuracy if I fired it as a single action.

"All right, you go first," I said tersely. "But as soon as you get on top, I want you to start running like a jack rabbit, and don't stop until you're back with Montoya. Don't worry about me, I'll be right behind you."

Her lips parted as if to protest. I think she knew I was lying. I'd hang back to give her as much cover as I could with the rounds I had left, but I knew in my gut that wouldn't be enough. I was going to have to stay, even if it meant throwing rocks at the men below, to give her every chance possible.

"Get going," I said gently.

She swallowed hard, made a quick sign of the cross, then headed for the fissure. Moving back to where I could peer down through the rocks, I waited until the man in the lead moved into a clear spot. Aiming carefully and keenly aware of how few shots I had left, I squeezed off a round. My bullet struck the boulder next to him and he swore and jerked back, hollering loud enough for me to hear him nearly three quarters of the way up the cliff. Two other men reared up to shoot in the next second. I drove them both back, but there was no sense of triumph in my accomplishment. Cierra had barely gotten started, and I was already down to just two rounds.

A shot from far below caught me off guard, as did the scream from above. I spun in time to see Cierra falling backward from the cliff's face, her long hair trailing upward like fluttering crow's wings. My heart surged into my throat as I scrambled to catch her, but I was too slow. She hit the ground hard, a solid whump that kicked up puffs of dust on every side. Groaning, she tried to sit up, but I dropped to my knees at her side and pulled her back into the cradle of my left arm.

"Are you all right?"

She nodded, but was blinking rapidly, as if trying to clear her head. My gaze was drawn to the narrow fissure. She hadn't been more than ten feet up when her assailant's bullet struck the cliff at her side. I pulled her arm around to examine the silken brown flesh that had been only a few inches away from where the bullet slammed into the rock wall. There were several small cuts, but only one deep wound—a tiny chip of lead or rock buried beneath the flesh, painful but not serious.

Watching me with her soft brown eyes, she waited patiently as I brushed away what dirt I could. Smiling with what I hoped would pass for reassurance, I said, "You'll be all right."

The words were barely out of my mouth when she rolled clear of my arms and stood. "I was wrong," she said. "We cannot escape that way."

I nodded solemnly, having already come to the same conclusion. Walking back to the edge of our cramped, I stared down at the approaching gunmen. Just fleeting glimpses, really—a hat here, part of a shoulder there—but all of them moving steadily toward our position.

"There might be another way," Cierra said quietly.

I turned. "Where?"

She pointed toward the far end of the rock we were hiding

behind, a part of the stone needle's slender base. "I saw it from above," she explained.

I looked and saw nothing. "What are we supposed to do, crawl underneath it?"

A smile came to her face. "Yes! Come on and I'll show you."

I followed, keeping low as the needle's base grew more stunted. Finally we both had to drop to our hands and knees to continue.

"Just around that point," she said finally, meaning the far end of the boulder. All I saw was the empty space beyond it.

OK, this is going to sound crazy, but I didn't believe her. I figured the fall must have jarred her brain, or that the fear had damaged her ability to reason. So, no, I didn't believe her, but I trusted her, which as I've already said is crazy, but there it is. And because I trusted her—don't ask me why, because I didn't even know her—I was willing to wiggle forward on my belly for another five or six feet, until there was almost no rock at all to hide behind. And do you know what happened when I got there? When I was just about a half-inch shy of turning around and crawling back? I felt a faint but cool draft of air brush against one cheek, that's what happened.

I looked around, but there was nothing to see. What little grass there was—a few stunted clumps clinging to the gravelly soil—were as still as photographs in the waning light. Glancing back, I saw Cierra at the other end of our shelter, behind the leaning monolith. Whirling, she hissed, "Hurry. They are just around the corner from us."Muttering a strained expletive, I scooted forward another few inches, and, as I came around the tip of the boulder, my eyes widened at the sight of a narrow passage, jabbed into the rocks like an open wound.

There was a shot from behind me and Cierra screamed. I spun onto my back, the Colt bucking in my hand. Twenty feet away, one of Kellums' plant workers stiffened under the impact of the .38 slug. He was carrying an old percussion revolver, something leftover from the Civil War, and, even as I watched, the gun slipped from his fingers. Jackknifing to my knees, I rocked the hammer back on my last live round. Cierra was at my side now, frightened but unharmed. Shoving her behind me, I jerked my head toward the hole in the rocks and ordered her inside. She complied without argument, sliding down feet first, her head disappearing with the sounds of her shoes skidding across stone.

"Chama!" The voice came sharp as the cut of a bullwhip. "Give it up, Chama. You don't stand a chance of gettin' outta here."

"Step out where I can see you, then tell me that," I taunted, backing toward the opening on my hands and knees. I recognized the voice. It was Elwood Hardisty. Feeling the earth end under my toes, I risked a quick glance over my shoulder. I'd reached the opening where Cierra had already disappeared.

"Come on out and I'll talk to the old man," Hardisty called. "He's mad as hell right now, but he'd listen to reason if I told him I promised you safe passage off this cliff."

It was a lie, pure and simple, and surely he knew I could see right through it. It didn't matter. Hardisty's wise reluctance to expose himself to my revolver gave me time to squeeze through the narrow opening. Even as I dropped from sight, I could hear the gunman still making promises he had no intention of keeping.

My boot soles came down on smooth stone maybe eight feet below the cavern's entrance, pitched so steeply inward as to be nearly sheer. I hung there, fingers straining on the rocky rim as my feet probed for a solid purchase.

"Wil."

It was Cierra. I tried to find her, but my eyes had yet to adjust to the darkness of the cavern's interior.

"It's safe," she called. "You can let go."

And there was that trust thing again. Loosening my hold, I was soon scooting down the slanted rock on my boot heels, coming to a stop in a cramped chamber probably twenty feet below the entrance.

The first thing I did upon reaching flat ground was to try to

stand upright. I swore when I cracked my head sharply on the low
ceiling, and scrunched down for a closer look. There was some
light seeping in through a vertical fracture in the outside wall,
but not much. There'd be even less when the sun when down. I
figured we had thirty minutes at most until full dark. After that,
if we hadn't found our way out, we were going to be in a lot of
trouble—no small accomplishment considering what had driven
us in here in the first place.

"Do you know where we are?" I asked Cierra.

"No. A cavern. There are many throughout these cliffs, although
we never explored them because of the rattlesnakes."

Well, that sent a shiver up my spine. Seeing it, Cierra smiled.
"Don't worry," she said. "We are very high on the cliff's face. Most
of the snakes will be farther down, where they can go out at night
to hunt."

That brought only a small measure of relief, and I mean small.
Tiny. I wasn't looking forward to stumbling into a nest of whirly-
tails down there in the dark. In fact, I'd wager to say I would have
given a good-size gold nugget to a lantern salesman right then, had
one happened past. As my vision adjusted to the fading light, I
began to pick out more details of the small chamber where we'd
been deposited. About five feet wide with a low ceiling, which I'd
already discovered. I was afraid at first that it might be a dead-end,
in which case it would likely also turn out to be our tomb, but
then I spotted a narrow slot against the inside wall, and stepped
around Cierra for a closer look. I perked up considerably when I
saw another shaft of light, maybe thirty feet ahead.

"Where does it go?" Cierra asked.

"I don't know, but I guess we'd better find out before one of
Kellums' men decides to empty his pistol down here, just to see if
he hits anything."

That startled her and she came close, hanging onto the tail of
my jacket as we pushed deeper into the cliff.

The light outside was fading fast, and I was more than a little worried that darkness would catch us before we could find a way out. Assuming there was a way out. That's why I hurried, and why I felt so disappointed when we reached that shaft of light only to find it seeping in through a crack in the wall only a mouse could wiggle through.

Or a snake.

I pushed on, the Colt held in front of me like a hollow nose, Cierra's toes bouncing against the heels of my boots just about every other step. We started to climb after a while, which I figured was a good sign, but as we did the air inside the cavern began to change. Cierra mentioned it first.

"It stinks."

"I smell it, too," I said. At first I couldn't place it. Snakes, what little experience I've had with them over the years, generally have a more musty smell. This was sharp and decidedly unpleasant, almost like ammonia. Then it dawned on me what it was, and I came to such an abrupt halt that Cierra bumped into my back.

"Wil, what is it?"

"Guano," I replied.

She repeated the word softly, not understanding it.

"Bat dung."

That brought an instant reaction. She pressed herself tightly against my back, sliding her bare arms up under my jacket as if to hide them. "Wil, I am afraid. Bats carry the brain sickness."

"Rabies," I confirmed.

"Their bites can drive a person insane."

I stooped low to peer ahead, as if that might somehow make a difference, but all I saw was darkness, although our route seemed to continue to climb. I could only hope it would lead us to an exit, a way out of this nightmare of bats and rattlesnakes and pursuing gunmen.

At that time I was assuming Elwood Hardisty and his men were still following us. I wouldn't find out until much later that

Hardisty's pards had refused to venture into the cavern after us, and that Elwood wouldn't go in alone.

"I'd do it, but I guess I'd better stay out here with you babies and make sure you get home safe, so's your mamas can tuck you into bed," was one of the versions I heard. That didn't really sound like the words of a hardened killer, but I've noticed a lot of tough guys will falter if they don't have a couple of boys along to bolster their courage. In the end, Hardisty and his crew hung around outside the entrance to the cave until darkness forced them down off the cliff.

Which, of course, was neither here nor there as far and me and Cierra were concerned. By that time we were basically lost. I'd followed the widest shaft I could find coming this far, but there had been others branching off into the bluff. And somewhere nearby was a whole damned colony of bats. The thought of walking into a mess like that made my skin crawl.

"We must go back," Cierra pleaded. "Please, Wil. Better to face El Diablo's killers than bats."

I hesitated, not entirely sure she wasn't right. Finally I said, "Let's go on a little farther. We've been climbing steadily. We might be closer to the top than we think."

After a strained silence, Cierra nodded bravely. "But not too far," she said. "The bats will leave their roosts soon, thousands of them."

Closer to millions, I thought grimly, pushing forward with the Colt in one hand, the other held protectively in front of my face.

With the light growing rapidly dimmer, I didn't know if our path was veering away from the cliff's face and its numerous fissures, or if the sun was dropping quicker than I'd anticipated. I was just about ready to give up and try to find our way back when I saw what I can only describe as the holy grail of lost cavers everywhere—a patch of gray light, forming a V-shaped opening large enough for both of us to squeeze through.

"We made it!" I shouted, a bubbling laugh slipping past my lips. Shoot, I felt like cheering until the echo of my words caused a dry-paper rustling across the ceiling, a sharpening of the ammonia scent, then the quick patter of urine and feces striking the floor. Throwing herself against my back, Cierra softly cried my name.

"We can't quit now," I said. "We're almost there."

But the more we spoke, the louder the rustling became, the more restless the rippling of the ceiling. Grabbing Cierra by the hand, I hauled her roughly forward, but the light between us and the patch of gray was nearly nonexistent, and we had to feel our way blindly. The odor became worse—a lot worse—and a sensation of nothingness expanded on my right. Stretching my hand in that direction confirmed that the passage we'd followed this far had widened into something much larger.

Overhead, a bat broke free of its mooring. I heard the flutter of its wings, followed within seconds by a thrumming of many more. Up ahead, fist-size shadows were already flitting through the patch of gray light that was our goal. But this wasn't the mass exit the citizens of Río Tinto had become used to every evening around this time. This was a smaller colony, and I knew from watching them in the past that there could be several more before the whole bunch broke loose, pouring from the cliff like smoke from an inferno.

The fluttering—I don't know what else to call it, what other single word quite describes that soft beating of tens of thousands of wings, the sense that the air itself had taken on a palpitating life of its own—swelled even louder.

Cierra's hand tightened around mine. Her fear was alive, too, coursing through her fingers, drilling into my palm. I was still carrying the Colt in my left hand, but had the inside of my left elbow pressed tightly over my mouth and nose to filter the stench. We were still climbing, but no longer on rock. Beneath a layer of damp bat dung, my boots were kicking up fine, chalky clouds of guano that disturbed the atmosphere even more. The bats knew we were there, intruders whose purpose they couldn't understand, and they reacted as any animal would, with their own fright and agitation.

The patch of light grew stronger but no larger, and, as we drew close, my heart sank a little. It wasn't the escape I'd hoped for. It was just the bottom of another steep chimney, like the one that had brought us down here. Stepping under it, we could see the entrance about ten feet above, the sky above it a soft pearl. It wasn't a vertical climb, but it was going to require the use of both hands as well as our feet. From below I could see only a couple of tiny crevices, neither completely horizontal—precarious holds for our fingers and toes, but better than nothing, I supposed. We'd have to be careful, though, that we didn't lose our grip and fall backward into the cavern.

"Wil," Cierra breathed, a shiver racking her body.

"We can do it," I said. "You can do it. Just don't panic."

"When … when I was a little girl … bats, hundreds of them, came into my room one night. They filled it with their squeals, their claws digging at the adobe walls. I screamed and screamed, but they …."

I gave her shoulders a pretty rough shake, her head flopping limply back and forth. Then her face changed and she looked at me with the same expression I'd seen just before she attempted to scale the fissure outside. She nodded determinedly. Pointing out a two-inch wide ledge, like half of a man's palm cleaved into the side of the chimney's wall, I said, "Give me your foot, and I'll …."

She shrieked then, and we both ducked as a dark, fluttering—yeah, there's that word again, fluttering—mass passed over and around us, swooping skyward like a puff of smoke.

"Wil, I can't," she cried, tears streaking those dusky cheeks.

"You have to," I said harshly, grabbing her and spinning her around. I jammed the revolver behind my waistband, then stooped and laced my fingers into a makeshift stirrup. "Put your foot in here," I barked.

Sobbing, she did as instructed.

"Ready?"

She nodded.

I rose fast, heaving her as high as I could. She grabbed the lip on top, managed to scrabble both elbows over the edge, then hooked the ledge I'd pointed out earlier with the toe of her shoe. She just hung there then, her chest heaving as she fought to keep from sliding back.

"You're going to have to pull yourself out!" I shouted.

The fluttering was growing louder, like the growing swell of rushing water, while ten thousand high-pitched squeaks—kind of an "eek eek eek eek"—filled the chamber behind me.

That's a real flesh-crawling sound if you've never heard it before, especially in the near pitch darkness of an echoing cavern. Above me, Cierra's foot, the one not jammed into the tiny ledge, was scraping frantically at the smooth stone, her bare brown legs flashing in and out of sight. Then a bat swooped past me, flying up the chimney, under Cierra's skirt. She screamed and kicked wildly and the bat came out, reversed course, then flew past her shoulder into the night.

The colony's riot was worsening as their fear made them both desperate and aggressive. The air around the chimney's lower mouth writhed with bats. I swear I could have swung a club and killed a dozen. There were even more in the chimney with Cierra, their leathery wings pummeling her sides and shoulders, skimming past her calves. At least two were tangled in her hair, and she twisted and shrieked, her free leg flailing, arms weakening. I thought she was going to fall. I was almost certain of it. Then something came over her, a calmness I'd already seen twice since leaping the wall of Kellums' compound. She tipped her head around, located an outcropping of stone that was little more than a lump in the side of the chimney's wall, and braced her right foot against it. The move, with her skirt, nearly blocked the bat's exit completely, but she kept her head and continued her upward struggle, flopping her waist over the top, then wiggling clear of the opening.

Like powder smoke from a fired musket, a mob of bats burst through the cave's mouth after her. I fell to the cavern floor and covered my head as the colony swept past. Millions of them. Tens of millions. They darkened the sky above the chamber's mouth, a climbing vortex that seemed to stretch on forever.

It didn't, of course. Half an hour later there were fewer than a dozen winged mammals passing through the narrow chimney every few minutes. With the worst of the nightly migration past, I poked my head turtle-like from beneath my jacket. Overhead, a voice called, "Wil?"

I looked up. Cierra was leaning over the opening, her head and shoulders barely discernible in the gloaming. "Wil, are you all right?"

I stood cautiously, reeking of bat feces and urine, my back and shoulders slimy with it. "I'm OK," I said.

"You've got to get out of there while there is still some light left."

I nodded again, my eyes scanning the chimney's walls. With darkness coming on, the little crevices I'd seen earlier had disappeared. It might as well have been a smooth steel pipe I was peering through. But Cierra had a better angle, and more light to work with. Pointing toward a spot on the wall not far above my head, she said, "There's a ledge there. You can't see it from below, but it's there. If you use that, you can pull yourself up to another small ledge to your right …"

And just like that, she guided me out of the darkness. On top, I flopped across the hard stone slope high above the Tinto Valley. There was a breeze off the river. There was always a breeze up there, and down below the lights of town glittered like flecks of gold.

Rolling onto my back, I saw Cierra smiling at me. Her hair was a mess, her blouse ripped from neck to shoulder, exposing a slim collar bone, and there was blood on her chin. I started to reach for the wound, then saw the filth staining my fingers and pulled my hand back. "Were you bitten?" I asked.

"I don't think so. A little beat up from throwing myself back and forth in the chimney, but that's all. Are you hurt?"

I shook my head. My ribs ached where I'd been shot, but I figured that was to be expected. Otherwise I felt all right. I'd check myself when we got back to Río Tinto to make sure I hadn't been bitten, but I didn't think I had.

Pushing to my feet, I took a look around. My heart sank to discover we were still stranded well below the rim, perched on a ten-foot-wide ledge sloping toward the valley floor. But Cierra took my hand, as foul as it was, and pulled me toward a narrow trail winding along the cliff's face. In no time at all we came to a split in the stone wall, a notch filled with debris, framing the top of the bluff nearly forty feet above us.

"Come on," she said, sounding exhausted. "We are almost there."

Staring wearily up through the detritus, I was inclined to agree.

WIL CHAMA INTERVIEW

∾

SESSION THIRTEEN

I won't waste too much space on your recording machine there telling about how me and Cierra got back to Río Tinto that night. We had to hoof it because no one knew where we were, and we avoided the Cut because we were afraid Kellums' men might spot us in the moonlight and pick us off with their rifles. Instead we walked south to the rim of the Tinto Cañon, then found a way down from there. That cañon trail is pretty arduous with carts, but not so bad on foot.

We washed as best we could in the tinted waters of the Tinto, but I think we were both still feeling pretty slimy as we made our way down the cañon. It was after midnight by the time we got back. I noticed Montoya still had men up on Bluff Street keeping an eye on Kellums' hacienda, but the rest of the business district looked deserted.

Inside the Bravo we encountered less than a dozen men scattered around the room, drinking mescal and talking quietly among themselves. Several were sitting with Amos Montoya at his usual table near the back of the cantina. Carlos Mendez was one of them. Gilberto Varga was another. A startled silence fell over the room when me and Cierra walked in. Then Gilberto abruptly shoved his chair back, kicking it halfway to the bar. A murderous look darkened his face as he stalked across the room.

"What are you doing here?" he demanded of Cierra.

She took a frightened half step back, then kind of sidled partway behind me as if to avoid the brunt of her brother's wrath.

"I brought her," I said, baffled by the man's reaction.

Wrapping a beefy paw around the handle of a butcher knife sheathed at his waist, he grated, "You bring only dishonor to this place."

I wasn't sure whether he was speaking to me or Cierra, but, either way, I was wishing I had more than one puny .38-caliber cartridge left in my revolver. Gilberto's knife was half drawn when Montoya ordered him to stop. Turning, Gilberto growled, "This is a family matter, patrón. It does not warrant your attention."

I could tell the *segundo's* reply didn't set well with Montoya. "You work for me, my friend," the older man said coolly. "If you wish to continue your employment, you will never again question my authority."

Remembering the way Gilberto had fawned when Montoya chewed his butt about wasting bullets earlier that day, the burly Mexican's defiance was surprising. He stood silently, jaws clenched in repressed rage, but finally nodded and stepped back. "As you wish," he replied, smacking the knife back into its scabbard.

Rising, Montoya came toward us, his gaze shifting speculatively between me and Cierra. He wrinkled his nose when he got close, but made no mention of our foul dress or lingering odor. "You escaped," he observed, although I couldn't tell whether that pleased or disappointed him.

My reply was a curt "Uh-huh."

"Where have you been?"

"Escaping."

He seemed to mull that over for a moment, then looked at Cierra and said, without any hint of gratitude that I could detect, "Return to your brother's house. The men here have business to discuss."

With her eyes cast toward the floor, Cierra dutifully left the cantina.

When she was gone, I said in American, "What the hell was that about?"

"Nothing that concerns you, Señor Chama."

I glanced at the table where Montoya's cronies were watching us. Gilberto stood where Montoya's command had stopped him, one hand still gripping his knife. "Do they know?" I asked, tipping my head toward the table.

"About the girl? Some do. Her brother. And Rosa, who took the information she brought to us. Kellums, in his arrogance, apparently didn't think the girl was bright enough to pass along information while she fetched water from the river with the other women."

"So now you're just going to let her hang there, with everyone thinking ... what they're thinking?"

"That she is a whore?" He shrugged dismissively. "Is it not the truth, Señor Chama? No matter the reason, did she not willingly go to Kellums' home, to his bed?"

"If she did, it was because you asked her to, god damn it."

Montoya's brows rippled in warning. "Again, my friend, this is of no concern to you. I did what I did to save the village. Sacrifices had to be made. There was no other way."

I had such a pile of words bubbling up from inside that they jammed solidly in my throat and wouldn't come out. Oh, I stuttered out a few assholes and sons of bitches, but I was just so damned mad I finally had to turn around and walk away. Looking back on it now, I wish I'd punched the old bugger in the nose, but I didn't think about it at the time.

Fairly seething, I walked over to the Cruz place and roused them from their slumber.

"I want a bath," I told Eber, and I guess he saw the anger in my eyes, because he didn't protest the late hour.

In the little stall where they kept the galvanized tub, I quickly stripped down to bare hide, flinging my discarded clothes as far as I could into the trees. When Elsa came in with a bucket of lukewarm water, I told her to burn them when she found them. She nodded wordlessly. It was only after she'd left that I remembered I was standing there buck-naked, my body sticky with dried bat urine. She must have thought I'd been bat-bit, and was already starting my journey into madness.

I cooled down as I bathed, both physically and emotionally, and by the time Eber brought me the clothes I'd left with them the last time I was there, I was feeling better.

Eber and Elsa seemed more relaxed, too, and Elsa volunteered to change the bandages over my ribs. That was my first good look at the raw, hardening flesh gouged between a couple of my short ribs, surrounded by a halo of black-and-blue flesh. It kind of scared me to realize how close I'd come to dying. Another half inch and the bullet probably would have punctured my lung.

I dressed lazily, slipping into my boots last, freshly cleaned and polished, and felt almost human again. Almost American again, wearing the Anglo clothing I'd brought with me from Colorado. I paid double what I normally did, and left with their good wishes. Circling behind the Bravo so that I wouldn't have to come face to face with Montoya or his surly *segundo* again, I entered the courtyard through the stable side gate. There was a light glowing in my room, and the door was open. I hesitated before approaching, wishing again for more cartridges for my little Colt self-cocker, then strode boldly forward.

I'll confess I was expecting to find Gilberto Varga waiting in my room. Instead I found Inez Montoya, sitting primly on the edge of a straight-backed chair across the room. She was still wearing her mourning clothes, although she'd removed the hat and veil. There was a wooden platter on the table, a coffee pot and tin cup beside it, fresh tobacco and papers next to that.

"Tía Rosa ordered me to bring you your supper," Inez informed me icily. "I was also instructed to wait to see if you required anything further."

It was tempting to tell her no, and to get out, but curiosity stalled my reply. Moving to the table, I poured myself a cup of coffee, then asked if she wanted any.

"No," was her stiff response, her gaze locked on the door as if considering making a run for it.

I took my coffee to the bed and sat down. "Why are you so angry with me?" I asked. "The last time you were here …"

She stood quickly, nostrils flaring. "If there is nothing else, I will go."

"Is it because of Flaco?"

You might have thought I'd popped her behind with a quirt, the way she froze up. Glaring at me with the same rage I'd seen earlier that evening in Gilberto Varga's eyes, she said, "It was supposed to be you who died. That is why Tío Amos hired you and Angelino Sandavol and Hector Flores, so that our people, the people of Río Tinto, wouldn't have to lose their own. Now Flaco is dead, and Antonio and Cesar, while you and Flores strut around town with all your guns and money and arrogance …" Her words broke off, and, with a cry of frustration, she swept from the room like a winter's squall.

I sat on the bed with a half-rolled cigarette in my fingers, until I finally dropped it to the floor, set the untouched coffee on the table, and kicked the door shut. I didn't eat, although I was famished. I didn't even bother to blow out the candle. I just fell into bed and closed my eyes. I woke up just once that night, hearing the distant echo of fading thunder, and hoping it would blow up a good rain that might dampen everyone's tempers. Then I went back to sleep.

I reckon I was more worn out than I realized, because it was late the next afternoon before I rolled out of bed, letting loose a host of new aches and pains to overlay the older ones. All except for my side, which was still the winner as far as hurting went.

The food was still there from the night before, a trio of tortillas wrapped around a concoction of beans and roast goat, and hard fried eggs sitting like cold scabs atop the greasy platter. The coffee was like ice, too, but I drank it anyway, then ate the tortillas, and finally the eggs. My stomach couldn't take that kind of torture nowadays, but I was young back then, with a cast-iron lining from in to out. Not much bothered me other than my occasional overindulgences of spirits, which is why I gave up drinking when I was young.

I rolled a cigarette and smoked it down, then rolled and smoked a second one while examining my Winchester. The saddle I'd ridden into town on sat next to the rifle, but it wasn't my rig. That one, as far as I knew, was still out at the Springs, buried beneath what was left of the hut. I figured my saddlebags were still out there, too, or someone would have brought them in.

Leaving the Remington's gun belt with its empty holster on the unmade bed, I shoved the Colt into the pocket of my trousers, picked up my rifle, and wandered over to the Bravo. The place was packed when I walked in, although quiet enough that you'd have thought you were attending a wake. Turns out, that's just about what it was.

There must have been two scores of eyes following me to the bar. Leaning the Winchester close by my side, I ordered a mescal. Carlos heard me, but for a moment he just stood there staring at the bar in front of him. Then he came over, a clay jug dangling from one finger. He set a short tumbler in front of me and poured, slopping some over the side as if trying to make a statement. Then he walked away, leaving his mess behind.

I stared after him for a moment, then let my eyes travel the length of the bar. Half a dozen men turned away when I looked at them. I hitched around to face Montoya, sitting in his customary spot at the table closest to the back wall. The old man returned my gaze silently for several seconds, then sighed and motioned me over. I went with my drink in one hand, the Winchester in the other. A man I didn't know stood up as I approached, and Montoya indicated the vacated chair with a faint tip of his head.

"You slept well?" he asked after I'd seated myself.

Not in the mood for trivia, I said, "What's going on?"

Montoya hesitated only a second. "There was more fighting, just after dawn." His eyes darted away, then came back. "We lost some men."

"Who?"

"Eber Cruz …"

"Eber!"

I'd just seen Eber the night before, and, after my mad had subsided, we'd laughed and joked while Elsa changed the bandages on my ribs.

"Yes, he and Gustavo Ramirez and Ernesto Valdez and," there was another pause, "the boy."

"What boy?" I asked, but then I knew, and it was like getting hit in the gut with a sledgehammer. "Felix?" I barely got the name out.

Montoya nodded glumly.

"What happened?"

"We became too confident. Gilberto decided to build a wall of planks across the back of one of the carts, then roll it toward the hacienda. He wanted to drive Kellums' hombres malos away from the outer wall, into the house itself. He didn't know Kellums kept dynamite in his house. He … we … had decided El Diablo must have sent it all to the Flats." Suddenly clenching a fist, Montoya slammed it down on the table top, upsetting a forest of squatty clay tumblers similar to mine, spilling mescal over the dark wood. Taking a deep breath, he went on, "Ernesto leaves a wife and a small daughter. Gustavo leaves a wife and three sons."

"And Felix?"

"He was alone after his father's murder. We will bury him between his parents, and they will be together again on earth. And if God smiles, they are together now in heaven. I pray that God smiles. The boy deserves that much."

Yeah, he did, I thought numbly. Then, remembering the thunder I'd heard the night before, I felt a massive weight settle over my shoulders. "What are you going to do about it?"

"I don't know," Montoya admitted, surprising me with his candor. "Perhaps our only recourse now is to wait them out. They are too well-armed, and if they have more dynamite, which I suspect they must, then it would be suicide for us to rush them." He drew his hand into a fist again, but didn't strike the table with it. "If I had dynamite, I would cram it down that devil's throat."

"Shove a fuse up his ass and light it from that end," another man said.

I stared into Montoya's sad eyes. "We could toss a stick down on top of them from the bluff. That would get their attention."

"True, but there is no more dynamite to be had. My men have searched the Red Devil plant and the stores along Bluff Street. The gringos howled, but we didn't ask their permission. Señor Landry says there is to be a new case of dynamite brought in soon, perhaps on the next keelboat, but that could be days away yet."

I was already shaking my head. "We don't have to wait. I know where there are two sticks of the stuff right now. If we can drop that down Kellums' chimney, he'd come scooting out of there with his tail between his legs, and his men would scatter like quail."

Montoya frowned. "Where did you get dynamite?"

I told him about the two sticks Danny Fuller had been carrying at Antelope Springs. "They should still be in those saddlebags, if someone hasn't taken them."

"Those saddlebags are considered your property," Montoya replied. "No one would have removed anything from them."

"Then I'll be right back." I started to push away from the table, but Montoya held up a hand.

"Carlos, bring me the saddlebags from Señor Chama's room."

The bartender nodded and left, and I sank back in my chair, sensing Montoya had more he wanted to discuss.

"Señor Chama and I would have a private conversation," the patrón said, and, although he spoke to no one in particular, his words cleared the table. When we were alone, the old man switched to American. "You should know that despite my earlier statement, I don't want Randall Kellums killed. I have already instructed my men in this matter, and I want to be very certain that you also understand my wishes."

"After all the trouble he's caused, all the men he's had killed?"

"There is a matter here that is larger than revenge." He sat quietly, watching me.

"You want the Red Devil for yourself, but you can't have it unless Kellums signs the place over to you legally," I said.

"It would be easier that way," he admitted. "For my people."

"Your people?" My words must have fairly dripped condemnation, because a muscle immediately started twitching in one of Montoya's cheeks.

"It might be wise for you to curb your anger, señor," he warned in a tone both soft and harsh. "My tolerance, as well as the tolerance of my people, has been worn extremely thin in recent days."

"Who killed Felix?" I asked. "Was it Kellums?"

Montoya shook his head. "No, of course not. It was the man called Layton who threw the dynamite. Felix was crouched behind the carreta with Ernesto and Gustavo."

"What was he doing there?"

"He was doing his part in the battle, as were we all."

"He didn't have a gun, did he?"

"He would have, had I enough to arm everyone. But no, Felix did his fighting with a leather sling and a pocket full of stones."

The old man smiled suddenly, his expression turning momentarily reflective. "The boy's aim was true," he said, then tapped his cheek, under his right eye. "One of the stones caught Layton here, and those who saw it insist the cut was to the bone."

I leaned back in my chair, my shoulders slumping. "And that's when he went to fetch his dynamite?"

"I am afraid so, yes."

Carlos returned with the twin bags that had been fastened to the gray's saddle. He set them on the floor at my side, then retreated to the bar to stand with the other men Montoya had dismissed from his table. I met the old Mexican's gaze quietly for a moment, then opened the left-side bag and extracted the two sticks of dynamite I'd shoved in there at the Springs. Twin fuses were already inserted into detonators at the tops of the sticks, then twined together so that they would burn evenly. The two sticks were held together with a piece of leather thong.

Eyeing the explosives warily, Montoya said, "You have experience with this?"

"No, but I don't reckon it'll be too hard to light a match, then give it a toss."

Switching to Mexican, he said, loud enough for the rest of the room to hear, "You will take these to the top of the bluff and drop them behind Kellums' hacienda. You will do this in such a way as to cause the maximum amount of damage to the building, yet not risk the lives of the men inside anymore than is necessary. Is that understood?"

I nodded stiffly, then rose with the dynamite in my right hand, the Winchester in my left. "I'm going to need a horse, a lantern, some matches, a belt and holster for the Colt, plus a couple of boxes of ammunition."

Montoya glanced at Carlos, who headed for the store side of the building. Motioning to a youth standing quietly against the wall, Montoya said, "José, bring a horse for Señor Chama."

"Sí, patrón," the kid replied, then darted out the front door.

After a moment's silence, Montoya said, "What are your intentions?"

"I'm going back up top, then come down on Kellums' place from above."

"But there is no ..." He stopped. Until me and Cierra showed up the night before, it had generally been assumed there wasn't any way up or down those bluffs, other than the one Kellums had carved out of the cliff's face. Not that Cierra and I had opened up some new route the townspeople could use on a regular basis, but we all knew that it was there. All I'd have to do was find it again.

Maybe sensing my doubt, Montoya said, "Do you remember the way?"

"More or less," I replied, although, to be honest, I wasn't all that sure that I did. I'd be coming at it from the desert side, for one thing, plus it had been dark when Cierra and I finally crawled out on top. I decided I'd have to figure it out when I got there.

The old man wouldn't let it rest, though. "There can be no mistakes, Wil. You have only the two sticks. You must make sure they fall perfectly, so that they come to rest against the rear wall of Kellums' hacienda."

"I'll find it," I replied snappishly.

"And I will help," said a voice from the storeroom door.

We all looked up as Cierra Varga stepped into the room, her gaze fastened on me rather than Montoya. "I remember the way."

"It will be full dark again by the time you get up there," Montoya reminded her brusquely, as if annoyed by her interruption.

Cierra had cleaned up after her journey through the cavern last night, and her dark hair was shining, reflecting the light from the burning lamps. She was wearing clean clothes again, too, although obviously well-used. "I have stood in El Diablo's backyard day after day, staring at that cliff," she told Montoya. "I can find it, even in the dark."

"That's good enough for me," I said.

Carlos returned with the items I'd asked for—gun belt and ammunition for the .38, a coal-oil lantern, and a tin of matches. Plus one other item I wasn't expecting, an old single-shot Philadelphia derringer, its barrel less than two inches long, the nipple freshly capped.

"Just in case," the bartender murmured, as if not wanting anyone else to know he was slipping it to me.

I eyed the old weapon silently for a moment, then lifted it from his arms, along with all the other stuff he'd brought me, and motioned for Cierra to follow me outside, away from the hateful stares of the men at the bar. Under the veranda I halted to check the lantern's reservoir. It was nearly full, and the seal on the tin of matches was unbroken. After unobtrusively slipping the derringer into my pocket, I shoved the rest of the supplies inside the saddlebags along with the dynamite, then moved away from all that flammable material to roll a cigarette. Cierra stood nearby, staring pensively at the rim of the bluffs.

"It is almost the same time now as it was when you came to the hacienda yesterday," she said.

"Are you thinking about the bats?"

"Yes. I started to tell you in the cavern about the night they came into my room. I was small, a child, and there were hundreds of them." Her lips twitched reflectively. "That does not sound so intimidating after what we lived through last night, does it?"

I smiled gently, but I could sense her fear, too. "You won't have to come with me," I promised. "Help me find that notch again, and I can make it the rest of the way on my own."

"No, I am not afraid, and it must be done. The people of my village are depending on me."

Cierra's words stabbed at me. "Is that what Montoya told you?"

She nodded solemnly. "It is all right, Wil. I know what the people of Río Tinto think of me. I also know that Montoya has used me for his own gain. But there is truth in his words, too. If El Diablo is allowed to take control of the salt beds, my people will become little more than subjects to his need for more money, more power."

I struck a match to light my cigarette, using it as an excuse to contemplate her words. The truth is, she was right. Randy Kellums was a man burdened with a lot of hungers, but the one that burned hottest was greed, and with greed came power, and the insatiable thirst for more. With Kellums in control, the people of Río Tinto would suffer badly. I was as sure of that as Cierra was.

Exhaling a lung full of smoke, I picked up the cartridge belt, broke open the box of ammunition Carlos had given me, and began filling the loops along the back. Crossing her arms under her breasts, Cierra moved to the edge of the veranda, gazing through the trees toward Bluff Street. "My brother is up there," she said quietly. "He leads the resistance for the patrón."

"He didn't seem especially happy to see you last night."

"Gilberto is angry about many things. Even though he knows it was Montoya who asked me to go to Kellums, he blames me." A trace of bitterness tinged her words. "Gilberto would never condemn the patrón, no matter what the request."

I strapped the gun belt around my waist, slid the Colt from my pocket, and quietly filled the cylinder.

"Do you have a sister, Wil?"

"No, I'm the only one. My father died when I was young, and my mother never remarried."

Cierra turned to offer me a sad smile. "So many deaths, so many orphans in the world."

Montoya had made a similar comment, I recalled.

"I am sorry for your loss," she added.

"Thank you." I dropped the Colt in its holster, wondering if I should say more. A few minutes later José showed up with the gray, the saddle I used already cinched down tight—the moment passed.

Handing me the reins, José said, "Go with God, señor."

"I ain't sure God would want to go where I'm going," I replied, but José stared back uncomprehendingly. I'd switched to American without even realizing it. "*Gracias*," I replied, forcing a smile.

Montoya must have been watching from inside, because he came through the door as I was leveling the reins above the gray's withers. Catching José's eyes, he nodded toward the trees that separated the two Río Tintos. "Tell Gilberto I wish to see him."

José nodded and took off like a shot. I stepped into the saddle, then reached down to hoist Cierra up behind me. She straddled the skirting behind the cantle, then quickly rearranged her clothing to cover her legs.

Halting at the gray's shoulder, Montoya said, "I will have my men in place and waiting. When you drop the dynamite, we will be ready."

"Do you intend to shoot them as they come out the door?"

He shrugged noncommittally. "Perhaps the hombres malos, the hired guns. The rest we will allow to surrender, if they desire. Otherwise ..." He shrugged again, as if the decision would be theirs, not his. "I care only about Kellums. I want him alive."

"Uh-huh," I replied dryly, tapping the gray's sides with my heels.

"Alive, Señor Chama!" Montoya called after me.

I eased the horse into a lope. Leaning close, Cierra wrapped her arms around my waist, tipping her face into my shoulder. I patted the back of her hand, hoping to reassure her, and maybe myself as well, that what we were going to attempt had an honest chance of succeeding.

It was nearly dusk when we rode out of Río Tinto. On horseback, we had to go farther upcañon to find a way out, but we were still making good time. On top, Cierra lightly squeezed my arm, then pointed to the west where a rising vortex stained the horizon.

"They are leaving," she said with obvious relief.

I watched silently as the main colony spun crookedly into the evening sky, then veered off to the southwest to begin its nightly invasion of Mexico. When the last of the bats had disappeared, I kicked the gray to a canter. The light was fading by the time we reached the edge of the cliff. I turned north, slowing to a walk as I scanned the rim of the bluff, looking for the notch we'd used the night before. I was starting to worry that we'd gone too far when Cierra spotted the shallow indentation in the cañon's rim.

"There," she said, pointing.

Heaving a relieved sigh, I reined toward the notch. We halted about twenty yards from the edge, and Cierra jumped to the ground without waiting for the offer of my arm. I stepped down lightly behind her, then began pulling gear from the saddlebags. I took the lariat, too, slinging it over my shoulder just in case. Cierra had walked over to the edge of the bluff to stare down at the town. She was still there when I came up beside her, and, when she looked at me and smiled, I think my heart melted just a little.

"Shall we go?" she asked, and I wondered if she understood the effect she was having on me.

"I'll go, but I want you to stay here with the horse. If he spooks and runs off, we'd have to walk all the way back to Río Tinto again. That's too far to have to do it twice in as many nights."

"No," she said. "I will come with you. You might need my help."

"I want you to stay," I insisted.

"I know," she replied, then gently stroked my cheek. "Come on, before we lose the light."

She started down through the notch without me, and, after a short hesitation, I accepted the inevitable and followed. It was slow going through the scree, and there wasn't much light left by the time we reached the sloping stone shelf that would take us to the chimney. We hugged the cliff's face as we made our way to the small opening. Dropping to my knees, I leaned forward to peer inside. My hope was that the entire colony of bats had left as one, but I knew there was a good chance a few had remained inside. The trouble with that was what folks nowadays call "relativity," and with those kinds of numbers, even a "few" could number in the thousands.

Getting down on her hands and knees at my side, Cierra poked her face over the opening. "Are there anymore down there?"

"I don't hear anything, but I expect there's some."

She gave me a sidelong glance, then, mustering a half-hearted smile, she said, "Shall we go?"

I told her, "No," and this time I meant it. "You're staying here," I added. "I might need your help climbing out, like I did last night."

"The sky was lighter last night," she reminded me. "I could see the handholds from above that you couldn't. It's too dark for that tonight."

"That won't matter. I'll have a lantern with me this time. All I need is for you to wait right here until I get back." I took the lariat off my shoulder and flopped it down on the stone ledge next to the opening. "You can drop one end of that rope to me when I get back, if I need it," I added.

Her lips were pressed thin in disapproval, but she wasn't arguing with me, which I took as a good sign. Breaking the seal on the tin of matches, I spilled a dozen or more into the palm of my hand, then dropped them into my shirt pocket. I started to slip the twin sticks of dynamite down the front of my shirt, but one of them caught briefly on the Cross of Lorraine I was still wearing against my chest. Setting the dynamite aside, I pulled the cross over my head and handed it to Cierra.

"I don't know if this means anything to you. Montoya gave it to me yesterday. He said it was the signal you two had worked out, and that when you saw it, you were supposed to get out of there quick as you could."

Tears filled Cierra's eyes as she accepted the heavy iron cross. "It was my mother's," she explained. "The only piece of jewelry she owned. I'm glad it was not lost." She kissed the primitive crucifix tenderly, then slipped it over her neck to lie against the gentle swell of her breasts. I was glad I'd remembered to give it to her before dropping through the chimney, what with everything that was about to happen.

Taking a deep breath, I said, "Wish me luck."

She took my face in her hands instead, and kissed me on the lips. When she leaned back her eyes were closed, her lips still moving slowly, as if savoring the taste. I stared at the soft oval of her face in what little light remained, and my heart began pounding crazily.

"Be careful, Wil," Cierra said, her fingers coasting gently off my cheeks.

I nodded, made some awkward attempt at a joke, then sat down on the edge of the chimney and kicked free of the rim.

Man, I'm glad I was young. If I tried something like that today, I'd break more bones in my body than I could count. It was a ten-foot drop to the bottom, and I plummeted down that narrow chimney like a sack of coal, bouncing off the walls and ripping my last good shirt beyond repair.

I'd forgotten about the angle of the floor underneath, too, so that when I landed, I fell sprawling forward, scuffing up a dusty, acidic cloud of guano that stung my nostrils and made my eyes tear up. The lantern sprung free of my hand, rattling off into the deeper darkness to my right, accompanied by the crackle of breaking glass and the sharp odor of spilling kerosene. I sat up with a smothered curse, then sneezed loudly, the sound unreeling in front of me, stirring up a restless fluttering of wings against stone. I swore again, but more softly this time.

"Wil, are you all right?"

"Be quiet," I called, no louder than I had to.

Rolling onto my hands and knees, I began fumbling around for the lantern. It didn't take long to find it, wedged up against a low, dung-coated rock. Feeling a cool draft against the underside of my wrist, I stretched my hand beyond the stone and found—nothing, and I mean nothing!

I jerked my hand back as if it were about to be bitten, then scooted back to where I'd originally landed, clutching the lantern close to my chest. My eyes were still watering badly from the stink of ammonia, not that it mattered since I couldn't see anything anyway. With just my fingers, I examined the lantern as best I could. The glass was broken out completely on one side, but only cracked on the other, and the wick was still in place, the reservoir intact. The coal-oil smell had come from the wick, while the lantern was rolling across the floor.

Digging a match from my shirt pocket, I struck it with my thumbnail. The sudden burst of light was blinding in the pitch-black chamber, and I had to turn my head away until my vision adjusted to the brightness.

Soaked in kerosene, the wick caught instantly. I shook out the match and tossed it away. Raising the lantern above my head, I pushed to my feet, staring in awe at the abyss dropping away in front of me. It looked bottomless, its walls dotted with furry brown patches that rippled eerily in the flickering light.

"Wil, what is it?" Cierra called, her voice hollow and distant as it rolled down the chimney.

"Be quiet," I told her. "There are still a lot of bats down here."

Her next words were barely discernible. "Be careful."

Examining my surroundings, it didn't take long to realize how lucky Cierra and I had been when we came through there the night before. Our destination had been the fading patch of light drifting down the chimney from the setting sun, and that had kept us on a more or less straight path. Had we veered from that course even a few feet, we could have easily plunged to our deaths.

Backing up against the wall, I unconsciously brought my left hand up to my stomach, as if to reassure myself that the dynamite was still there. Instead my fingers touched warm, bare flesh, accessible through a gaping tear in the fabric of my shirt.

"Ah, hell," I groaned, running my hand around my waist as if the explosives might have retreated to the small of my back for safety. But the dynamite was gone, ripped loose in my drop through the stone chimney.

Panic crawled up in my throat like bile as I searched the narrow, dung-encrusted shelf for those two slim red cylinders, but they weren't to be found. After a couple of frantic minutes, I backed up to the wall and placed the inside of my free arm over my mouth and nose, just to filter out the ammonia stench.

I'd lost the dynamite. I couldn't believe it. My eyes went to the rim of the abyss. There was no other explanation.

Half sick with anguish, and maybe a little from the smell of ammonia, I eased over to the lip of the ragged crater, holding the lantern out at an angle so that it would shine downward. Even then, all I could see was more of the same—clumps of rustling bats and a gut-chilling drop into nothingness.

Returning to the bottom of the chimney, I called quietly for Cierra to toss me the lariat. I guess she'd already figured out something had gone awry. "What's wrong?" she demanded.

"Just throw me the rope."

"Wil, tell me."

I hated to admit the truth, but I hadn't lied to her yet. "I lost the dynamite."

Total silence greeted my confession. It stretched on for so long that I began to wonder if she'd gotten disgusted and left.

"Cierra, are you there?"

"Oh, Wil, we can't fail now. We're so close."

"I tore my shirt coming down the chimney. The dynamite must have fallen out then. There's a pit down here. If you give me the rope, I can lower the lantern inside and maybe find it."

"How deep is the pit?"

"God damn it, just drop me the rope," I replied, louder than I meant to. I heard a distant squeak, like a starter's pistol, then a rapid fluttering as a group of bats released their grip on the wall.

"Watch out!" I called, then ducked out of the way as a smokelike cloud of the tiny, winged creatures swept past me, up the chimney and into the night. When it was over, I moved back to the bottom of the opening. "Cierra, are you all right?"

After a long pause, her reply drifted back to me. "I've tied the end of the lariat to a rock large enough to hold us. I'm coming down."

"Don't be a fool," I said, my words sharp but low. There was no answer from above, but a few seconds later the end of the lariat tumbled down the chute, followed almost immediately by Cierra, dropping gracefully into the chamber. She turned slowly to examine our surroundings, and I admired the way she tried to mask her fear.

"Where is the dynamite?"

"Over here," I said, picking up the end of rope and moving to the edge of the pit. Cierra followed, leaning tentatively forward to stare into the yawning cavity as I fastened a quick slipknot to the lantern's bail. Bracing myself against the pull of gravity, I began slowly to lower the rope, keeping the lantern a foot or so away from the wall. Despite my care, its heat and light disturbed the bats hanging on the near wall, and a batch launched itself away from the light, their faint warning eeks like tiny scratches against my eardrums.

The pit wasn't bottomless, but it was deep. A lot deeper than we could have reached, even if we had the whole length of the lariat to play with. What made it worse was that we could see the twin sticks of dynamite, barely visible at the edge of the lantern light, maybe fifty feet down.

"Oh, Wil," Cierra breathed. "How will we ever reach it from here?"

It was a good question. The walls of the huge pit were smooth, not a handhold anywhere. We'd need a lot of rope to get down, and, considering the narrowness of the guano-slick ledge we were standing on, it would probably take a sturdy set of block and tackle to get us back again.

Swaying back from the crater's edge, I reluctantly shook my head. "We can't reach it," I said. "Not from here. It's too far down."

It took Cierra a few more minutes to accept our defeat, but in the end she had no choice.

"We were so close," she whispered in disbelief. "Just a few more varas and we could have dropped it into Kellums' backyard. Now," she made a vague motion with both hands, as if tossing flower petals into a grave, "we might as well throw rocks at them, like poor Felix did."

She sobbed once, no doubt thinking of Felix, but her words sparked an idea for me, and I turned it over and over in my mind, blocking out the odds against it.

Leaning forward, I took another gander at the drop. The dynamite was easy to see, the two sticks lying flat. I turned to the wall behind me, gauging its thickness, its stability, remembering the cracks of light that had guided us through there the day before.

"What are you thinking?" Cierra asked.

"I'm thinking maybe this is far enough," I replied. "It's not what I wanted, but I think it'll work."

"I don't understand."

"If we could light the fuse here, it might just bust out the side of this cliff, send a bunch of it down on Kellums' hacienda."

"But what if it doesn't? What if the blast just travels up the shaft without damaging the wall?"

I looked at her, taking in the smoky softness of her eyes, the dusky smoothness of her cheeks. Then I smiled. "I say it's worth a shot. It's either that, or go back to Río Tinto without having even tried."

She smiled. "All right, what do we do?"

I peered over the edge, studying the wall more closely, measuring the force of a faint, upward draft against my palm. "We'll have to get a light down to it," I said. "I can see the fuse. It's angled toward the middle of the pit, which should help, but I don't want to risk trying to drop the lantern on top of it. If I missed, we'd be out of luck."

"Matches?"

"Too small. They'd blow out before they got halfway down." I handed her the rope. "Start pulling that up," I said, then peeled my shirt over my head.

"What are you doing?" she asked, watching me even as she brought the lantern up in a hand-over-hand motion.

"I'm going to make a torch. Something large enough that it won't blow out when we drop it, and heavy enough that it will fall straight."

Cierra stopped pulling. "You're going to drop a torch on top of the dynamite? Will there be enough time for us to get out?"

Picking up a stone about the right size to wrap my shirt around, I said: "Not right on top of it. Just close enough to light the fuse."

"But how can you be sure? What if you misjudge? Even a thumb's length …"

I stopped what I was doing to meet her eyes. "All I can do is try."

"Wil, no. It is not worth dying for."

I reminded her of the sacrifices she had already made, and others before her.

"But they did not set out to die. They wanted to live."

"So do I," I assured her. "And I'm going to do everything I can to get out of here, if you'll help."

"Of course I will help. Anything. You need only to ask me."

That was what I wanted to hear. "As soon as I'm ready, I want you to get out of here." I quickly threw up my hand to stop her protest. "I'm going to have to move fast once that fuse is lit, and I don't want you in front of me. As a matter of fact, I don't want you anywhere nearby."

"I won't leave you," she said quietly.

"I'm not asking you to, but I need you up top with the gray. I want you to be mounted and ready to ride, and, as soon as I get up there and swing on behind you, I want you to dig your heels into that horse's ribs like our lives depend on it, because they very well might."

I stopped talking. She was watching me silently. After a long pause, she nodded. "All right. When you are ready for me to go, I will."

I took the rope in my left hand and swung the lantern topside, allowing it to come to rest at my feet. "I want you to go now, Cierra. I want you on that horse before I light the fuse."

She nodded and swallowed and said OK, squeezing the words out between clenched teeth, her throat taut with emotion. I took her in my arms and held her tightly and, Lord help me, I told her I loved her. And I guess I did. Crazy, huh?

"Go on," I said, giving her a little shove.

She turned toward the chimney, stumbling a little. I followed and gave her enough of a boost to grab the upper rim of the opening and crawl out. She looked back just once, her eyes glistening wetly in the light of a rising moon. Then she was gone, leaving me alone in that hellhole, the air alive with darting bats, reeking of fresh feces.

I went back to the lantern, then counted slowly to two hundred, figuring that would give her enough time to find the gray. Then I arranged my gear in front of me and blew out the light.

The darkness was instant, although not quite complete. It took a couple of seconds for the bright orange crown of the wick to quit glowing. After that it was like sticking my head in a bucket of black ink and opening my eyes. I couldn't even see my hand in front of my face if I wiggled my fingers. I know because I tried. I gave the lantern a couple of minutes to cool off, then opened the cap and splashed about a cup of coal oil over what was left of my shirt. Then I closed the reservoir and moved away from the kerosene-soaked rag and relit the lantern. The light was quick and blinding, and I jerked my head away and squeezed my eyes shut until they'd readjusted to the lantern's flame.

Returning to the edge of the pit, I lowered the lantern over the side, then went back to grab my shirt. After that I just stood there a moment, staring down into the light. Although I'd tried to display as much confidence as I could with Cierra, the truth is, I was worried. Hell, I was scared. If I missed and dropped the torch too far away, the fuse wouldn't catch. But if I missed the other way, and set off both sticks before I got out of the cavern, there wasn't going to be enough left of me to scrape together for burial. Then I remembered Felix, and that miner's kid up in Hogup, and I scraped a match alight and held it to one saturated shirt sleeve.

The fabric burst into flame. Holding it over the edge of the pit, I took aim, then dropped it. And I'll swear it was a bat that brushed up against it as it fell, knocking it ever so slightly off target.

I cursed bitterly as the bundled shirt thumped into the ground just inches shy of the fuse. So close, yet it might as well have been in Mexico for all the good it did me. I was trying to formulate another plan, when the heat from the flame forced one end of the sleeve into the air. Kind of like it was waving good bye. Then the burning material flopped over on top of the fuse about halfway down its length, and a heartbeat later the nitrate-soaked cord started to sputter and pop.

I stood there just a second, transfixed by this sudden turn of luck. Then I saw how fast that fuse was burning, and I spun out of there like a good cutting horse. I raced for the rope dangling from above and jumped and grabbed it as high up as I could, then caught the rim with a heel and rolled on out.

Cierra hadn't done as I'd asked, and it made me mad when I saw her waiting at the bottom of the scree-filled notch. I suspect she wanted to be within hearing, in case it turned out I needed help after all. I yelled for her to run, then I did the same, my legs pumping like a steam engine's drivers as I raced along the outer ledge to the bottom of the notch, then started up through the debris.

I hadn't quite reached the top when I heard a muted whomp. Then the earth heaved upward beneath me, flinging me toward the stars. Far below, I watched the side of the cliff explode outward, followed by a second blast that seemed to shatter the night like a sledgehammer coming down on a shelf of fine crystal.

That much I remember clearly. The rest is just a hodgepodge

of sights and sounds and odors, along with an artificial warmth that seemed to hurry me along like a giant hand at my back. The earth spun crazily, alive with jagged stones and screaming bats, my own hoarse cry of protest muffled within it all. Then the gentle hand curled into a fist, and I was hit by—well, I was hit, hard, my world exploding in a final burst of heat and pain before discarding me into darkness.

Excerpts from
Why the Bat Is Our Friend

∾

by Victor Milano

[O]ne of the more common species of bat found in Texas are the Mexican Free-tailed Bats (*Tadarida brasiliensis*). In some locations these colonies can number into the tens of millions.

* * * * *

It should be noted that bats are not the "winged rodent" of common folklore, but are instead true mammals ... the only flying mammal known to exist in the Western Hemisphere, as other familiarly termed creatures, such as the "flying squirrel," can only glide.

* * * * *

A single Mexican free-tailed bat can consume up to 1,200 mosquitoes per hour.

* * * * *

[A]lthough there are no gender-specific terms to differentiate between adult male and female bats, baby bats are called pups. Only one pup is born to a female per year ... bats can live to between forty and fifty years of age.

* * * * *

Despite its strongly disagreeable odor, [bat] guano is an excellent organic fertilizer ... also highly flammable because of its heavy concentration of ammonium nitrate. These propellants, like similarly nitrated explosives such as nitroglycerin and TNT, are converted into a nitrogen gas upon ignition, releasing massive amounts of potentially destructive energy.

WIL CHAMA INTERVIEW

❧

SESSION FOURTEEN

Gentle hands tugged at me. They poked and prodded and just plain disregarded all my efforts to swat them away. After a while the probing ceased, but the annoyances didn't. Fingers briskly caressed my face, and a woman's voice urged me to return. I wasn't sure I wanted to, but she insisted, refusing to let me go where I longed to flee. I don't recall now exactly where that was, only that it seemed a lot nicer than the place I'd just vacated. I fought her cajoling with growing impatience, but she wouldn't give up, so I finally did. With surrender came all the aches and pains I thought I'd left behind, and a few more besides.

"Wil?"

My eyelids fluttered open. I was lying shirtless on the stony ground, my shoulders and head propped on Cierra's lap, my legs splayed before me like the forked branches of a distant road. It had been Cierra's hands roaming my body in search of fresh wounds or broken bones, Cierra's chiding that had eased me back among the living. I didn't thank her for it. The place I'd been was far too comfortable to relish leaving.

Rolling suddenly onto my side, I gagged and choked until I hacked up three or four globs of what I hoped was muddy phlegm. When I finished, I spat a few times to clear my mouth, then wiped my lips with the back of my hand. God, I hurt. Everywhere, everything—like I'd been hung up in a tree and beat with clubs.

"Wil, can you hear me?"

I nodded weakly.

"Can you speak?"

I croaked out an affirmative.

"Can you stand?"

I wasn't as sure about that, but I told her I'd try, and with her help I managed to not only get to my feet, but to hobble over to where the gray was standing hitched to a scrawny mesquite.

"I need you to get in the saddle," she said.

I replied, "All right," then sucked in a deep breath and looked around. "Was I unconscious?" I asked.

"Yes, now give me your foot. We need to get back to Río Tinto to see what happened."

I nodded and pushed her hand away, then hooked a toe in the stirrup and crawled into the saddle. Moving back along the gelding's flank, Cierra loosened my old canvas jacket from the cantle. Glancing at the sky, noting the progress of the moon and the stars, I said, "How long was I out?"

"Too long," she replied, handing me the jacket. I slipped my arms through the sleeves and buttoned it partway up. Loosening my left foot, I motioned toward the stirrup. "Climb up."

"Maybe I should lead the horse by hand," she murmured.

"No, it's too far."

"We can use the Cut."

I shook my head. "Too risky. If Kellums' men spotted us, we'd be sitting ducks on that cliff."

Her fingers tightened momentarily on my knee, although it

was a gentle pressure. "I don't think so," she replied, then moved up to take the gray's reins near the bit.

I started to protest, but she took off without warning, and for the next several minutes I was swaying back and forth in the saddle like a beaver-gnawed aspen in a high wind. Deciding to shut up and concentrate on hanging on, I wrapped my right hand over the horn, then cupped my aching ribs with my left. It was less than half an hour's walk to the top of the Cut, but I was feeling a lot better by the time we got there. Cierra halted the gray at the top, giving me my first clear view of what remained of the cliff. Barely able to comprehend the altered landscape, I slid cautiously from the saddle, then moved up beside her.

"Damn," I whispered, staring at the rocky slope, its pitch sharp but no longer sheer.

Let me say right now that I had no idea, and I mean none whatsoever, that bat droppings, under the right circumstances and in large enough quantities, can be nearly as volatile as dynamite. Sure, the smell of it had stung my eyes and clogged my sinuses while I wandered around down there, but, hell, I'd been striking matches and lowering that lantern with its open flame up and down that shaft like I was sitting on a rain-soaked raft in the middle of a deep lake.

From what I've learned since then, it takes a pretty big chunk of guano and the right environment to set it off like that. Well, there ain't no doubt there'd been a lot of bat dung in those caverns, and I'm guessing there might have been a buildup of methane gas at some of the deeper levels. I've never been able to determine if I was just lucky that my lantern hadn't set off an explosion, or if something as piddling as a match was even potent enough to trigger a reaction, but there was no doubting the results I'd gotten from dropping a couple of sticks of dynamite down on top of several tons of cavern-enclosed guano. Studying that broken cliff face, I figured we were lucky we hadn't blown the whole damned town across the Río Grande into Mexico.

We started down the Cut, paralleling the slide. Cierra led the gray while I walked beside her, enjoying the feel of the earth beneath my boots, the cool breeze off the river. The lower we got, the more I could see. The explosion—the second one, from the guano—had taken off nearly the top third of the bluff directly above Kellums' hacienda, then deposited a sizable chunk of it on top of the house. The entire rear section of the building had been crushed to powder by boulders, a couple of them as big as stagecoaches, and the rest of the structure was cocked westward at an angle just short of collapsing.

There were still tendrils of dust swirling around the head of Bluff Street when me and Cierra got to the bottom. Someone had kindled a bonfire in the middle of the road, about where Montoya's carts had been sitting before Layton turned them into splinters; its light cast an odd, wavering glow over the scene, kind of spooky, actually. I spotted Kellums and several of his men sitting in the dirt in front of the cactus-crowned wall surrounding what was left of his hacienda. A handful of Montoya's men were standing guard over them with their old Springfield .50s.

Amos was there, too, all gussied up in a tan vaquero's outfit with black velvet trim and silver-inlaid spurs, bossing his men around like a strutting general. A lot of the townspeople were looking on from a distance, likely waiting to see which way their next year's profits were going to fall. Over at the edge of the trees, Carlos Mendez was supervising the construction of an awning, with a small writing table and several chairs already placed beneath its gently flapping canvas.

I was watching Carlos' men tighten the guide ropes when a lanky Tejano came over to tell me the patrón wished to see me. Cierra hesitated when I started toward him, but I stopped and held out my hand.

"You're with me," I said, and after a moment's pause she took my hand, but I could detect her wariness through her fingers.

Montoya was nodding approvingly as I came up. He even took time to offer Cierra a small but formal bow. "It would appear that we

have won the war, Señor Chama," the older man stated with undisguised delight. "And due in no small part to the efforts of both of you."

"What happened?" I asked, nodding toward the debris sitting
atop the remnants of Rattlesnake Hill.

Montoya's smile turned into something close to a sneer. "There
was no battle, no final, courageous conflict. By the time El Diablo
managed to drag himself from what remained of his home, all the
fight had been taken out of him. He surrendered with the dignity
of a dog giving up its bone, but he did surrender, and to my terms
as well. We will have a formal signing at dawn, a Declaration of
Surrender, if you will, with a contract sealing his relinquishment
of the Salt Flats."

Although Montoya was as happy as a goose on the day after
Christmas, something felt wrong to me. It didn't take long to figure
out what it was.

"Where are Kellums' gunmen?" I asked. "The only fish I see
here are the small fry."

Houck and McKay sat next to Kellums, but the others,
huddled in a group farther down the wall, were all plant workers
and stable hands. Tom Layton and the rest of his gunnies were
nowhere to be seen.

"A couple of Kellums' worst did manage to slip away," Montoya
acknowledged. "The man called Johnny Potter was killed when
the cliff came down on top of the house. I am informed he was
badly burned when this young woman," he nodded toward Cierra,
"managed to throw a boiling kettle of pinto beans into his face."

"She saved my life doing it, too," I interjected, although
Montoya seemed either not to hear or not to care.

"Elwood Hardisty and Emillio Robles were captured and
disarmed," Montoya continued. "I had them taken to the jail,
where my men can keep a better watch over them. Unfortunately
Tom Layton and Ike Bannon managed to elude capture. I have
men out now scouring the chaparral, while others watch over the

main avenues of escape." He glanced toward the eastern rim of the horizon, considerably lower this morning than it had been the day before. "It will be light in another thirty minutes. We will have the official signing at true dawn, and afterward, if they have not yet been rooted out, I will put all of my resources into finding them. They will be run down before midmorning, I assure you."

Carlos came over, his bald head shining with perspiration. "The awning is ready, patrón," he announced. "I could bring a lamp, if you wish to begin now."

"No, we will wait. A document of such importance as this should be signed in the light of day."

The thought of what was about to take place must have given Montoya a lot of joy, for he started smiling again, and was still at it as he walked away.

After Montoya had moved out of earshot, Carlos said, "If you two are hungry, there is food in the courtyard behind the cantina."

I looked at Cierra. "Breakfast sounds pretty good to me." I cocked an elbow out for her arm. "Would you join me?"

She hesitated, then shook her head. "It would be best if I didn't," she replied. "The patróna would not look kindly upon my presence."

A quick roar of heat swept through me, but I knew she was right. After all she'd done, everything she'd risked and sacrificed, the old trappings of formality would not be denied. Not in Río Tinto, and sure as hell not by a Montoya.

"I know a place where we can get some food," I said, picturing the New Harmony Café, recalling the warm aromas of Mama Belle's fried eggs and flapjacks and good, cinnamon-flavored coffee. But before I could insist, there was a gunshot from down the street, followed by another, then a ragged staccato of revolver and large-bore rifle fire.

I stepped in front of Cierra, using my elbow to keep her behind me, but none of the bullets were coming our way.

"That is from the Red Devil!" she exclaimed, standing on tiptoe to peer over my shoulder.

Agreeing, I moved back along the gray to ease into the saddle.

"Wil, no," Cierra cried, tugging at my jacket sleeve as if to unhorse me. "You have done enough."

I pulled free. Although I was staring down the street toward the Río Grande, in my mind's eye I was seeing Felix's face on the day Montoya asked me to go the Flats with Angel, and then the blankness of his expression upon our return, when he discovered we'd been too late to save his father.

"Stay here," I told Cierra, then bounced my heels against the gray's ribs.

The sporadic gunfire guided me toward the Devil. When I drew close, I spied Gilberto Varga and Hector Flores huddled behind a front corner of the Red Devil's main office, overlooking the salt processing plant. Dawn must have been coming on faster than I realized, because I could see blood dripping from the tips of Gilberto's fingers from thirty yards away, like tiny rubies spilling out from beneath his sleeve.

Hector looked around as I galloped up, then motioned for me to take shelter behind the office. Dropping from the saddle, I let the gray's reins trail in the dirt as I joined the two men at the corner.

"Is it them?" I asked. "Layton and Bannon?"

"They were trying to get to the wharf," Hector replied calmly, punching empties from his revolver to reload. "I think maybe they wanted to cross the river on the ferry. When they were discovered, they made a run for the plant."

I risked a quick peek. "Both of them?"

"Sí."

"Any idea where they're holed up inside?"

Hector shook his head.

"They could be anywhere," Gilberto added, then spat in disgust. "If I get Bannon in my sights, I will make him pay for the bullet he put in my shoulder, that son of a foul whore."

"Are you familiar with the interior of the plant?" Hector asked me.

"I've been through it a few times, but I don't know it real well. It's long and narrow, but fairly open from one end to the other except for the steam room at the south end and a small office at the other end."

"There are many places for a man to hide inside the Devil's lair," Gilberto tersely corrected me. "A person would be a fool to describe such a building as open."

"He's right," I told Hector, trying to ignore Gilberto's provocation. "It's open, but cluttered. It won't be easy to root them out." I glanced at Gilberto's shoulder. The dark stain just under the joint looked wet and heavy, the fabric of his wool shirt frayed where the bullet had entered. "How bad is that?" I asked, nodding toward the seeping wound.

"Do not concern yourself over my shoulder," Gilberto replied curtly. "When the time comes, I will not be found wanting."

Hector shifted around to eye the wound. After a bit, he said, "No one doubts your courage, Gilberto, but I think maybe Chama is right. If we go in after those two, we cannot take a wounded man with us."

"Chama is also wounded," Gilberto replied hotly. "Look at the bandages under his jacket. That is not a red dye staining his bindings."

"Chama's wounds are not recent," Hector replied calmly. "His body has had time to recover from the shock of the bullet's passage." He fixed Gilberto with a hard stare. "You could fall unconscious at any time, as Chama did outside the Bravo on the day he was shot."

"I will not ..." Gilberto started to reply, but Hector cut him off with a sharp, slashing gesture of his hand.

"No, you will stay behind. Wil and I will go in after Layton and Bannon. If we fall short of our goal, it will be up to you to finish the task."

Gilberto clamped his lips shut, like a man who'd unexpectedly swallowed a bug but didn't want anyone else to know. Turning to me, he said, "If you fail Hector Flores as you did Angel Sandavol and Flaco Montoya, I will kill you myself. Do you understand?"

Gilberto had been prodding at me for a long time, and I'd mostly turned a deaf ear to it, but he touched a sore spot, bringing up Angel and Flaco, and my temper took off like a bottle rocket.

"You've got a big mouth, Varga," I growled, leaning forward as if to wrap my hands around the blowhard's throat. "When this fandango is over, I think I'll take you down a few notches, just to show you how easy it can be done."

"When this is over, and, if you are both still alive, I will supervise the fight for you," Hector said impatiently. "But today we have another task that demands our attention."

He sounded mad, and being older now myself, I can appreciate his feelings, but at the time I just continued to glare at Gilberto, ready to pounce.

Pushing to his feet, Hector said, "I'm going now, Chama. You can come if you wish."

I hesitated, fighting the urge to slam my fist into Gilberto's fat nose. Then, gritting my teeth, I turned my back on him and followed Hector.

We made our way to the rear of the office building, then paused to study the lay of the land between us and the nearest entrance into the Red Devil plant—the loading dock doors, where I often backed my rig after returning from the Flats with a cargo of salt.

"That might be our best bet to get inside," I told Hector.

"What lies beyond those doors?" he asked.

"It's mostly open, although that's also where they park the steel-wheeled wooden carts they use to haul the salt around the plant. It could be crowded if everything was put away before they shut the place down."

"Are you sure we can get in that way?"

"Pretty sure."

Nowadays most folks will lock their doors at night or over the weekend, but back then, and especially in places as isolated as Río Tinto, it generally wasn't considered necessary. Fact is, I wasn't even sure there was a lock on those doors

The stables were about halfway between the main office and the plant, although at an angle so that, if Layton or Bannon were watching from one of the high ventilation windows, they'd likely spot us real quick. On the other hand, going through the stables would cut down on the amount of time we were exposed to their guns, which suited me just fine.

Glancing my way, Hector said, "Give the word, amigo, and we'll make a run for it."

"Let's do it," I grunted, then leaped forward like a rabbit startled from cover. We sprinted downhill side-by-side and reached the shelter of the stables without drawing fire. A couple of Montoya's men were already inside, watching the east wall of the plant from a gap between the shutters on one of the windows. They'd seen us coming, and looked relieved that we were there.

"El Diablo's killers are inside!" one of them shouted, excitedly motioning us over.

"Hush," I barked, scowling. "Do you want them to know we're here?"

The eyes of the man who'd urged our approach grew wide, and he quickly shook his head. "No, I want you to go in there and kill those two, so that we can put this foolishness behind us and return to our jobs." His reply brought a soft chuckle from Hector.

Stepping in beside them, I put an eye to the gap between the shutters. "Where are they?" I asked.

Both men shook their heads, as I'd expected. "We have not seen them since Gilberto sent us here," the second man asserted. "Where is Gilberto, anyway? Will he send us more men?"

"You do not need more men," Hector replied. "If you cannot stop those two from here, then you have no business standing guard."

"I never did think we had any business standing guard," the first man stated solemnly. "It makes my stomach jumpy to think of them charging us."

Hector glanced at me, and I could tell he was struggling not to laugh. "Nevertheless, you two are to remain here until this matter is settled," he said firmly. "Wil and I will go inside and chase down those two bad men for you."

"The sooner the better," the second man said, making a quick sign of the cross.

"Come on," Hector said to me. "Before the cowardice of these two salters rubs off on us."

Hector and I made our way to the stable's rear entrance. From there only a simple pole corral and thirty yards of hard, bare ground separated us from the loading dock. We studied the distance for nearly a minute, then I looked at Hector. "Well, we can take our chances and make a run for it, or we can die right here of old age, waiting until we're sure it's safe."

Hector grinned. At least I think it was a grin. It might have been indigestion, although I understood what he wanted to convey. Hector Flores was scared. We both were. But he'd come here to do a job, and he meant to see it through. And by God, so did I.

"Come on," Hector grunted, surging to his feet.

I was at his side the whole way, climbing the corral fence and jumping down on the other side, then racing across the vast emptiness between the two buildings like twin bolts of lightning. I was gasping by the time we skidded into the shelter of the loading dock, although not from exertion.

"So far the Virgin has smiled upon us," Hector said, puffing just as heavily as I was.

"Let's hope she keeps on smiling," I replied, then scrambled onto the dock and over to a small side door, next to the bigger twin doors the men used to cart the salt inside. The latch rose silently under my fingers, and the door swung partway open. With the Colt out front, I slipped sideways through the door. Hector followed close behind, making no more noise than a passing shadow. He closed the door quietly behind us, not wanting to advertise our presence in case we'd managed to sneak into the plant undetected. Pausing with my back to the rough adobe wall, I looked around for a couple of minutes.

I don't know if you've ever been inside a building like a sawmill or a gristmill, some place where they hammer, stamp, or grind between massive weights to make large things smaller—like fifty-plus-pound chunks of red-veined salt into something you can pinch between your fingers to sprinkle over your meat—but it creates a hell of a fine dust that covers just about everything, inside and out.

I've seen laborers—those who worked the stampers especially—come out of the Devil at the end of a twelve-hour shift coated in pink from head to foot, the gritty dust clogging their sinuses, burning their eyes and throat. Everywhere you walk, everything you lay your hands upon, leaves an imprint. It's why I never spent anymore time than I had to inside the Devil, and why just about everyone I knew who did wore leather gloves, tight-fitting goggles, and a bandanna over their mouth and nose—and woe be to the man or woman who showed up with a fresh cut or a piece of raw flesh, for it would be constant agony until the wound was healed.

I didn't know where Layton and Bannon might be hiding, or if there were better paths to follow than the one I eventually led us to, paralleling the iron-slatted conveyor that ran from the waterwheel at the upper end of the plant to the steam room at the bottom. It just seemed like a natural route, and I fell into it without thought, Hector right behind me.

I've already mentioned how the Red Devil plant was mostly open from one end to the other, and it was. But Gilberto had also been right when he said it wasn't. The building's interior was thickly cluttered with an assortment of machinery, carts, and crates of spare parts to keep everything running smoothly. There were small mountains of kegs of grease to lubricate the gears, pallets stacked with five-gallon tin cans of oil to keep the leather belts pliable, and five-hundred-pound rolls of coarse brown paper to cut, then wrap around the salt cones as they came out of the steam room.

Additional kegs containing red ink, used to imprint the Devil's trademark dancing imp with its giant crimson salt shaker upon the paper-wrapped cones, were stacked on pallets along the walls, and even more crates were filled with the finished product—twenty-four cones to a crate—crammed away wherever there was room to await shipment downriver. It was all a pretty simple operation, as long as everyone did their job and nothing broke down.

Although the building might have been relatively free of walls—except for the steam room at the south end and Jim Houck's office next to the loading dock on the north—Gilberto had also been right when he said Layton and Bannon would have a dozen places to hide. After covering maybe fifty or sixty yards, Hector tapped my shoulder and told me to hold up. Although still in a crouch, I dropped even lower, then half turned to ask him what he wanted.

"They know we are here," he whispered. "I can feel them watching us."

I felt it too, like I had bull's-eye target pinned to my chest. Pivoting on my heels, I studied the mishmash of salt-dusted machinery, the ridges of supply-heaped pallets surrounding us like a rust-colored jungle. I'd said there were a dozen places to hide? Hell, there were a hundred, probably more. At the creeping pace we'd settled into, it could take all day to flush out our quarry. Glancing over my shoulder at Hector, I said, "There's one way we could find out where they're hiding."

Hector returned my look. "How is that?"

"We can ask them."

Hector stared at me silently for a moment, then he laughed out loud. "I think maybe you're right," he said. "It could save us a lot of time." Duck-waddling across the narrow aisle to where he'd have a better view of the south end of the plant, he called out in passable American, "Hey, you two gringos, why don't you come out where we …"

I suspect Hector was going to ask Layton and Bannon to come out where we could see them, but a shot from somewhere up ahead cut off the invitation before he could finish it. The bullet sprang off one of the steel brackets on the side of the wooden trough through which the conveyor belt ran, spitting pieces of lead into a pile of burlap sacking at our side. Me and Hector hit the floor fast, but no other shots came our way.

"I guess that tells us what we need to know," I said.

"It tells us where one man is hiding," Hector agreed, reverting back to his native Mexican. "But there was only the one shot. The other man could be anywhere."

I shrugged, figuring we'd gotten about all the reply we were likely to, and lucky to have that much without one of us getting hit.

Spotting a path winding through the clutter on my right, I said, "You stay here. I'll go see where that takes me. Maybe I can slip around behind whoever took that shot at us."

Hector nodded, then slid behind the stack of baled burlap sacking. "Don't get killed," he advised drolly. "I don't want to have to flush these two gringos out alone."

"I'll see what I can do not to inconvenience you," I replied.

You might wonder at such flippancy, considering the situation, but I'll guarantee you it wasn't a deliberate attempt at humor. I think we were trying to assure one another that we were as ready as anyone could be under the circumstances, and that we'd do what we could to cover the other man's back. In other words, we weren't planning to run when the shooting started. I don't know how Hector felt about it, but I appreciated the reassurance.

Pushing off in a crouch no more graceful than Hector's awkward waddle, I crawled under the long wooden trough, then made my way along a winding channel between cases, crates, and five-gallon tins. It was slow going, and it wasn't long before I began to feel a steady burning across my ribs—salt working its way under my clothing and through the bandages across my ribs. I gritted my teeth and continued on. I'd probably covered another thirty yards along the serpentine path when gunfire erupted from behind me.

I dropped flat as peels of thunder rolled and bumped down the long, narrow building. My pulse was loping. Getting up on my knees, I peeked over the top of the cart just in time to see Ike Bannon burst from cover near the south end of the plant, a revolver bucking in each hand as he made a dash toward Hector's position behind the pile of sacking.

Bannon was firing swiftly but accurately, his bullets thudding into the stack of burlap, each one releasing a cloud of shredded brown fibers. Before I could react, Hector launched himself away from the low, coarsely woven mound to roll smoothly inside the shallow-walled trough, then crawl up behind one of the big five-hundred-pound iron stampers. Bannon, meanwhile, had come to a halt behind a stack of crates. I was taking aim at the gunman's position when a shot from the opposite end of the building sent a bullet whizzing so close past my ear I swear I felt its movement in the air.

I ducked as two more shots slammed into the heavy planks of the cart's side wall, then popped up real quick to snap off a couple of rounds of my own at Tom Layton as he ventured out from behind the belt's controls at the opposite end of the building.

Sometimes when I think back on what happened next, I believe I actually knew what Layton was going to do before he did. I started to call out a warning to Hector, but then had to duck back down as a round from Bannon whistled over my head. And in just the second or two that it took me to find my voice, I heard the clank of an iron lever being shoved into gear, the groan of straining machinery as the whole operation shuddered to life under the slow, creaking power of the water mill.

Hector shouted a startled curse as the iron-slatted belt in

the bottom of the trough lurched forward. One of the iron slats caught his heel and he tumbled backward, arms flailing. The track ground slowly forward as the stamper rose on twin gears, and like a one-hundred-seventy-pound chunk of squirming, pink-veined salt, Hector was roughly deposited onto the heavy iron screen beneath it. The massive block paused for a fraction of a second about five feet above the stocky Mexican, then the ratchet tripped past top-dead-center and the stamper dropped with a shrill, metallic scream.

Silence followed as the clatter of gears and track was abruptly stilled. I stared in horror, frozen immobile. Then a bullet from Layton drilled into the side of my cart not six inches from where I was gripping it with my left hand. I yanked my fingers back and whirled to return fire, but my feet skidded out from under me on the salty floor and I went down hard.

Drawing in a ragged breath, I quickly rolled onto my hands and knees. I knew better than to raise my head, though. I could picture both gunmen posed, their revolvers cocked and aimed, just waiting for me to show myself. I listened for their approach. What I heard shocked me all the way down to my socks.

"Wil!"

The word came raspy and dry, and I instinctively ducked a little lower.

"Wil, get me out of here!"

I shook my head in disbelief, even though there was no one around to see me. Crazily I wondered if it was a trick, yet I knew it couldn't be. The stamper had fallen. Hector Flores had been under it. So the question became, how badly was he injured?

"You'd better go help him, Chama," Layton taunted.

"Go to hell," I replied.

A gunshot roared from my left. A bullet rattled along a workbench behind me, kicking up a line of spare parts across the oil-blackened top. Still on my hands and knees, I began crawling toward where I'd last seen Hector. He must have heard me, because his next words came so softly I had to stop to be sure it was him.

"Wil, I'm stuck. Get me out of here before one of Kellums' dogs decides to rush me."

"One of Kellums' dogs is already here," Bannon cried triumphantly, and I came up like one of those jack-in-the-box toys they sell at Christmas time, snapping off a shot just as the wiry African stepped into the center aisle alongside the conveyor.

Bannon grunted sharply as my bullet spun him partway around, then dropped him from sight. In that same fraction of a second, I saw Hector hung up in the conveyor belt, the huge stamper halted less than a foot above his legs. Then I hit the floor as a shot from Layton cleaved the air at my side, tugging gently at my jacket sleeve as it passed.

"Bannon?" Layton shouted. "Damn it, Bannon, where are you?"

"He's dead," Hector returned in American; we were all speaking more English than Spanish now.

I didn't know if Bannon was really dead or not. It was possible I'd gotten lucky with the snap shot, but Hector might have just been mocking Layton, too, hoping to goad him into something foolish. Either way, I wasn't going to chance it, and kept my head down as I wiggled through the clutter toward the stamper. No matter what Bannon's situation was, I knew Hector was in a tight spot.

I got to within about ten feet of where Hector was stretched out on top of the heavy wire mesh under the stamper before I had to stop. I couldn't see Bannon, and I didn't have a clue where Layton was holed up, so I didn't dare move in for a closer look. What I could see from where I was crouched was bad enough. The stamper had been blocked about eighteen inches above the metal screen, with Hector's right leg somehow caught under it. I couldn't tell what was obstructing the hammer's fall, but I was dead certain that if it gave away with Hector's leg still pinned beneath it, there wasn't going to be anything left of the stocky Mexican's limb except a bloody mush.

Spotting me hunkered down behind a pallet of grease kegs,

Hector used his eyes to draw my attention to a spot maybe twenty yards away, where several steel-wheeled carts had been haphazardly parked. I nodded my understanding, then eased up just far enough to get a better look at the stamper's iron-framed tracks, rising vertically above the screen. There was a cog outside each track, and I caught my breath when I saw what was wedged between the teeth of the nearest one—the muzzle of Hector's revolver, jammed between the gear and the frame.

The pressure against the crushed gun barrel must have been tremendous. What was worse was that all but a handful of teeth had already been sheared off the cog. What few remained looked bent and cracked, ready to fail at any time.

I couldn't see what Hector's leg was caught on, but I figured it had to be pretty tight or he would have already squirmed free. I was still staring at the damaged cog when two more teeth gave away with a sudden pop, pop. The stamper lurched down another inch, and Hector howled while jerking frantically at his leg.

Shrill laughter rang out from the upper end of the building.

"He's gonna get squashed if you don't drag him outta there, Chama!" Tom Layton shouted. "Don't be shy, boy, go ahead and help him. I won't shoot."

Well, that was a damned lie, and we all knew it. Still, I had to do something. Hector's situation was becoming more desperate with each passing second.

"Wil, my boot is caught, and I can't get my foot out of it," Hector hissed. "Every time I try, the entire frame trembles like it is about to collapse. Someone has to get around on the other side and cut me loose."

"Hang on," I replied tautly.

Hector's eyes were boring into mine. I could see the fear in them, the silent plea—the same look I'd seen in Felix's eyes, that morning in the Bravo Cantina, just before I agreed to ride out to the Flats with Angel Sandavol.

I leaned back, swearing in quiet despair as I fed live cartridges through the Colt's loading gate. My eyes swept quickly over the stamper and its frame, and it was just as I dropped the last round into place that I spotted something I'd missed before—a shallow, open-top wooden box bolted to the outside of the frame. Inside was a hodgepodge of tools, including a common mechanic's wrench, the kind used to adjust the stamper's mechanism. It was a fairly large wrench, maybe ten inches long and hefty, with a tapered handle and a three-quarter-inch head, and as soon as I saw it, I knew what I had to do.

Leaping into the open before I had too much time to think about it, I got off two quick rounds at the carts where Layton was hiding. Then I was at Hector's side, shoving the revolver into my belt with one hand, grabbing the wrench from the tool box with the other. I tried jabbing the U-shaped head under the stamper the same way you'd jam a broom handle under a window to hold it open in summer, but I'd misjudged the gap. If I'd been just a few minutes earlier, before those last two teeth broke, it probably would have gone on in as slick as silk over a baby's butt. Instead the tip of the handle snagged short, a half inch too long to fit into the track.

Layton saw what I was doing and popped up with his revolver leveled. I swore wildly and pushed on the wrench with everything I had. I felt the cog give just a fraction of an inch, and knew I had only seconds to wedge the handle in place before another tooth snapped.

But Tom Layton wasn't going to give me the time I needed. He was stalking toward me, his eyes burning with hatred, his cheek where the stone from Felix's sling caught him seeming to glow cherry red. He fired, the bullet slamming into the frame at my side. I hollered at the fresh bite of shattered lead digging into the meat of my right arm. I could hear Layton laughing as he closed the distance between us. He had to know that, even if he killed both of us, he'd never get out of there alive. I don't think he cared anymore. Maybe at that point, all he wanted to do was take as many men with him as possible. He was advancing steadily, almost at a run—thirty yards away, then twenty.

Even as I struggled against it, another tooth on the cog began to bend inward, a hairline crack spreading across its base. I was shoving on that wrench with everything I had, but it wouldn't budge.

There was a tug at my waist, the Colt sliding free of my belt, then a single shot from in front of my belly. I saw Layton stop abruptly, sucking in his gut as if someone had taken a swipe at him with a large knife. Hector fired again and Layton dropped to one knee, bleeding heavily from a pair of wounds in his torso, one right above the other. Then the last two teeth in the cog snapped, and the stamper dropped.

I figured Hector's leg was a goner for sure, and maybe Hector, too, but instead, for some reason I've never been able to figure out, the cog rolled backward for just a fraction of a second before slamming downward. And in that fraction of a second, because I was still pushing on it, the wrench snapped into place like a precision instrument, the huge iron block jerking to a stop once more.

I stepped back to give Hector more room. Layton was still up on one knee, his lips peeled back in a bloody, soundless snarl. I glanced at Hector, wondering why he didn't shoot. He was looking at me with panic in his eyes, holding the Colt up where I could see it. The trigger flopped loosely inside its guard, a spring broken— springs were always breaking on those early self-cockers—rendering the gun as useless as a stick.

"You greasy, bean-eating bastards," Layton grated, spraying a bloody froth over his hand as he lifted his revolver.

I breathed, "Jesus," and yanked the little Philadelphia derringer that Carlos had given me from my pocket. I spun toward Layton, the stubby gun coming up fluidly, as if independent of bone and muscle and thought, its single bead of a front sight coming to rest on Layton's chest. It all happened so fast I wasn't even aware of the derringer going off, neither hearing its blast nor feeling its recoil, but I saw Layton's reaction at the other end of the sight. Saw him stiffen as the thumb-size round ball ripped through his heart, the revolver falling from nerveless fingers. Then Layton fell on top of it, his face striking the hard-packed dirt floor, nose first.

I turned to seek out Bannon, but the little gunman lay on his back several yards away, a gaping wound in the side of his throat where my bullet had struck him earlier. He was dead, too, and after a minute of stunned silence I numbly pocketed the derringer, then dug a barlow from my pocket, opened the blade, and began cutting Hector's boot free of the conveyor.

WIL CHAMA INTERVIEW

❧

SESSION FIFTEEN

I've got to admit that you surprised me when you asked for another recording session. You're the first person who ever wanted to know what happened afterward. Most folks just want to hear about what it was like being on top of the Tinto Bluff when all that bat shit exploded, or about the gunfights behind McGivens' grocery store and inside the Red Devil plant. It makes me believe you when you say you want to hear as much detail as I can remember, and that's been a lot more than I expected when we first started recording.

Like we discussed while you were setting up your machine, the deaths of Ike Bannon and Tom Layton brought an end to the Tinto War, at least for me. I guess for a lot of others it was finished before that. Old Montoya had pressed ahead with his Declaration of Surrender, making it kind of a big deal to touch ink to paper just as the sun crested what was left of the bluff. They say he didn't pay a bit of attention to the gunfire that kept drifting up from the plant, although Kellums did. From what I heard, Kellums flinched at every shot, but he went ahead and signed the document as it was presented—not that he had much choice in the matter.

Basically what Kellums signed that day was relinquishment of any mineral claims to the Tinto Salt Flats, and water rights to any spring, lake, or well in that part of the country. I don't know how legal any of it would have been in a state court, but there'd never been much law in Río Tinto other than what the people who lived there could enforce, so the courts were never called in.

I'd wondered earlier if Chad Bellamy had managed to get word to anyone at Fort Duncan, and it turns out he had. The commanding officer there sent the word on to whoever it was you sent it to back then, and a few days later a couple of United States deputy marshals showed up aboard the keelboat *Yolanda*. Them two huffed and puffed like the wolf in that kids' story, but there wasn't much they could do, since most of the witnesses were in Amos Montoya's pocket by that time. New Town's businessmen, Jay Landry and that bunch, ended up siding with the Montoya faction, which pretty much put an end to Kellums' complaints. When the *Yolanda* cast off for its homeward journey three days later, those federal officers were on board, their handcuffs still in their bags.

Although Kellums stayed on to get his Red Devil Salt Works back in operation, it soon became obvious that his stranglehold on the community had been broken for good. Montoya offered to buy him out, but Kellums vowed to burn the place to the ground before selling it to a pepper-gut. Montoya took the insult in stride and withdrew his offer. Three days later, Kellums sold the whole shebang, right down to a barrel of worn-out mule shoes, to Jay Landry for about a third less than what Montoya had offered. I don't know if Kellums' change of heart had anything to do with the color of Landry's skin, or if he just finally realized how few options he truly had. After the contract was signed, Kellums caught the next keelboat south, and, as far as I know, he never set foot in Río Tinto again. But here's the kicker. The day after Kellums left town, Landry sold the Red Devil operation to Amos Montoya for one dollar and a Cuban cigar. You can draw your own conclusions as to what kind of shenanigans went on behind the scenes on that deal.

Randy Kellums may have left Río Tinto with his tail between his legs, but he didn't leave Texas, or even the Río Grande Valley. He settled in Laredo, where he made a whole lot of money in real estate after the Tex-Mex Railroad came through the following year.

Hector Flores went back to Mexico, where I heard he wound up raising cattle and horses that he shipped to the United States via the same Tex-Mex line that made Kellums rich. I don't know if they ever ran into one another again, but I always kind of doubted it. It would have been an interesting encounter to witness, though, if they had.

Although Amos Montoya made a pitch to have Elwood Hardisty and Emillio Robles arrested for the murders of Antonio and Cesar—ironic, since Robles hadn't even been in Río Tinto at the time of the twin hangings—the marshals refused. Carlos later told me the lawmen had been so disgusted with the politics muddying the waters of their investigation that he doubted they would have arrested anyone unless they actually saw the person commit the crime—which is probably what kept me and Hector out of the Brownsville jail.

They say Elwood Hardisty went to Missouri and got a job teaching school in the Joplin area, although I don't know how true that is. Emillio Robles supposedly went back to Chihuahua, where he was killed by Apaches a few years later. I don't know if that's true, either, but it sounds a lot more plausible than Elwood Hardisty as an educator.

Inez Montoya married Jay Landry later that summer, cementing the relationship between Amos and the New Town businessmen that began with Amos' purchase of the Devil. Bob Thompson stayed in the saloon business until his death from a heart attack twenty years later. Chad Bellamy and Frank Gunton continued working for the Devil under Montoya, although Bellamy gave up his badge. Amos gave it to Gilberto Varga, but Varga lost the job in the next election to an Anglo brought in by Montoya. Man, the politics that went on in that little town could make your head spin. I don't know what became of the rest of the people I knew back then.

Something that's always fascinated me about the Tinto War was that, after the explosion that brought such a big chunk of the bluff down on top of Kellums' hacienda, both the bats and the rattle-snakes that had given the knob its name practically disappeared. I don't know what became of the rattlers, and I doubt if anyone who lived there ever mourned their loss, but I know a lot of people said the mosquitoes got real bad after the bats vacated the Tinto Valley. I was reading an article in, I think it might have been the National Geographic, not too long ago, that claimed if you disturbed a colony of bats too much, the whole bunch would likely pack up and move on to another location. I kind of figured that's what happened with the Tinto colony, since it was the dead of night when the dynamite went off, so I doubt many of them were killed in the blast.

You might also be curious about what became of the town of Río Tinto, the Red Devil Salt Works, and the Tinto Flats, because if you look at a map today, you aren't likely to find mention of any of them.

Amos Montoya took over the Red Devil plant after buying the operation from Landry, but Montoya, as powerful a presence as he was in Río Tinto, lacked Randy Kellums' business skills. Or maybe that was Kellums' doing, getting a little revenge from down in Laredo, him being about as underhanded as he was unethical. Anyway, I figured once the railroad came in at Laredo, the Devil would flourish, but it didn't. Don't get me wrong, Montoya continued to sell salt well into the 1890s, but the heyday of the dancing imp had passed with Kellums' departure. When the salt flats began to peter out in the late 1890s, Montoya shut the plant down for good.

The Tinto War occurred over a large chunk of March of 1880, and by May of that year I'd left town for good. Not by keelboat, though. I took the gray I'd brought back with me from the Springs, and brought the little bay filly along on a lead rope. The bay carried a light pack consisting of a few odds and ends of camping gear and enough food to last as far as El Paso. Cierra Varga rode behind me on the gray, and she's been riding with me ever since. In my opinion, it's been a damned fine journey.

END TRANSCRIPT

Obituary from
The Alamosa Examiner-Journal

JULY 28, 1946

∞

WILHELM KARL CHAMA

April 6, 1856–July 27, 1946

The town of Alamosa lost one of its leading citizens yesterday with the passing of Wilhelm Chama, a devoted husband, loving father, and admired grandfather and great-grandfather. Chama passed away at his home late last evening after a courageous battle with pancreatic cancer.

Known throughout the San Luis Valley as "Uncle Wil," Chama was a lifelong resident of the area. Although born near San Luis, he settled in Alamosa in 1880, where he worked for a time for Trans-Valley Shipping and Freight. He also ran a small gun repair business out of his home on Ansel Avenue for a number of years, before opening a hunting and fly fishing shop on Main Street. In 1899, Chama founded the Tinto Springs Sporting Goods chain, which now includes stores in Alamosa, Pueblo, Denver, Santa Fe, New Mexico, and Cheyenne, Wyoming.

In addition to numerous business ventures, "Uncle Wil" was also the founder and past president of Tinto Valley Farms, which supplies a variety of food products to needy children and their families throughout Colorado and New Mexico. Through the TVF, he founded the Cierra Vista Boys and Girls Club in 1922, a summer camp recreational facility located next to the TVF at the northern end of the valley.

Nationally known for his philanthropy for children's organizations, Chama was officially recognized by two recent American presidents, Herbert Hoover and Franklin D. Roosevelt, for his efforts to bring orphaned boys and girls from large city slums to the Cierra Vista complex, where they were tutored in horseback riding, camping, firearms safety, archery, and indoor skills such as auto repair and sewing.

Wil Chama is survived by his wife, Cierra, their six children— Felix Arturo, Samuel Karl, Maria Theresa (Chama) Winchell, Consuelo (Chama) Smith, Hector Theodore, and Gilberto Thomas. There are fourteen grandchildren and one great-grandchild.

Viewing will be held tonight at the Cleveland Mortuary from 6:00–9:00 p.m. and tomorrow afternoon from 1:00–4:00 p.m. Graveside services will be at the Santa Maria Cemetery at 4:30 p.m., followed afterward by a wake at the TVF Recreational Center from 6:00–8:00 p.m. The Chama family has asked that in lieu of flowers, donations of food and clothing be made to the Cierra Vista Boys and Girls Club.

RIP, old friend.

AUTHOR'S NOTE

In order to avoid any confusion, let me state right off that *Río Tinto* is a work of fiction. So is the American Legends Collection. That said, the rest of the Works Projects mentioned at the beginning of this novel did exist, including the Folklore Project, which is where I got the inspiration for the American Legends Collection.

I love history. It's what made me want to be a writer when I was still in middle school. In my research of the nineteenth century American West, I've uncovered stories that boggled my mind. Fascinating characters and unbelievable accounts of daring and accomplishment. But the trouble with reading history is that it can be so damned boring. Hair-raising excitement, buried inside a muck of tedium, like flecks of gold dust in a miner's pan.

I love fiction. I love its ability to lift readers out of their chairs and plunk them down right in the middle of the action. I love the way it can illuminate a time or place, or add clarity to an historical event.

Maybe it's because I love both so well that I wrote *Río Tinto* in the style that I did. I saw it as a way to present a story in a more exciting manner, yet still give the reader a sense of reality, the feeling that he or she is hearing about the incident firsthand. My goal was to impart the same thrill I experience whenever I stumble across a gripping drama that I'd never heard of before. I hope I accomplished that.

Río Tinto is the second book in my American Legends Collection series. The first was *City of Rocks*, and the third in the series is *Leaving Yuma*. Check my website at www.Michael-Zimmer.com for a complete list of past and future novels.

—Michael Zimmer

ABOUT THE AUTHOR

Michael Zimmer grew up on a small Colorado horse ranch, and began to break and train horses for spending money while still in high school. An American history enthusiast from a very early age, he has done extensive research on the Old West. His personal library contains over 2,000 volumes covering that area west of the Mississippi from the late 1700s to the early decades of the twentieth century. In addition to perusing firsthand accounts from the period, Zimmer is also a firm believer in field interpretation. He's made it a point to master many of the skills used by our forefathers, and can start a campfire with flint and steel, gather, prepare, and survive on natural foods found in the wilderness, and has built and slept in shelters as diverse as bark lodges and snow caves. He has done horseback treks using nineteenth century tack, gear, and guidelines. Zimmer is the author of ten Western novels, and his work has been praised by *Library Journal* and *Booklist*, as well as other Western writers. Jory Sherman, author of *Grass Kingdom*, writes: "He [Zimmer] takes you back in time to an exciting era in US history so vividly that the reader will feel as if he has been over the old trails, trapped the shining streams, and gazed in wonder at the awesome grandeur of the Rocky Mountains. Here is a writer to welcome into the ranks of the very best novelists of today or anytime in the history of literature." And Richard Wheeler, author of *Goldfield*, has said of Zimmer's fourth novel, *Fandango* (1996): "One of the best mountain man novels ever written." Zimmer lives in Utah with his wife, Vanessa, and two dogs. His website is www.Michael-Zimmer.com.